A Star in the Face of the Sky

A Star in the Face of the Sky

a novel by

David Haynes

American Fiction Series

©2013 by David Haynes
First Edition
Library of Congress Control Number: 2012950069
ISBN: 978-0-89823-283-7
e-ISBN: 978-0-89823-290-5
American Fiction Series

Cover design by Rachel Brixius
Interior design by Richard D. Natale
Author photo by Hillsman Jackson

The publication of *A Star in the Face of the Sky* is made possible by the
generous support of the McKnight Foundation and other contributors to
New Rivers Press.

For copyright permission please contact Frederick T. Courtright at
570-839-7477 or permdude@eclipse.net.

New Rivers Press is a nonprofit literary press associated with
Minnesota State University Moorhead.

Alan Davis, Co-Director and Senior Editor
Suzzanne Kelley, Co-Director and Managing Editor
Wayne Gudmundson, Consultant
Allen Sheets, Art Director
Thom Tammaro, Poetry Editor
Kevin Carollo, MVP Poetry Coordinator

Publishing Interns:
Katie Baker, Hayley Burdett, Katelin Hansen, Richard D. Natale,
Emilee Ruhland, Daniel Shudlick

A Star in the Face of the Sky Book Team:
Sydney Gill, Andrew Mendelsohn, Naomi Nix

New Rivers Press
c/o MSUM
1104 7th Avenue South
Moorhead, MN 56563

And it's 'cause you've thrilled me
Silenced me
Stilled me
Proved things I never believed
The face on you
The smell of you
Will always be with me

> "Three Babies"
> —Sinead O'Connor

1995

That Janet Williams hadn't liked children all that much she blamed on the boy's mother. Children annoyed her, frankly—all that incessant energy, the enthusiasm for obnoxious music and inedible food, their general and relentless neediness. When pressed, however, she would admit there was something special about this one, this Danny, her five-year-old grandson. On that day—that god-awful day—he'd mostly amused himself, trying out all of the chairs in the living room, plopping himself on the new loveseat and scootching his little bottom around, testing it for comfort, twisting his face around like a bad actor portraying a food critic. Goldilocks with nappy hair.

"There's not a thing wrong with that sofa," she'd admonished him as the phone rang. He'd blown a quiet raspberry to demonstrate his immunity to her goading.

"I don't know what I'm going to do with you, boy."

The call had been from Keisha, the second of the day from her, her voice reminding Janet of some other time, although just then she had been unable to put her finger on when that might have been.

"Mama," her daughter had sighed—a happy sigh. "Mama, His will be done, has been done. All praises, all praises."

"None of your foolishness tonight," had been Janet's response. That girl, her sanctimonious ravings. Who needed it? She never knew what it might be with her daughter, had never known. The new thermostat didn't work. Cryptic passages in obscure books of the Bible needed interpretation RIGHT THIS MINUTE. Mama, please how do I crisp these collars? He wants them just so, like all the deacons have. You know how Jerrold gets.

Me, me, me, me, me.

"What do you want, Keisha?"

"I've sent them across, Mama. My angels. Sent them across to Him."

The boy in Janet's house made sputtering noises and blew spit bubbles. Maybe this was normal for boys. She reminded her daughter that another of her angels happened to be right here in her face, right this very minute thank you very much, and that all day long he had been giving her the fish eye and various other exotic expressions.

"Damn boy's about to eat me out of house and home," she told her. Danny mugged shoveling handfuls of food in his mouth. Janet tossed him another pack of Skittles, which he caught with his teeth. No lie! He tore the packet open and dumped what looked like half into his mouth. You'll choke, she mouthed—wondered if that sounded less like worry and more like a wish.

Through the phone she heard something that might have been singing, but it was hard to tell. When Keisha had been the age of her son, she "sang" entire operas to herself, part Diana Ross, part screaming banshee. Janet heard something about tempests raging and peace, the phone line flattening all of it to a sad monotone.

Keisha's earlier call, before noon, Janet remembered. Same phone, here on this counter, beside it, a to-do list—things to be accomplished before the trip to Rend Lake with Wes. She'd warned this girl (hadn't she?) that she had no time for mess, that a weekend away with her (potential) new stepfather was more important than anything that she, her sorry-ass husband or any of their crumbsnatchers had cooked up. It would have been the weekend that Janet closed the deal, and on the list had been the tools of her trade: the makings for a knockout supper, fine champagne, a sexy CD. Wes enjoyed a soprano sax.

What became of that list? That boy had better not be over there scribbling on it.

Now, across the wire, her daughter sang something about being here and how because of that the rest of us need not worry.

"Keisha," Janet prompted.

"We are bathed in His glory," came the reply.

Enough! Honestly these people and their drama. What hope did Janet have but to snag this man (Any man!) and convince him to move as far away from this crew as they could find. Tasmania. Tuvalu. Some place with bad phone service.

"Wes and I want to be on the road early, so I need to go to bed. Is one of you coming to get this child? Or I could send him in a cab."

I'll bill you.

Danny hummed and sang and pretended to draw. Mostly he looked around the room at nothing in particular, a million miles away, no doubt. Couldn't be more like his mama. Sometimes.

For what it's worth his mama had been lucid during the earlier call.

I need you to pick Daniel up after kindergarten. Keisha, classic demand mode—damn anyone else's needs. Another childhood trait, it had been. Get me a new dress for school. Eggs for breakfast, and they better not be runny.

Please, Janet would remind her. Puh-leeze. Again and again and again, she'd remind her, and Keisha would always look at her as if she had been speaking another language.

"They're like angels, Mama. Wrapped in white, that He may receive them."

Miriam, Sarah, and baby Hosea—and they had been angels, too. Bundles of brown beauty, perched on their parents' laps in some Sears photo studio, dressed to the nines, posed in front of a neutral backdrop, muted earth tone smears. Big brother, bigheaded Danny, beaming, down on his knees, in front.

"Keisha?" Janet insisted. The girl just hadn't sounded right, but when had she ever, really? "What's the matter, Baby? Talk to mother."

Just then Janet remembered what the air-thin whispers put her in mind of. Years ago (Time passed so quickly!) she had dropped Keisha off at some teenage friend's house. (And who knew what that girl's name could have been. Since she had married Jerrold Davis and joined New Purpose she had cut off her friends from "the world.") Keisha had called from the party, pointedly whispering into the receiver. "Mother, they're *doing* things here." "Things?" Janet had prompted, and in reply all Keisha had said was, "You know. *Things*." Her voice had been full of both fascination and horror. The rest of the call had been mostly breathing and giggling from Keisha's end. "Do you want me to pick you up?" "Are (whatever her name had been)'s parents there?" More giggling and wheezing. "I can be there in five minutes. Keisha?"

"Talk to me, Baby." She'd said it back then, and she'd said it on the terrible day, too.

"It's Jerrold, Mama. He's so heavy. I must prepare him to be received."

"Keisha? OK, sweetie, mother's coming right over. I'll get the boy together and . . ."

"Uh uh. Don't bring that boy over here. Don't."

"Keisha?"

"You heard me, Mama. Do not bring that boy over here."

"All right, Baby. It's all right. Mother will do whatever you need. Just talk to me. Keisha?"

Some nasal humming. (Could that have been a sob?)

"Keisha?"

"There's someone at the door, Mama. The deacon. I called him."

"Keisha, don't hang up. I'll wait. Don't hang up."

"Blessings, Mama, on you and your son."

Keisha? Baby? Keisha.

The phone clicked off.

They waited and the boy spun on the barstool. What a compellingly odd person he was—even back then he had been so. Butterscotch-colored with a large blocky head that he would grow into when he inherited his father's good looks—which he would. He'd grow into the strangeness, too. He'd use it to attract people, to endear them.

On that night he had hummed and he'd spun and he'd hummed. Hadn't he been listening to her conversation? Hearing his mother's name called in alarm by her mother: Wouldn't a normal child know to be alarmed?

She paced. Now and again she'd look down and there he'd be, right up next to her, head tilted back like a turkey in the rain, ear-to-ear insipid smile like a primitive cartoon.

Then again it had been a good thing, after all. Certainly on some days oblivion is a form of grace.

Hadn't she herself packed it all away since that night? Press clippings. Memorial cards. A tiny teddy bear she'd plucked from atop the mountain in front of his family home, black button eyes, its bow of white ribbon crumpled and stained with blood-brown chocolate.

Words lingered: Premeditation. Cyanide. Insanity.

Images, too. Three tiny coffins (So small! Who imagined such things?) arrayed around a large one. Cameras—dozens upon dozens—aimed at her and at the boy. She'd layered a shawl across his face.

More than anything: the blank-eyed bliss on her daughter's face. Try forgetting that.

When the doorbell rang, it, as expected, had not been her daughter.

"Ms. Williams? Ms. Janet Williams?" A policeman. That deacon, the young one, from their church.

"Ma'am, I'm afraid . . ."

She'd put her hand up—the universal sign, for just-one-damn-minute. They reeled back, as if her fingers contained lightning bolts.

"Danny. Daniel!" Sometimes he didn't seem to know his own name. Keisha had that, too: selective deafness. The boy stopped his spinning and humming and dropped from his most recent stool, staggering like a drunk, overcome by the sudden motion of the room. When the spinning stopped he seemed to recognize the deacon and made to rush for the door.

Get him out of here. That had been her instinct. Go take a bath. Fish through the smutty books in my underwear drawer. Find my purse and steal me blind. Just get the hell away from here. Now.

She held up the same hand that had stopped the officer to stop the boy in his tracks. She concocted some errand—some picture to be torn from *Essence.*

"Leave the magazine on the bed when you're through."

The boy had called out something to the deacon, but on her life she cannot remember what he had said. He knew something was up (don't they always) but considered the look on her face and decided to comply. She had set her jaw and affected the slightest of squints; it was the face she used on recalcitrant employees at the phone company. Foolproof, dependably so.

"That's a good boy," she encouraged. God, how she hated easy compliance. They'd work on that, the two of them would.

She turned and faced the men.

What she remembers most from that night was feeling sorry for them. What an awful thing, what a grim business: the giving of bad news. The officer had been young—perhaps barely out of the academy. Peach-fuzzy, he was. Blond, chunky build, ex-military—his haircut announced that.

The other man, the deacon, she had seen glowering self-importantly next to the pastor of New Purpose. A friend of Jerrold's, she remembered, but she couldn't retrieve a name. Something Germanic perhaps. Barely out of his teens, clean as a whistle and self-righteous as a snake. Good Lord, could there be anything more smug than a handsome young man who thought he had God's ear. That night he had a bruised quality about him, like someone off an all night flight from Tokyo.

Instead of sadness she saw fear in their eyes; and she was the cause of that fear, she knew. What, after all, would she do when they told her what Keisha had done?

As it turned out, not much. Hang her head. Accept a hug from the boy deacon. Note the probable next steps: autopsy, funeral arrangements, jurisprudence for her daughter. Lots and lots of media, they warned, and she agreed that would be the hard part.

But, really, until they spoke their truth, these men had no idea how she might respond. None. And for a moment—just for a moment—she savored her power, the sheer deliciousness of it. How often in life did you have a man—two men—at your absolute disposal? What wouldn't a man do for you in a moment like this—and she could see in their eyes that the longer she held them off, the harder it pained. Once, maybe twice in her life she'd had this power. Sex with her now long-dead husband. He'd be helpless—she'd stun him, he'd buy her the moon. And then there was that nasty piece of work down at the office—a lineman—up to his whiskers in gambling debt, rude and evil, him sniveling in a chair in her office, his fate in her hands. Beg me, she'd thought to herself. Beg me and maybe I'll save your worthless behind from the unemployment line. She'd stared the bastard down while he cried like a little girl—the same way Keisha would always do, in fact—swearing, as would Keisha, off his bad behavior, promising to be good forever. She had reared up, slightly, up over the worm. Who cowered. She'd had to dispose of that chair (one indiscernibly shorter than her own that she'd kept across from her desk—for the little people). He'd peed his pants a little, ruined the damn thing.

The eyes of the frightened: They were peerless. In front of her, these two men: Waiting for my fangs, boys? You! Blondie: in that kitchen and clean up the mess my grandson left on the counter. Preacher boy! Yes, you, hot stuff: Up on that roof and clean those leaves from the gutter. In the bedroom when you finish, the both of you. I'll be waiting—and I'd better not be disappointed.

On occasion over the years—rarely—she revisited this moment in the doorway. She'd entertained the identical pedestrian fantasies that all her fellow humans did: She'd frozen time right there. Wouldn't life be . . .

Except Janet, good determinist that she was could never finish that sentence. Janet had been nine when she had settled on the stoicism that would shape her entire life, and she had told her mother that her path in life contained no choices. Her proof had been the fact that all of the things that had happened to her had in fact happened to her. The other choices had not. Her mother—who had as much as made a religion out of resolute common sense—had ordered Janet to stop talking nonsense. Frequently and never with anything remotely resembling tolerance she would cut off Janet's little pseudo-philosophical ramblings at the nub, handing her a clean dishtowel and ordering her to get on with the matter at hand—another philosophy that had always served Janet well. So be it, then. She'd put these men off as long as a person decently ought to.

Like the big girl she'd always demanded her crazy ass daughter be, Janet squared her shoulders, took a deep breath and nodded to the men, signaling that it was time for them to take their best shot.

2007

Chapter **One**

Accrording to Estelle, condos in West Palm were hotbeds of depravity, geriatric Peyton Places—would put a blush right on that Angelina Jolie, may God strike me dead.

"Honestly, Janet, two hot mamas like us? We'll make Queen Bee in no time—we'll alternate mornings and afternoons. I'll take the early shift."

Estelle took another pinch off what remained of the gooey butter cake she'd brought over for brunch, another of those foods unique to St. Louis that Janet had never developed a taste for. A lifetime in this city and somehow it still didn't quite feel like home. Those boys had made good work of the bulk of the treat, leaving poor Estelle crusts and edges. Jesus, they'd eat anything, those boys would. (What were they doing up there anyway?) Janet fingered the envelope that had arrived today from the prison. She hadn't opened it. She never opened them.

Estelle recounted the story of a man in his eighties—the Sarasota Seducer, the papers called him. The old coot had apparently been working a couple of ladies in every building on Longboat Key. At least until the public health department got involved.

"A walking gonorrhea dispensary, the man was. Two good legs and a beach view condo: The ladies couldn't get enough. It's that Viagra, Janet. There's a whole new world out there. Time to get back in the game."

Bless her heart, Estelle meant well, but this was certainly the wrong tack for convincing a person to uproot herself from her home of thirty-five years and move to the Sunshine State. Low prices, mild winters, and a rich cultural life: That's what the brochures touted. Janet was pretty sure the chambers of commerce preferred to keep the STD outbreaks on the QT.

Estelle had been working her hard, here lately, selling the shared retirement home idea like a used car salesman. Not that Janet needed much convincing, frankly. She was as anxious to get on with the next phase of their lives as her friend here, but there were . . . loose ends. Alas, Estelle read her caution as foot dragging.

"We're not getting any younger, kiddo." Estelle's mantra, trotted

out in every conversation the way promises of low odometer read-
ings and almost-new transmissions would be—and Janet would
joke back as to how sixty was the new forty-five. And, what the hell:
They were two nice-looking women "of a certain age," as Estelle
preferred to refer to them. They had money in the bank ("We're
comfortable." Also Estelle.) Their old bones didn't creak too badly most days. Weekend mornings they walked the paths of Forest
Park, after which the two of them thought nothing of spending the
rest of the day at The Galleria—shopping, movies, a bite to eat at
the Cheesecake Factory. They ran circles around girls half their
age down at the phone company. Between Estelle in Accounts Re-
ceivable and Janet in Human Resources it was pretty much impossible to make a move in the company without their say so. The
Dynamic Duo, the young hens called them—to their faces. Behind
their backs: the Witches of West County.

"I keep trying to imagine you and me in each other's pockets day
and night." Janet's standard delaying tactic.

"Face it, kid: We're companionable." Estelle's standard response.

And they were. When she was a younger woman, Janet had been
the type to wonder at the vagaries of life—how people ended up
who they were, where they were, and with whomever it was that
peopled their lives. Not so much anymore. Things had changed
after Keisha; all of the what ifs, why nots, and wherefores seemed
rather beside the point. She imagines that if someone were to ask
her how at this point in her life she had ended up parenting a teenage boy and having a best friend who was Jewish, she would laugh
at them. Life happened. If you were lucky. What could you control
of any of it?

"I keep going back and forth between the Gulf and the Atlantic.
You're a sunset person, aren't you, doll? But the prices . . ." Estelle
held a hand up in front of her heart, shielding it, no doubt, from
the shock of real estate inflation. "Here's the plan: It's hurricane
season. We'll pray for action on both coasts. Pick up something
cheap on the other end."

Just as she always did, Janet checked Estelle on her tackiness—
check of which Estelle immediately blew off: The bitch gave her
the finger. Actually it was one of the things Janet loved about her
friend. All that in-your-face, go-for-the-jugular practicality. Es-

telle—a woman who grossed well into the six figures, considering salary, investment income, and a late husband's nest egg—thought nothing of pulling the car over at the world's most tawdry garage sale, greasy cardboard boxes stacked on card tables in some worn out part of Florissant or Maplewood. "Treasure knows no borders," she'd say, twisting the rock on her ring finger. You had to admire a woman who equally valued a diamond tennis bracelet and a barely used All-Clad roasting pan—"Eight bucks for this, can you imagine?"

"I printed out the brochure for that two-and-two in Boca—both bathrooms en-suite. It's pricey, but we'll talk it down." She fished in her pursed for the copies.

Ah, ha! Unauthorized copies! Nothing Janet relished more than a Xerox scofflaw. She closed one eye and aimed a pinky at Estelle, ready to demand key-code documentation or a time-dated receipt, when Estelle put her hand to her mouth. This, Janet knew, could be a bad sign.

"What?" Janet prompted. Estelle put her finger up, indicating she'd need a minute.

Good Lord.

"I wasn't going to say anything," Estelle gulped. And then she didn't say anything.

Janet waited.

"Well?"

Another finger in the air. Queen of the dramatic pause.

"There's no easy way to say this."

Apparently not, since once again she hadn't said whatever it was needed saying. Janet fetched a box of Kleenex from the counter. Sometimes with Estelle it helped to provide a prop.

"Bless you, Darling. Where would I be?" She put a hand to her heart, sobbed, dabbed, sobbed some more. Janet was pretty sure that Estelle had had those permanent cosmetics applied. There never seemed to be any mascara on her Kleenex—and the woman went through Kleenex like, well, Kleenex.

Estelle girded herself. "I'm pressing you on this Florida thing because . . ." Tick, tick, tick, tick, tick: that old kitty cat clock. All those years she'd had to keep that Danny from climbing up there and touching that tail (—and what on earth could those boys be up to? What kind of a noise was that?)

"I think that I have found the exact perfect place for Poppa's money."

That? All this for that?

"Honestly, Estelle. A person would think . . ."

But Estelle propped a hand to rebuff the rebuke.

"A miracle, I know. How often have I said to myself: Estelle, you'll be hauling this trough of money—this albatross—to your grave. Poppa's legacy squandered on probate lawyers. A shander!

"But, kid . . . [dramatic pause] . . . with any luck we'll soon see the last of St. Louis ice and slush. Goodbye road salt; hello Mai Tais by a pool in South Beach."

"There's the matter of Daniel," Janet offered. When Estelle was in steamroller mode it sometimes helped to raise the specter of the boy.

"Like sands through the hourglass, sweetheart. And how nice, your Danny and my grandson becoming friends. It's a mitzvah."

Upstairs something crashes to the floor and there is some sort of wild animal noise. Janet cringes but Estelle seems oblivious. She had tried reading Estelle's face for hidden (or not so hidden) flying quotation marks around the word *friends*, but didn't see any. The poor dear, what was it? Cluelessness? Denial? A genuinely progressive heart? Janet couldn't read her sometimes. One minute it was this and that about the right wing asshole governor, the next it was liberal vultures pick-pocketing her hard-earned wages, "death taxing" her beloved Bernie's—may God rest his soul—life savings ("A man who slaved every day of his life in that savings and loan, and where does all his money go but to teenaged chippies, riding around in their Lincoln Continentals and flushing money down the slots at Harrahs.") It wasn't as if Janet knew for sure herself about those boys, but she'd seen them look at each other, and, yes, it was *that* look. Or maybe it was. When was the last time she'd been looked at that way? That Wes? Wes, yes, that was it. In any case, she'd definitely be knocking on the door and announcing her presence before delivering any surprise snacks. On second thought, better to just avoid the upstairs altogether. She'd suggest Estelle do likewise. She fingers the envelope, spins it on the tabletop. It seems thicker than usual, marked "Personal." She didn't remember the others being marked so, but then she hardly looked at the things anyway.

"It's a blessing," Janet concurred, and, regardless of the nature of their relationship, she's pleased that the gods have finally smiled on the boy. Her Danny: Friends had been hard for him, always. That was the way it was sometimes with bright boys. Too smart for their own good. Another trait he and Estelle's grandson shared, that Ari. Sometimes she'd like to slap Ari silly, what with his crooked sneers and his not-quite-under-the-breath smart remarks. Who did he think he was messing with? Too clever for his own good—a schemer, there was no doubt about that. Cute as a button—big and cute and rather beefy. An armful of man, that was for sure. She could see what Danny saw in him.

"So we just go off and leave those boys to fend for themselves?"

"Our dear angel grandsons are off to college in—what?—a year, give or take. It's them doing the leaving. As the good book says, it's the seventh day: Our work here is done."

Could those be the actual words? Estelle plucked another crust off the corner of the gooey butter cake. The calories in Janet's imagination rolled like the numbers on a gas pump.

"And it's not like you go visit *her*." Estelle's eyes traveled from the envelope up and met Janet's.

Something for Janet not to like about her friend: straightforwardness without boundaries. And sometimes you were in the firing line.

"Roommates should share," Estelle preempted—neither a prompt nor a tease. Janet's silence about Keisha had been a long-standing source of tension.

And they weren't even roommates. Yet.

They'd become friends almost immediately, just after Estelle's transfer in from a small satellite office in West County, back during the consolidation in the late nineties. Janet's response to the requisite "any kids?" question had been, "A daughter, but she's as good as dead." What else was there to say? Estelle, Janet knew, had researched the ugly details on her own—searched the *Post*'s archives and pieced together the rest of it from bits of office hearsay. Over the last ten years, now and again she would push Janet to talk about it. Compassionately, as would be her way, one mother to another: "Janet, what could she have been thinking?" Or, "Can you imagine the grief?"

As a matter of fact, yes she could.

Like a chewed-over dog bone, it was. Leave the damn thing alone, for heaven's sake. Bury it.

But no, people could not leave it alone. Ask enough questions, they believed—ask the *right* question—and the secret vault in your head would pop open and out of it would emerge a logical and acceptable explanation for killing three babies and your man.

The religious types were the worst—choir mistresses, ushers, stalwarts of the Ladies' Aid. According to them, Jesus would reveal all—if only Janet prayed hard enough.

How are you feeling, Sugar? the opening gambit in every conversation back then; prelude to the probe: "Have you figured it out yet?"

She changed her number; quit her club and her old friends. Started a brand new life for her and the boy.

Across the table Estelle's brow knitted, undone by the enduring paradox. Janet resented this even as much she knew that Estelle came out of an entirely different bag. Her parents had survived the camps. Unanswerable questions and imaginable grief had been part of the texture of Estelle's childhood, coloring her life the same way Janet's parents' stories of Jim Crow Tennessee had done.

But Janet would always shut her down, her quiet inquiries, however well intended.

Until today.

Something about today. The letter perhaps. The happy boys upstairs. Estelle's dogged determination to get them both retired and relocated to a luxury apartment on the beach. Open the damn door, Janet. It's time.

She held up the envelope. Department of Corrections stationery.

"You realize," she said, "that he'll be responsible for her."

"She's responsible for herself, Janet. This is something Poppa made sure I understood. 'Stell,' he'd say, 'Each one of us . . .'"

Janet shook her head, signaling Estelle to stop. "Hear me. Please."

Estelle set her coffee cup down, folded her hands in her lap.

"These letters that come, they're next-of-kin letters. At least some of them are."

The ones that weren't marked "Personal."

Estelle's eyes rimmed with tears. (Drama queen! This woman would cry at anything—pet food commercials, sappy pop songs, a particularly luscious bite of cheesecake at their favorite restaurant.) Janet tapped the Kleenex box as a reminder of its availability.

"When an . . . inmate . . . is considered vulnerable—juveniles, the elderly, and mentally ill—and if there is someone out here who . . . cares . . . the Department of Corrections provides you with information about . . . them."

Them. A lovely, vague denominator.

Estelle trembled, in full dab mode now, one step from all out blubbering. "Updates, progress reports. I know just what you mean."

In reply Janet offered a non-committal half shrug, half nod. Ten years back the last letter she'd chosen to read had come from some prison psychiatric worker, reporting that her daughter had been docile, tolerating her medication well, and generally compliant.

"The point is that someday—maybe soon, maybe later—Daniel will be her next of kin."

Because she killed the rest of us.

They sat quiet. Estelle sobbing silently (well, almost silently), comforting herself with large bites of gooey butter. (500 calories. 500 calories. 500 calories.) She extended a hand toward Janet, her standard projection of empathic comfort.

"He'll be a man then," she said. "He'll do what he has to do. He'll do the right thing."

Which would be exactly what? Janet wondered.

"Come," she ordered Estelle. She led her friend down the corridor past the open stairwell (down which poured a variety of noises—what the hell?).

"Sounds like they're having fun up there," Estelle enthused.

"Boys enjoy a roughhouse," Janet concurred. To her the noises sounded obscene, positively pornographic. "In my office," she directed.

Janet fished a key from where she kept it secreted beneath a leather-bound collection of "Great Books" and spun open a lock on the credenza. Inside: files, envelopes, videotapes, a book or two. She tossed the latest letter on top, avoiding with her eyes an acknowledgement of what lay jumbled before her. Estelle reeled. (Genuine or fake? With Estelle, why bother distinguishing. Estelle didn't.)

"Bless your heart," she cooed.

"There it is. All of it. Every sordid detail."

Estelle lifted a photo from the drawer. Janet's heart quaked.

"So precious," her friend cooed. "The angels." The poor woman positively broke down looking at that photo.

Six years she'd been prying; six years Janet had put her off. Be careful what you ask for . . .

Estelle set the framed picture back on the file. She swallowed the last of her hysteria, dabbed a bit, and then stepped back, assessing the contents of the cabinet with appropriate professional distance, the accomplished accountant on the case.

"Such a mess," she pronounced, her opening appraisal.

So this is why I opened the door, the drawer. Outside consultation, and didn't we all need professional help now and again.

"I think I see the problem here." Estelle lifted a yellow legal pad from atop the credenza and selected—as if the damn things were bonbons—from among the tumbler of ever-sharp pencils. "How much of this has he seen?" What's-his-face, upstairs, she indicated with her head.

"We don't discuss . . . this."

Estelle nodded, neither shocked nor surprised.

"Will they be out of our hair for a while?"

So, OK: The woman *was* clueless then.

"They're occupied. You know how boys are."

Estelle waved her tell-me-about-it hand. "I'll need just a minute." She had already begun drawing boxes on the page, numbering a list in the margin.

Knock yourself out, Madame Comptroller.

"I'll be in the kitchen."

"Say, you know what, Hun: Boys need some protein in the afternoon. Rustle up a snack, how 'bout it?"

Janet walked away. She hummed as she walked by the steps: At the moment it was quiet up there, but a person couldn't be too careful.

Closed coffins. That had been the best deal she could get at the time. She'd wanted a private service. Jerrold's parents wouldn't hear of it. The whole enchilada in all its breast-beating glory: Nothing less would do.

"Think about the boy," she'd implored. Janet couldn't imagine getting him through it—through any of it. Jerrold's mother had gotten in her face, pulled rank, hissed, "At least your child is alive."

Coming into the church the boy had melted into her side. The place had been packed—who were all these people? Jerrold and Keisha, they had no friends—or none that Keisha had ever mentioned. Danny pulled into her tighter; how scary it had been for him.

Across the aisle, Jerrold's mother railed and raged and wept and howled. "My babies!" she'd screamed. "Jesus!"

Danny rose up to Janet's ear. "Can we go?" he'd begged. A thin-voiced whisper, oddly absent of despair.

She kissed his head. Close cropped, as was his father's, there in the big box, the one in the middle. (Those tiny coffins. Good Lord!) Enough, she said.

"Give me your hand."

She pulled him close, walked him out.

All those people, and what had happened to common sense? Don't stare at this child. Janet cut them dead. ("Killer Mom's Mother: Her Bitter Wrath." An actual headline! Janet's face just below, her grandson pulled into her side, his own face covered by her shawl. Estelle would find the picture there with the others.)

A bench in a small garden courtyard: They'd sit there, she decided, until the ritual thrashing ran its sordid course.

The boy held her hand. Not too tight, she remembered. More little-friend-like.

"Well this is sure something," she'd said to him. Danny nodded in reply. He hadn't been much of a talker back then, at least not to her. Recently the hormones had changed that somewhat—transformed him into an often surprisingly chatty adolescent. Chatty and furtive at the same time, they'd sit at this table and converse quietly over breakfast or—more rarely these days—over dinner. And, no novice about creatures such as teenagers, sure she knew there was plenty he chose not to discuss. All the same she cherished his willingness to offer whatever of himself he was willing to share.

Now and again a swell of music had penetrated the windows of the church, pressing into the courtyard the same way that a loud bass in a passing car does. She hated funerals, always had. It will make you feel better, she'd been admonished. People need ceremony. Who in there felt better, she wondered? How did any of this help? While she walked the boy out, the young deacon who'd broken the news to her had been up there behind those coffins blathering about God's will and how none of us knew the plan. "We ask you to look over Sister Keisha," he'd implored (to whom?), and it had been all Janet could do not to turn around and say, "How dare you? How dare any of you?"

You and your Jesus! The delusions you placed in my daughter's head. People don't wake up one day and just decide on their own that the devil has possessed their children's souls. Someone tells them that shit. Normal daughters don't send Mother's Day cards saying things such as "I hope you don't go to hell." Something had happened to Keisha in that church—to Keisha and perhaps Jerrold and the rest of them, too. They were just . . . wrong.

Janet had felt herself breathing faster and Daniel noticed it.

"It's OK, baby," she'd said. She petted him, calmed them both. "This dress is just cutting me funny. Grandmother is just fine." She kissed him on the head. Goddamn your mama to hell.

"You getting hungry?" she had asked him. He nodded eagerly. Boys: pretty much eating machines. There was never enough.

She wagged her chin and winked. That came to be their sign. It meant, "Stick with me, honey: I'll hook you up."

She remembered there was a Popeye's down around the block. They'd go get a couple of three-pieces and a coke. Fuck this funeral.

If anyone noticed their absence, she never knew. They had their chicken, and later they had stopped by the multiplex to see one of those cartoon musicals. Danny had laughed at some silly African animal—which made her want to cry. She had cried, there in the dark, silently, the bright Disney colors blurred into meaningless mush.

Later that night, the boy deacon rang the bell.

"Evening, ma'am," he'd said when she opened the door. She said nothing.

"Just thought I'd stop by and check on you. And the boy." In his eyes, the same deer-in-the-headlights fear from when he'd come to break the news. She told him they were fine, thank you for your concern.

In that moment he seemed to remember that he had a baking dish in his hands. He thrust it in her direction.

"In case you all are hungry. You know. You should eat."

He really was a good-looking young man. A little yellower than she preferred, but pretty brown eyes and a nice build on him. She noticed that the skin around his left eye had a purplish cast—the kind she'd see on the insomniacs down at the phone company—and there was what must have been a detergent rash around his neck. Just a baby, he was. Barely took care of business.

She accepted the casserole, thanked him. He stood there, looking awkward. Make him sweat, Janet.

"I should be going then. Just wanted to check in on you."

She nodded.

"How is he? The boy, I mean. Danny."

"Daniel is fine. Thank you for asking."

"All right then." He started down the walk, turned back. "My name is Craig, by the way." He turned and headed off.

"Craig," she called after him. He turned again. "Craig, don't come back here again." He opened his mouth but did not speak. She closed the door, took the food straight to the garbage cans in the garage and chunked it in, dish and all, didn't even see what it was.

And she set about making a life for the child. She had already done it for one child; she could do it again.

And there was the problem. Maybe she'd done it wrong: Ample evidence supported that theory. But what else was there to do, after all? The boy was here. Alone. Oh, sure, Jerrold's people had a fine house in St. Charles and a garage full of fancy automobiles, but leave her grandson with those fanatics? Over her dead body. (And it told, didn't it, that they'd never come for him. She'd fully expected them to—she'd lined up lawyers and social workers just in case, but they never came.) He was hers.

What the hell? A couple of degrees in industrial psychology: She'd figure it out. Step one: Lose the post-mortem. Off to Famous, where she bought the lovely credenza that matched her desk, and in went the lot of it—condolences, the business card of that obnoxious court-appointed attorney. All of it, she swept it in there, shut the door and locked it away: Good riddance. One thing she knew for sure: She'd not raise him under a cloud. His life lay ahead.

And they'd done just fine. He grew. She got promoted. Into their lives came a wild and funny Jewish woman.

Who walked into the kitchen and dropped the yellow legal pad in front of Janet. Estelle had covered the thing with notes—three lists that Janet could decipher, at least two marked "Plan A."

"The verdict?" Janet prompted.

Estelle sighed, adjusted first her hair then her bra. She rubbed her hands together and licked her lips, much the same way she did when she sat down the senior management and explained to them for the ten-thousandth time the meaning of the words *due diligence.*

"Well," Janet prompted again.

Another sigh from Estelle. These conversations: Who knew where to begin?

"First things first," she pronounced. " It'll be a small condo and there's no way this mishegas is coming with us to Boca."

Upstairs it sounded like the lion's den at the zoo. Janet smiled benignly at her friend. The doors had been opened and the horses let out of the barn.

Lots of doors. Lots of horses.

Chapter **Two**

Upstairs, those boys.

"Like this?" Daniel proposes. He sits astride Ari, grinds his hips. A sound comes from Ari's mouth. A scream or a giggle. Daniel isn't sure; neither is Ari. Ari rolls Daniel off. Grabs his own junk. It feels so good. Ari giggles some more. They kiss.

Ari reexamines the photo. It's confusing. The guy on top: There's his dick, but you can't really see where the other guy has his. Well, OK, you know where it is (sort of) but, like, how's it in there? Assuming, of course . . .

"Let me see that again," Daniel orders. Daniel owns the clinical eye; Ari's the technician. Ari turns the laptop sideways, rights it again. Shakes his head. "Whatever," he giggles. He adds, "Beats me,"—and waits for his laugh. None comes. Daniel doesn't do puns. Fuck him.

"At least this one's cute," Ari lies. He points to the blond—the one underneath.

Not as cute as you, they both think. They're sappy that way, each more than the other and each more than the other knows. They kiss. Ari grunts like a pig through the kiss, which does earn a laugh.

How'd that sound get out, Daniel wonders, their tongues tied the way they were. So mysterious, all of this. And exciting. "So that's your type," Daniel says. "Figures."

"Blond and dumb as a post. What's not to love?" What a skeeze, this blond—airbrushed, glossy—posed in a sailor's hat, no less. Meth addict, Ari figures. It's been a while since these website photos lost their erotic charge for him; it's the cold calculation of the whole enterprise that draws him back. Here, for example, someone had gambled on the probability of people being attracted to rail-thin Aryans with unflattering haircuts. The model owned the generic look of every blond child star on television. Swarms of his type buzzed through the halls of Parkway South—Ari'd never given them a second look. By the same token, nowhere in these pages did one find men like Daniel. Or himself, for that matter. The message couldn't be clearer.

All the same, the power of the crap fascinates him. A glossy, fakey, not particularly well composed photo of two not particularly (at least to him) handsome men: Drop it in the lavatory of the high school, paste it inside your locker, let your parents find a copy of it in your underwear drawer. All hell would break loose.

"Hand me the list," Ari orders, but neither can come up with it.

They rummage around the misaligned bedding, the scattered printouts. Daniel digs up the legal pad; Ari fishes the pencil from his Jewfro. He readjusts his shirt, which has wound itself around his body in some weird way. Daniel does the same.

"Give me a name for it," Ari demands.

Daniel clicks through the website. Never any names on these positions. What was up with that? There should be arrows. Labels. When he becomes emperor, that'll be his first command: More instructions on the porn. Daniel still finds the pictures titillating, but in an indirect sort of way. In the place of the generic studs, he pictures himself and Ari—and it drives him crazy.

He suggests, "Ride 'Em Cowboy." It's the sixth position they've cataloged.

Ari's pencil poses above the page: "My list or yours?"

The legal pad lists sex acts and positions they plan on trying out the moment one of them triumphs in this stupid contest.

Good question, Daniel thinks: to ride or be ridden. Who could say at this point? He's pretty sure it's like the exotic vegetables his grandma's always foisting on him: one of those you-won't-know-it-until-you-try-it kinds of deals. And who decided which one did the riding and who got rode? What a gorgeous man Ari is. You wouldn't notice him at first, but when you looked again, good God! Those big old smart smoldery eyes. They slay him! He stretches out next to him, wraps his leg over his friend's leg, khaki over denim. Is it his sweat or Ari's sweat that pastes them together? The woman could turn on the air conditioner maybe for once. It was Memorial Day, dammit!

Their legs wrap tighter—arm wrestling's nasty, hotter cousin, this game is. Ari grunts again. Neither of them can remember who came up with this stupid contest or what possibly could have possessed them to do so.

Maybe I'll lose, Daniel decides. He leans over and sucks Ari's lower lip into his mouth. Ari hadn't shaved today and Daniel combs the bristle of lower lip hair with his teeth.

Ari trembles. Moans. Exhales briskly, the way he did when his mother put Mercurochrome on a cut. "Asshole," he pants. "Get the fuck off me." He shoves Daniel off again, and wonders if there's any such thing as a lip orgasm.

Daniel lies on his stomach this time, rubbing himself against the bed. The rules allowed for that, but maybe it was a bad idea. It felt good (It felt great!), but it also made him want to snatch off this boy's clothes and get it the hell over with. Ari would love that, would probably pass out or something. Ari liked it on the rough side. You could tell.

If they compared notes, they'd discover their notions on the wager are somewhat out of sync.

Daniel (You'll beg me for it, you little bitch) believes that he has bet on one succumbing to the other's carnality.

Ari believes (I'll wake up one morning and you will so be sucking on this shit) almost the mirror opposite—that one or the other will be defeated by his own raging lust.

Close, to be sure, but not exactly the same idea. They've been too busy researching and rehearsing for sex to revisit the subject of why exactly they aren't having any at the moment. Furthermore: Whatever the hell the wager, neither remembers the stakes. What an embarrassing thing to forget, and it wasn't like you could ask. Was it money? More sex?

Daniel hopes it was more sex. Ari hopes the same.

Daniel's still prone and Ari mounts him. He forces apart Daniel's knees with his own until Daniel splays like a frog. He wraps his arms around, pinning Daniel's to his side, massages Daniel's nipples through his shirt. "Give up," he pants. Over and over, slowly, a mantra. All of his mass he presses into this boy, this man, beneath him.

Yes, Daniel thinks. *I give.* The other boy's penis presses against his back. Ari outweighs him, twenty pounds, easily. He's a big boy—solid, not fat. Daniel is smothered in Ari, who trembles above him and presses him into the bed. He has sweated through both their shirts. *More*, he thinks. *More. Press harder. Don't let go.* A noise comes in his ear—some sort of high frequency thing from the back of Ari's throat. Dogs will be summoned.

Ari squeezes tighter. (Oh! or No! or Don't! from Daniel. Ari doesn't give a fuck which.) This boy: He'd swallow him whole if he could. Ari: every inch alive, pulsing. Un-fucking-believable.

I'm dying, Ari thinks. An attack of some kind. Curse of the Birnbaum men: Bubbe warned me. Birnbaum men, dropping dead like flies. A shande, she called it. But what a way to go.

And you so could die from it, too, what he felt for this boy. It's as if Ari's heart has swollen to the size of this house, had a mouth and cock of its own. It pounds like a tympani; it hums, tunelessly but incessantly, the same way his granddad had done. He could love this boy or he could rape this boy. Two things that didn't belong in the same universe, let alone the same thought—and what if the wrong impulse prevailed? He could tear this boy's clothes off and beat him senseless. Who do you think you are, making me feel this way? It could happen just like that, out of his control.

Or he could hold him forever, just this way. Whisper in his ear, then suck in his earlobe, tender morsel of baby flesh that it is.

"Tighter," Daniel orders, and Ari complies.

Love was dangerous: Win the bet, lose the bet, you could die. ("The Birnbaum heart: like porcelain.") Best to postpone the inevitable.

As for Daniel, Ari has read it right; lust will be his undoing. Some sort of a fiend, he was—never stopped thinking about sex for one minute, and he's two seconds from peeling his clothes away, but, no, he won't. Give in now, and seal his fate—both of theirs. He could see it now: There they'd be, the next sixty years, derelicts, washed up in the kind of cheesy motel you found out by the airport, fucking like maniacs. (As it happened it would be a series of increasingly elegant townhouses, far from washed up, these two, never anything remotely resembling cheesy.) Because once you got started how could you fucking stop fucking? You could bottle this shit. It was better than grape soda.

Above him Ari vibrates like the fancy chairs in the Sharper Image store, like a purring cat. He is hot and Daniel is warm but it isn't the heat. Something radiates through Daniel, like warm hands are massaging his insides. He hasn't felt this way since the others left. He doesn't deserve this.

"Oh God," Ari moans. He closes his jaw around Daniel's neck.

Daniel feels the teeth. Pleasure, pain, slobber. Two perfect grade point averages on the line. Time to pull the plug.

Roaring like a lion, out and up and as hard as he can, Daniel pushes, expands like the Incredible Hulk. The bedside lamp falls. When his head clears, he finds himself standing in the middle of his own bed. Dripping with sweat. Ecstatic. He roars again, pounds his chest, king of the jungle. His nipples pull like cinders against his sodden shirt.

Ari has landed standing on the floor. Stunned. He pants like a mile runner. The crotch of his pants looks swollen and absurd.

"Motherfucker," he says to Daniel, but as if it were the most tender endearment in the world. He crawls into the club chair, mops up perspiration with some clothes, his or Daniel's—it doesn't matter. The sweat has defined every muscle that Daniel can see. Ari hadn't expected this body—his own—but here it is. He hadn't even worked for it. "Where'd this buff bastard come from?" His father said that last week, catching him shirtless, shaving. Ari had no idea.

Daniel dead-man-drops down onto his bed—which is damp and clammy. He rolls himself into a sheet all the same. Across the room Ari, still panting, glowers like a boxer between rounds. It is a look that is fierce and that drips with lust. The Elvis sneer. His hard-on tents his pants—Damn, it was like a coke bottle in there. (Who could handle such a thing?) Daniel's eyes stick to it.

Ari stares at himself too. Or he stares at Daniel over himself. He pushes at it, strokes it a little though his pants, relishing Daniel's admiration. Love it. Worship it. "What are you smirking at, bitch?"

Asshole. Animal. Daniel exposes his collarbone. "I ought to drive a stake through your heart." He doesn't even have to look to know there is a lurid bruise on his neck—indigo against brown.

"I got your stake right here." Ari flicks at the monster with his middle finger. "Get your ass over here and finish it. I dare you."

"Fuck off." The Ivy League: definitely on the line.

And then Daniel is skulking off the bed like a cat. His graceful, angular body. He licks his lips, does his own curled lip sneer—which makes Ari shudder. Daniel leans in, and Ari thinks, *Holy Shit! Here it comes. Goodbye cruel world.*

Daniel kisses him tenderly. A short one. Then a longer one. Then another. Ari reaches up—to touch something, anything—but Daniel bats his hands away. Lips and tongues only. A sweet little peck to finish them off.

Which melts the sex monster in the chair—it filters away like so much smoke; in its place, the rather addled geek boy his grandmother delivered here last fall along with a bushel of freshly picked apples. A big adorable teddy bear.

Inside, Ari roils. Both boys do. Chemicals stir, synapses flash.

"Let's go fuck with people," Ari suggests. Daniel sniggers in agreement. Those fucking people out there: Fuck 'em—they deserved to be fucked with.

Fucking with people: the hobby for boys without hobbies. Two sweet boys, with one big flaw: They liked fucking with people, treacherously good at it in the way only smart boys can be.

"What do you want to do?"

Do some more sex shit, Ari thinks—seventeen, already a monkey on his back. Oy! "Something at the mall maybe?"

Daniel considers it, said, "Nah." They were on to them at The Galleria—a little miscalculation with a bag of laundry detergent and a fountain. He doubted they'd even make it through the door. Fucking stupid shopping mall and fucking stupid people who shopped there.

Ari considers Daniel's flawless, perfect skin. It was as if someone had poured honey into a glass mold. Golden brown and smooth as silk. His own face has cleared as of late, but his back would flare now and again, and he would wonder if Daniel felt the bumps and if they bothered him. He hadn't seemed to notice. Bubbe blamed the cheap fabric softener her daughter-in-law insisted on buying—"tighter than last year's girdle, your mother. I should have such a precious angel to splurge on!" She'd peel off a twenty.

Neither of them knows why they enjoy making trouble. It's not something they talk about; it's just something they've both always done. Long before they met, they'd been baby hackers, each of them, unwittingly and ironically, feeling pride over minor computer disruptions that had actually been caused by the other. Both had graduated to the more satisfying realm of social mayhem—scrambled music during orchestra performances, undermining the weekend plans of their snobbiest peers, student council election tampering. Between them, a whole West Wing of dirty tricks.

Separately: good clean American fun. Together: Frankly, they scared themselves. And because of that each had an array of de-escalation techniques—stop this shit before it got out of hand.

Ari attempts one now. He flops down next to Daniel on the bed. Maybe if they kiss for while, no one will get hurt today.

Both of them both do and don't want the other one to jump his bones. Instead they lay side-by-side, arm contact only. (But such contact, good Lord! Ari's peach fuzz ripples with life, Daniel feels it, and it's as if there are insects between their skin. There's a name for this [Think, idiot: It's an SAT word. Beat this asshole on the test or there'll be hell to pay!]—animals whose entire sensory life is a universe of fine hair. Ari busies himself trying not to feel the flow. The brown arm next to the olive arm may be the most beautiful thing he's ever seen. Hands back-to-back, their fingers interlace, a perverse game of cat's cradle.)

Ari, whispering, "We should go to the graduation dance, get right out in the middle of the ballroom and, like, totally make out, totally hard core."

I'd so do you right there. Honest to God, I would.

Daniel scoffs. Taking your boyfriend to the prom: so last century. "You come up with something then."

I'll put you in a thong and a dog collar, bitch. Drag you into that dance on all fours—you'd love it. And Daniel is pretty sure this is true about Ari. He lingered a bit too long on the fetish websites, got a little bit of a thrill watching their victims squirm when they went out and fucked with people. Maybe not so little. He'd be their downfall one of these days—caught on the sidelines, snickering too vigorously, a little bulge in the shorts perhaps, all the while some pompous and deserving store clerk cowers in shame. (That asshole in The Gap—boy, did he have it coming.)

Assholes only: a rule enforced with vigor. Purveyors of cosmic justice, equalizers.

A Willy Wonka styled moralist, Daniel liked the crime to fit the punishment—let the greedy starve, let the vain be covered with boils.

Ari's motto: Payback's a bitch, Bitch. Just let a person hurt one hair on this beautiful boy's body. The hounds of hell would be loosed.

Most days it was paralyzing: Where to even begin in a world just teaming with deserving recipients? The streets of America ran with all sorts of scum: arrogant high school socialites, corrupt politicians, child molesters, that dim bulb who couldn't get your order right at the Jack in the Box. People needed to pay.

Ari walked into this house last fall, and they'd each thought the same thing: Who the hell is this fucking loser?

One look at that curled-lip sneer and Daniel had a plan—a logistical nightmare, for sure, but do-able. The bucket of dog crap would be the hard part, but assholes needed shit.

Another stuck-on-himself pretty-boy, Ari had thought. Give me cause, dickwad: speak to my Bubbe the wrong way—look at her cross-eyed even. You're gonna wish you were dead.

"You boys. Go upstairs and make nice. The grandmothers have business to discuss."

Daniel turned on the X Box. At least he wouldn't have to talk to the jerk.

Each turned out to be both the worst loser and the worst winner the other had ever met—albeit there hadn't been much competition. Loners—another thing they shared: too many jerks in the world. Better to keep to yourself.

New Year's Eve: one of those road rally games.

"Cut me off again, fucker. You'll wish you hadn't."

Daniel cut him off. Sniggered.

Ari dropped his controller and stood over Daniel. Glowered.

Daniel stood up to him. "What, motherfucker? What?" He made himself bigger the way he'd seen the out-of-control kids do in the cafeteria.

Ari was thrilled and Daniel was thrilled: all these new vulgar words, all this badass behavior. Life was good sometimes.

But there was a problem, of course: As it would be with a lot of things, neither of them was sure what was supposed to come next. Sure, they'd seen lots of fights, and Ari had even instigated one or two (try proving it) that never went beyond glowering and name-calling. They were pretty much virgins at this, unbloodied.

There they were, nose-to-nose—or chin-to-scalp, more like it; Ari's a good head taller.

Which intimidates Daniel. The whole package does, really. Ari is

solid. Square, built like the shithouse that he is. Looks blubbery—
but that's only because he dressed like a blind person. This is a big
man and he just might hurt me bad.

Neither is badass, really. Each suspects that's true of the other, but what if it weren't. Things could go south here pretty damn
quick.

Over the fall they'd become friends, more or less. Turns out they
hated all the same kinds of things: teachers who made mistakes but
then pretended they were just "testing you"; the way high school
just wouldn't end even though they both knew they'd learned everything these people had to teach; the way their grandmothers
would introduce them to other ladies and then talk about them like
they weren't even there; the clone-ish sorts of kids who populated
their parts of St. Louis County—stamped out of cookie cutters, the
same clothes and hair and makeup and body sprays.

Ari'd never tell this creep, but he actually looked forward to Sunday mornings, when his Bubbe came over here for coffee. She'd
pick him up at his parents' house and stop at the Dierberg's store
for a treat—a little nosh, no biggie. Sometimes his parents had
plans that included him and he couldn't come. God, he hated that.
He got Daniel's number. He called. They played games on line.

Daniel felt the same. The big lug kind of grew on you after a
while.

Daniel was pretty sure that the stand-off part of this wasn't supposed to last so long. In the cafeteria . . . Oh, that's what was missing here: In the lunchroom, the other kids doled out instructions
and advice. Kick his butt. Bust him upside the head. An audience
would help.

Ari had similar thoughts. This being a badass was more work
than it looked like, that was for sure. He figured that since Daniel
had called the last name, it was his move. That was the holdup
here. He pushed up on his heels another inch. He could wedge this
boy's head in his armpit now if he wanted to.

"Punk," he said. He blew two hot streams of steam from his nostrils.

Trash talk: That's the spirit. Daniel was a big fan of trash talk. It
hadn't been two weeks ago he'd completely fucked up the number
two and three students at Clayton Prep—two snotty little Ladue

bitches. A carefully timed, "You're gonna choke," before a biology exam. Worked like a charm, but in this particular case a more subtle hand might do. This Ari: Perhaps he was a crier, a big baby. Daniel'd bet he was. Always go with your first impressions.

Ari was noticing Daniel's eyes. Brown: Who knew? Maybe a little green in there? Wasn't it funny how you could hang around with a person for a couple of months and neglect to notice what color his eyes are—so, you see, a stare-down had its advantages. Daniel's eyes are the color of shiny new pennies. It surprised Ari how good it felt to call someone a punk. His parents had raised him to be a good boy, as had Daniel's grandma. Good boys didn't call names.

They are good boys.

They did their chores and they did their homework. Each is at the very top of his class.

They are good to their grandmothers—love the old girls to death. They are polite and solicitous and attentive to these women. They pick them up treats when they are out and tell them how pretty their dresses are and ask them if that's a new perfume. Both boys know that older ladies like to be flirted with. None of your fresh mouth, say the grandmas. Both boys are flirts.

They like museums and tourist traps; hate the mall, are neutral about zoos. Ari loves dogs; Daniel can take them or leave them. Given a choice they'd eat pizza at every meal.

They believe that the hungry should be fed and that the homeless deserve shelter. Healthcare is a right, not a privilege.

Each believed in the supremacy of his own intellect—not even the other could be more brilliant. Over the months since they met they have also come to believe that the man in front of him is pretty much the only human who just might, on his very best day, maybe—maybe—be slightly smarter, perhaps only equally so—and only on *his* very best day, and then only maybe, and then only with a few critical caveats thrown in. This about them would never change, not over their entire lives together.

Call me a punk, will you. "Say it again, fat boy." That ought to get him . . . (to do exactly what, Daniel isn't entirely sure).

They had come to know each other well that autumn—which might explain how easily Daniel had located the magic button. Before the solidly built man, had come the butterball boy. Say the secret word . . .

Daniel had been surprised to find himself upside down, then flying through the air, his bed coming up behind him. Only somewhat less surprised to see that the large person who'd thrown him here had set himself up for the crush, and he'd thought to himself, *I probably shouldn't be lying here when a man this size comes crashing down on top me.*

He'd thought that last thought a second too late.

His next thought: This is what the fly feels like after the flyswatter.

As for Ari, he hadn't been entirely sure of the words coming out of his mouth as he wrestled the boy on the bed. Some sort of speaking in tongues, perhaps—he'd heard this could happen, it was a religious thing. Some sort of spirit took over and nonsense came out. If this was that, it was rather enjoyable—like all the angry words that you wanted to say to all the mean kids who ever called you fat all came out of your mouth at the same moment. At some point he found himself with a mouth full of bedding. Apparently he was trying to bite something. (Actually, Daniel had indulged his regular desire to stuff something in the mouth of people who talked too much.)

Ari imagined that they had reached the time where pummeling was required, but you could hurt someone with your fists, couldn't you? Pretty badly. Recently he'd grown these big "guns" as his father called them. Who knew what the things could do? Maybe if he just squeezed. So he squeezed.

Concurrently, Daniel had been wondering if throwing punches could damage a pianist's hands. Not that he was a exactly a pianist, or at least not a concert pianist, but he did noodle around—pretty good probably—and who knew? A lot of times he preferred visual art. It was good to keep your options open. Did Vladimir Horowitz have fistfights?

And so there they were. Wrapped together. Entangled. Sort of mad. Sort of not so mad anymore. You let go. No, you let go. You first. You.

Each believed and would spend the better part of the 21st century believing that the other was the single most stubborn person he'd ever met—would over all those decades bask in self-satisfaction at his own mature self-sacrifice for his lesser and yet beloved mate.

After a while you relax. And then . . .

And then you both sort of know, simultaneously, that if you don't let go now, it'll be too late. It's already too late.

Let go. No, you.

You.

Neither does. And then the big boy trembles.

"Isn't this something," Daniel whispers, and pets the other boy's thick silky black hair.

On this late spring morning that New Year's Eve feels part of a distant dream—a filmy memory from the old world. They can hardly remember the boys they had been, lonely and scared and lost. Look at them now: giants among men. Dangerous boys who know they are dangerous. Bad boys who can back up their badness with proof. A bad combination.

Oh, but couldn't the whole thing have gone so wrong! Say the muscles on the big boy had been made in a bottle of chemicals. Say the darker one fit the stereotype. Say one leaned into the other, said: Dude, we could *so* go get us some rifles.

Smart boys, they are aware of the powder keg they sit on—and it's a blessing for everyone else that they are.

"Well?" Ari prompts. Surely somebody out there deserves payback for something. The law must be served.

"I'll think of something in the shower," Daniel replies.

He rises from the bed, strips his shirt like a burlesque star. His honeyed skin lacks hair, save the trail from his bellybutton south.

Enjoying the view? his look taunts. He pops his buckle and lets his pants fall to the floor, peels away his briefs, stands there in all his glory.

When he remembers to breathe, Ari in fact snorts. He's seen hundreds of naked boys before. In the locker room at school, and the two of them have been looking at porn for months, prepping for the big day ahead.

He has never seen this naked boy.

What had Bubbe said were the telltale signs of heart failure?

Yes, this is *SO* unfair, Daniel agrees—but life was unfair—trust someone who knew. No adrenaline junkie he—he's too smart for that—now and again it stirred Daniel's blood to walk right up to the edge of something. From his first sight of Ari, he'd known the boy was nine-tenths marshmallow and one-tenth maniac, the homicidal kind. (Decent percentages, as the human race went.) Nothing pissed Ari off more than a dirty fight. If Ari killed him, Daniel hoped he'd be quick about it.

Daniel saunters slowly on his way to the bathroom—give him the leisurely take on the rear view. See how the little bitch liked them apples. It's your move, Fat Boy.

Chapter **Three**

Estelle has lost patience with the Weather Channel. She's listened for hours, and a person couldn't get a tropical report to save her life—it's all tornados and flash floods these days—not a darned thing to get the South Florida real estate market churning. And, OK, so hurricane season didn't get fully ramped up until August. Mother Nature had her ways. Storms could be ravaging West Palm even while she sat here in traffic. Perfectly good—albeit water-damaged—two-and-twos could be dropping in price even as she tried to catch a left into the high school (and could these people get a light here, for the love of everything human, and what these people didn't know about landscaping. Could there be anything worse than a striped petunia?)

She spots her grandson slouched against a pillar, out of the sun. Just look at the posture: A scolding is in order, for all the good it would do. A genetic failing, it was. The boy's father had slouched just as had her own—may he find eternal happiness. The man died with a hump.

You had to admit it looked good on the Birnbaum men. Leaned back into a tree or a telephone pole, one leg bent at a right angle. They crossed their arms, tipped their heads down—slight angle only, just to hood the eyes a little. Swiveled their eyes around the way Secret Service agents did. The boy's father—her Aaron—would chew gum when he slouched, his jaw rotating slow and languid like a cow's. Like gangsters, the Birnbaum men. Pussycats, every one of them, but look at this boy—who'd know? If you saw him coming down a dark alley you'd turn and run the direction you'd come from.

Could he be the most gorgeous of all the Birnbaum men, this Ari? The Hillyers, too—her father, mind you, no ogre, thank you very much, a regular Tony Curtis he was, and her Aaron no troll either; had his choice of women (and take a look at what he ended up with—the anorexic bitch—the woman should spend eternity eating the garbage she served this poor dear child, the only good thing she ever did in her life.)

Ari had seen her, she was sure, but it was Ari's world and Ari set the pace. Look at that sneer on him. Smile, damn you. Fifty thousand dollars of orthodontia: all I get is an incisor. More of the Hillyer in him—just look at the boy. He looked like the sort of men Meyer Lansky would hire to break legs. Huge, menacing and the dim bulb gleam around the eyes. A certain kind of woman loved this sort of thing—and, well, OK, so I'm one of them—could you blame me?

The slow walk, is it, then? Two can play. She popped the door of the Lexus.

"Ari, darling. Yoo, hoo! Grandmother's here. Over here, precious."

Live by the sword. And a little snickering from your peers—it could do a person good—like an eagle stirreth his nest, to quote Janet. When he bought their companies and foreclosed their house trailers they'd be sorry they snickered at Ari Birnbaum.

Still walking slow. Estelle hated to admit how endearing she found it. Big, macho tough guy. As long as they both knew who was in charge.

And could that be a swagger on the boy? What the hell. Well, the wonders never ceased, did they. Here he came—as if trained by James Dean himself. His center of gravity had shifted south lately. Used to lead with his shoulders, he did—Frankenstein with a curly perm: Chest out! she used to order him. This new walk—it spoke to a person. It was comely even.

The outfit: not so much. Less James Dean, more *Señora, I trim bushes now.*

"Completely uncalled for," he pronounces her little show. She peeled away from the curb, which causes him to roll in her direction, which allows her to place a kiss on his cheek—an opportunity rare as a straight flush here lately, so she pounced on it—such a cutie, this one.

"Damn, Estelle! Let a person get his leg in the car, would you."

"Indulge me: Grandmother's time is short. Errands to run, people coming by." And I see you rolling your eyes, she doesn't add. He rubs away her lipstick and slumps down into the seat—at least as far as he could slump. Poor boy kept forgetting he wasn't a little butterball anymore.

"Where we going anyway?" A lovely mixture of exasperation, indolence, and genuine curiosity. As recently as six months ago, she'd have reached over, pinched his fat little cheeks and said something teasing such as "Just you wait." The fat little cheeks not so fat anymore—in fact, angular now, chiseled even. As for the touching business, these days it was no-fingers-in-the-produce as far as grandmothers were concerned.

At least she could read the boy—unlike his parents, for example, on whom by this point in the interaction he'd have declared World War 5000—the previous 4997 having been waged weekly, sometimes hourly over the last seventeen years.

He's . . . difficult, Aaron had cried to her. On a regular basis, he'd cried this—and she'd wanted to say Puleeze: Will you look who's calling names here. Aaron: a person who still insisted that ordinary vegetables caused gas, ate them by the bushelful, called her nightly to report on his bloat problems. It's the diabetic candy, you idiot who doesn't even have diabetes and then eats the crap cause it's low cal or low carb or whatever and then putters around the house like a toy boat. One could of course not say such things to his royal gassiness, who, adding to the irony, also complained about his son's "sensitivity," and, again, look who's talking. "Everything I say to the boy, it's a tantrum or tears. I don't know, Mama. We've had it over here. I'm through."

What choice did she have? Ari became her project. Some women gardened. She had a grandson. A delightful boy, might she add—an actual blessing in a dark world, and just look at the thugs walking up and down the streets even in such a nice area as this. Absolutely, the boy was sullen, temperamental. Often downright ornery. Which would distinguish him from other seventeen-year-old males exactly how? Boiling skin-bags of hormonal soup—that's what teenager were, and it had always puzzled Estelle the way parents—his parents—former bubbling cauldrons themselves—had forgotten what it was like to be trapped in these bodies.

"I hate the fucking Galleria."

A perfect example for you. The boy knows good and well that the "f" word was not a word to be said in front of the grandmother. He wants to start something, wants her to say, "Young man, I have asked you time and again to mind your language, and therefore your punishment will be . . ." to which he would respond with some sort of escalation, etc, etc, etc, all of which merely serves to change the subject, which had been:

"These clothes . . ." After which she'd put her hand to her heart. She could die. Really. What this family has endured so a certain person could dress like the homeless.

"They're clothes. They're clean. End of discussion."

What? Estelle Birnbaum: Struck blind? The shapeless, hideously colored T-shirt she could live with, *maybe,* but:

"Ariel. High waters! Come on. *Come on!*" Normally she'd offer a few tears at this point, but the left into The Galleria was tricky under the best of circumstances. She pulls into the garage next to Dillards. And just look: He's embarrassed now. The Hillyer men's olive skin purpled when shamed or enraged. Let him sit for a minute, Estelle. Let the bubbles simmer down, wait till the breath came easy.

Damn Hillyer pride. Just like her father. Boy grows an inch this month, and she swears she could kill his parents: too busy with Hannah and too busy being "The Gateway City's Top Docs." This one here, she could kill him, too: Too proud to ask for money for a pair of pants. Wouldn't take it if it were offered. Would rather filch it from their wallets—and Aaron and that woman must be on to him and hiding their cash—what with the ankles emerging like this. Soon he'd be stealing it from his sister, a witch who counted her cash hourly. Who would then call the police on him—as she had done before, accusing him of domestic violence (and, for the record, Estelle would have shoved her too. Honestly! A princess with a mouth like that on her. Let me get her in a game of Hold 'Em: I'll teach the girl a thing or two about cash flow.).

Usually with the men in this family, the plan was to make them think they'd thought of it themselves, but desperate times called for desperate measures. Boys as unpopular as Ari didn't need their inferiors walking behind them asking when the flood was expected. And look at this boy: a diamond in the rough. What a person couldn't do with raw material like this. A blessing!

"All right, fuck it, let's do this." He slammed out of the car and stalked toward the store.

"A minute, please." She exaggerates her toddle after him. (Although the heels in fact were precarious. She'd picked these out with Janet just last weekend. Six-inch stilettos, black, strappy, and—go, ahead and say it, sure—sexy. Adorable.) "Help an old lady, would you." She signaled him to grab her elbow.

Which always worked with Ari—a Boy Scout at heart, and don't tell him you know it. He supported her arm and she petted his hand with her free one, sent all her calming energy into him. "Aaron, you could hug the boy maybe once and a while," she'd offered as advice to those two, but, no coddling—the mother's rule—although if coddled wasn't what Hannah was, then maybe they'd changed the meaning of the word and neglected to forward the memo. It's the rage that scares his father. Aaron had been—still was—all bluster. Debate and fuss and complain and cajole: This was the boy's legacy. A millennia of sitting around old country campfires seeing who could outtalk whom. Look at one of them sideways and he'd go off and sulk. Ari seemed a different breed, somehow—her mother's people, surely—scrappy Russian bulldogs. Estelle's greatest fear: the day Ari popped his father in his loud mouth—and sure, he'd have it coming, her son, the verbal bully—but that would ruin all their lives. Such a day must never come. She'd see to it that it wouldn't.

"Do Grandmother a favor, sweetheart. These retail types—they take some handling. Just follow my lead here."

More eye rolling.

Two clerks approach. She waves off the one in the cheaper suit. "We need some . . . assistance, if you will. My grandson here . . ." She indicates with her hand the problem area, fishes for the word. "Let's be frank: a . . . makeover. There: I said it." Ari, mortified, she's sure, rifles through a hanging assortment of perfectly atrocious tops, pretending, she knows, that he isn't there at all. They'd not be buying anything on that rack or anything resembling anything on that rack. He shoots her the evil eye—another gift from his mother's people.

The clerk gives Ari the once over. He's a young guy, twenty-something, smart haircut, appropriately smarmy. "What are you into, man?"

Ari shrugs or scoffs. The same treatment she got—more of the slow walk.

Who has time for such nonsense? "Here's the deal," she started.

Ari's exasperated sigh. She puts her finger in his face, a warning.

Just like at the office: You had to remind these people who was in charge. She lays it out the way she would the case for changing software vendors: rising senior, Parkway South, top of the class.

"Congratulations, man."

Another shrug from Ari.

"Bottom line, he's the best. Make him look it." And then she outlined the rules: Quality material, quality tailoring. None of that hip/hop gangster crap. And:

Estelle walked behind her grandson. She grabbed his T-shirt and gathered the fabric together, acres of it, there was. "Fit."

Show off this body. Poor boy. One day you're a butterball, and then one day you wake up with this. It took some getting used to. For him, for her, for everyone. And, OK, so repackaging the goods would surely change things—for him, for everyone—and who knew what that might lead to? But she figures it's like inheriting an expensive Italian racecar. The sooner you learned to drive the thing, the better. As for the speed, well, wasn't that the other drivers' problem?

"How about if we start with a great pair of jeans?"

"Off you go." She'd wait here by the register until Ari got in the groove. He'd set up his protesting already, whining to the sales boy as to how none of this "shit" fit him, blah, blah, blah; she didn't want to hear it. He'd settle down. He always did. Then she could kibbutz. Another thing with these men: Prime the pump, they'd do the rest—and they'd be grateful for the favor (but don't hold your breath for a 'thank you").

The clerk is good, he knows his inventory. He extracts five or six pairs of denim with a range of cuts and washes on them and orders Ari to the dressing room.

"Whoa!" says the clerk when he finally re-emerged. "I think we got a winner."

Could they be more perfect, these jeans?

Ari's about to burst with pride, she can tell—he's feeling those jeans, as Janet would say. When pleased, the boy's mouth had a way of tilting off to the left—all the better to air those canary feathers.

"How they fitting?" the clerk asks. "Let me check the waist."

Ari hauls his T-shirt off over his head. Beneath it he had on one of those sleeveless T-shirts, wife beaters the kids called them, and what an awful name for something—but he's a shvitzer, like all her men have been. You had to wear something underneath, and notice the light dusting of talcum powder if you will. She'd have to ask Janet about darker powders. Surely they made such a thing.

"Dude, you are built," says the clerk, way too solicitous and way too something else, as well. Hands off the merchandise, she wants to say, but her assistance had clearly not been required. She'd noticed Ari's momentary embarrassment at the compliment, then also noted the change in his expression—replacing purple with the half-smirk, half-sneer thing he employed when looking down on his classmates with lower GPAs—which would be all of them, thank you very much. Arrogant contempt you could call it. He's in charge now, just the way she likes to see it.

Despite the overeager hands and the fact that he has clearly fallen into some kind of stupor, the clerk does have an eye; she'd figured as much when she'd reviewed his outfit. And he also knew how to dress a young man—particularly after he'd gotten the full picture of what he has to work with here. He'd fetch the perfect khakis and cotton knits, knew which designers cut their clothes for actual men (as opposed to skinny beach boys). And wasn't it amazing how many people didn't know what colors went with olive skin (because, frankly, if he'd hauled down the yellow Polos, she had a few choice words ready).

She watches her grandson play this man—a half-decade his senior, surely—the way a card shark played a small-time rube. Offering a bit of a smile here and there. Swaggering past him, asking how a pair of cargo pants looks from the rear.

"These are kind of expensive," Ari'd complain, looking the guy right in the eye. As if it were his credit card on that register.

"No worries. I'll hook you up." The sales clerk would wink, and Ari would strut by him again, obnoxiously close, offering back enough to keep him in the game.

There was something cruel about that sneer-smirk thing. Rhett Butler with a little Clint Eastwood gunslinger thrown in for the good of the order. This clerk's had some experience in the world, she imagines. Knows the score here—although, who knew, maybe he'd never been up against as genuine a pro such as her grandson.

She's watched this boy work his parents—no chumps they—watched his uncanny ability to read people, see their weakness, turn it to his favor. He exploited his mother's love of academic success, his sister's vanity, his father's obsession over current affairs, over any news from Israel in particular. Wanting love, he'd drop at the breakfast bar full of praise for the right wing's latest crackdown on the territories.

"Finally putting those Gaza assholes in their place, I guess."

More regularly—as in the episode that set up this particular exile—he'd mouth some platitude from the peace-niks.

"They're going to have to learn to co-exist with those people."

"Co-exist! Co-exist! What, are you nuts, Ariel!" Estelle could imagine the leering scoff on her son's face as he went after the boy. "You can't co-exist with animals."

"Typical," Ari had mumbled.

"What was that?" Aaron demanded. She's fairly sure he'd heard exactly what the boy had said, but it was more fun (Fun! What was her son thinking?) to come around the breakfast bar and get right in the boy's face and bluster a bit—just as Aaron's father had done with him. But Aaron isn't Bernie and Ari isn't him. Some weren't for taunting, and this boy was one of those. Seventeen years! Didn't he know the boy at all?

"He said 'Typical,'" volunteered Hannah—no help under the best of circumstances (although, as it happened, invaluable in piecing together the details of the battle).

"Typical *what*, Ariel?" Aaron had wanted to know. By this point they were face-to-face—or face-to-chest: Ari is the tallest of all the men in her life—and the testosterone held sway.

"You should have seen it, Bubbe. It was on!"

That Hannah: For her it's all fodder for the ongoing theatricals she kept stirred in her own life. The girl would call her now and again—often when her conscience bothered her. She'd come to believe that her grandmother in some way supported her shenanigans and used her less as a confessor and more as an unlikely confidant. Estelle played along: better the poor deluded creature talk to someone. Honestly! Some families needed two Bubbes. Six of them!

And apparently it *had* "been on," as per Hannah, although Estelle imagined she'd never get the full story of how it had gone so badly wrong.

"Get off me," Ari ordered his dad.

"Answer my question. Typical what?"

"Get off me."

At which point, Aaron (damn him) had cowed the boy in some way: barked or screamed something in Yiddish or some ridiculous thing. The idiot. Just when he needs to make a joke or pass gas (an expert on which he is), he takes the wrong tack. Whether or not the intention had been to make the boy cower, that had been the effect, however briefly, and when the child had recovered himself it had been too late to take it back: He'd been shamed. And had Aaron backed down at last? Of course not.

"Daddy called him a name."

"Your father did no such thing," Estelle protested.

"Believe what you want," Hannah sighed. You didn't need to be in the room with the girl to know that her face had been set in smug certainty. Her brother had landed on Estelle's doorstep later that same day, a hastily packed gym bag in hand.

"Fuck those people," he'd said, and made himself at home in the guest room.

He saunters out of the dressing room in his boxer-briefs and the wife beater and tosses the jeans to the young man

"I can wear these today, right Estelle?" Somewhere between a question and a demand, her being only a bystander in this show, she knows. A thin carpet of curly hairs mats his upper chest. He'd be hairy like her Bernie had been.

"Anything for you, dear," she tells him. He signals his appreciation with one finger, as if he were Sinatra and she'd just sent him over a drink from the bar at the Sands. The clerk busies himself with a seam ripper, removing tags and security devices. If she turns her back, she's sure he'll sniff them.

They cleared Dillards with three loaded shopping bags, Ari in the new jeans and a black cotton knit top that clearly had been made for him. His power thrills her: She can't recall being prouder to be seen with a man. Damn his parents. So obsessed with the princess sister that they don't see the king in their midst. Unlike this boy, Hannah emerged gorgeous from the womb, a natural beauty. Like all the men in the clan, this boy had to grow into his looks. As had happened with Aaron, one day it was just there, but Aaron had been a different young man altogether. Insecure enough to need the approval of his peers, he'd cultivated his oily charm at an early age—as a placeholder until the real attractions developed. None of that had ever mattered to Ari—he'd seen through the game at an early age, and the Birnbaum arrogance had kept him from stooping to play. Ari preferred his classmates' contempt to toadying for their affection. He was smarter than his father in that way—in almost every way, for that matter.

Which is what scared the boy's mother about him. Dr. Rebecca Westman Birnbaum had always been the smartest on whatever block she occupied, and then along comes this thing. Someone better at your manipulations than you were. Better to have strangled him in the crib. Bested once too often (and Estelle could just see the bitch, in the designer bedroom of her Twin Oaks McMansion, bolt upright in her California King realizing that the boy had tricked her), she had been more than happy to go along with Aaron's plan: "Mother can help the boy," and Rebecca, she was sure, would have made the requisite look-what-a-good-job-she-did-with-you joke. In any case, she'd offered no protest at the removal of her only begotten son from her dream home.

"Thanks for the rags, Estelle."

"You'll owe me."

Of course he did not. She'd rarely known such pleasure. This must be what an artist feels, she thinks. Look what I made. Yes, there was work yet: the hair, for example—which frankly wasn't that bad. The messy, tousled look could work, but she'd run him up to Regis. She bet if they thinned it . . .

But that would have to wait for another day. That fellow from the settlement house would be by in an hour, and they still had to stop at Janet's.

Which fills Ari, she notes, with a kind of crazed energy. He seems alarmed at her sticking a key in Janet's door.

"You can't just walk in people's houses, Estelle," he said, a plastic bin tucked under each of his arms.

"Watch me."

"What time is it? Daniel's home at 2:30. What if he's in here?

Doing something?"

"Would you like a sedative, sweetheart? Otherwise calm yourself and do as Grandmother says. Put the bins on the desk there and go pour us some tea. Janet should have things set up on the counter. You know where everything is: Hurry along, would you?"

She keys open the credenza and begins unloading the contents into the plastic bins. Sad and awful, every handful of it. Imagine such a tragedy, then imagine this: an archive—this . . . museum to it.

"Be a love and grab two coasters, across there in the living room."

"What's all this stuff?"

"Nothing for you to be concerned with. Make yourself useful."

Everything is as she left it when Janet allowed her a first look last week. Heartbreaking. She commences to sort between the two bins, but soon recognizes the larger task at hand. At which point, she begins loading randomly.

"Eye-witness news, June 2, 1995," he reads, lifting a videotape.

She slaps his hand. "Why don't you run up to your little friend's room? Leave him a note or something." Perhaps it had been a mistake bringing him here today, but she needed someone to lift these bins.

He slumps into the armchair and glowers at her—his I've-got-my-eye-on-you glower.

"If you must know, I'm doing a favor for Mrs. Williams. If she wanted you involved, she'd discuss it with you, I'm sure."

Ari mocks her, and she stops herself from turning and jumping down his throat. You choose your battles with these smart boys, and this one needed to learn that not everyone would take his bait. Some of us weren't born yesterday, buddy. She tossed him one of the yellow pads.

"The note to your little friend."

He brushes it off his new jeans onto the floor. More provocation.

"I sent him an e-mail before you picked me up. They have a full day today at Clayton Prep. He's probably already answered me from the computer lab.

"Fine, in which case you should go check. You boys are always on that computer up there."

"Estelle, you know sometimes maybe a person just wants to sit and enjoy a cool drink and not have all this . . . static."

She can't help but smile: If her Bernie, God rest his soul, had said that to her once . . . A last dusty bundle fills the first bin.

"When his Highness finishes his drink, he should deliver this to the trunk of the royal coach. Sooner rather than later, I'd prefer."

The sneer/smirk indicates he's considering a smart answer, reading her to see how far to push. (She'll tolerate an "Aye, aye." A "Ja, Voll" and she busts his ass.) He understands the limits, but just how big a man is he these days? As would his father, she'd have to have her showdown with him one of these days. No violence between him and her, surely. A few sharp words, a few weeks in each other's exile. They'd survive, and today's as good a day as any. Bring it on, Mr. Big Stuff.

He saunters up to the bin, sets his glass, sans coaster, on Janet's lovely oak desk. He hefts the bin.

"Anything for you, dollface." Purses his lips into a mock kiss.

Saucy. Inappropriate. One silly milliliter inside the line—and right this minute a slap would surely satisfy a person, but she lets him walk, puts the smack in the bank for when it would really come in handy.

She buffs the ring quickly, clears the glasses, puts away the tea. This kitchen—neat as a pin, tasteful (in a 1989 sort of way). In all the years she's known this woman, nothing here has changed. Preserved, like a historical home in a state park, like the medieval rooms at the art museum: You've seen one, you've seen them all.

It's the past, girl, Janet would say. I've moved on.

Raised a mausoleum to that past and buried yourself in it, more likely. Her sad and beautiful friend.

"Enough," she says to the room.

She'd sort through the ghosts and lay out the exorcism. The final step—leave this house, this city, these memories. No, of course you couldn't forget—her father had made that clear. The camps stayed with him every day, but he also knew that forgetting was beside the point. The pain: You made a place for it, and then, like an arrested tumor, you could grow your life around. If not, you became someone like Janet—dragging the past behind you like a hermit crab, all the while pretending it wasn't there at all.

"Yo! Estelle. Let's roll." Ari's in the door with the bin.

He's eager to be out of here. Something with him and the boy, no doubt. She'll not ask. Ari didn't do questions.

At home the truck awaits.

"Unacceptable," Estelle says, approaching the man. "To keep you waiting. I so beg your pardon."

"I just drove up. And you're doing me the favor, after all."

So gracious, this man. "My manners! This is my grandson. Ari, say hello to Pastor Mitchell."

They shake hands. Ari, as always, draws into himself—withholding judgment, weighing his options and keeping them open.

If Ari'd read the article she'd read, surely he'd warm up. Pastor Mitchell would appeal to the social crusader in her grandson. It's still too soon for her to judge, but she's pretty sure this man is some sort of saint. For years she'd searched for someone doing just the right thing—some place for Hiram Hillyer's money, his legacy.

"Leave the museums and the hospitals to the rest of the Jews, Stell. There's lots of folks worse off than us: Find someone who's doing something about it."

Three years, she's searched—attended volunteer fairs, co-chaired, along with Janet, the United Way campaign at the phone company. Somehow nothing seemed to be exactly the sort of thing her father had in mind. Until Sunday, in the Everyday section of the *Post*, this man, the big smiling picture of him. (Well, OK, it wasn't really a smile. Like Ari here, he didn't seem to have that expression in his repertoire.)

"Pastor Mitchell's here to pick up a few things—you'll help won't you?" and no, that wasn't a request. She directs the man to some chairs in the garage, asks him if he'd like to begin with those.

"We can always use seating," he replies.

Ari follows her into the mudroom.

"I've tagged some things back in the great room and down in the basement. Help him load them will you." She'd start small with these people—some furniture, canned goods. Take her time to feel them out. A lot of these operations: fly-by-night. The high-and-mighty type out front, poaching the poor like suckerfish, skimming their nickels and dimes to buy a brand-new car each spring. Have a hot meal, but kiss Jesus' behind first: Not with her father's money, they wouldn't. From what she'd read, Mitchell here was the real thing. All about full stomachs and warm beds and respite from the chaos of the world. She'd have to dig deeper of course. But so far . . .

"That's a perfectly good love seat you're giving away."

Ari had inherited her Bernie's penchant for announcing the obvious.

"Your point would be?"

"You could give it to me. I'm just saying."

This lovely floral chintz loveseat in that abomination you call a bedroom?

"If you want furniture, we'll make a trip."

"I was just saying. You redecorating or something?"

"Or something. Let's just say I won't need all this where I'm going. I am, in the words of Dr. King, taking the champagne flight to the Promised Land. Help the nice man with those bookcases, please."

Ari gives her one of his looks the whole time they load the truck. A nightmare, it must be, to go through life questioning everyone's motives. He one-word-answers the pastor's innocent questions, barely meets the man's eye. When they finish, Estelle suppresses her desire to apologize for her grandson's rudeness. Ari wouldn't tolerate it. Furthermore, she figures this is a man who on a daily basis works with much tougher customers than this oversized brat. She'd let it ride—this time. She sends the pastor on his way, promising a visit to the day center, soon.

"So. You don't need furniture in the Promised Land?"

"What would make you believe that everything in the world is your business?"

"Don't answer me, then. Fine."

Estelle has just about had it with this boy. Badgering, bad enough, but for him to believe she's subject to the petulant act! He has, to quote Janet, worked her last good nerve. She orders him to come, puts a finger up in his face. It's a good two and a half heads above her.

"I don't know who you think you're dealing with here."

He begins the eye-rolling bit—perhaps the only trait he shares with that sister of his—but she grabs his chin.

"You listen to me. Everyone has her limits. Even me. Do you understand me?"

"Whatever," he scoffs. She grabs an earlobe.

"Is that really the smart move here? Is it Ariel?" She feels him dissolving.

"If you must know, and not that it's any of your business, in the not too distant future, Mrs. Williams and I shall quit these vicinities and set up operations in a more temperate clime. And if you say *hell* you'll wish you hadn't."

Never leave a Birnbaum with a straight line.

"The Promised Lands of Boca and vicinities—maybe the Gulf, who knows? A nice condo on the beach somewhere, and I'll tell your father when I'm good and ready."

"Daniel's moving?" She'd misread the panic as insolence.

"Don't you worry. Everything will be fine. Be a love and get the bins from the car."

While he retrieves Janet's awful burden she hopes that is true; wonders if she can make it so. She has to believe she can, that she can make it work out for all these people. Her friend. These boys.

"This crap in these boxes. Florida. It's all part of the same deal, Estelle."

"Ariel Birnbaum, boy genius." Strong back, bad ally. "Let Grandmother fix you a nosh, what do you say?"

He shrugs his "sure" shrug. She loads a plate of his favorite goodies and turns on KWMU: *All Things Considered.*

"You know I'm going to find out what's in those bins." Neither threat nor taunt. The Birnbaum confidence: You had to love it. She offers him back one of his trademarked insolent shrugs. He'd have to find out the hard way that there were some things you wished you didn't know.

Chapter **Four**

Removing the bedding from the cupboard, the pastor first unrolled the foam camping pad and then wrapped the sheet around it, tucking the cotton between the peaks of foam and the cot beneath it. He was pretty sure you were supposed to sleep on the peaked side of the thing, but for him it was more comfortable with the flat side facing up. He was bone tired—as he is every night at this time—and would just as soon skip the whole bed-making routine, but it's a ceremony of sorts, a ritual. Rituals; they are part of what makes us human.

Willis the Wino, a fixture in Old North St. Louis for a generation, since long before the settlement house had landed on this block, had abandoned the camping pad a while back. Willis had requested that the pastor "hold" the pad for him while he took care of a little business out of town. That had been the winter before last and had also been the last time anyone around here had seen the old man. A rumor had gone around that he'd frozen to death on a sidewalk a block or two from the Savvis Center. Such rumors were beyond verification, of course; people like Willis existed outside of the refined documentations that ordered the rest of the universe. The Willises of the world came and went in patterns that defied logic. Last week a bedraggled Chinese man had found a place at evening supper—someone the pastor suspected to be much younger than his grime-obscured face let on—and had not been seen since. Men who had been fixtures on the cafeteria tables over the five years since the settlement house had opened its doors would one day just be gone. Pastor Mitchell knows that a regular check of "John Does" down at the morgue might at least offer closure to some of their narratives, but each day here offered more than enough pressing concerns to keep him busy: another new face or even a returning one, someone who was still alive and needed what little he had to offer them. There's neither time nor energy for benediction.

He fluffed his pillow and as he headed out to check on the folks in the sleeping area he notes the box of assorted canned goods he'd picked up at the woman's house this afternoon. Tucking them away would have to wait for morning. He remembers the woman's (quite insistent) promise to pay a visit to The House of Hope, and he sighs. With any luck she'd not turn out to be another West County do-gooder, the kind who thought another star might bejewel her crown if she stooped down to see how the other half lived. (More and more these days it is the other nine-tenths.)

Schmidtty waits just outside the cloth panel that divides his "private" alcove from the rest of the center.

"I got them all settled in," he reports, and the pastor says thanks. Schmidtty: another old guy who has been around here long enough to appoint himself dorm master.

"Did anybody find Similac for the woman with the little one?" The poor thing had dragged in here just before they were full and claimed the last of the beds.

Schmidtty coughs—deep and full of phlegm—and reports that they'd located the can, almost empty, deep in one of the spare refrigerators. The pastor made a mental note to try to get another donation of formula or of some money to buy some formula. Since he'd made the night shelter exclusive for women and kids, they went through a lot of the stuff.

"There's a lady and a little boy. Outside under the awning. Wasn't out there when we put out the light."

Pastor Mitchell sighs, massages his temple. What to do? Early June: At least the nights were warm. But a woman and a young child, out at night, in this part of town? He knew who was out there with them: A lot of them used to be in here, and he knew full well what they were capable of. But there are no more beds.

"How old?" The child he means. In the cold calculus needed to divide nothing amongst those who have even less, who knew what might tip the balance. Schmidtty guesses he is four, and the pastor mumbles the word "fuck." He's not leaving a kid that age out on those streets.

"Let them in," he orders, and reading the desperation on Shmidtty's face, he says, "I don't know where to put them either, but they can't stay out there." He squeezes his eyelids together, in vain, as always, in hopes that the location of the extra bed might appear. The industrial-sized can of sweet corn. The two thousand dollars to keep the lights on. A building appropriate to the mission.

The woman—the Jewish woman—hinted about wanting to put some money into the operation, but who knew. The article in the *Post* had been a blessing and curse. It raised the visibility in the funding community, but also with the community of people in need. More of the latter, alas, and to too many of the former, "help" meant an opportunity to unload useless crap from their basements. Or you could just give me cash, he wanted to tell them, but who knew better than he about beggars and choosers, and some of them—the Jewish woman, for one—actually had things that were useful or could at least be sold to buy other things that were. He'd gone himself to pick up the donation, and she'd made the appointment to "see what else we might do for you." Alas, among her furniture had not been another bed nor a few more square inches of floor space.

"Give them this cot and the pad," he says, loading out his spare blanket from the cupboard.

"No, sir. Uh uh. Them's yours and they ain't getting it."

Mitchell starts to argue as to how it was his decision to make, but he can see that Schmidtty has his heels dug in, and Schmidtty wasn't the kind of man easily persuaded, particularly at this hour. Even in the near darkness he can see that the man's pallid complexion has reddened.

"We'll figure something out, the women and me. You need that shut eye."

The pastor has slept on the ground plenty of times, and had he energy he'd argue how it's better for the back. Today he has nothing left, not even for that white lie.

Schmidtty does take the extra blanket and heads toward the front door.

"Schmidtty," the pastor calls. "Narrow eyes, OK?"

Narrow eyes: their code for closing down one's peripheral vision against whomever else lurks in the shadows outside. Like lifeboat directors on the *Titanic*, their job: to parcel out the scarce seats and decide who faced the icy Atlantic on her own. When he'd opened the settlement house his idea had been simple: Give people a place to come in out of the cold, a simple meal at noon, and someone to hear their story. But there was, he noticed, more and more need, not so many of him, and almost no money at all. He'd walked away for a week or two. Padlocked the doors and hidden at an old friend's house out in the county, where he called upon the Lord.

Do something. The words had come into his head. He'd years before turned his back on the idea that Jesus might speak to him directly, and yet the words had been there in his head all the same. *Do something.*

After which it came down to simple arithmetic. With this much (of him, of money, of sainted old souls like Schmidtty, of beaten-down square footage on a beaten-down old block) you could feed this many, sleep this many, and offer this many a comforting word or a shoulder to cry on.

As for the rest . . . well, you coveted miracles of loaves and fishes, and sometimes—not often enough, alas, but every once in a while—a truck would appear out of nowhere and drop off a few dozen cases of food that were actually fit for human consumption. Sometimes—often—the truck didn't come or the apples were full of worms. On those days you mixed an extra quart of water into the noodle soup and prayed for myopia. If you can't see it, it's not there. And you and everyone else knows that your solipsism is a lie. So you open the doors wider and the peaceful oasis becomes a warehouse of chaos. There are fights over the last slice of stale white bread, and fifty people yet in line.

You walk away again, but still there is that voice. *Do something.*

You retrench and you relearn the trick of selective sight.

As for the mother of three who is around the corner tonight, just outside of the burned-out confectionery: Well, there is no mother of three around the corner by the burned-out confectionery. Or none for whom you have anything to offer.

She knows that, too. Knows, as do they all, that once that light in the foyer is out, there is no more room at this inn. The woman at the door with the boy: She must be new—evicted as recently as this morning, perhaps, from some affordable rat's nest being bulldozed for new condos or simply being stripped for the now-fashionable old fixtures and the copper piping inside the walls.

Pastor Mitchell watches as Schmidtty ushers the woman and the child into the auditorium/dining hall/gym/sleeping space. How solicitous he is, and Mitchell imagines they see him as some kindly old uncle, the kind they surely never had. Schmidtty had spent the latter half of the twentieth century in an alcoholic stupor, wreaking havoc in the lives of more women than whose names he could remember, holed up in one flop house after another, and surviving on the kinds of jobs that no longer existed: pumping gas, bagging groceries, breaking tens in the toll booths of the crumbled up parking lots that used to ring the core of the city. He'd wandered in here drunk off his ass about four years back, asking, "What the fuck am I doing, son?" He'd slept off that bender, cleaned himself up, and had been here since, seeing to the needs of all of them.

"You've been touched by the Lord," the pastor had ventured after that transformation.

"Believe what you like, sonny boy," and, saying that, Schmidtty had patted him on the arm, less in condescension than with the fatalistic certainty of someone who had learned that dogma and a dime wouldn't buy you a cup of coffee in this town.

Back in those days, Pastor Mitchell still retained at least a fleeting belief in the power of magical thinking. If we all prayed hard enough, he believed, the bellies of the poor would be full and the grace and light of the Lord would pour down like rain. And thus he would pray—and once again he would be crushed by this world and retreat to someone's musty guest room.

Every time he returned, there Schmidtty would be, passing around whatever scraps he himself had scrounged, wishing Craig good morning and setting him again to the task of just doing something.

From the shadow of the alcove where a nun came by sometimes to sit with the little ones and read them a story, he watches as Schmidtty does what Schmidtty does so well. The woman from out front is collapsing in relief—the way someone reprieved from the gallows might—barely able to stand, trembling, perhaps at the thought of what might have become of them (what might become of them still—tomorrow night or the next). The little one has the stunned look he's seen on the faces of people walking away from car wrecks. The other women, settled in for the night, offer welcome, encouragement, make what room they can. There is little grumbling—there rarely is—then only from the few slightly older and dotty women whom he is still able to shelter. (The ravers cannot be here with the little ones.) Someone has room on an old gymnastics mat next to her little girl, and there's a place nearby for the woman to spread enough soft things to make it through the night.

He should go out and greet them and tell them it will be OK, but he is superfluous in this moment and also overcome by his witness. As they often do, such displays of selflessness fill him to bursting and drive him from his feet. He collapses on the cot, weeping, and he presses his hands into his chest because he feels as if his heart is trying to come loose from its mooring. Back at that old church he would feel this way—all of them would—and people would collapse from ecstasy, filled, they believed with the Holy Spirit and the love of the Lord. How bogus it all had been. The singing, the bliss, the false fellowship, the passion. And he curses sometimes the time he had wasted back then believing that God's love was all about seat time in that awful building. God's love was a woman without a pot to piss in making room for someone else's child on a worn out gym mat in a decrepit auditorium in a forgotten corner of a dying city. It was the last four women in line tonight dividing the last slice of Wonder Bread into four squares, laughing about it, then dropping their heads together to give thanks for the blessings of this day.

He still prays. And tonight he asks as always for God's forgiveness and for the strength to continue doing whatever it is that he does for these people. Back at New Purpose, back in his deacon days, he'd prayed as if God were a genie with a box full of favors. All you had to do was say the right words—and of course *really* mean them—and the enchanted satchel would open and out would pop peace on earth, a winning lottery ticket, and victory for the Cards. And who knew, maybe that trick bag does exist up there in heaven, and if you're filling orders tonight, Lord, please send down a case of infant formula and maybe could the Jewish lady write us a check to get the electric company off our backs.

Whether or not there is such a bag he has no idea, nor does he spend any time thinking about such things. He's lost all interest in theological debate. He is here; believes that were this also His time, Jesus would be down here with him. Here or someplace similar. He thanks God for that, and then he closes his eyes to sleep.

One more thing, Lord: *If* there is a satchel and if it is open tonight, please encourage Flo the bag lady not to defecate in the children's play area. Thanks and I'll see you in the morning.

Chapter **Five**

Daniel knew that when you were on a public terminal it was probably a bad idea to open any e-mails from the screen name "goldenair." Fortunately, the campus DSL lines were clogged with late afternoon surfers and pirates, and Ari's ISP had a crappy interface that took forever to load graphics. He'd been able to click the red dot before the image fully revealed. The angle of the photo, the lewd expression on Ari's face: He didn't have to see the rest of it to know what probably filled the bottom half. Not that he didn't want to see what was on that jpeg—more than anything in the world he'd like to see what was on that photo—it's just that the folks in charge of this joint didn't care for dick pictures showing up on the library computer screens. The little bitch would pay for this.

Daniel is supposed to be working on a draft of his last essay for his Rhetorical Styles class. Why don't we all write about summer plans with our families—we'll make this last assignment an easy one. Tell me what you, your mom, and dad, and siblings will be up to while school's out. Make it funny, like a fake travel book or a my-nightmare-vacation kind of thing. Have fun with it.

Have fun with this, Daniel thought, wishing he could actually give the man the finger.

You got used to it after a while. Eleven years of Parents' Nights and Father/Son Cookouts and Take-Your-Child-To-Work Days. Grandma, God bless her, was fierce. In fact, he had to protect these people from her. "Every child does not live in the same kind of home, and you need to have more consideration when you make these assignments." She'd get all up in their faces and shit, and it was fun to watch, but in the long run, hardly worth the cost. She'd go into the principal's office and close the door and from that day forward he'd get that "you poor kid" look. Who needed that? He'd learned that if he didn't complain to her, she tended to stay away from these dumps.

Hell, no. He didn't need or want their pity. There's nothing they have here that he needs or wants, and he's known that for a long time. Filling time, he was—and he, of all people, knows there are worse places to do that.

He considers his next move. Ari Birnbaum, you have been a bad, bad boy, and we all know what happens to bad boys. They get punished. You had to be careful with Ari. Like all good chess players, he was a half-dozen moves ahead, every contingency planned. Put frogs in his bed and he's already prepared the dipping sauce.

Ashley Winston plops down at the terminal next to him, smiles sweetly, and adjusts her "What Would Jesus Do?" wristband.

"Started on your essay?" she asks.

"OK, sure," he responds.

Ashley is pleasant in her pretty pert blond way—but also frosty to him, the way all the kids at Clayton Prep are. Gives them street cred that they know the black kid at school—only better if he were captain of the football team rather than #1 in the class. Were he dealing, he'd be prom king.

So much the better, their lack of warmth, since the ruthless competition at the top of the heap made friendship pretty much impossible among all the best students. Frankly, Daniel couldn't care less who became valedictorian. Won't change his life one way or the other, but it was sort of fun to watch—the frenzied clawing for position. It was a game that was easy enough to play and it cost almost nothing as far as he was concerned. A well chosen ass-kissing now and again, burning the midnight oil when needed. You did what you had to in these dumps.

"You're so cool about everything," Ashley gushes. "If I don't get an A in this class, my mom and dad will kill me." Daniel already had his A—extra credit had covered that. This paper was gravy. Mr. Thompson's name would look good on his college applications; the man always worked in his own matriculation from one of the favored Ivys. The perfect little summer vacation essay ought to help close the deal.

Memorial Day rolls around and everyone in the Davis household airs out the backpacks and sleeping bags. Shortly after the last bell of the last day of school, the Davises hit the road and head west. Yellowstone Park, here we come. Yogi Bear, watch your back!

Mr. Thompson cottoned to a breezy tone. He liked the sort of sunny essays they played on those NPR shows that Ari's grandmother listened to. The people who read them always had interesting sounding names—the women for some reason always had at least three of them. They read those essays as if they included the secrets of the universe, but if you listened closely (and how could you not, as loud as Estelle played them—and they were always on during after-school-snack time), they were usually about how cute their dogs were or about the cranky but still dear old man who worked the counter down at their small town post office—and wouldn't America be a better place if we all had endearing but cranky old men selling stamps. These radio people all seemed to live in small towns, in places such as Vermont and Martha's Vineyard, the same cranky old guy making their lives the charming pleasure it always seems to be.

Mom's been shopping for weeks, loading up storage bins with healthy snacks for the family to enjoy on the trip. There's nothing that Keisha Davis loves more than the hustle and bustle of getting her family ready to hit the road. My sisters like the various trail mixes she packs, but my brother and I always manage to sneak a few bags of chips and some candy bars in with the rest of the provisions.

Here's what he should do to that Ari Birnbaum: He should mail him a nasty towel, crusty with sperm. Stuff it into one of those big padded envelopes and have it delivered out to Parkway South right in the middle of the school day by some sleazy male stripper type.

"My mom's taking me to Paris this summer," Ashley announces.

"Paris, huh." Daniel feigns interest. Ashley's the kind who expected only a nod or at most an audible grunt from the men in her life, be they her father or casual acquaintances in the computer lab.

"For some shopping and stuff. My cousin's going, and Mom says she may let us go to some clubs and stuff. You can get in over there if you're sixteen, you know. No IDs or anything."

The Davis family vacation begins with an early morning stop at the Denny's off of I-70 in St. Charles. Every family has their traditions, and for the Davis clan, traditional means a belly full of pancakes augmented with a rasher of crispy bacon.

Fucking asshole, that Ari Birnbaum. A normal person would have given up by now, and the two of them could be enjoying what the Health and Wellness teacher had referred to as normal and routine sexual relations. There's a problem, he's discovering, with smart people: The way that every deal with them was played like

it was a game—didn't matter if it was buying a Popsicle or negotiating peace in the Middle East. Some guy says, "What's up?" in
the hallway, and your garden-variety intellectual thinks "I wonder
what he *really* means by that?"

The twins, Miriam and Sarah, prefer the middle seats of the van,
while Say (short for Hosea) and I like to sit way in the back. One
thing about Dad: He knows that you need a good van in order to
travel well. While the girls chill out to taped episodes of *The Real
World*, Say and I plug in our pods and run our own personal play
lists. Who even knows what the parents do up front? It's like their
own separate world up there. Every now and again Mom swivels
her head around to make sure us kids are behaving back there.

Ashley says, "You're not going to that party at Melanie's are you?"
and see right there, Daniel thinks. A statement she's made—but in
the form of a question, just like on *Jeopardy.* Ashley knows very
well that he wouldn't be invited to a party at Melanie Thorndike's
house, also knows that the only way to announce the fact that she's
invited without either bragging about that fact or seeming like
even more of a bitch than the one that she knows people know
her to be is by diminishing her God-given social superiority with
a question that laments the terrible burden that has been heaped
upon her and that, luckily for him, he has been spared.

"It's going to be so lame," she continues. No need in such conversations, of course, to pause for an answer from him. "You know
who I heard was going to be there?"

"Who?" Daniel responds, filling his designated role in this trans-
action. He, in fact, can recite the guest list from memory, as can
everyone else at Clayton Prep. Check the listings of live births
in certain zip codes for the years 1990-92: that would give you a
pretty good jump on the invitees. Ashley names one of the usual
suspects—a trust fund job, ranked somewhere down in the middle
of the pack. One of those headed-off-to-Dad's-alma-mater types:
Daniel rarely had dealings with his ilk.

Clayton Prep was full of these Ashleys—neurotic blonds who
never ate and who inhabited their social melodramas as if their
lives depended on it. For some reason, Daniel seemed to them to
be the sort of person upon whom they might unload all their fears
and angst about the fetid shark tank that was the social whirl of

high school life. This despite the fact he offered them almost no encouragement to do so—neither opinions nor advice.

Daniel wishes he could tell Ashley to shut the fuck up. That's what Ari Birnbaum would do. To paraphrase his grandma, he's a little cantankerous, that one. Apparently down at the phone company Estelle kept grandma entertained—or horrified, depending on your perspective—with stories of Ari's latest rude behavior. Must be nice, Daniel thinks, to not give a fuck what people think of you. He's sure that's the way Ari thinks, even as much as he also finds that impossible to believe. Everyone wanted to be liked, or at the very least they wanted people to not think much about them one way or another. Not Ari. The fact that telling Ashley Winston to shut the fuck up would result in his being relegated to social purgatory Ari would consider a badge of honor. The boy collected snubs the same way some boys collect merit badges.

"How do you spell Cap D'Antibe? It doesn't seem to be in the Word dictionary."

Daniel points her to the atlases over by the windows.

"Forget it," she says, and spells M-o-n-a-c-o out loud. "Like someone like Thompson knows the difference," she scoffs.

In his own essay, he steers his brothers and sisters deeper into the West, overnight in Denver and then north up Interstate 25, parallel to the Front Range. Miriam, the crankier and bossier of the twins, complains when the boys take off their shoes or tap the back of her seat in time to the music. Say, the youngest of them, can't resist tormenting her—the two of them feed off each other. As she always does, Sarah tires of the commotion—even before the parents do. (Mom is so patient with them.) Sarah distracts her sister with something on the video. Say returns to his Gameboy.

Daniel wonders what Ari might be doing at the moment. His school had a half-day today, lucky bastards. He was surely on lockdown: Last week, evidently, he'd thrown a lamp through the picture window in his parents' living room. He only has the outline of that story—Grandma's not one for gossip. Your little friend has a temper on him: That's as much as he could get out of her, and Daniel thought, *Well, maybe. If a lamp went through a picture window and Ari Birnbaum was the one who threw it, a person could be damn sure he'd thought through every detail of his performance.*

"The thing is, if Jake shows up like everyone says he will, then the party is liable to get totally crazy, if you know what I mean."

What was it about bad parties that the people who went to them thought that the people who weren't invited cared to know the details? In this case, the party hadn't even happened yet, and here he was, having to listen to this crap. It was like those radio shows that Estelle listened to, where some asshole would come on and tell you what the president was going to say in tonight's speech—in which case why bother to give the damn speech anyway.

He's a bully and a coward, Ari Birnbaum—a bad combination for him, but a good one for the rest of the world. Maybe Daniel's the only one onto that coward part. If Ari pitched a lamp through the picture window, he had his parents more cowed than Daniel believes possible. He is *so* onto that boy. So is Estelle. Hunch your shoulders at him and he shrinks back like the chicken he is. That's what he should do: forward this e-mail to his parents. God, that would be great.

Now it's time on the family vacation where everyone's nerves are on edge.

"I swear, you kids: I don't know why your father and I take you anywhere. Jerrold, you better find the damn campground fast, and those hot showers had better be nearby like you promised."

Dad, like all the dads driving around Yellowstone, is tight-lipped and placid. He's taking those special dad pills that they issue with your first baby. They work real well, unless your kid wrecks the car and they raise your insurance premiums. Finally, Say and the twins fall asleep, and up front, Mom and Dad are able to relax a bit. Thirteen-year-old boys and fifteen-year-old girls should not be confined together in small spaces.

And if you took naked penis pictures, weren't you pretty much asking to have them distributed on the Internet, and then Daniel realizes, Wait—that's probably exactly what he wants me to do: Put his nasty business in the street because he's too chickenshit to do it himself. That's just how the boy operated. Daniel tries to wrap his mind around just exactly how he's expected to react to this jpeg. He's stuck.

What a way to live, he thinks, as he imagines the calculus involved in the smashed window operation. Ari would have un-plugged the lamp earlier in the day—Daniel would bet on that. Yanking the cord from the wall would undercut the dramatic effect, and you couldn't risk the power in your throw being undercut by the tension from the plug. He'd have walked the room, calculating the best angle from which to heave the thing. The risk, he would have figured, would be the lamp not smashing through—to have it just bounce off—which it would do if it thrown at the wrong angle or with the wrong amount of force. He'd have made sure to ar-range the curtains just so.

Daniel can see him stalk the room after the throw. He'd have al-ready selected a few things to heft—just for punctuation, the main show being over, of course. Ari! Son, calm down! Please, don't hurt yourself!

Suckers.

Ari would have called glazers that morning and recorded bids on replacement costs; already priced lamps on the Internet. Daniel wonders what Ari got for that performance. Must have been good, something that over the top.

"Jennifer is such a whore."

Tell me something I don't know, but Ashley is genuinely in-censed. Bad shit is going down at this party tonight, and it's all that slutty Jennifer's fault.

And now for the epiphany—the time in the essay where the fam-ily gathers around the geyser and the beauty of nature draws them closer and makes them appreciate all that they have and all that they mean to each other. Mr. Thompson appreciated a good epiph-any. A good essay, he told them, repeatedly, should open the read-er's heart in some way. He should have a feeling of soaring.

Soar they would.

"What's this?" Say demands to know. "A big puddle of mud?" But our Dad tells him to just hang on another minute or two.

Of course Daniel doesn't actually know that there's a penis on the bottom half of the photo. He's only guessing: There could be other things. A vulgar sign, perhaps. Something Ari stole from Daniel's room.

It's uncalled for, whatever it is. Rude and outrageous. Oh, yeah, it's a penis—he's sure—and Ari must pay.

"Jen told me that when Jake comes in, she's gonna so make sure he catches her making out with that Mark from Trig class. She wants to see the fight. She's so like that."

"Hang on," says my dad. The ground beneath us begins to rumble and the twins wrap their arms around him.

'Every seventy minutes," he says. "You can set your watch to it."

Right there in front of us, a column of water with all the power of the earth rises toward the sun. Say jumps up and down and the girls cling to our father and scream with joy.

"That's the most beautiful thing I've ever seen," Mom says, and there are even tears on her face. She's an emotional person, our mother.

"She doesn't even like Mark. I mean, who would? You know?"

Could it be our Ashley's had a useful insight? At the very least she's prompted a brainstorm.

I imagine I am standing behind our family, looking at us looking at Old Faithful. The summer blooms before me—opens up like a fresh rose. I am already there.

Enough, Daniel decides. This fucking essay: He's making himself sick with it. But, that's the way you played the game around this joint: You had to give these people what they wanted. Thompson would lap it up—post it on his website, for sure. He'd love the part where Miriam and Say double-team Sarah, both of them tired of her obnoxious maturity. Mother had made her sit by Daniel for the rest of the day. And speaking of Mom, that surprise birthday party out in the park, where the candles glowed atop Hostess Cupcakes and Twinkies and where Dad walked around with whipped cream on his nose—until the flies drove him crazy. Irresistible: Why, it wouldn't be long before Daniel himself was on NPR. He didn't know any curmudgeon post office dudes, but how hard could it be to locate one?

"One of these days Jen's so going to go too far."

As had a certain Ari Birnbaum. And "Thank you" to all the slutty Jennifers of the world: You've always known best how to make bad boys pay.

"Later," he says to Ashley and she wishes him in the sugariest voice imaginable to have a really good day, too. He's off to scan the library and to consider who around this joint might be into posing for a picture or two.

Chapter **Six**

Estelle had sorted the contents from the credenza into four bins and then placed those containers in her formal dining room. "Make yourself to home," she offers, sliding open the pocket doors to a room she has almost never welcomed anyone into in all the years that Janet has known her. A tasteful and charming room it is, elegantly appointed in the traditional style both ladies prefer—oriental rugs, rich woods, and the kind of substantial drapery that didn't look like you'd picked them up on the sale table at Penney's. They also both preferred a simple meal in the breakfast nook over a fancy sit-down job here, thus its rare use, but having a showplace dining room did tend to say something about a person; and in any case the things on that table are not here to be eaten.

"At your pleasure," Estelle offers as if presenting a feast. Then she drops her hands to her sides, solicitous as a funeral director, awaiting the go ahead from her friend. On the table are two smaller boxes—the size for storing a few sweaters for the season. On the floor, a tired-looking cardboard box that at some point had delivered a computer monitor. A larger plastic box on the table matches the two smaller boxes (leave it to Estelle to color coordinate the grizzly task). And there is the envelope.

For a moment—for just a moment—Janet considers backing out. It wouldn't be so hard. What she'd have to do, she knows, is simply turn around and walk out the front door. But that would be a one-way trip. There'd be no coming back—to this task, perhaps not even to this friendship. Still, it was so tempting.

Estelle knows this can't be easy for her friend. Were that not the case, surely the poor woman would have dealt with it on her own. Or, perhaps not. Stronger people than Janet Williams had been brought down by burdens lighter than this one. Estelle is pleased at what she has done here, arranging and archiving the contents of the credenza—or as pleased as one can be with such a task. History, Trash, Yours, His: She's ready whenever Janet is. As far as these things are concerned, Estelle sees herself as something like the Metamucil of Janet's emotional life. Sometimes things got stagnant down inside you somewhere, and before you knew it your whole life became one unproductive moment after another. Enough! Time to get this stuff moving through the system, for Pete's sake.

As for Janet, she knows that starting the collection in the first place was a mistake. So much more sensible it would have been to just dispose of it all immediately.

Trash:

Several dozen leftover programs from the memorial service, replicated on ordinary copy paper, folded and stacked in a stationery box. Business cards, numerous duplicates of more than a few of them—many with familiar names of journalists from a wide variety of print and broadcast media. Other cards, too: realtors, ministers, attorneys. A handwritten recipe for jam thumbprint cookies (the only thing Estelle copied for herself). Several of the kinds of printed paper bags used for dropping off film at the drugstore, clearly used but empty of their contents, containing no information about what had been processed or when. Pre-school refrigerator art, watercolors faded to pale gray smears. A dozen extra copies of the obituary page from the *Post*. Lots and lots of receipts, amounts and vendors no longer legible. A blank book.

Estelle waits patiently, but Janet feels paralyzed. Even though everything is packed away neatly, it is as if each item were on display—had been blown up poster-sized, the way they did on those celebrity trials on Court TV. She's trying to remember her rationale for collecting these things, but none comes to mind. Maybe there had been none. Maybe it was like that catchall drawer in everyone's kitchen, the one that contains duct tape and superglue and someone's abandoned cigarettes. An ancient bottle cap or two. At some point such drawers had designated roles in the life of the house—this is where we keep the matches—but over the years things happened. Someone dropped in a loose key or a fast food restaurant condiment, and then all bets were off. There was no going back. Alas, Janet knows all too well what this manifestation of her out-of-control life contains. Letters. Those pictures. She won't be looking at those—that's one thing for sure. She'd rather go blind.

They broke Estelle's heart, the photographs in the credenza, and it had been a hard call knowing what to do with them. For instance, the wedding album—where did that belong in the scheme of things? Janet's daughter, as they all do, had had a copy made for both of the mothers, and Janet's copy had ended up at the bottom of the mess, buried beneath everything else. It's unremarkable, as wedding albums go—standard shots of the bride and groom and the bridal party, with perhaps a bit more religious iconography than she's seen. In one photo, the bride and groom stare adoringly into each other's eyes under the benevolent gaze of a generic-looking Jesus, golden brown tresses and all. She's guessing an autumn wedding—burgundy satin bridesmaids. One image in the album had stopped Estelle, amazed her: Janet, stunning in pale pink, in sharp contrast to the jewel tones on the others—and had there ever been a more elegant mother-of-the-bride? What a beauty. *Have you seen this gorgeous creature?* she wants to ask her old friend. Janet should revel in this woman—hire an artist to paint a life-sized replica for above our fireplace. (Should they have a fireplace in Florida?)

But Janet had buried this deep, this album, and Estelle, reading the drawer like an archaeologist would, figured that meant something. She placed the wedding book in the history box where it would keep until Janet or her son wanted it. If or when that might happen. And if it never did, that was OK, too.

It's the photos Janet fears most. The babies! Those faces! Who could look? She turns to leave. She couldn't abide it.

"Janet." Estelle's voice is patient yet insists, and it stops her in her tracks. "We'll take our time. The hard part's been done. As you can see. There's no rush."

OK, then, Janet thinks, and she realizes that she has fixed herself but good this time and that there is no walking away. She should have known; she did know—Estelle Hillyer Birnbaum disdained cowards. Together they would see it through to the end. Come on, Janet: Be a big girl. Get on with it.

Ah, but the photos. Estelle has made duplicates at Wolff's. Such beautiful little ones, and as she'd processed these pictures she'd considered the fact that almost all black babies seemed cute to her, had wondered if that thought was racist or looks-ist or something-ist. Didn't "good" people think all babies are beautiful, even if everyone knew that was a lie? Racist, shmacist—this is what she believes. And whose business was it anyway.

History:

Articles from the *Post Dispatch* documenting the deaths and the court case, now adhered semi-permanently to archival paper, sorted by date—duplicates in the trash box. Already compiled videotapes of local news coverage. Someone (Janet?) had started the VCR just as the story began, stopped it just after. Six hours' worth of this. A copy of a legal brief filed on behalf of Keisha Williams Davis, including depositions from psychologists and social workers, and a passionately argued addendum from a women's rights advocate, stamped "Received" (where?) October 10, 1996. (Could this be the one who had saved the woman's life?) Birth certificates for a Hosea Mark Davis, a Miriam Mary Davis, and a Sarah Ann Davis. (Estelle searched but could find none for Keisha Williams, but had located a DMV learner's permit in that name and a high school diploma—University City High School, class of 1988.) And the books. There were three:

a 2003 copyright academic book, written by someone named Weiss at one of the California state universities—a study, it was, of mothers who murdered their children, full of statistics and tables and written in the driest prose imaginable;

a lurid 2005 text called *Mothers from Hell*, on the cover a cowering and clearly crazed Keisha Davis being led into the courthouse;

and the local best seller—1997's *Keisha, How Could You?* — chock-full of speculation and accusations about what caused her to break and why.

To each certificate of live birth Estelle has paper-clipped the corresponding certification of death. No corresponding documents for Jerrold Davis. Of course his own mother would have those.

Pulling through the contents of the drawer, Estelle had at least a modicum of sympathy for the authors of those miserable tomes. So much to digest, so many conflicting theories. To this extent she fully understands Janet's desire to deep-six the whole mess. It was more than any one person could grasp, regardless of her distance from the horror.

Janet has always rejected even the possibility of sense. The woman killed her husband and kids—where was the sense in that? Or, worse, maybe that *was* the sense and it was just that simple. What she wants from Estelle is not sense, but order, a plan—and she can see one here in front of her: four boxes and an envelope. Tears streak paths through her face powder. God, how she hates a crier.

Loose, rolling around in the drawer, Estelle had uncovered five assorted pieces of jewelry. Two rings, a bracelet, a gold chain, and an earring for which she could locate no mate. She placed them in the boy's box. He should have something from the mother, something personal, and there is nothing else here that fits that description. She makes presumptions, of course: that the jewelry belonged to Keisha, that the boy has a sentimental side, that he is a saver—a person such as herself, whose every closet and dresser drawer is packed tight with keepsakes. Many things she presumes, but that, after all, is part of the job she'd volunteered for.

Yes, the boy did have a sentimental side. She's sure of that, at least.

Janet takes a step forward. Well, old girl. You asked for this party; might as well embrace the celebration. She nods for Estelle to begin.

"As you wish." And as if she were one of those skinny models on a television game show, Estelle points to the collection and Janet almost has to suppress a chuckle—the unintended melodrama; Good Lord, this is my doing. If some attendance scofflaw at the phone company performed thus I'd personally escort her to the state unemployment office.

Estelle indicates:

"History": the big box,

"Trash": on the floor,

"Yours": one small blue,

"and His": the other.

And Janet orders, "Wait!" What the hell? Who said anything about *his?* There's no *his* here.

His:

Pictures: his parents, his siblings, some with all of them together. (By all evidence the Davis family appreciated the Sear's Photo Studio. Five or so years of annual updates, the new members added to laps along the way.) The jewelry she'd found. And the letters.

"The things in this box belong to your grandson."

Janet starts, "I'll not have that boy dragging around . . ." but Estelle puts up a hand to stop the speech. She repeats her statement of the facts.

"It's for the boy to decide."

Of course she's right, Janet knows, but still . . .

"What's in there?" She had rights here, too (didn't she?). She snatches open the lid, sees the pictures right there on top, recoils as if they were rattlesnakes.

"They're not the originals. You can be sure."

Janet nods in understanding. She sees through the translucent box bearing her own name the chunky frames that had once populated her bedside table. So efficient, Estelle—damn her. She should have offered this task to that Tammy who she'd fired from customer service last week, a girl unable to distinguish the file cabinet from the shredder.

"What else is in there?" Janet demands to know.

"Letters. From the mother."

"Oh, hell, no. Absolutely not." She lunges for the box, but Estelle steps in her way.

"The boy has a right."

Rights my ass, Janet thinks. His rights, my responsibilities: A person only needed to see one raving missive from the crazy bitch to know that, if anything, the child had a right to be protected from her madness.

Reading her mind, Estelle indicates the trash box. "The crazy ones are here."

"You read them?"

Estelle turns her hands up: of course, part of the service, no biggie. The letters from deep in the pile had been the oddest things she'd ever seen—the girl had been hallucinating apparently, visions of fiery chariots and marauding horses. Estelle can't imagine whoever had been in charge of the medical unit allowing her to mail such nonsense. Sometime in the late 90s her medication had kicked in, perhaps, or therapy at last had taken root. If never forthcoming, she was at least increasingly lucid. By comparison to her earlier offerings, the routine obnoxiousness of the recent letters might offer some comfort with their benign, predictable unpleasantness.

"Mostly she reports on her day and how she's feeling. That sort of thing."

Janet is incensed. "I don't want to hear that."

"Well they're not addressed to you."

The most recent letter Estelle found from Keisha to Janet had been dated sometime in early 2001. Begging her mother for contact—a note, a visit, an . . . anything. She figures the girl gave up. That last letter from Keisha—it's the only thing not accounted for in this room. An unadjustable—a loose end that fit nowhere else on the audit. She's sure the contents would not surprise her friend— equally sure that Janet would probably prefer not to read it, but it wasn't addressed to her. It's to the boy. But what good would it do to read such a thing? Maybe it belonged in this box of trash. As was the case with all the awfulness that her father put away, maybe the world would be a better place without it. But it belonged to the boy—his right to read it now or read it later or burn it in the fireplace. And, what was the rush? For now, she'd placed it in her nightstand up in the bedroom until . . . well, didn't sometime lightning strike or bushes catch fire and the man upstairs tell you what to do about such things? She'd keep her eyes peeled for the sign, see how he did with the rest of this before hauling him down that road.

Estelle had archived Keisha's earlier letters to Janet in the history box. The lucid ones, that is, along with the letters from the prison reporting on her condition, and she'd placed a representative sample of those official letters in the boy's box as well. Who knew? It might help the boy to know that even people such as his mother were looked after with at least some degree of professionalism.

(Part of her believes they are a lie, those letters. An edifice constructed to conceal the gulag that is the federal prison system. And didn't she deserve to rot, that girl—didn't a lot of them deserve it—and the hard part of this whole project had been the ghost of her father over her shoulder, berating her hard heart. Stell, please: They're people, not animals. *OK, fine, Poppa*, she'd think—to this day never understanding how a man who'd suffered the bayonets of animals just like Keisha could show such compassion. And she knows it's that dead spot in her own heart and in everyone else's hearts that allows such animals to do their evil work.)

Janet openly weeps, but she already feels better for some reason that she is not entirely sure of. She asks Estelle about the history box, and then is repelled by the whole idea that there needed to be an official record of some kind. For whom, exactly?

"Why not trash it?" she asks.

Estelle tells her it's for the boy—for when it's time for answers, but Janet just shakes her head.

"Daniel doesn't need to know any of that."

Perhaps she is right, Estelle tells her, and she knows that it is entirely possible that the boy would be one of those who would let sleeping dogs lie. In any case, everything in the box was public information. Nothing here that he couldn't find on the Internet with a couple dozen keystrokes, no more.

"Better to not have to dig for it, wouldn't you agree? For . . . *if* he decides he wants to know."

Which will never happen, Janet is sure.

Estelle lifts the history box from the table—it is the heaviest by far. She'd have to have that Ari move it one of these days—her back, all this lifting. What use a healthy-as-an-ox grandson if not to do the heavy lifting? She slides it out of view, against the window seat.

"Don't you worry, OK? I'll store it for him. For if . . . *if* he asks for it, OK?"

Out of sight out of mind, Janet thinks. The best plan for the whole mess. She approaches the table, the box with her name on it, the one with his.

"OK, then," she concurs. "And, now? Next?"

"Two things, then. Both concerning the boy."

And again Janet flinches. The boy: Couldn't he just be a boy? An ordinary boy?

Estelle places a gentle hand on the container that Janet would just as soon didn't exist. "In my opinion—which I offer only in my capacity as an outside advisor—advice you are, as always, free to accept or reject—the boy—the young man—is more than mature enough to deal with what's in this box. It's a matter of when. I say now. The decision would be yours."

"What if I don't know?" And what good are you if you don't tell me what to do?—(and then make me do it when I refuse).

"Nothing's on fire. There's no rush at the moment."

"At the moment? Meaning, until?"

"Until he's eighteen, Janet. Then you will give it to him . . ."

Which to Janet sounds like an order and she opens her mouth to protest, but then Estelle finishes her thought.

" . . . or I will. The matter's settled."

Estelle isn't sure if this is the time for moral persuasion—or legal niceties, for that matter, since she's pretty sure that Janet has broken the law diverting mail directed to her grandson (not that there was a judge in America who would convict her). But someday—maybe by the pool in Florida—they'd have a long talk about all that she'd attempted to conceal from the boy. It's not so much that Estelle has the answers—she does not—or that she believes that her friend has done the wrong thing. She would simply like to understand what Janet had been thinking—the same way she had wanted to understand her own father's silence about the camps. Maybe Janet was like Poppa; a man who believed that evil was a weed that thrived on being spoken of. Keep your mouth closed and it was likely to die.

"Then there's this," she says to Janet. The last thing, the envelope. The one thing Janet would not be able to hide from. Estelle would not allow it.

"Which would be?" From Janet's face, Estelle would bet that she's being disingenuous. The woman either knew or had intuited the existence of this letter or one just like it.

"This envelope contains a letter from Keisha's attorney. It's addressed to you."

Janet lowers herself slowly into a chair—one of the padded, armless ones. She and Estelle had spent many happy afternoons shopping fabric for these chairs—four years back had that been? Janet had advocated for some kind of nouveau, striped ticking that had been the rage back then, but Estelle's more classical tastes had prevailed, thus the ivory satin tone-on-tone floral. She turns the manila envelope in her hands, lifts the unsealed flap—just enough to get an eyeful of the long-familiar letterhead.

"I'm guessing I won't like what this says. Will I?"

Estelle nods her concurrence. She imagines this attorney to be a good-hearted person—someone active in the prisoner's rights movement, no doubt. In fact, she vaguely knew the girl—she's related in some way to those Cohens at the synagogue, she'd met her, if she remembered correctly, at a bat mitzvah a while back. To her everlasting credit she had stuck by Keisha Williams Davis at every step along this bleak and dismal road, beginning as a newly minted from Wash U legal aid attorney, excoriated in the tabloids for daring to defend a child killer. She'd carried the case files into her defense practice—pro bono, of course. (Janet had offered not one cent in the daughter's defense.) Had saved the crazy woman from the death house, and continued to advocate for her humane treatment—appropriate psychiatric care, in particular. At the bat mitzvah, she'd seemed to Estelle to be a ragamuffin—just another of that whole generation of barely put together working girls, the kind you weren't sure if the mis-ironed blouse was slovenliness or a fashion statement.

"She wants money I presume."

Well I'd be cynical, too, Estelle figures. Who wouldn't? Janet by all evidence had no intention of reading the letter, so Estelle did what she considered to be the most important part of this awful job.

"Your daughter would like to see her son."

Janet's bitch fits were nothing new to Estelle. She'd seen this woman go off down at the phone company over things much less trivial—messy microwaves, a sloppy print job on a batch of W2s. And while she'd just as soon not be subjected to the string of vulgarity that issues from her dear friend's mouth—some demanding actions Estelle is fairly sure are anatomically impossible—she does understand, and she lets the woman vent. The poor soul deserved it.

As for Janet, as was often the case when she went off, she's sure she's saying things she'll later regret, is glad those boys are off at the movies somewhere—because God knows that they didn't need to hear such language. Her own mother had been a ranter—had taught Janet everything she knows about carrying on—in public and/or private.

She's expected this letter for years. For twelve years, to be exact. Over the years she'd invented elaborate schemes for what to do when Keisha did try to contact the boy, had contemplated creating a fake news article documenting the shrew's being stabbed to death in the prison shower. Anything to keep her away.

"For what it's worth," Estelle adds, fully aware that it might not be worth anything at all, "It's a request, not a demand."

Couched, of course, in appropriately dunning language—but Estelle'd sent and received enough lawyerly letters in her life to read between the lines. The Cohen girl blustered and shamed, but the custody papers right there in Janet's box would keep her in check until well past the time the boy would be able to decide for himself. She also believes that those papers and the letter itself are entirely beside the point. She reaches for Janet's hand. "I say this with love, my friend. At the risk of our friendship, I say this to you. This is about the boy and his mother."

Janet is surprised to find herself nodding in agreement. How would her friend feel if she told her that in this very moment she wished for the same thing that she had wished for on that god-awful day in 1995? That her bitch of a daughter had drank the poison herself.

So what's the play, Madame Accountant? How exactly did one broach this subject?

Say, Daniel, you know that mother of yours that we haven't discussed in a dozen years? That bitch who is cooling her heels in the federal penitentiary and who will remain there until she begins her consecutive terms—in hell? Well, guess what?

"It's his choice, love." As it should have been to this point, as it shall be henceforth. Estelle doesn't add this, of course. Instead, says, "We'll all help him, whatever he decides. You and I. And Ari, of course. They're very close, you know."

(Both of them wonders exactly what Estelle means by that, wonders just how much the other knows about the subject—probably not enough—and is pretty sure that now is not the time to say any more about it one way or the other.)

"You know what I would do? Take the boy to a nice dinner."

"Do you think?" Janet replies. Daniel loved a good steak—not the Golden Corral type, but prime. She'd have to spring for Flemings, maybe. Sometimes you had no choice but to butter them up.

Estelle seals the lid on the "His" box and places it in front of Janet, sets the letter from the lawyer on top. "Do it all at once, I'm thinking, huh?" Janet at first balks, but then concurs. Might as well get it all over with.

"And as for this?" Estelle asks, sealing the box with Janet's name on it. Janet would be surprised to know that her box is the lightest of the four containers. The frames and their glass had heft, but other than those, it was paper and ink, a few pages, no more. Nothing compared to the boy's load—and she knows that at some level at least Janet knows this—but she also knows that all suffering is relative. Poppa had taught that lesson well, and therefore she is not surprised when Janet shakes her head. Estelle gets this. She understands and she tells her friend, "So be it. Let the books be closed for now."

"Meaning?" Janet asks. She's like her Aaron when the doctor would tell him there'd be no shot today—relieved of the pain, disappointed to not get to cry about it; the gods of ambivalence with their enduring battle royal for her son's soul.

"Let me put this away for now. For when you're ready," Estelle says. She places the box in the bottom of the breakfront and clicks closed the latch. "We'll open together, OK? One day soon. For when you're ready."

Janet nods. She knows that day will never come. She hiccups: Her crying jags always brought on the hiccups.

"Poor baby," Estelle coos. "You're a wreck aren't you?" Her friend's pride will not allow her to acknowledge the truth of that.

"I'll tell you what," Estelle offers. "You and me: There's a turtle cheesecake in that kitchen, just dripping with chocolate and caramel. Best we get to work on it before those boys find out it's here. What do you say?"

Cheesecake, sure, Janet thinks: Strudel, stolen, Danish, cobbler, turnovers, frosted and stuffed chocolate chip cookies, and seven-layer coconut cakes with lemon filling. Bring it on, bring all of it on. Let's nosh our way to oblivion, why don't we?

Damn this woman—her damn efficiency, her damn responsibility. Her damn turtle cheesecake and her common sense, too.

"Come, then," Estelle offers, proffering her hand and what Janet recognizes to be her brave face. "Come. We move forward, then. Come."

A smile, at least, Estelle sees, and it relaxes her for the first time since she's sorted the credenza. Indeed, they would move ahead.

And it's the joke of that which has caused Janet to smile. People and their foolish positive thinking: as if moving forward ever solved a thing. As if the road ahead were any better than the road you were already on.

Chapter **Seven**

So Janet calls the steakhouse—no time like the present. Made the call herself, didn't even put Beth on it—Beth the stunningly efficient yet somehow vague administrative assistant whose job it is to manage the phones, the correspondence and the appointment book—then she sent the boy an e-mail and told him what time to be ready. A response pops up immediately. <Why?> and she finds herself insulted by this. "Why" was not the response to an invitation to a lovely dinner, but then she remembers that it has been a while since they've done anything of the kind. In their early years together, she'd often just throw the boy in the car and run off to the movies or out to a pizza joint. Now and then on a Friday, on an impulse, she would pick him up at school and drive him up to Chicago for the weekend. What fun they would have; what a perfect companion he could be. She realizes that here lately they are like some long-married couple who've become nothing more than companionable roommates, she busy with work and with Estelle and the various adventures she cooked up; Daniel always on that computer or here lately with that Ariel Birnbaum. Like forever-married couples, they passed each other in the hallway now and then, she and Daniel did, exchanged a civil word or an occasional peck on the cheek, and other than that pretty much kept to themselves. And rather than pleasantries, too often she'd needed to advantage their passing to hector the boy about his chores or the orange juice (that the fool couldn't seem to remember to set back inside the damn refrigerator, and there's no cup in sight so she just knows he drank it right out of the spout, and just let her catch him at it: Then his ass will really be sorry).

Daniel's birthday is months away, so she e-mails him back to tell him that dinner is to celebrate the end of another success-filled year of school (the penultimate before college—where had the time gone?). Her little Danny: once again with the perfect GPA. The other purpose for dinner would, alas, have to be a surprise, and as pleased as she is to be reconnecting with her grandson over a nice meal, the other agenda depresses her to no end. She suspects she will chicken out, hopes that the lead Estelle poured into her spine—

served alongside what really had been a delicious cheesecake (just the perfect amount of pecans!)—holds up for another few hours.

"Being a parent isn't for wimps, Janet. Like a great man once said: You take the good, you take the bad."

Estelle had continued to work on her; hectoring her, applying her sometimes circuitous but always—ultimately—sound logic; counseling her the way she needed to do when Janet was headed up to the management suite to break her foot off in someone's behind. But Estelle had misread her: What seemed to be reasoning errors were in fact nothing more than simple rage. Damn that Keisha, putting her—them—in this position in the first place.

"You've been lucky. He's a good boy. Alas, the water gets rough, and it's time for you to step up."

They had rehearsed some words for her to say to the boy. Janet can't remember much of it, but Estelle, in typical dramatic fashion, favored the sort of prefatory statement also favored on *The Young and the Restless*: Daniel, I'm afraid there's something I have to tell you. On Estelle's story, they always cut to a commercial after lines such as that one. During which, of course, some professional writer fed the actors their next lines. Regrettably, she and Daniel were on their own.

<Cool> comes the instant message back from her grandson, and Janet thinks, well that was easy enough. It usually was with Daniel. Even when she nagged him about setting out the garbage bins or about the damn orange juice, the most she would get was that expulsive little thing he did with his lips—half scoff, half sputter—or the hand by the ear that had come to mean "I heard you the first ten times" (In which case why am I standing here running my blood pressure up?).

Then there is an e-mail from Estelle.

<J, Good news! Category five in the Atlantic with a bead on Boca. Fingers crossed. E.>

And then an instant message from the boy: <Can Ari come?>

Hell, no. The last thing she needed tonight was that big goofy thing in the middle of their business.

<What do you say, G? Two for the price of one.>

Well, hardly: more like two for the price of six. That Ari—she swears the child has a hollow leg! She's never seen a person pack away food the way that boy did—and Daniel is no piker in the eating department himself. A human vacuum, that Ariel Birnbaum. She had to admit that it galled her to find that boy rummaging through her cupboards looking for something else to inhale. Not that he wasn't welcome—her home was his—but a person would like to hope that the box of raisins she'd bought for emergency oatmeal cookies (Daniel's favorites) would still be there when the spirit struck. She'd taken to hiding her leftovers—she'd learned her lesson the hard way after leaving a couple of fried chicken legs loose in the refrigerator. He'd even shredded the remnants of that Easter ham she'd been saving for a sandwich or two—stripped it to the bone, barely worth tossing into a pot of beans when he'd finished with it, and apparently kosher wasn't an issue with some people.

"What the hell have you done to this ham, boy?" she asked him.

"Sorry," he'd said, and he had even teared up so she'd had to go pet him a little.

"I can never get enough," he'd shrugged, a confession accompanied by a wry smile but also with a hint of teary-eyed chagrin. She'd patted the boy on his back and directed him to a box of cheese crackers in the pantry.

No wonder his parents sent him to Estelle: Who could afford to feed him?

<Another time> she tells Daniel, and then makes herself a note to tell Estelle to find something to keep that Ari out of their hair tonight.

So different, raising a boy. Keisha had been born a fussy eater. A fussy everything as far as that went. The poor girl had been cursed with the Williams metabolism, her father's people—charter members of the tribe of the hefty, not a slender one in the bunch. If Keisha had eaten the way her son ate, she'd have weighed four hundred pounds, died young the way that the rest of the Williamses had. A normal diet—three decent but by no means excessive meals—had kept the girl on the plump side, she'd starve herself to get anywhere near the neighborhood of normal. Forget the damn experts: Some people just couldn't eat like others.

Daniel had Janet's genes. (Or perhaps his father's? No: Jerrold had been tall, but built out large the same way Ariel Birnbaum is.

Daniel is lanky, as her people had been.) Definitely her genes in him.

He is ready and waiting when she arrives home. (He has also inherited her intolerance of people who seem incapable of being on time.)

"You sure Ari can't come? I'll text him. We can swing by."

"I've got a taste for a good steak," she responds. The boy knew better than to ride her on this. "With a perfect baked potato," she adds, gilding the lily a bit.

"Butter *and* sour cream?"

"And some of that creamed spinach thrown in. To help us pretend like we're not being so naughty."

He's disappointed she didn't take the bait about Ari, but there's also a little something on the positive side mixed in there as well. It's strange times these days with the boys. Like lining up outside the locked Nordstrom on the morning of the annual shoe sale—a national holiday on Estelle's calendar. Everyone pretends to be calm, but all it takes is a turn of the latch and all bets are off.

She lets the boy drive, another rare treat, and Daniel relishes it. And such a good driver he is tonight: all full stops and careful corners. The trip from the house out to Flemings: like gliding on air. (Driving a BMW 760 XI didn't hurt, of course. Janet's one indulgence: a divine and divinely expensive car.) She should let the boy get a license. Maybe?

They'd decided, she and Estelle, not to encourage the whole car thing so much. It didn't seem like all that great an idea, they'd concurred, two boys with free run of the Missouri roads—particularly these two boys. It wasn't that they weren't responsible—you didn't become potential valedictorians by slacking off. Neither boy drank (did they?) and neither of them had the kinds of friends who'd fill the car and then go out and lose control. (Well, neither of them had friends, really.) They hadn't really talked it through, she and Estelle. They both just sort of knew. Daniel and Ari and a couple of tons of motorized metal: Might spell trouble. And, yes, so it meant a few extra hours in the week for the two of them hauling boys to and from school and from this appointment to the next one. As Estelle always says: Better safe . . .

Such attentive valets they have here, and Daniel has barely

parked the car before one of them trots over and opens her door. Daniel, she notes, eyes the boy carefully, making sure he's treating his grandmother with proper respect. Satisfied, he nods to the young man—his version of a compliment, no doubt—and hands off the keys like a pro. Daniel then holds the restaurant door for her and approaches the maitre d' to ask after their table.

"Right this way, Mr. Davis." She'd left reservation in his name; she knows that it's the little things men appreciate. He's strutting a bit, and people are looking at them. She's sure the other guests are wondering if Daniel is her boy toy. They hardly resemble each other—in any way other than body type, that is. You saw a lot more of the Davises in him. Janet has kept herself up (despite everything) and so who could blame a person for wondering if maybe she'd invested a few dollars in a pleasant male companion of an evening? According to the papers, she'd not be alone. It was all the rage, this January/June thing, and those other cougars should only be so lucky as to be seen with a fine catch such as this. Eat your hearts out, ladies.

And talk about a young man who looked good in a suit. Her Daniel is *wearing* this sports jacket—navy blue classic cut with a cream-colored mock turtle underneath, a couple of shades up from his skin tone, that shirt. She worried sometimes about the child's vanity. He didn't have that "I can't get enough of my reflection" type that some beautiful people had. Instead, he possessed pride of a more problematic variety: the kind that wouldn't allow him to leave the front door if a seam were out of plumb or a speck of lint dotted his pants. Two short steps from compulsion, she feared he was, and it wouldn't surprise her at all to find him someday, trapped in his home, unable to face the world in his less than perfect state.

So different than his mother—a child for whom clothing had been often no more than the costume required for whatever role she was playing at the moment: wannabe gangster, sullen Goth, pious church lady. She was a girl who with some frequency left the house with the hems of her sleeves inadvertently curled back upon themselves, not fashionably but as if she'd risen from bed and thrown over her head the first thing she found on the floor and not bothered to adjust it properly, as she often in fact would.

But for tonight perfection reigns, and Daniel waits to seat himself until the host has settled her in her chair and offered her something from the bar. If Estelle were here, she'd order a carafe "and
a glass for the boy," signaling her lack of concern for both the law
and the liquor license. It amazed Janet how often Estelle had gotten away with that, but she'd not dare try it. She orders a Chilean
Merlot for herself and a Coke for the young man, please, and notes
almost immediately the set of Daniel's lips, indicating he'd be happier if his grandma let him be the host for the evening (even if she
would pay the bill). Duly noted.

They settle in with the menus, and Daniel, she can see, is perfectly at ease here. Unbidden she remembers that cigarette jingle from
back when she was a teenager: You've come a long way, Baby. And
in a perverse way it pleases her to know that her grandson would
almost certainly never in his life entertain such a thought—the
idea that he might not be welcomed in an establishment such as
this one. For Daniel, such treatment is a sidebar in a social studies
textbook. And there were surely many who regularly reviewed with
their children the price that had been paid for their privilege, but
Janet isn't one of them. And certainly there had been a price. Joe
Jameson, her father, had returned from the Second World War and
joined that generation of folks who were bound and determined
to move up in this country. He got himself a teaching certificate,
rooted his wife and daughter in an area of solid brick bungalows
not far from O'Fallon Park, and set about clearing any and all im-
pediments on their daughter's path to a fine life of her own. No, it
had not been easy. And, no, it had not been her parents there in the
headlines, sitting-in and having their skulls busted. Instead, for
the Jamesons it was the day-to-day grind of standing your ground
in the department store when the clerk pretended you were invisible, flourishing your property tax receipt in the face of the bitch
who refuses your daughter a spot in the school-sponsored Brownie
troop. A death of a thousand cuts, it was, and the price they paid
had been their health, both parents dead in their early sixties from
stroke and diabetes—surely, Janet feels, attributable to the stress
of being born when and where they were.

But, no she will not hold any of that over this boy's head. His
ability to sit over there—so smug and calm and safe—that is his

birthright. Paid in full, as Estelle would say. Janet knows that this is exactly what her mother and father had dared imagine in their wildest dreams: this confident young man, their descendant, in a high-class joint, inhabiting the masculine elegance of the place with effortless and unreflective comfort.

And so what if it had taken an extra generation? The boy's mother, she'd be in that chair, glaring around at her fellow diners, eyes set hard in characteristic paranoia. (What had been the name of that place they used to go eat at back in the day? Shortly after Wallace had died.) They would barely be seated before Keisha started whining to go home. A perfectly ordinary family-style place it had been, not far from the Esquire Theater. (What is the name of that place?) She opens her mouth to ask the boy, but catches herself in time. More and more frequently here lately she has almost made this same mistake—has almost asked her grandson about things that had happened well before he'd been born. The marital status of Keisha's third grade teacher. Whether Keisha had preferred Pepsi or Coca-Cola when she was in high school. Sometimes she'll be remembering some moment from her life with her daughter and there he will be in the middle of it—*this* Daniel, the young man Daniel. At a high school choral performance in which Keisha soloed, there the two of them are, greeting his mother and telling her how well she had sung. "Do you really think so?" Keisha beams. For the life of her, Janet can't imagine who, if anyone, might have actually been by her side that night. Wallace had been dead by then and Keisha didn't have a boyfriend. It's a nonsensical and even a trashy cross wiring of her imagination. Totally impossible and yet somehow entirely plausible to her, which perhaps explained why it persisted.

"I bet you're thinking what I'm thinking," he says, the flirtatious and always transparent way he had of enforcing his will.

"Could we have the bruschetta, right?" she responds. Far be it from Daniel Davis to outright ask if he can order an hors d'oeuvre. Janet feeds right in, of course—would also rather like something savory right now—and, after all, it is the boy's night. Deciphering men had always been easy for her—so much so that she scoffed at the kinds of magazines and books on every newsstand these days purporting to lay out operating instructions for these "difficult" creatures. Look at him: What was difficult here? Like all of them, he wore whatever simple emotions he owned right there on his sleeve. The key word was simple—and the mistake that most women made was in believing that simple equaled shallow. Bad idea. Men were like the beautiful celadon porcelain most people walked right by at the flea market. A simple green vase, people thought— only because they never stopped long enough to see the depth and richness of the glaze. If you dropped that vase, it shattered into a million pieces. There was a lesson in that.

"What do you think about a twelve ounce filet?" he asks her.

Clearly a boy who didn't understand much about women.

She decides on the petite—will probably have half of that wrapped to go. Their drinks arrive and so does a boy with a basket of baked goods. Daniel and the boy exchange greetings—it's likely they're classmates or something. The boy announces to Daniel (not to his "date," of course) that the waiter will be right along. Daniel says something such as "thanks, Dude," breaks into a roll and settles into small talk.

This small talk: It's a gift to her and a blessing, she knows. God knows she's watched her peers perched awkwardly across the tables from sons, grandsons, nephews—husbands, even—some sundry lamebrain who can't even ask her how her day has been. Lord knows her daughter never carried on a civil conversation, and look at poor Estelle! That Ari Birnbaum: a grunter if she'd ever seen one. Not Daniel Davis. He'd ask about her work, ask about her friends, ask after characters on her story.

"Enough about me," she'd have to protest. "Tell me about school. Tell me what you're reading." And off he'd be, every mother's dream: a chatty teenage boy, telling you all about his wonderful life and how much fun he's having.

Daniel hates school. Janet is fully aware of this fact. He didn't hate learning; rather he disdained the place and the people and teachers and the ritual and all of everything else that went with it. His innate intelligence is his saving grace, along with his curiosity about the world. He was savvy enough, for example, to understand at an early age that because of his history people didn't expect much from him, particularly not in the brains area. Some kids would have been done in, but Daniel Davis may be the most goal-oriented person she has ever known. Mind made up, there was nothing he wouldn't do to get what he wanted, and just after he'd come to her he'd made his mind up that he was going to the best college in America. "Which one is that, G?" he'd asked her, and she'd brought him home the list from her outplacement files, after which he laid plans on how to get himself there.

He stuffs a roll in his mouth. And another roll.

"You'll choke yourself. And you might want to save some room for your meal."

Typical male: What she intends as maternal concern is read as infantilizing—hardly worth acknowledging. He places a roll on her plate, next to the half-eaten one already there, then signals to the busboy—so much for anything you might have to say, Granny dear.

The busboy complies. If Janet were in charge here, the boy's hair would be tied back in a ponytail or something. Or cut. Turns out Daniel does know him—from God knows where—and their small talk about mutual paths their lives have trod infuriates her to distraction. She's about to remind a certain member of the junior staff that extraneous chit chat from his ilk was not the custom here, but she's spared the need for supervision by the waiter, who is by all appearance also peeved by the all-you-can-eat decorum that has been on display. Janet quite enjoys the subtle eyebrow raise and head tilt that sends Gabby about his business.

"Sir, ma'am: Welcome. My name is Steven and it will be my pleasure to serve you tonight. How is everyone this evening?"

"Steven, we are just terrific, aren't we, G?"

Janet hardly knows how to respond. She's unused to this public ebullience, not sure what to make of this particular Daniel, whether or not he is someone she should encourage or someone to squash like a fly.

"There are a couple of specials I'd like to tell you about. I won't go through the wines, since I see that you're set, but for next time I do want you to remember we've got a great cellar here, everything from affordable to high end. All quite drinkable."

Steven's a tall one—Ari Birnbaum's height without the bulk. Mid-twenties, handsome in the non-threatening sitcom star kind of way. Professional waiter or grad student, perhaps. She'd make her decision about that as the evening progressed.

"The chef is doing a special appetizer tonight—a bruschetta . . ."

Daniel gives her a goofy grin and a thumbs up.

". . . It's a simple prep. Tomato tapenade, caramelized leaks, and Gorgonzola. Simple but really delicious."

She's reminded again why children annoy her. Honestly: Neither the description of the food nor the anticipation of it ought to prompt that kind of silly face. (Well, at the very least the bruschetta sounds like the kind she prefers: She'd not looked forward to the "house smoked" salmon that they often featured. Estelle sucked down lox like nobody's business, even while Janet failed to be charmed by what was in her opinion no more than a slimy salty mess.)

"We're serving a yellowtail tonight. If you haven't tried it, I really recommend that you do."

"What's that like?" Daniel prompts—always a mistake with this kind of waiter.

"Oh, man, I just had it when I came on. Let me tell you: The chef soaks that tuna in a ginger soy marinade, pops that bad boy on the grill, serves it rare with this balsamic ginger reduction, a little wasabi in there. It's the best. Anytime we get in some fresh tuna, I'm all over it."

"Sounds great. And you're the man who'd know."

"Everything here is great, of course. I'm biased. Think about that yellowtail, while I tell you what else is on the board."

Steven runs down the specials. Every now and then he smiles over at Janet, but the show is mostly for the man of the table.

"You folks ready? Or . . . I can come back."

Like a good date, Janet looks to her man for guidance. (Frankly, she'd like to get on with the meal, but Daniel's enjoying himself and due to the coming attractions she needs him in a good mood— in the very best of moods.)

"You know I think we *are* ready, aren't we G?"

She'd warned him about this "G" garbage. (And that Ari Birnbaum had picked up on it and one day she was going to put his large behind in his place, and she didn't care what Estelle thought.)

"Don't tell me," Steven smiles. "You're going on the yellowtail." No pen and pad, a pro.

Daniel makes a big show of hemming and hawing. He sighs,

looks to heaven in mock exasperation. Janet should kick him under the table, but her legs aren't long enough.

"You know what, man: I got to go with the steak. I got to have a steak."

"You can't go wrong with the steak here. That tuna is out of this world, but if you got to have a steak . . . Filet? No, the strip, right?"

"Give me the strip."

"Rare."

"Absolutely."

"A man who knows his meat."

"And for the lady?"

Janet goes to open her mouth, but is pre-empted.

"She'll have the filet. Petite. Medium rare. Right, G?"

Daniel Davis, were I not about to ruin your life, your ass would so be sorry right about now.

Just then the busboy delivers the bruschetta.

"Dude, get my man here another . . . what is that, a Coke? Diet?"

"Sure thing," Gabby agrees. They are so happy with each other, these men.

Daniel takes a big bite out of the crispy treat. Janet's appetite has waned, but she tastes it for the good of the order.

(It *is* good—would be great tomorrow at about 2:30, in her office, with a diet ginger ale!) She hauls two pieces onto her small plate before they can be wolfed down by the man of the house, who is insulted, evidently that she would have the nerve to actually remove her share—less than half, for the record—before he had the chance to offer them to her (or to eat them himself, more likely).

"We can order more," she says, and he pretends not to know what she's talking about.

Daniel eats and follows the busboy and Steven with his eyes. She wants to tell him to stop staring at those people—it's embarrassing, but they don't seem to mind. Gabby with his scraggly hair stops by to top up the water glasses and Steven needs repeated assurance that everything is just fine.

He delivers the steaks, and the strip on Daniel's plate may be the largest piece of meat she has ever seen in a restaurant.

"Oh, man, dude. You hooked me up!"

"I told you I'd take care of you."

They high-five.

Seventeen: Hadn't that also been Keisha's whorish age? Couldn't take her anywhere! She'd doll herself up with the most vulgar teenage fashion of the day, designs the sort of which have never been made with the full-figured gal in mind. There she'd be, that awful daughter of hers, stuffed into some tube of a blouse that left her midriff pooching out. Just as disgusting as the too-pleased-with-himself look on her grandson's face.

Back on my agenda, she decides.

"I don't know about you, but I'm getting nervous about those practice SAT scores."

He looks at her as if she's lost her mind. It's the same look that she herself gives people at the phone company who ask if the Family Leave Act applies to house pets. He scoffs, slices a big hunk off his big steak. He won't even dignify her foolishness with a response. He's angry, she can tell. Or insulted—neither emotion useful for her needs tonight.

"How's your steak?" she asks, hoping yet another subject change will calm the waters.

"Terrific," he says, mouth full. He swallows. "The best." He gives her the thumbs up and doesn't ask about her meal. So that's to be her punishment: cool charm for the wait staff, chilly indifference for her.

Men and their egos: One slight misstep in the conversation and now she has to pay.

Of course, I'm not nervous, damn it.

All she wanted was to shift the boy forward to well beyond tonight, to beyond even the awful subject of that awful mother of his and whatever the hell she might want with him. Eyes on the prize, mister.

He's mad, she's sure, because he assumes she's worried he'll somehow falter and allow one of his hapless classmates to slide past him into his coveted Ivy-league berth. Fat chance that would happen. He's too accomplished and way, way, way too vain . . . and, frankly, there was something wicked about the pleasure he obtained from sitting on top of a pile that he so clearly disdained. When he regaled her with tales of the joys of high school life—the ordinary and sordid comings and goings, the absurd day-to-day existence of adolescents and those responsible for their growth—that disdain simmered in the subtext, the carefully noted flaws in every personality, the idiotic simplicity of each assigned task. This vanity often comes dangerously close to making the boy insufferable. But it also has its uses, and despite her slight shame, she exploits it to get the evening back on track.

"You know the great thing about that jacket? Not only do you look good in it, it goes with so many things."

Chewing his meat, he checks out the brass buttons on the—as one would expect— expertly shot cuffs. Preening, the boy is.

"In Famous last week, Estelle and I saw a teal-colored raw silk shirt that would go perfect with that."

"Oh, G: You're too good to me."

That's for damn sure. They are interrupted by Steven, who circles around again, this time delivering two small plates to each of them.

"Compliments of the chef," he says, and he winks at her grandson, and she wants to tell him to back the hell off.

But the tuna *is* absolutely out of this world; Daniel falls back into his chair, an ecstasy on his face that no grandmother should see.

"We'll have to come back," he sighs. He's eaten half a cow and she can't even imagine how he wedged that bite of tuna in there.

Yes, we'll do that, she thinks. We'll push through this hard patch ahead, and then we'll all come back here: me, your boy Ari, and Estelle.

He's stuffed and happy and as adorable as the day he came to her.

"Your mother has asked to see you."

Which is nothing like the way she had rehearsed it with Estelle or over and over again in her head as she lay in her bed last night unable to fall asleep. She had been leaning toward a speech that began with a phrase such as "at times in our lives" or "in the course of human events," and she'd entertained shamefully childish fantasies that at this very moment—the moment following the actual statement of fact—the earth would shake violently or the ceiling would blow open and they would rise and be spared this unpleasantness, or that something else might descend and put that god-awful girl out of her misery.

Could it be even so that the room around them did darken and that all the other customers and the waitstaff dissolved away into the night?

Perhaps more that her every sense is focused on the boy.

Who does nothing.

He meets her eye with an expression on his face that she imagines he employed when across the table from an able opponent at a chess tournament: reading her for seriousness, for sincerity, for bluffs.

She starts to demand him to say something, damn it. But it isn't that sort of party.

Thankfully (or unfortunately—she's that conflicted) here comes Steven again, offering coffee and soliciting additional reports on their satisfaction thus far.

"Want to hear those dessert specials?" He offers this to Daniel with the oily seductive charm of a heroin dealer.

"Oh, man, I'm stuffed, but . . . what the hell, tell me about them anyway."

As if she's not said what she'd said.

Steven, she is sure, gives the performance of his life, each compote and every glacée dripping with deliciousness, and Daniel is one brandy sauce this side of drooling all over that lovely blue coat.

"It sounds *so* good and I am *so* full," he whines, and then says to Janet, "What do you think, G?"

"I'll have the check now," she orders, and just before he shrugs to Steven that he'll pass this time, Daniel's eyes flash with anger.

So they're both angry, which had not been the emotion she'd predicted for tonight. They drive home in silence, and the entire ride Janet berates herself for not being the adult here. He drives with a thuggish gangsta-lean (which she can't imagine where he learned), and all the way home all she wants to do is tell him to sit up straight and put his other damn hand on the wheel and to wipe that scowl off his face if he knew what was good for him. He glides into the garage and to her surprise comes around to open her door.

"Thanks for dinner," he says, and he prepares the carafe of ice water he keeps by his bed at night.

She crosses her arm and blocks his exit to the kitchen.

"What?" he asks, and because she can't think of anything else to do, she shoves him with her purse.

Which causes him to shake his head, as if to say "Isn't this a shame?" And what he does say is, "What a mess, huh?" He's calm—centered, even—as he has always been. At every step on this ugly road he has been this way.

Such a shame, and she concurs that a big goddamn mess it is.

"You afraid of her, G?" He pets her arm the way he did when she complained of her pressure being up or of headaches.

She shakes her head, and he says "good," although she isn't sure they are talking about the same thing.

"We'll go together then, huh?"

He gives her a goodnight peck and heads on upstairs with his water.

Well, I'll be damned. She looks around the kitchen for something to smash against the wall. She'd imagined a lot of awful reactions from the boy, but somehow she'd never imagined anything quite this awful.

Chapter **Eight**

T hat Ari Birnbaum is a bad, bad boy. First, he'd arranged to have himself thrown out of the house for what will probably be at least three more weeks. (He'd dubbed his sister "Queen of the JAPS" and "The St. Louis Cunty Whore," monikers that had been accurately calculated to send his mother into a full-fledged conniption and to order him from her sight until further notice. Then he'd hitchhiked up 141 to Creve Couer. (Estelle Hillyer Birnbaum: "Jews do not hitchhike." His mother and Estelle had pillowcases embroidered with that motto.)

And now, in the guise of being downstairs looking for something to read, he is rifling through a big blue bin, part of the crap he'd helped Estelle load out of Daniel's place last week. Looking through the bin of crap is a convenient and necessary diversion to lying up in his bedroom and playing with himself while he considers new ways to seduce his boyfriend, a pleasurable but dangerous pastime, seeing as how his fantasies here lately generally ended with him giving up first.

How convenient, he thinks, *of Estelle to leave this treasure right here in the open where it is so easy for me to find*, and he figures that because it isn't hidden, she really does mean for him to have officially examined its contents, whereas if she'd made him look for it, his perusal would be unofficial, which would mean that although they both would know that he knows all of the interesting things that he's about to find out, they'd both have to pretend like he didn't know them. Whether his official knowledge is ever acknowledged is another matter entirely.

The Birnbaum/Westman/Hillyer clan: What a crew! They operated on a complicated matrix of official and unofficial knowledge: history, misinformation, rumor, myth, verified truth, and outright speculation. Some of what people knew could be publicly acknowledged, other things could not. Occasionally a member has the full story, usually people knew about half the facts, and now and again (rarely) someone is entirely out of the loop.

Ari's mother, for example, knows that Hannah smoked pot regularly last summer with her best friend at sleepover camp, because

Ari's mother found Hannah's diary (because Ari put Hannah's diary where Ari's mother could find it). But because Ari's mother doesn't want her daughter to know that she has read said diary, Ari's mother's knowledge must remain unacknowledged knowledge, meaning that at the same time that she is free to lecture her daughter about the evils of drugs and to wring her hands at the breakfast table while airing her "suspicions" about her daughter's sketchy behavior, she cannot, alas, lower the official boom. Similarly, Ari's mother believes that Ari also knows about Hannah's druggie ways, because Ari's mother is no fool and she knows that diary didn't land in her path by accident. But because she cannot acknowledge that she has in fact read the diary, she is also unable to confront her son about violating his sister's privacy or for having left it there for her to read in the first place, nor is she willing to give him the satisfaction of either reveling in his sister's punishment for what is in fact partially his own moral failing, nor for that matter can she acknowledge her son's crime to his sister, which would then, she knows, allow Hannah to occupy the moral high ground, which she most certainly does not deserve. She is further unwilling to validate for that manipulative bastard of a son of hers—who has of late mounted a vigorous campaign to catch her in the act—the fact that as a mother she does snoop on her children—*as is her right*—but because she wants her children to believe that she believes in "children's privacy" and "children's rights" (values the children's father holds dear and that he also believes that he and his wife share—even if the truth is that she believes her husband to be full of shit—about this and about a lot of other things as well) she cannot acknowledge browsing her children's notebooks, computers, dresser drawers, and jeans pockets in search of evidence of their self-destructive and/or illicit behaviors (and haven't her suspicions in fact borne fruit—witness the condoms and strangely-colored pills and seed-like things in Hannah's pockets, among other sordid findings just these past few months, and don't even mention the diary) and therefore she also has to officially pretend that she and Ari both don't know what they do know about his sister and each other, which would include most or all of the above, depending on which of them you're talking about. And for the record, Ari also knows that the diary that he left for his mother to find is not, in fact, Hannah's real diary. That tome, a phenomenally badly written and deliciously lurid accounting of his bitch of a sister's actual life experiences, Hannah did a much better job of hiding. The fake diary has been created, Ari knows, for the same reason that he left the fake diary for his mother to find—so that Hannah can, first, verify once and for all what an evil and hateful shrew their mother really is to invade her privacy in that way and, second, to deflect the stupid woman's attentions away from behavior that even with Hannah's own perverted moral barometer she knows are well beyond the pale, and toward the gentler and more mildly out-of-control Hannah, the girl you might sit down with for a stern and loving chat as opposed to the girl you would send to military school. In spite of an effort that both her mother and brother acknowledge merits commendation, but still unbeknownst to Hannah, Ari and his mother have both located the secret compartment built into the back of the inside of her mother's—and there's the genius part—French provincial vanity, constructed from duct tape and a used jiffy bag. And although with a family like this one you could never be sure, Hannah feels confident in her genius and in the fact that her secrets are safe; and while it is unfathomable to Hannah that her mother would refrain from confronting her on the activities documented in the book, what is actually unfathomable to her mother is that Hannah's behavior could possibly be any worse than that which is reported in the fake diary, and therefore Hannah's mother has been unable to bring herself to actually read the real one. In her least rational moments, she convinces herself that the real diary documents the wholesome adventures of a chaste and naively sweet Jewish girl from the southwest suburbs of St. Louis, obsessed with puppies and with the latest gossip about the equally wholesome and chaste teen star, who, also a virgin, will wed her daughter in a stunning garden ceremony, preferably in the late spring. Even on her best days Hannah's mother can only sustain that fantasy for a matter of minutes, and she has faced the realization that in some perverse way the existence of the real diary confirms the awful truths contained in the fake one, truths, which by themselves are all the evidence she needs to operate in full prison wardress mode. So Hannah's mother watches her daughter like a hawk, which Hannah's mother also knows thrills that brother of hers to no end. Neither Ari nor his mother knows for a fact that the other knows of the existence of the real diary, from which Ari has read on numerous occasions and with what he feels is an appropriate amount of horrified disgust. Every word is true, he knows, in the way that only a slightly older brother can know such things: Boys talk.

In his most charitable moments Ari believes that it is his duty to protect his parents from the ugly truth—because wouldn't they absolutely die if they knew just how much of a major skank they had living under their roof?

But charity not being his strongest suit, he knows that he would have zero qualms about dropping a filth-filled bomb of Hannah on his parents' heads, and, therefore, he hoards his lewd jewels the way Estelle hoarded sourballs. You never knew when you would need a little something-something, as Janet Williams has been known to say, and in his case one of these days he would be busted for something major, and when that happened, the big guns were loaded and ready to blow (as apparently was his sister much of the time).

When Ari arrives at the breakfast table each morning (when he is not in exile—which is rarer and rarer these days) he smiles a big and friendly smile to his mother and to his sister, one that to an outsider says "What a nice young man," but to them and to him means, "I've got you bitches in check, and just try fucking with me and see what I won't do to your asses." This, he knows, is just one of the many reasons that a lot of the time his loved ones wished he would just go and be someplace else—the park, the zoo, Antarctica—anywhere else, it didn't matter—and so he often did. But they say good morning all the same, and they ask him if he's slept well and how he'd like his eggs done. If nothing else, everyone here knows the importance of a good breakfast.

Estelle, queen of the office supplies, had hauled out her deluxe label maker and had lettered and spun out a white strip with the word HISTORY on it, the word centered perfectly on the white strip, of course, as is the label on the box. Estelle liked a system. She alphabetized the spices in the cabinet to the left of the stove as well as the flavors of canned soup.

Ariel Birnbaum, if I open this cabinet one more time and find the tarragon next to the basil, I'll . . . I'll . . . Usually she'd peter out on the threat because she would instead have to yell at him about mocking her or rolling his eyes or both simultaneously. He never cooks and she never cooks either—this despite having a kitchen that has been featured in a local magazine—and therefore this banter is just another part of the fun, the Estelle and Ari Show (Ari and Estelle, he'd insist), the same way that the loud guy on the sitcom has to come in every week and make a joke about how fat the funny guy is.

He's already rearranged the soup today, so now there's this. Inside the box he finds three large ring-bound notebooks and several videotapes, each with dates covering several weeks in 1995. Ari would have been five back then. About a half-dozen manila envelopes, some regular-sized, some legal sized, are stuffed thick with paper. And there are three books in the box. One has a plain cover on it—a dull-sounding title in simple block letters. The other two books have the kind of loud covers on them that one saw at the supermarket checkout counter: Good for you, Janet. Daniel's grandmother was the kind who was always complaining about other people's trashy media habits.

"Ari Birnbaum, I'm not running an all-night convenience store here. Unless you're paying the electric, I suggest you turn out those lights down there and come up to bed."

"Yes, ma'am, right away, Grandmother Birnbaum."

"He starts with the smart mouth at this hour. You've been warned." He heard her bedroom door close up there. Unlike some people, Estelle chose her battles well. His mother would be down here, slamming stuff back into this box and then she would stand in the door, silent, and pointing up the stairs like he was a collie or something. Estelle knew the score, knew that there was no percentage in making people sneak around and do shit that they were probably going to do anyway.

Poppa told her: "Stell," he said, "life's too short to worry about gnats." Damned if the woman didn't love that man. With Estelle it was always Poppa this and Poppa that. What a great old guy, Poppa Hillyer. His great grandfather had been dead since Ari was ten, and his grandmother still grieved every day, he knew. Ari's father couldn't speak of him at all without his eyes brimming up.

Janet Williams, evidently, harbored a secret love of true crime stories, or at least this is Ari's initial understanding of the artifacts in the storage bin. Daniel's grandmother was the kind to pretend like she hated stuff like this, but just look at this shit—and Ari flushes with thrill. Sniffing out hypocrites was one of his favorite hobbies (alas, here lately supplanted by seducing a certain beautiful, caramel-colored boy). The contents seem to be the "history" of one of those grisly domestic murders—the kind that was the subject of every news magazine and made-for-television movie, the kind that only people who were Estelle and Janet's age ever watched. Boring, he thinks, and certainly nothing worth skulking around about, and he's ready to haul the whole mess out to the storage shelves in the garage—which he's fairly sure Estelle will be asking him to do in the morning anyway. Opaque plastic tubs with dark blue tops got stored (in alphabetical order by contents) on the shelves in the garage.

Davis.

The name Davis is everywhere in this box, and as he snaps the lid he has one of those moments that people have five minutes after the exam is over and they remember the Fibonacci Series. Damn it to hell, they think, and Ari thinks, "Double-damn it," because Ari Birnbaum does not have those kinds of moments; only amateurs do.

Davis, as in Daniel Davis, and therefore this box and everything in it deserved a closer look-see.

"Pay attention, Ariel," his great grandfather would say to him. "If you look for them, the signs are there. They always are."

"What's this old timer telling you?" his own father would tease.

"Nothing," Ari would respond. His great grandfather had been fragile as far back as Ari had been able to remember. He remembers a constant tremor, but sometimes in Ari's memory it is one hand that shakes and sometimes it is the other. Poor old guy, his father would say. You never know where his mind is these days, and Ari had to credit the truth in that. Sometimes he approached the man and the eyes that he looked into would be so full of pain and fear that they frightened him. Poppa Hillyer, he'd say, quietly, and then he would be back from that other place. "Look who's here," his great grandfather would say, and it would be as if there could not be enough Ari for him to take in—that was how hard he would stare at him.

"You got to take anything the old guy says with a grain of salt," his father would say, and even at the time Ari felt his father's equivocation had been a little on the desperate side.

The newspaper articles have been cut carefully—razored out, perhaps—and pasted onto individual pages. On top of each page Estelle has pasted the dateline, and in her elegant script (which he'd recognize anywhere) she has written the name of the paper and the page number on which the article appeared. He begins to read the story of a Keisha Davis. Daniel had never mentioned any Keisha Davis, but then again Daniel never mentioned any other Davises. Ari never thought much of it—has always figured that this is another of the many things that the two of them have in common—the fact that both of them seemed perfectly content to not to think about the rest of their clans at all.

It scares Ari sometimes how much Daniel and he are alike, and he wonders if that was how it worked: that people always fell for people with whom they had a lot in common. And then he can't believe that he's got a phrase like "fell for" in his repertoire, and he shudders a bit—what was he, some sappy Parkway South bitch, swooning over some jock? *There should be some manual or something*, he thinks, giving normal people—such as himself—better words for this shit than the worn-out ones on soap operas and in the movies. *I am up to my fetlocks in the swamp of your love.*

Back in the box, the story sucks: The crazy bitch had mixed up a batch of cyanide-laced Kool-Aid and offed her husband and kids. God, there were some fucked up people in this world, and they really were everywhere, just the way Poppa Hillyer warned they would be.

"Ariel Birnbaum, don't think that I won't come down there and unplug some fuses on you."

"I'll be right up, Grandmother, dear." Ari isn't quite sure what these fuses are that she's always threatening him with, but he figures that at some point they had been a constant headache to the old gal.

"More with the smart mouth."

He flips her off (or her voice, at least) and reads on in the files. It was the voices, she'd said, this Keisha. Each and every day, *life here under Satan's Dominion became increasingly morally debased. Every earthly path had been strewn with the Devil's traps, and at any moment any one of us could become ensnared, even her precious babies.* The choice was simple: Keep them here and risk them falling from the light, or *send them ahead, unsullied and pure, on into Eternal Care.* One envelope contains pamphlets from some place called New Purpose—some kind of church—and all of the language is bossy and abstract, with random words capitalized for no reason that is apparent to Ari. She'd saved her babies from Guaranteed Heathendom, snatched them from the Devil's Maw, and many articles quote some guy named Deacon Craig—a guy in the photos not much older than he and Daniel—spouting the usual clichés about the "Mysteries of God's Will" and how "Sister Davis herself had fallen away from God's Grace" and how he hoped that we would "all join him in a prayer for Deliverance from Evil." Deacon Craig seems vaguely familiar somehow, but these were the sorts of people he'd been warned to avoid at all costs.

"It's the so-called Christian ones, Arye." Poppa Hillyer always said his name as if it were the old country version. "They're the ones to be careful of." Ain't that the truth, Ari thinks. The hallways of Parkway South swam with bliss cases, spouting their platitudes and competing with each other to see who could find the most ostentatious crosses to hang around their necks. If the administration allowed it, those fuckers would construct full-sized models on the soccer field and nail each other up.

In the news photos, this Deacon Craig looks crazy—glassy-eyed and paranoid, like he's getting ready to break some skulls with a baseball bat. If he walked into a bank, you'd press the security button. Kind of hot, too, this Deacon Craig, but not in the Daniel Davis league.

About whom he has found nothing so far, but in any case he has a bad feeling. Only fools borrow trouble, Estelle would always say, also quoting Poppa Hillyer. Meaning, he knows, it's bad luck to write ahead in life's story; better to let it unfold on its own.

But sometimes it can't be helped, so he pages through the news clippings faster, looking for the one picture that he knows will be there.

A few weeks later, during a more careful, detailed review of the evidence—one precipitated by the need to both verify and solid-ify his case against the human scum, Pastor Craig Mitchell—it would occur to Ari that of course Janet Williams had employed every means possible to shield her grandson from the madness surrounding the case. He found no pictures because she had al-lowed no pictures to be taken, had herself shunned the press, in-cluding, by evidence of the envelope full of letters from producers and agents, the opportunity to whore her story to the highest tab-loid bidder.

Estelle has catalogued separately from the rest, in its own ma-nila envelope, what must have been the sole photograph, identified on the outside only as "PD 1995." The article, assuming there had been an article, had been placed in the ring-bound book with the others. All that is pasted here is the photo and the caption.

In the photo, looking very much as Ari expected he might have looked, a young Daniel Davis holds his grandmother's hand as he is escorted up the steps of a church. Janet, in the color pho-to—front-page news, to be sure—wears a pale pink suit—hot pink, perhaps—the photo surely has faded. Daniel wears a classy little suit. Man, what a big head on that boy, and for a moment Ari sa-vored his newly found ammunition, but quickly remembered that there was nothing to joke about here. (And Estelle, needless to say, chomped at the bit to haul out her own cherished photos of her precious little butterball. Best to crush this impulse at the root.)

Beneath the photo, a typical and appropriately flat caption reads "Grandmother Arrives with 'Miracle Boy' for Memorial."

"They hide in the grand palaces they build to their Jesus. Sing his praises, all the while planning the end of our people." *A building like the one in the photo*, Ari thinks: This is exactly what Poppa Hillyer had in mind.

Following the by-lines, Ari infers it had taken the press more than a few news cycles to figure out that Keisha Williams Davis had another child and that the boy had survived the bitch's murder spree. Janet Williams spirited him away somehow, and she kept the boy out of the public eye for as long as she possibly could. And then, for a few days, he had been a sensation: Lucky Danny. Grace-ful Dan. The Fortunate Son.

Yes, said Deacon Craig Mitchell, the late Brother Davis and Sister Davis were blessed with *four* children. By all evidence, Craig Mitchell didn't have a media-shy bone in his body. He is quoted frequently, although saying pretty much the same old shit about God being the only judge who mattered and about the importance of accepting Jesus as one's own personal Lord and savior. His photos oozed the same hard-edged earnestness.

Janet Williams had been consistently unavailable for comment.

Ari, the scholar, had been reading the box as he would a historical artifacts project in his Ancient Civ class—cracked vases, fragments of parchment, sundry miscellany out of which to construct a plausible story of the life and times. So it surprises him, the whelm of emotion that knocks him over in his chair. He inhales sharply the way that his father did when he was eating too fast. ("Good plan, Aaron: Die and leave me with these rotten kids.") But this isn't choking. His breath heaves in and out all the same, and then there are tears on his face. What is this? Ariel Birnbaum doesn't cry. Suck it up, motherfucker.

Daniel, he thinks. And he wonders about the cost of all of this. He wondered how people went on with their lives. Poppa Hillyer: all those people in the camps that he lost. Daniel and all the people who loved him. He wonders what the rent looks like that has been ripped out of the souls of these men.

A vaguely people-shaped hole, perhaps. Maybe something more precise, sliced out with an X-ACTO knife just the way these articles had been.

He's blubbering now, ashamed and shamelessly, both at the same time.

"Enough." Estelle closes the notebook and places it back in the box. "Enough for now," she says, snapping the lid in place.

She reads the accusation there in his eyes.

"It wasn't mine to tell," she tells him. "And as Poppa used to say, when I'd ask him about his own dark times: 'Stell,' he'd say, 'some stories you're just better off not knowing.'"

She puts a hand on Ari's shoulder—which he shakes free. He doesn't need her damn comfort.

"You leave that for now. Come on. I'm not asking; I'm telling."

He follows her to the bottom of the steps. He hates his big awkward ugly body.

"Estelle," he calls up behind her. The steps wear on her some nights: Tonight she grips the rail to pull herself.

"It's bedtime, son."

"Estelle. Why didn't she kill him, too?"

She stops, doesn't turn around.

"Let God forgive you for that, Ariel Birnbaum."

Chapter **Nine**

Those boys: a stalemate.

At the mall, incognito (a lie they are both almost ready to stop believing).

The security guard—Sgt. Hitler (not his real name)—follows them at a distance. Today's plan: Make Sgt. Hitler follow us around the mall us until he drops from exhaustion.

And who wouldn't notice the other one, the other one thinks, and both are wrong for excluding himself from that conclusion.

"Nice pants," Daniel compliments.

"Estelle bought them."

"They're nice."

"Yeah."

Daniel has another new plan: Say nice things to Ari to break down his resistance. Ari, he feels, is the sort of person about whom not enough people say nice things—because he looks like the sort of person who doesn't give a shit what you think anyway, which is also true. Daniel figures that people like that ought to be a sucker for a compliment or two.

"How 'bout the shirt?"

"What about it?"

"She buy that, too?"

"Yep."

"Uh huh. It's nice, too."

"Yeah, it is."

It's hard to talk in the mall. Not that it's noisy at The Galleria, or any noisier than any other mall. It's just that a lot of the things they have to talk about are not the sorts of things that people walk the mall chatting about.

"Go in here?"

"Sure."

They pop into Foot Locker. Sgt. Hitler pops open his cell.

"Asshole," Ari says.

"Yeah," Daniel agrees.

They pick up and put down samples of the kinds of shoes that the kinds of people that they hate prefer. Ostentatious, expensive but lacking in class and sophistication. People and shoes both.

Daniel, to his grandmother's delight and chagrin, is developing a taste for Italian leather. Ari is discovering that an old school shoe fits his new style: a black and white Vans or a red Chuck Taylor.

"So she just bought you some new shit? Or what?"

"Something like that."

"Something like what?"

"Something like she just bought me some new shit. Something like that."

"Just for no reason she bought you some new shit."

"Is there a problem with that?"

I don't know, Daniel says, but the hummed version of that. And, yes, he does have a problem with it, and he's looking at it. And thanks to Estelle and her credit card so is everybody else in this joint. The boy is wearing the shit out of this pair of jeans: Damn! And people all over this mall are enjoying themselves a look.

Ari also sees them looking, but he assumes that they are looking at Daniel, who looks, as always, like some sort of movie star. As for Ari's plans, they have changed. Because now, instead of the really hot guy who is your boyfriend and who you want to trick into wanting to have sex with you before he tricks you into wanting to have sex with him, instead of that, Daniel is now all of that and he is *also* the boy whose mother killed a whole bunch of people, all of whom happened to be his family members. This is the first time they've hung out since he read the file, and he isn't entirely sure if and how things are different, but they had to be, right?

"So are you gonna be, like, wearing new shit all the time from now on?"

Ah hah! Ari thinks. If the game is still on—and that's a big if—then he's definitely got game today. Don't answer him; that's the play. Instead he says: "What's on at the show?" and again Daniel hums "I don't know." They go down the escalator to check, and Ari makes sure he gets on the escalator in front of Daniel, because he knows that the view drives him crazy. He sneers back at Daniel who has his lip curled up as well in the way that he did when he was getting ready to say something hateful about someone.

The movies all suck, so Daniel suggests they get some fries and Ari agrees. Both boys feel for a variety of reasons that he deserves to be treated to his snack by the other one, but neither can think fast enough of a way to make the other one pay, and the cashier thinks that their rude grimaces are directed at her because the fries cost too much, which they do, or because maybe they have already spent their generous allowances on the movies and are having to cough up their last few pennies for a few ounces of nasty potatoes, which she wouldn't eat if they paid her to, and they did. They look like the sort of dudes who got allowances as opposed to her who is the sort of girl who has to work for her spending money. But they're cute. Real cute, the both of them, and she wonders what's up that they aren't checking her out. It's these stupid hats they make us wear. God this job sucked. And then she notices that a whole herd of other rich Ladue types have lined up behind these two and are checking them out, as is also that gross security guard, the one whom she knew for a fact hung around the dressing rooms at Banana hoping to catch a peek. I saw them first, bitches.

It's too bad, Daniel thinks, that Ari still ate like a pig. New clothes and a new haircut and there he is still hunkered over his food and shoveling it in his mouth with his hands. Disgusting. He wondered how long did you have to be someone's boyfriend before you could correct all the things about him that made you want to vomit. He liked the new haircut, though, but he's not going to mention it. Big boy would only use that to start some shit.

Ari's pretty sure that Daniel has noticed his new hair, because he's seen Daniel looking at it. His hair looked the same, only better, and only someone who looked at you close would know that it was the same but better. Daniel is looking at him, he knows, but now Daniel, he sees, is looking at something else.

"What?" he asks.

"What?" Daniel replies.

"You got a problem of some kind?"

"Do you?"

Then Ari sees his problem. He shouldn't eat like this. Estelle tried to warn him, but did he listen? No. And now this asshole has control of the ball again. Damn it! Think fast.

He figures that if he embraces his greediness he might win points for being up front with it.

"Good fries, huh?" he says.

Sure, Daniel agrees. He should rub it in, but the game is getting tiresome. Not just because he would like to go ahead and get on with the sex part of the program, but also because he's thinking that at this time what he needs more than a sparring partner is someone to help him think through this whole business with his mother. G is furious, still, for some reason he doesn't quite get. Just when she makes one little step off the dime and it looks like she might be ready to deal, she comes apart on him. All these years he's been so careful to not bring up the others, and then she finally mentions them herself but then immediately goes off. Ari will know what to do.

Ari gets a devilish gleam in his eye. "I should take these greasy, salty, ketchupy hands and smear them all over that fucking shirt." What a great shirt it is that Daniel wears, black and woven with those stripy things. When he was here with Estelle, he wanted to try one on, but clothes dude said that guys like him needed more structure or whatever, and he kept feeling on the tip of Ari's shoulders to make sure that the seam lined up. Hey, here's a plan. They should go over to Dillard's and get sales boy to wait on them hand and foot. He waves his greasy hands at Daniel again.

"What do you say? I know just the place to buy you an even better shirt."

"Grow the fuck up," Daniel growls, just above a whisper.

"What did you say to me?" People look over at them. Ari's voice carries.

"You heard me. Go wash your hands."

Ari calls him an asshole and shoves his chair back, which causes Sgt. Hitler, they both note, to make his presence known by moving closer.

Talk to me that way: Who the fuck does he think he is? He washes his hands and then splashes water on his face because it's hot and he is also afraid he is going to cry, which isn't allowed. And then he is just afraid. Because, drying his hands, he knows that when he opens the door there is a possibility that Daniel will have ditched him, and then what would he do. These past five months have been the best part of his life—a part of his life he never believed that he would have. And for a moment he cannot even open the door to the men's room, because if he looks out and Daniel is not out there across the food court still sitting at the table, he will crumple on this floor and he will just die, just like that. Natural causes, as Estelle will tell her friends. Curse of the Hillyer men. A shande!

One, two, three, he counts, and he hopes for the best and swings the door wide.

"Boo!" Daniel says. Right there outside the door. And then he says. "Hitler's right behind me, isn't he? We should just start making out like dogs right here—free show. What do you say?"

"The bastard would get off on it. Let's go sit in the vibrating chairs."

So they go to Brookstone and try to think up a strategy to get Estelle to invest in a pair of chairs for her media room. They both agree that she's more likely to buy them than is Janet, although Janet would get more use out of them. The store is only partially busy—folks browsing Father's Day and graduation gifts. The sales clerk heads their way and the boys figure that they are about to get eighty-sixed, but instead dude says they "look hot" in those chairs and gives them the thumbs-up, and they figure, fuck it, we'll chill.

"It's like we're the store's models and stuff, huh?" Ari says, in his best imitation of the dumb West County boys that they really both hate a lot but figure other people probably think that they are, and then Daniel says, "Dude," and then they bump fists. Neither of them really knows why they act like and talk like those other boys; each is pretty sure it's just a phase.

And then, ironically enough, just when the thought of models causes Daniel to remember his plan to fix Ari Birnbaum for sending him that dick picture, who should walk in the store but the waiter from Flemings. "Hey! Davis, right?"

"That's right. And you're Steve. Good to see you." Steve looks much younger out of his work clothes, more like a guy their age, really. He's got the shadow of a goatee, which Daniel figures they make him shave for work. But, damn, it looks good on him. Here in the fluorescent store lights his eyes are much bluer than they had seemed in the candlelight of the steak house.

Ari also notices those eyes. He hates this motherfucker, whoever he is.

"Good to see you, too," the bastard says. "You just hanging out, or what?"

Ari's fairly sure that the "you" in that sentence was the third person singular—like he isn't sitting here with his boyfriend having a quiet afternoon, modeling furniture. What, bitch, you're just going to stroll in here and get all up on my man. Your ass is about to be in for some big hurt.

"We're just chilling," Daniel tells him. It interests Daniel that he's now able to feel the energy coming off the boy in the other chair. There's more vibrations coming from over there than either of these motors could muster: Ariel Birnbaum is pissed.

"What brings you into the store?" Daniel asks. "Can I interest you in a deluxe massage chair? My associate and I would be happy to give you a test drive."

The saying of which sends Ari ping-ponging with emotions: snickering at how nasty that sounds, and then wanting to choke that nasty Daniel for the look he's giving this guy, and then sort of being really a whole lot turned on by the way that this guy is now looking at both of them, and then the guy's looking at just him and then he wonders what would happen if he adjusted himself in his pants because he sort of needed to and then he does and then the guy raises his eyebrows.

"Check you two later, OK?"

"Sure thing," Daniel replies. They sit there for a minute and Ari wonders if "Check you guys later" means that the guy was coming back over here and one or both of them would have to make good on the test drive offer. He's pretty sure but not entirely sure that they weren't talking about lounge chairs.

Daniel thinks almost exactly all those same things at the exact same time, and they are both wondering about the ramifications of a threesome when you haven't actually had a twosome yet.

"Let's roll," Daniels says, which both frustrates and relieves Ari. Because, who knows: play their cards right, and whoever that was could have taught them all kinds of stuff, and to hell with the bet.

"Who was that asshole?" he asks.

"Just some guy," Daniel replies, and he's pretty sure that this little episode has been just as good as the pictures he would have convinced Steve to take (although in his planning he hadn't quite gotten as far as figuring out how he was actually going to convince some guy who he primarily knew as a waiter to take his clothes off and pose in lewd positions).

Ari is interested at the moment in the part of himself that wants to shove Daniel over the railing into the lower floor of the mall, and he thinks, *OK, so this is how people end up on the police blotters for beating the shit out of their boyfriends and girlfriends.* And what if this feeling was related to the other feeling: the one that made a person mix up a batch of poison fruit punch and exterminate your husband and kids. (Or at least most of your kids. She'd poured the concoction into a baby bottle and for the older girls into their favorite cartoon cups. One of the books made a big point out of this detail and included photos of the cups that the cops had taken at the scene.)

Some girls—the same ones from in the food court—walk too close to Daniel going the other way, and they giggle and Daniel brushes up against Ari to step out of their way. Ari thinks that what he ought to do is shove Daniel hard for bumping him—like real hard: hard enough to go knock over one of those mannequins in the door of the store—and he looks around to see where Hitler is, although he doesn't really care if they get thrown out today. The mall is boring.

Hitler's not there, but some girls from South are, and they say "Hey," and he says "Hey." They're just some skanks. Behind the skanks are the girls from the food court and then a couple of guys he's noticed also walking around today. Across the atrium the "some guy" who wants the test drive happens to be headed the other way and nods in greeting. Ari gives Daniel the secret signal—the one that means "check it out." He indicates that Daniel should look behind them, but without looking—which he tries but fails to do. The skanks say "Hey."

"Hey," Daniel says and then he thinks, *What the fuck?*

Ari says "Cookie break."

They get cookies and then get white chocolate lattes at Starbucks and sit at a little table. Just like that the Starbucks is busy. The skanks order fraps. Daniel recognizes a sophomore from Clayton Prep: The dude accosts him in the lunchroom once a week or so for tips on how to get over on certain teachers.

At about the same time, they're both thinking *How about this shit?* Apparently what each had been using to work on the other, worked on other people, as well. Across the café, Steve raises a toast to them. What an exciting and intriguing development this is.

And a scary one. Options had not been part of Ari's game plan—options for either of them, but particularly not for Daniel. Daniel is supposed to be his little secret. He feels like one of those fairy tale queens who locks her beloved daughter in a tower for safekeeping—only to discover that the frog prince knows the secret code for the alarm system. He wants to run interference—like a defensive linesman—mow down anybody who gets within an inch of this boy. Across the café, that guy that Daniel knows for some reason continues to stare at them, and Ari wants to go over there and beat him back into the twentieth century. And then he sees that the guy is looking at him in the same way he is looking at Daniel and smiling, too. (Is that in admiration or is he leering at us?)

Great, and so now everyone can also see, Daniel thinks: *Damn you, Estelle Birnbaum!* He wills Ari to stuff big crumbly hunks of the cookie into his face and chew with his mouth open—show these people what a pig you really are—but it doesn't work: Ari takes dainty breaks of the cookies, catching the crumbs with his napkin. Damn it, damn it, damn it.

They are like countries with brand new nuclear weapons: that delicious frustration that comes with having a new toy that it's a pretty good idea not to use.

Desperate times, desperate measures; and Daniel feels that the best way to retain his fast-fading foothold is to pull out the big guns, but Ari beats him to the punch.

"Whatever happened to your mom?" he asks, and then immediately recognizing the mistake, amends, "Your parents, I mean." He isn't sure why he's going there now, but if this was the end of the line for them, then at least he could get some questions answered.

Odd, Daniel thinks at first, Ari asking him this, but then he feels Estelle's hands pulling strings here—everywhere—as always. She's talked to Janet or Janet's talked to her, and somehow Big Boy's picked up the vibe. So he answers:

"I don't know."

And then, "They're around."

And then, "Why do you ask?"

Answers that are bad and wrong, he knows, but he hasn't had much practice with this sort of thing. He's spent a dozen years working hard to be the sort of person to whom people didn't ask any questions of at all.

Ari feels as if someone has punched him in the chest. He wants to reach across the table the same way Estelle would right about now. Wrap Daniel's upper arm with his fingers and gently massage it, saying "It's OK, sweetheart. Bubbe's here and nothing will hurt you again." His instincts tell him to try again, try another tack, but he second-guesses them and says nothing.

Ask me again, Daniel wishes. *You're the one I can tell it to, and together we can figure out what to do about the whole awful mess. So tell him yourself*, he thinks, but how did you do that? The words are unspeakable and hideous to say.

Around them, the mall whores are getting restless. Only the most skilled sippers will be able to stretch their drinks much longer. Someone needs to make a move here.

Be a man, Ariel. No games: This is the person you have chosen for your life . . . No: Life chose you, placed you together. Step up and be a man.

"You ever go to the prison?" he asks.

Daniel shakes his head, and it's like someone has released a band around his chest and he is able to breathe for the first time in his life.

"Estelle helped your grandmother organize a bunch of . . . stuff."

G. had left his box on his bed just the night before, "Daniel" printed on top, all customized and official.

He'd long ago forgotten what the others had looked like back then. The girls, as they'd gotten older, had retained their oblong, angular faces. Miriam would become taller than Sarah—by an inch, and only the family could see this. The baby fat that he didn't remember surrounding Say's face would melt into his round handsomeness.

He tells Ari that he hasn't seen his mother since before, and that makes Ari sad, he can tell.

"I guess she's asking for me. I guess that's what this is all about."

The nasty sleeping dogs, Ari figures.

"You going?"

His favorite song: I don't know.

"I guess I kind of wonder what she wants."

Ari starts to note that the woman is his mom; realizes in that moment that issues of progeny are WAY beyond the point. He's saved from all of his dumb responses by Daniel, who adds: "And I think that if I go that G should go, too. Do you think that's wrong?"

And it interests Ari greatly that his brilliant friend hasn't figured out that if Janet Williams had wanted to visit her daughter she would have done so a long time ago. Or maybe he has figured that out and doesn't approve of her decision.

It occurs to Daniel that Ari Birnbaum knows a lot of the story—perhaps even more than he does, which is good, he thinks. It might come in handy.

And it occurs to Ari to trust Daniel to ask for what he needs. The door is open at least.

"We'll figure something out," he tells his boy, and he watches Daniel relax—like someone letting the air out of balloon, it is.

And in the meantime, the management is getting antsy—it's time to turn these tables.

"What do you say?" Daniel asks, "Shall we walk the gang down to the Pottery Barn?"

"After you, my good man."

In the rush for the trash bins, one of the skanks spills leftover foam on Steve's trousers and ugly words are exchanged, but by this point Daniel and Ari are at the staircase, practicing pretending like they can't see the volunteer entourage that would accompany them in a wide variety of configurations for many years to come—for the rest of their lives, in fact. Both boys recognize their newfound power for the mixed blessing that it is. On the positive side and at the most basic level, it is nice to be admired, even if it is for reasons that both of them hold in low regard. All the same—just as with their intellect—both can and fully intend to exploit their gifts to enrich their own lives and each other's as need be.

Still, on this particular afternoon, neither is as of yet quite sure how to operate these new machines, but they're confident that between them they can figure it out. And, as it happens, there are bigger problems out there in the world.

Chapter **Ten**

Surely MapQuest has made some sort of mistake. Estelle has heard of none of the streets on this printout; after the command to exit I-70 at Salisbury, it's pure gibberish as far as she's concerned. Which is why it's a good thing those boys are coming with her. They could navigate; and if they couldn't navigate, they could communicate with the locals; and if they couldn't communicate, they could fight them off, and then while they were getting their behinds kicked she could make a break for it and run for help. A terrible thing to think this way, she knows: Poppa would die. But after all, Pastor Mitchell is serving the neediest, and where the needy are, there are also the people who take advantage of the needy and of everyone else as well. Better safe than car-jacked, and she figures with two large-looking male types in the car, the odds at this particular table swing back toward her favor.

What's keeping those boys?

She'd rather not know, in all honesty . . .

. . . that Daniel sits astride Ari in the soft chair, arms and legs wrapped around his boy. Or that both boys fight lust as well as wrinkles, each in the other's favorite new shirt. That they have never kissed more tenderly, each never more aware that there are parts of himself that are separated by mere inches of fabric from the corresponding parts of the other. Tenderly—all the same now and again one cuffs the other in the head or tugs at a clump of hair or an earlobe.

"Ariel! There's an old woman down here getting older by the minute."

Ari holds the boy to his chest and promises himself that he will protect this boy forever.

"She's waiting," Daniel whispers.

"Let her wait," Ari responds.

"Ariel Birnbaum!"

She's up to two names now, which means it won't be long before steps are stormed and doors are thrown open. They peel apart and turn their backs on each other as they straighten and tuck, oddly embarrassed for two people whose tongues moments ago had been inside each other's throats. Daniel spies a spot of lint on Ari's shoulder and plucks it between two fingers. Then he spins the boy slowly, double-checking for others. Ari—at first disgusted (What are you, my mom?)—gets with the program quickly. He tugs at the hem of Daniel's sleeve, evening one with the other.

The doorbell sounds the exasperated aggressive pattern that signals fire or frustrated Jehovah's Witnesses. Estelle's ready to blow. Down the two of them strut. Ari has told Daniel that they ought to stand there and smile until they received the compliments that they deserved. He is stunning in a rich grape-colored T; Daniel, a charmer in a crisp denim shirt and black jeans. They secretly think this way about each other these days—as if one is on a fashion runway and the other is offering color commentary to the discerning consumer. (Of the two, Ari is less sure of the language for all of this, but he knows that this boy looks damn hot in blue.)

It's all Estelle can do to ignore them, smiling there like idiots, and particularly after trifling with her schedule in this way. What might the pastor think of her, straggling into his place of business with no apparent regard to his busy day. Here were a couple of young men who had A LOT to learn about the way the world worked.

"Let's go," she orders, but they stand there posing like they're in a J.C. Penney Father's Day ad.

"Fine. You're gorgeous. Are you happy now?"

"Thank you, Bubbe." Ari bends to kiss her. He's amazed how a toothy smile still works on the old girl.

"You," Estelle orders, handing Daniel the maps. "Be a love and navigate, would you? This one I want up front," she says, grabbing her grandson's arm. "Shotgun, and I'm talking in the actual meaning of the word." She had considered loading the .357 into the glove box, but neither of these two needs to know she owns such a thing (although it wouldn't hurt them to know that she'd not think twice about using it).

Ari begs her to let him drive: It kills him that Daniel is now Janet's primary chauffeur, but everyone in this car knows that Estelle is not in charge of Ari in the way that Janet is in charge of Daniel.

Daniel leans up and makes a comment admiring the pick-up in the Lexus. His eyes are on Ari when he says this. He can hardly keep from snickering, enjoys the flush of rage that he sees run through his boy.

"Eyes on the map, Magellan." A pair of cards, these two: Jokers. No: deuces, at best. Estelle has already laid down an initial set of rules for the day. Number 1: no pissing contests.

She's never known two people to compete with each other the way these two did: Who could down his juice in one gulp, which one got the highest score on some awful video game (so violent!), who knew the answer to arcane trivia questions that not even *Jeopardy* would ask. Here's hoping they stayed relatively sane and didn't take up one of those extreme sports—and then it would be who can go the longest without opening his parachute, and they'd both end up squashed like bugs on a windshield.

Ari wants to drive this car so bad it is killing him—and damn that Daniel, who could probably cruise up and over this ramp from I-70 to Salisbury like he was born with a steering wheel in his hands. Ari's parents have forbidden Estelle from teaching him—and fuck those motherfuckers anyway. Next year he and Daniel will so be out of this pile of shit city. They'd move to Cambridge (or New Jersey or Pennsylvania or New York), get their own place and then Daniel would teach him to drive a car that the two of would pay for with their own goddamn money. How dumb not to have thought about summer jobs before all the good ones were taken.

As for Daniel, he's not so sure there are good jobs. He's not wearing some funny hat and coming home smelling like grease, and he thinks it's probably a bad idea standing in the store waiting on the sorts of people who shopped. ("Have you *been* to the mall?" he asked Ari, when he suggested they fill out applications at one of those shoe stores. "Not only would we have to touch people's feet, we'd also have to pretend to be nice to them.") As far as that went, he's not sure about jobs of any kind. How did people choose careers? How did Janet and Estelle wind up working in the business world? Why are Ari's parents doctors? Why did people have to choose?

Driving by Lambert reminds Estelle of Florida, and so she dials the X-M to the Weather Channel. Sadly, the tropics are calm. Why was there always construction on this highway? She ought to have gone in on 40, but the damn MapQuest hadn't heard of that road— and it's only been there her entire life.

Daniel licks a finger and then reaches around to the side away from Estelle and runs it gently down Ari's neck, slowly, through the downy hair that began where his curly hair ended. He had that soft hair everywhere.

Ari suppresses a shudder, gets that evil sneer on his face.

Honestly, Estelle thinks.

"Bubbe, doesn't the law say that all children in the backseat must be belted in?" This is, of course, only the first part of Daniel's punishment. Might be time to get that digital camera out again.

He's a street brawler, her grandson. His idea of a fair fight is one that he wins. There isn't much she imagines he wouldn't do to make that happen.

"Sweetheart, do Bubbe Birnbaum a favor and buckle yourself in. Just in case." Because heaven knows there'd be hell to pay should that beautiful young man come flying through this windshield, God forbid it should happen, and not only would Janet have another unbearable tragedy, but it's highly unlikely she'd be willing to share a condo with the woman who brought it on. "And keep an eye on that map, would you?"

Ari turns around to give Daniel the look he gives him when he's trounced him on that stupid Star Wars game. Daniel hates that look. Ari thinks it's hot that Daniel is stealthily giving him the finger—has it parked, an arrow pointing to his crotch.

They're hardly past UMSL and Estelle figures that if she's going to survive this trip it's time to distract.

"You boys may not believe this, but I remember a time when this was all farms and fields."

"Before they invented cars and everything, huh?"

"Daniel, your friend up here thinks he's funny—a regular Shecky Green. I'll tell you something, Shecky: You should be so vibrant at my age."

Neither boy is sure exactly who Shecky Green is, but that was true of most of Estelle and Janet's references.

"Bubbe's got it going on, doesn't she, Daniel?" He's teasing her, but Estelle is in fact, Daniel knows, an attractive older woman, as is his own grandmother, whom he is worried about to the point of distraction.

Estelle tells Ari to watch his fresh mouth, but Daniel can tell that she is thrilled that her hunk of a grandson is flirting with her—who wouldn't be? He decides to stay out of it.

"It's too bad that Janet couldn't join us," Estelle says to him. Not just because Janet could be helping to keep a lid on these rowdy boys, but also because should this settlement house prove to be everything she imagines it is, Human Resources should add them to the list of certified charities.

Daniel tells Estelle that Janet had a lot Saturday morning errands. Actually, she had no more errands than usual—and both Daniel and Estelle know that for a fact, each of them knowing the woman's routines as well as their own. Janet has remained chilly to Daniel, refused to talk about why—about anything much at all. What do you want for supper? Keep the noise down please. Tell Ari that Estelle will pick him up at 9:00.

Estelle too has noticed that Janet has made a turn for the worse since the drawer has been sorted—something she would not have predicted. Down at the office she hardly touched her lunch and had been snippier than usual with everyone, regardless of how timely their "Bi-weekly Mandatory Departmental Productivity Inventories." She'd hoped that today's outing might offer a pleasant diversion—something to take her mind off of whichever old demons had been released from that box—but no dice. Janet blew her off coldly, although Estelle could tell that it had been a struggle to maintain her tough-cookie persona with her friend. She'd even asked—rather pathetically, Estelle thought—begged really—for her to call her later in the afternoon. Estelle certainly would do more than that. She'd stop by that Schnucks and pick up one of those gooey butter cakes that Janet loved and have a good lingering cup of coffee when she dropped off the boy, and in the meantime she figured that the least she could do was get these two out of everyone's hair for the day. They'd check out the mission, she'd take them to one of those trough restaurants and let them eat their fill, and if they behaved like the gentlemen she knew they could be, she'd throw a movie in for the good of the order. Or, she could drop them at the movies anyway and then swing by Estelle's, so they could talk without these oafs under foot. Which seems like a pretty good plan, seeing as how the gentlemen part of the deal kept going from bad to worse.

Ari is trying to grab Daniel's knee with his hand that is closest to the car door, but it is a tight fit. Daniel is trying to angle other parts of his body close to the hand, or alternatively, to think of something disgusting to put into that hand. (Daniel can't actually think of anything that Ari wouldn't enjoy.) Ari finds that his arm is stuck. Estelle checks the rear view mirror, catches a glimpse of the devious smile on the one back there, says: "I'm thinking that this Pastor Mitchell may be doing great things. Simple, but great. He should be an inspiration to you boys."

The name sounds familiar to Daniel. He wonders if Mitchell is one of those rich preachers and maybe he has a kid at Clayton Prep. Ari is sure he has read about this guy in the *Post*, wondered what this one has done: molest some kids, swindle old people, just generally be an asshole.

He wrestles his arm free and almost spills Estelle's purse, which is there in his lap (*thank goodness*, he thinks).

Estelle thinks the look on his face is the crazed look that comedians have when they are about to sing a vulgar song on the Jay Leno program.

"Poppa told me, 'Stell,' he said: 'I want you to find someone who is doing good work and I want you to help with that work. That's all I ask.'"

Ari has heard this story perhaps a million times. He has one basic question for the do-gooders of the world: What's in it for you? It's not that he doesn't believe that people do good things, it's just that he's pretty sure that there's something in it for them somewhere.

Daniel isn't sure what he thinks. They've crossed into the city, a place he'd almost never been, except to go to the zoo or the stadium. Top students got free tickets to the Cards. He and Ari had gone last month and ditched the game to see if they could sneak onto the casino boat: Ari had a "foolproof" card-counting scheme he's dying to try out and plans for the two of them to use it to clean up at blackjack tables around the world.

"Poppa wouldn't want his money going to line anyone's pockets. He'd want the hungry folks fed, people getting a hand up, that sort of thing."

"I'd like to get a hand up," Ari says.

His look, Estelle sees, is meant to provoke her—or at least partially. She ignores him.

"So many of these charities: It seems like they exist primarily to raise money so they can raise more money. Poppa would roll in his grave."

Her Bernie had had a smart mouth on him, too. And randy as a goat, he was. Like this one here . . . like these two. Thank God the pill had come along: She'd have littered yearly like a brood sow.

"Do me a favor, boys: Keep your eyes open when we're in this place. Be on the lookout for anything that looks out of place: fancy jewelry, expensive shoes. You know what I'm talking about."

"Because poor people aren't supposed to have nice stuff, right?"

"Ariel Birnbaum: I'm up to here." She indicates her eyebrows, which she realizes are at the same level with his chin—and she's sitting on cushions as it is—and may leave him with the impression that there is room left in her for further shenanigans. There isn't. She exits the freeway and asks, "Where the heck are we now?"

"Take a right here, Mrs. Birnbaum," Daniel tells her. This place is both exciting and scary to him. He doesn't see the gangsters and thugs that Janet is always warning about, but they've got to be around here somewhere.

And he also thinks that Ari had better chill. His grandmother would put up with a lot, but he can tell that she's about to go off up there.

Ari knows that, too, but he knows that the good thing about Estelle is that when she does finally goes off on him, she'll get it out of her system and then move on with life—unlike the people at home, who went off, stayed off, and never let you forget that you were the scum who made them lose control in the first place.

"Hang another right," Daniel orders. He sees the "I'm not letting go of this bone" look in Ari's eye—the one he got when he debated . . . hell, when he talked about anything, really, since every conversation with Ari Birnbaum was pretty much a debate.

"If I were you, I'd take Poppa Hillyer's money and walk up to . . . say, that homeless guy, right over there, drop the whole wad on him and say, 'Hey, Joe Bum, it's your lucky day. Knock yourself out." Because, Ari thinks, for all the good that money would do otherwise you might as well do something like that, and even Joe

Bum over there would be right back here in six months, his life the same reeking bag of crap it had certainly always been, but at least he'd have a hell of a six months between now and then. How much else could the money do: buy a couple of bowls of soup? A toothbrush or a blanket or two?

"You know nothing," Estelle tells him, immediately disgusted with herself for taking the bait, except she knows that he's not baiting her. They'd lived too easy, these two—as had many in this country of their age. They'd not had to, as her father had done, drink from a ditch to survive, stagnant water with human waste floating in it like ice cubes—one of the few stories he'd even share. Fartik! he'd shout. Those days are past! She'd not carry that horror in her life, so stop asking about those terrible times. And just like these boys she has never in her own life known a day of hunger. A blessing, perhaps, that the real life horror of her parents' lives in the camps didn't play in all their heads (the way that she knew it had in theirs) day and night like a commercial for laundry soap. Perhaps the tradeoff for that innocence was the boorish selfishness here in the seat beside her. Poppa would smile and call it even.

"So spoiled," she mumbles, and when Ari rolls his eyes, it's all she can do to not knock him in the head with her purse. The boy in the back tells her to make a left.

They enter a block that had at one time been vibrant—as evidenced by the range of boarded-up storefronts. She imagines that a school had been in that vacant lot—the rusted gibbet of a swing set remains along with a slide and some abandoned basketball stanchions.

"What a shithole," Ari says. You'd think the city or somebody would come through here and tear down these raggedy firetraps, run some of these people off.

Daniel is both appalled and thrilled. That people lived this way had mostly been a theory in his head, confirmed annually by the Hundred Neediest Cases that the *Post* published during the holidays. Janet did not talk about people like this, except to warn that boys who messed up their lives would end up with them, and so he'd conjured from those images in the paper and on TV a fantasy version of this place. To have verified the truth of his imagination appalls him and also causes a perverse kind of thrill—which always rushed through him when he discovered the power of his own mind.

Estelle engages the childproof locks. "Listen up, the two of you: You know what Grandmother expects." And then, when they don't respond, she prompts: "Well?"

"Yes, ma'am" is their answer, and she's satisfied that while there may be a snigger or a rolled eye, they'd keep their goofiness to a minimum. She presses the button that frees them.

Ari watches some really scary types eye the Lexus—the scary kind you had to shoot in the head on Grand Theft Auto or they'd keep after you. He takes hold of Estelle's arm and tries to signal Daniel to get on the other side. He has no idea what he'd do if something goes down here, but at least they could protect the grandmother. Daniel, alas, doesn't pick up the hint.

Daniel's mesmerized by these people, this building. He can't imagine what this place might have been. Its now flat, windowless front has been coated over in beige stucco with a sandy texture. It bears no signs. Had it been a bank? A grocery store? A library? He opens the door for Ari and his grandmother. Ari, he sees, has on his this-better-be-over-quick face—one of his sullen ones. Inside an old man with translucent skin chases a bird around with a long pole. Daniel isn't sure what the plan is here, or if there is a plan. Is he trying to skewer the pigeon? Or did he plan to beat it to death? Not that the bird needed fear either fate. It hopped from I-beam to I-beam, only mildly annoyed, surely, by whatever that was down there stirring up its air space with some shiny thing.

Pastor Mitchell sits with the mother and her young son. They had returned for a second time last night, late, just before the wind that had blown open the hole that had let in the pigeon that he hopes Schmidtty has as much luck getting rid of as he had getting everyone re-settled after the storm. He sees that the Jewish woman has arrived right on time, bringing with her the sullen hulking grandson who had been around when he picked up the furniture. And another young man as well.

He excuses himself from the woman: just as well since she's not talking, although she hadn't seemed to mind him sitting there with her and with the little boy.

"What's your name, son?" Craig asks, and the boy whispers what

Craig deciphers to be Malik. He petted his mother and refused to leave her side, despite Craig's encouragement to go play with some of the other little ones. The mother neither supports nor encourages his efforts.

The wiry old timer manages to shoo the pigeon onto a ledge where a beam meets the cinder block and the two combatants call a truce. Estelle can't determine his age, but she can see he's got many miles on him. She smiles for the pastor as he approaches, but not too broadly. Enough to put him at ease but not to allow him to think she's an easy mark.

"How good of you to come, Mrs. Birnbaum," he says, and then Ari remembered: Him. The one who hauled off the best video game chair from the media room. He hadn't liked him then and saw no reason to change his opinion now. He dripped with smarm just like all these Bible thumpers. Something else familiar about him as well.

He's familiar to Daniel, too, in a way that makes Daniel slightly discomfited—the way he felt when now and then he would be momentarily unable to call up the correct word on a pop quiz, the awareness that the information was right there but for some reason he just couldn't locate it. Although sometimes there was no information to be had. Sometimes like, for example, with the regulars that his grandmother chatted up in the aisles of Dierberg's. They only seemed familiar, but they were in fact just strangers exchanging a friendly word. On the other side of Craig Mitchell about a half-dozen kids chase a ball around incompetently. There are as many colors of skin as there are boys.

"Pastor Mitchell." Estelle extends her hand. He did a good grip: Poppa would approve. "You know my grandson Ariel, and this is Daniel, another member of our little family." She wags her chin to get them to take the man's hand. A seminar in manners lurked in the near future of a couple of young men of her acquaintance.

The old coot who was chasing a bird with a stick is now over by a wall trying to stack what look like cots. They tumble over, then tumble over again. Ari wants to laugh, but knows that Estelle would have his head for doing so. The name "Mitchell" begins to register with him.

"Careful," the pastor calls to Schmidtty. "Some of the kids want to shoot hoops, so we've got to move the cots. Short-handed as always." And then he yells at the old man to "Hang on a sec." He waves his hands at Estelle in the way that means that he'd love to talk but this was more pressing.

"Boys, go help the man while the pastor and I visit." There's eye rolling, she knows, but to hell with them. She smiles at the man, giving him a moment to center himself before she prompts the show that she's confident he gives regularly and with ease.

"Saturdays are hectic," he says. "Every day's hectic, really."

He had the tired but serene face she'd seen on the faces of on-cology nurses and others who worked with the dying. Bright eyes undercut with bags draw her attention. His weariness he carries in his shoulders, which now and then snap to attention as if a whis-pered reminder to mind his posture had been dropped in his ear.

"Remind me how many you serve here." Her first prompt. Would his number match the papers?

Lord, how he hated that question. How to even count? How did they count bees in a hive? Two flew in, five flew out.

"Meals, we can serve a hundred dinners most evenings. It goes up toward the end of the month." He recited the rest of the figures to her: the amount of cereal and milk the kids went through, how often the nurse from public health dropped through to check on the endless colds that circulated through the mothers and toddlers. And for lice. The standard figures he filled in with regularized dil-igence on the 100-to-1 odds grant applications that he filled out even despite those odds.

"We can sleep sixty. Comfortably."

"In a dormitory?" she asks, and he tells her that this is the dormi-tory, shows her the wheeled bookcases, coat racks, and the other various jury-rigged apparatus that he and Schmidtty rolled into place to divide the room into somewhat cozier smaller places.

Across the room, her grandson helps the old man slide the rest of the beds from under the hoops.

"It's that kind of place, I'm afraid. You can eat or you can sleep, but not at the same time." He laughs and she laughs with him. Or the beds could be there and the art supplies there and there'd be no basketball, or the art could go in the changing room and then the boys could shoot hoops, but then the women would have to use his office to get ready to go to their jobs or job interviews.

One of the little boys grabs Daniel's arm and orders him to come on.

"You be on one team and him on the other," and Daniel says sure, even as he knows Ari won't be happy about this one bit. Ari hated Physical Education more than anything in the world (with the possible exception of his sister Hannah). At least Daniel would pretend to enjoy the damn class—anything for that A. Ari had cobbled together a file of bogus medical excuses to get himself assigned to one of those gym classes where you played checkers and copied pictures of the muscle groups from anatomy textbooks.

Ari can't believe what Daniel's gotten himself sucked into. He's surrounded by a whole herd of rugrats—the dump's overrun with them—and he's actually gotten the little bastards organized into some kind of ball-passing game. But he looks happy, Ari sees, in a way that he has not seen his boy look before. That's the real laugh, he knows, not the fake I'm-laughing-at-these-assholes one.

The bird flutters down, flutters back up. Another—his mate—enters through the hole through which the white blue St. Louis summer sky can be seen.

"The roofers are on their way?" Estelle asks, and the pastor chuckles, looks at her as if she'd asked him when the queen's coach was expected.

"Give me a minute," Estelle orders. She speed dials Janet, who takes her time picking up—something really is off with this girl. "Sweetheart, you were busy with something?"

"Oh, Estelle. It's you." Janet is relieved although she can't say why. "Just . . . puttering. You know."

Estelle doesn't believe her for one minute. But talk would wait for later.

"Do me a favor, doll: In your hall closet, pull down the Yellow Pages. The good one, the one we used when we were looking for new lawn services. Got it? Good. Look up roofing companies . . . I'll explain later. Do you have the Weather Channel on over there?"

God, yes, Florida, Janet thinks. They'd all escape to Florida.

Estelle leads Janet through to the listing for the guy her Bernie used in his properties, then tells Estelle she'll see her soon, real soon, as soon as she finishes up here, be a doll and brew the Kona.

Hurry, Janet doesn't say.

"County Roofing will be out Monday," she announces to the pastor, and lifts her hand to indicate she's no interest in either his
protests or his thanks. Across the musty room, she wishes her
grandson would get in there and play with his friend and the little
ones. Look at his face. A more sad and touching expressing she's
not seen in her life. That heartbreaking longing to be just one of
the boys. And absolute adoration.

Ari can see that Daniel is the big brother—the father—that none
of these boys have. He knows what they are to him.

"Ari! You come be on these guys' side."

He starts to protest, but half the herd stampedes his way and
drags him into the middle of things.

It tickles Daniel the way that Ari towers over the boys. Many
ages here, preschool to maybe eight. *All the ages and sizes of Say.*
These guys think that Ari's clumsy clowning is the best act they
have ever seen (have no idea that much of this clumsiness is real).
He falls on the ball and rolls with it and they chase him around and
they laugh and he does his goofy laugh right back at them. That's
it, Big Boy. Let it all hang out there. He never allows himself to just
let go in this way.

The pastor also laughs heartily at the antics. "You have no idea
what a gift this is for them."

"The regular staff doesn't work weekends?"

"You're looking at the regular staff."

She asks for the rest of the grand tour—to the few small side
rooms that serve as kitchens and changing rooms and quiet rooms
and crying rooms and storage rooms and safe rooms to hide from
the gunplay that happens inevitably on a street like this. She listens as he tells her about the two retired teachers from Illinois
who drive in every Wednesday afternoon to work with some of the
mothers on their GEDs; the young couple from the south side with
the matching mohawks who came up two nights a week and were
able to make delicious and filling casseroles out of the most unlikely combinations of whatever had fallen off the truck that day. How
surprised he seems to be, she thinks, that it all works. She can also
see that the surprise is undergirded by some kind of uncanny calm,
like the figure skaters that she liked to watch who by all evidence
believed that jumping in the air, spinning three times and landing

on a blade as thin as a kitchen knife were the most ordinary things in the world.

In one of the side alcoves, some of the mothers sit with an array of babies and toddlers, rocking them, encouraging their crawling and cooing. They nod good morning to Estelle: Some of them are used to, apparently, being part of the pitch.

In the main room another of the mothers—"Donette" is the name Estelle hears—announces that it's time to set up for lunch, and she hustles the ball players over to one of the two bathrooms to wash up and get drinks. Other mothers open out accordion tables—salvaged from that long-gone local elementary school—as another phalanx appears with paper plates and bowls of salad.

"We do it family style at lunch. Small group today: A lot of the families are out on Saturdays."

Doing what, she wonders?

The boys—her boys—stumble over, panting and shoving at each other, laughing. Sweat stains the pits of the shirts they had modeled so elegantly this morning, and Ari's has a layer of dust from his clown act.

"That was fun," he pants—words neither Estelle nor Daniel have heard uttered by him in any way but cynically, if ever.

"Where do all these guys live?" Daniel asks. This man is so familiar to him.

And to Estelle it looks as if the pastor is at first ashamed to answer the question. (Again, Poppa, the tradeoff.)

"They live . . . here," the pastor tells him. "This is their home. For now."

For a week or a month or six months. Donette and her two kids would pass their one-year anniversary in July—and so much for the six-weeks-and-out rule he'd imagined imposing on the place. She worked forty hours a week at the discount store, but the asthma inhalers for the boy and her own blood pressure medicine continued to eat up apartment deposits. What could he do? Show her to the door? And, besides: No one, not even Schmidtty, organized a meal the way Donette did.

Daniel must have heard incorrectly. Children didn't live in places like this. He looks to Ari, but Ari only looks confused or hurt or something.

"My boys here are looking for summer jobs you know."

Good for them, the pastor thinks.

"I'm sure we could work something out. Right boys?"

Ari, Daniel sees, is staring at the man. Rudely. Perhaps Ari recognizes him, too.

"Ariel?" Estelle asks. He's been pestering her like a gnat about picking up some piece of a job, although what he needed money for, God only knows. And, OK Poppa, so I spoil the boy, too. My pleasure—and what's that look on the boy's face? Like something smells and like that something is the pastor. "Ariel?"

"Excuse me, sir. You said your name was Mitchell, right?" They hide in plain sight, Poppa Hillyer had said. You couldn't be too careful.

Daniel can't imagine why he's familiar. He didn't know any church people. Janet hated churches and particularly the people inside them.

"It's Pastor Craig Mitchell, Ariel. I swear the damn music machines make these children deaf."

Craig Mitchell. Older. Worn. Oily as shit. Dangerous.

"The boys and I will talk in the car. But what do say you, Pastor Mitchell? You could use a couple of spare hands for the summer, I'm sure."

The part of the pastor that is ecstatic with the thought of what might happen around here with two high-energy young people at his disposal declares war on the part of him that is confident that having these two around may be the worst mistake of his life. (Or the second worst, perhaps.) The brute is bad news, and as for the other . . . well he'd always wondered what had happened to the child. How many years has Craig spent hiding from the memories that the boy has already triggered?

"We'll consider their salary the first of what may just turn into a significant . . . endowment for your fine work."

Which (and he's chagrined at the expediency of his ethics) tips the scales in favor of his two newest staff members. For some reason the large one glares at him with absolute hatred. The one he already knows keeps casting glances in Craig's direction and then averting his eyes. He doesn't remember me. How could he?

"Until next week," Estelle says, extending her hand. Something has gone off with these boys, and it's time to move on. She hands him her card. "Call me when the roofers arrive and if there's any problems. They'll have Estelle Birnbaum to deal with."

Out in University City, Janet Williams peels back the living room curtains that she has kept drawn for the past week, stealthily looking to see what might be there. What could be keeping her grandson? She hopes he hurries home.

One of the ballplayers, one of the little ones, tugs at his shirt. "We playing after lunch, right?" A smear of peanut butter connects his mouth to his chin. Daniel thinks he said his name was Malik.

"We've got to go for today, but we'll be back, right Ari?"

"Sure, kid," Ari agrees, with a mean-sounding snicker.

Mr. High-and-Mighty; God's One and Only; Pastor, former-ly-known-as-Deacon Craig Mitchell. Boy wonder and head recruit-er of New Purpose Temple of Faith, the shit-hole of a cult that had once had more than five thousand members. Deacon Craig Mitch-ell: promoter of lies, stealer of innocent people's cash. Murderer by proxy. A man, according to everything Ari has read, at least par-tially to blame for the fact that Daniel has no family of his own.

Oh, hell, yeah, he'd be back.

Chapter **Eleven**

Once, during his years on the street, the boy had visited Craig: a dream, the most likely explanation, but it had been so vivid, so real. He would swear to this day he'd been wide awake and the boy had been right there—he could have touched him had he dared—but he hadn't dared, and who would even believe such a thing? Not even a desperately alone and homeless drunk. People like the man Craig Mitchell had been at the time saw all sorts of things, all the time. Sometimes during the dark years, he would go for days without food, and hunger did astonishing things to the imagination. Tennis balls turned into McIntosh apples, ordinary gravel into chocolate bonbons and peppermint Life Savers. People on the streets learned to distrust the most basic sensations: the relative warmth of a free cup of soup or whether the peach fished from the bin behind the bagel shop smelled rancid. It had been in such a state that the boy had appeared to him: Daniel Davis.

Dressed in the same suit he'd worn to his father and siblings' funeral, he'd materialized next to a stack of wooden pallets. This part of the dark years often found Craig bed down in the alleys off Forest Park Boulevard, a forlorn industrial district just west of Grand, a part of St. Louis ripe at the time with abandoned factories and warehouses. A lot of his brethren of the street peopled these grimy warrens: the Salvation Army just up the road offered a hot meal, if you could stomach the side of religion served with the bean soup. (Often Craig could not.) He'd unpacked himself from his nest of newspaper and cardboard one morning, and there the boy had been, and it had startled him, as it would anyone—waking up to an improbable gaze.

He'd recognized the suit before he recognized the boy. What a sharp little outfit it had been, and the gathered media back in the day had noted as much—no discount store off-the-rack special, this one. Black and crisp and tailored to his little body like a second skin. Back, after it happened, the grandmother had offered no response to Craig's request to escort her to the Davis home to retrieve some things for the boy, including something to wear to the services. He'd heard—in the few months between the tragedy and the time he'd finally disappeared from the life he had known—that she'd angrily rebuffed requests to come and see to her daughter's possessions (what little there had been) and a sister from New Purpose (whose name he has forgotten) who had delivered the box of meager keepsakes—mostly family photos and a few pieces of jewelry—had abandoned the box on the grandmother's porch when no one had answered the door.

The boy sure kept that nice, Craig remembered thinking of the suit. And then he had realized who it was who had taken such good care of his outfit, and he startled again, blinking his eyes at the unlikeliness of it all, had shaken his head to clear it. It would not be uncommon back then to wake up still drink-muddled or otherwise out of his mind.

Yet the boy remained, staring at him, his arms crossed in the same way his mother's often would be, with that mixture of defiant strength and defensive self-confidence, his head tilted almost imperceptibly to the right, his face set with that what-kind-of-creature-be-you curiosity often seen on boys visiting the zoo. When the door had opened that day and there his older self had been with Estelle and her grandson, Craig had looked across the room and seen those same crossed arms and a rush of hot acid had seared his heart. Merciful Lord.

In the capricious way that luck often would shift, shortly after the woman had arranged for the roof repair and then headed off with the boy and her grandson, a truck pulled up out front, loaded with cases of canned goods and trays of day-old bread. Schmidtty wheels in palette after palette—the effort seeming to exacerbate a pronounced wheeze that has troubled the old man for the past week.

"We're eating good," says Donette, who helps Craig unload the palettes and pack the food into the cupboards. As is often the case, Donette is ready with a cheerful and helpful hand; Craig's not asked for this help, but this is her way. When something needed doing, she's up doing it, be it a toilet that needed scrubbing or a child needing comfort after a fall.

"May have to last us a while," Craig tells her, and she sighs and says that she supposes it may. He berates himself for bursting her bubble. What would it hurt, after all, to have an extra vegetable on the tray tonight or to toast up the bread and spread it with butter and let them all eat their fill for once? Which of them didn't need it?

"There's more where this came from," Donette assures him, patting his arm. "You'll see." Her voice has the chipper positive tenor of an air-headed news anchor.

Oh, well: Someone, he guesses, has to keep the faith. He says nothing.

He has this theory that just the same way some people were unable to digest milk, others—like him, for example—lacked the ability to imagine the future. Or perhaps what they lacked was the ability to imagine it to be anything worth anticipating. A projection, surely, that theory, of his own aimlessness as a young man—of the way that he'd never been able to picture life outside the walls of his parents' bungalow, let alone beyond the constrictions of that awful high school out in Overland, the one whose name, as did all school names in St. Louis, marked his class and status as effectively as a tattoo—in this case as a permanent member of the striving classes. It was a given and thereby accepted among parents and teachers and neighbors and friends that dreams for the likes of him were not only deferred but had largely been cancelled by fiat and were therefore beside the point. How much imagination did it take, after all, to join the military or to get a job on the loading dock? All things considered it was probably just as well not to fantasize oneself with a broken back or otherwise as cannon fodder.

His parents, whose love of piety and obedience only slightly outweighed their disdain for ambition or whimsy, daily praised Jesus's gift of a humble home and simple sustenance. Eugene and Shirley Mitchell stored their treasure in heaven, and sometimes when Craig caught their eyes, he swore he could see reflections of the mansions built on platforms of clouds and of the roads paved with gold. When rewards waited in heaven what did it matter your enterprise on earth? He'd been unmoored, just about the age that Daniel Davis is now, and hence easy pickings when approached by the youth minister of New Purpose and encouraged to attend "fellowship," which he agreed to do out of boredom more than anything else. The first step on the long road that led him here to this place and these people.

He is not bitter about this or about them—any of them: his parents, Jerrold, Keisha. He cannot be—and what good would it do: all that water, all those burned bridges.

What kind of man heaped blame on the likes of his parents—who wanted nothing more than to raise a healthy happy child and to serve the Lord in the best way that they knew how? Craig can, in fact, only remember being happy as a boy—nurtured and cherished—perhaps even to the point of smothering. And there was the point perhaps.

"The new girl . . ." Donette begins, and Craig sees her catch Schmidtty's eye. Schmidtty juts his chin in a way that signals her to continue. These people's caution around him often troubles Craig.

"What about her?" he prompts, recognizing too late the aggressive and even petulant quality in his prompt. Donette stammered a bit—uncharacteristic for someone with her stout confidence—and he's unsure if he's intimidated her or if she's hunting for the right words. Once again it had been Schmidtty to the rescue.

"She's trying to tell you that the girl's off her rocker. Nuttier than a nickel fruitcake."

"I was trying to be polite," Donette demurs. She hands Craig a few stray tins of sardines.

Sardines. Typical of the odd lots that found their way into these shipments. One bottle of hickory-flavored ketchup. A couple of jars of mint jelly. An entire case of "potted meat product," a bubble gum pink abomination that had always been a favorite of Craig's mother.

"Crazy how?" he asks the two of them—and he manages a bemused quality this time. It's clear they want to talk. They've paused in their unloading of the groceries, awaiting, he can tell, whatever wisdom he might deliver.

"I don't know," Donette responds. "She's . . . skittery or something. I don't know."

"She's up to something," Schmidtty adds. "That's for sure." Donette shrugs.

Not useful information as far as Craig is concerned. It might describe about half the folks out there.

"You know folks who when they're talking to you, you feel like they're not really talking to you? Like their mind is somewhere else."

Craig nodded.

"It's like that. Like . . . I don't know. Like we're just part of her plan or something. But not in a good way. You know what I mean?"

Sure, he knew. That had been his first impression of Jerrold Davis, the young evangelist who had knocked on the door of his parents' Breckenridge Hills home, alongside a man who called himself Reverend Brickell. They'd come announcing Jesus's kingdom here on earth and the advent of the New Purpose Temple of Faith.

Rocky ground, those Mitchells had been, and many had been the door-to-door preacher busted a hoe attempting to sow their seeds among these dyed-in-the-wool COGIC stalwarts. All the same, his mother positively adored the idea of evangelism of any kind, and she would open wide the door for the Mormon boys in their crisp white shirts and had for years a regular Jehovah's Witness lady who dropped by copies of *The Watchtower*—an older white woman, who as did his mother, Craig figured, cherished their quarterly visits to set aside the mundane routines of their modest lives and simply talk quietly for a few moments, less about Jesus as he remembers than about progeny, the always impressive summer heat, and the high price of cabbage at the farm stand.

And thus without qualm Shirley Mitchell had opened up for the New Purpose team, ushering them in out of the scorching sun and inviting them to sit a spell, an offer easily agreed to. Jerrold had been "in training" that day, and after declining the offered "glass of ice water," he had slid into his spiel. Green as baby snot he'd been, his proclamation of the good news prompted from a scribbled stack of 3 X 5 cards. His under-rehearsed and stumbling presentation had contrasted sharply with the oiled perfection of his too-well-put-together appearance. He looked like a mannequin or like one of those people in the newspaper ads for Famous Barr. In Craig's experience, real people didn't look this way—not unless they wanted something from you—more often than not for you to buy whatever the hell they were selling.

Jerrold said: "Wouldn't it be wonderful, Sister, to live in a world without care?"—his smarmy equivalent of the used car salesman's "You can afford a couple a bucks a day, right?" But Pastor Brickell, old warhorse that he was, cut Jerrold off before his close.

"How long have you been saved, Sister?" he asked Craig's mother.

Had it been the amateurish oil painting of a cloyingly sincere Jesus that tipped him off—the one mounted above the sofa and lit by a portrait lamp? Perhaps the gospel station blaring from the kitchen? Any of five hundred similar clues? Whichever, Shirley Mitchell bit the bait and once again offered her witness, less a story of salvation than an ecstatic declaration of everlasting devotion. Transcribed by Berry Gordy, it could have been a hit for Marvin Gaye, and the New Purpose crew punctuated her testimony with their own Hallelujahs and a final "Amen, Sister."

Satisfied, they'd moved onto what they must have imagined to be more promising quarry. An afternoon off from his summer job flipping burgers, Craig had arrived just in time for this performance.

"And what about you, young man?" the reverend inquired.

"He's a heathen," his mother had informed her guests, her voice laden with self-righteous shame. The previous winter, halfway through his junior year in high school Craig had finally mustered up the courage to defy his parents and to not get up for Sunday services. Subsequently he had been reproached daily by his mother, who promised him eternal damnation, the works, including the hellfire, the brimstones (whatever the hell they were) and his own personal beady-eyed, pitchfork wielding Satan.

She mightn't have asked for a better son, truth be told—his goodness less a consequence of piety or some innate decency than it had been an accident of where he'd come of age and when. Upon his birth, his parents had also purchased their home, and a blessing for them it had been: priced cheap and cradled among stable working class folks like themselves. Alas those working folks had been in their seventies, eighties, and even older. He was the only child—within miles it seemed. And as for the character thing, he hadn't been the kind to wander off and find those who were also looking to make something happen. A few streets over, his inner gangster might have been nurtured under the half-assed tutelage of a gaggle of mostly harmless suburban bangers, but nothing about those boys had been appealing to him at the time, and as surprised as he had been to find himself dispossessed during the dark years, he had not been surprised to find a few of those lost boys among his peers in the back alleys of the city.

All the same, as far as Shirley was concerned, his resignation from regular church attendance was as straight up gangsta as it got.

"My own personal cross," she had moaned to the reverend.

"Have heart," he cheered. "A boy needs saving, that's all." Halfway in jest, he'd said this, as encouraged by his new prospect as a hooker in a convention hall. "Have you heard the good news, young man?"

"I may just have," Craig had responded, nodding for the first time at Jerrold—the casual nod that young brothers give each other on the bus or in the mall. He had nodded at the young man and then had averted his eyes. There had been some sort of shiny appeal about Jerrold Davis—something like the sun, compelling at the same time it was impossible to look at. What a handsome man he had been.

"My son has turned his back on our Lord," his mother lamented. "Can you help me?"

Yes, Reverend Brickell could.

"Jesus loves you, young man," he assured everyone present, and then he suggested they all lower their heads and pray for intervention.

It had been all Craig could do to not to bolt from that room, let alone close his eyes. He remembered nothing of the prayer, being as it was, one of countless thousands of similar ones he'd tuned out and for as long as he could remember. He did remember his mother whimpering quietly, as if begging for his life—and after all, hadn't she been doing just that? It broke her heart, the idea of her son down there—all those demons and all those lakes of fire.

And she wouldn't have understood, he still believed, how much it wrenched his own heart to watch her clip coupons and water down the canned soups in order to scrimp together an offering for her own minister—and watch those nickels and dimes buy a brand new Bronco every year and a new dress at the Lane Bryant every other weekend for the minister's wife, a woman who could barely suppress her bemused contempt at Craig's father's run-over shoes and his mother's dimestore frocks. Better they imagine him a heathen than confront them with what he believed to be the folly of their own poor choice of congregation.

"Amen," spoke the reverend, announcing the end of his supplications, seconded by all except Craig, and then the reverend added,

"He loves you, son," which prompted another round of praise.

He already knew about that love and he believed in it—which would almost certainly have surprised them all. The presence of that love had been proven to him by its occasional absence, by those times over the years—during the dark times, for example— when he would find himself lost, absolutely bereft, blind with the fear that we had all been abandoned here and left to our own sinister devices. Even as a boy he had felt a light in his life, and ironically enough when the reverend and Jerrold knocked on the door it had not been a particularly dark time; even more ironic that he owed to that light the strength he had found to defy his parents' demands that he rise and walk to their chosen services and to the then novel certainty that his spiritual path was and would always be of his own choosing.

All the same—and despite his mother's melodrama and the reverend's feeding into it—and despite Jerrold's air of arrogant smarminess—he hadn't been entirely repelled by their attentions that summer afternoon. Some people needed these door-to-door preachers, he imagined, or needed people like them, and they seemed harmless enough. It must be difficult to knock on strange doors and face whatever you found on the other side. And so the partially whispered invitation by Jerrold to "maybe drop by a little thing at the temple for the young folk" found—if not fertile ground—at least a person with some sympathy for their difficult work. Craig palmed the "business card" Jerrold slipped into his hand, hiding it from his mother. Sure, it might have taken the edge off her fears for his soul for her to know that he had it; at the same time he could do without her hectoring him to "call the boy and go see about being saved." He'd call Jerrold on his own time, thank you very much.

"What should I do with these?" Schmidtty asks. He kicks at a pallet of industrial-sized cans of baked beans. They're a blessing, Craig knows, these beans—nutritious and filling, even if the cans didn't quite fit the makeshift shelves in the pantry.

"Stack them," Craig orders, nodding toward the wall against which he usually aligns his cot. Schmidtty is as usual one step ahead of him and already clearing a space for the cans.

Donette opens an unmarked carton and squeals with delight at her discovery that half its contents are baby formula.

"The Lord does provide," she sighs.

Craig reminds himself to hold his face still and to not register any impatience with Donette's platitudes. He'd learned this skill early in life, reared as he had been on his mother's frequent vocal pieties. His training came in handy at the House of Hope, where the discourse would often dissolve into sanctimonious inanities about how blessed they all were (to be living in an abandoned supermarket eating donated canned goods and expired baked goods). Such cynicism is cheap, he knows, as much as he knows their platitudes are a form of whistling in the dark. Better after all the happy talk than the dark truth of the reality of their lives.

He has never been entirely sure why he made the call to Jerrold Davis later that same summer, suspicious as he'd been about organized religion and as unimpressed as he'd been with the young preacher. Even the way the boy had answered the phone had rather set him off.

"Hey, it's you. Thought I'd hear from you." After which he'd said nothing.

Craig had resorted to small talk—never a great strength of the Mitchell clan. His father almost never talked at all; his mother spoke only to or about Jesus and in either case almost always about which part of her hurt today and what she hoped He'd do about that.

When it became clear that for whatever reason Jerrold had no intention of bringing up the reason he'd slipped Craig his card in the first place, Craig took the initiative.

"I'm calling about that thing?"

No response.

"You remember? When you came by to talk to my mama?" The thing, the get-together, the fellowship, the whatever the hell it was the Jerrold had called it: the possibility for Craig that something might alleviate the tedium of that long summer.

Still no response from Jerrold.

"You said I might want to come . . ."

"How about 6:15?"

"Beg your pardon?"

"6:15. I'll swing by and get you on the way. It's casual, OK?"

Now and again Craig wondered what his life would be like had he, for example, taken that extra shift at the burger joint—as he'd been asked to do on that day his mother let them into her house— or perhaps if he had later that same day dropped Jerrold's card in amidst the coffee grounds and grapefruit rinds and abandoned it at the curb with the rest of the trash, his semi-weekly chore for as long as he could remember—and he'd almost done just that: tossed it away and forgot entirely about the New Purpose Temple of Faith. Surely they'd have never returned to St. Benedict Court; surely there were too many other souls that needed saving out there—and surely to those men Shirley Mitchell seemed well in the hands of at least some reasonably acceptable version of Jesus. How different his life might be.

Perhaps he would be suited and tied and ensconced in some office park, pushing papers and spending his morning worrying about where the gang would have lunch. Or in the Bay Area, per- haps, with a cozy little apartment and a lively circle of friends.

Jerrold Davis drove a horrifying wreck of an old car, which he'd apologized profusely for, assuring Craig that sooner rather than later he'd pick him up in a ride more befitting gentlemen of their standing in the community.

"Do you think Jesus cares what kind of car you drive?" Craig had asked him, but Jerrold had only scoffed in response.

The original site of the New Purpose Temple had been in a run- down strip mall on Natural Bridge just west of the University of Missouri. Surrounded by nail salons and chop suey joints, the storefront presaged none of the ersatz opulence of the future sanc- tuary, a building nearing completion on that night in 1986, one Jerrold assured him that would put New Purpose Temple of Faith on the national radar.

"We're growing, my brother. And you can be a part of it."

The young men and women gathered around Jerrold that night impressed Craig and attracted him. So calm and so not frivolous.

So happy to see him, including the girl with the intense eyes.

The bored, the aimless: always ripe for the plucking, Craig knows. Just as easily mightn't they have been a guild of motorheads on a recruiting binge, cars on blocks and Harleys on the brain instead of Jesus; or mightn't it have been potheads at the door, a clutch of them, Craig's misspent youth alternatively misspent on endless loops of jam band music and childish cartoons, a decade of blissful ennui?

Sometimes he believes that the big business of life is the business of finding the people you're supposed to go on this journey with. How poorly Eugene and Shirley had equipped him for this work.

His current fellow travelers help him stack the last of the season's bounty—these usually short-lived seasons of serendipitous generosity. The old man wheezes like an un-greased hinge; Donette rubs his back and shoots Craig a look: Do something. But this is another thing Craig has no idea how to respond to. So he changes the subject.

"That girl . . . You were saying about that girl."

It frustrates him when he once again gets shrugs as a response.

"It's just a feeling," Donette offers. "You know how sometimes you get a feeling about a person."

Keisha Williams had been the New Purpose girl's name. Another person delivered by fate—and he'd had a feeling about her, as well. She had eyes that toggled between summer warmth and winter chill, moods that flipped unpredictably, at her whim it seemed. He knew right away to fear the chilly side.

"The reverend and I delivered Keisha the Good News just a few weeks back. Look at you both: all fresh and new." Jerrold beamed, a hand on both their shoulders.

Craig told her he'd been pleased to meet her; noted she had not reciprocated. He had wondered that night if Jerrold's proprietary interest in the girl had been anything more than the pride the successful salesman has over his latest trick. He'd kept a hand on her shoulder longer than seemed appropriate, particularly considering the venue, and Craig found himself surprised at his own mild irritation over this. She hadn't been, after all, Craig's type—as much as he might have had a type. She was chunky and borderline sullen, the sort of unpleasant girl he found himself stacking burger buns next to at work. All the same, she'd compelled him. Who could say what pulled people together?

He is feeling Donette's need and Schmidtty's need and it is beginning to annoy him and scare him and he feels himself ready to flee this dump.

"Look, just keep an eye on her, OK? That all we can do—keep an eye out."

He closes himself into some paperwork on the counter—his signal to them that he has had his fill of the social side of things.

"And the boy . . ." he adds to their backs. "Keep an eye on her boy."

"Malik," Donette says, but Craig only hears nonsense and grimaces.

"The child's name," she says, a hand extended in a way that signals she is not offended. "And, yes, we'll keep an eye out."

The boy: all the lost boys. Malik. Daniel Davis.

Danny: Craig had recognized him instantly, from the moment he had set foot in the settlement house with Estelle and her grandson, and as it often had been, his first instinct had been to run— the feeling he had whenever he thought about what had happened back then, the feeling that had caused him during the dark days to hide in alleys and in the wild areas of the park, numbing his brain in every way he could, anything at all to forget the crazed eyes of the boy's mother on the day she had called Craig and ordered him to come see her handiwork. Eyes glazed with confusion and vengeance and even a kind of demented glee.

How blessed Danny had been to inherit the best of both parents' beauty. Jerrold's square jaw and high cheekbones, the intensity and dark depth of his mother's eyes.

What have you done? Jesus. Lord. What have you done, girl? Where's Danny?

Someplace you'll never get him.

What did you do?

He had always wondered what had happened to the child. The grandmother had withdrawn him from sight almost immediately. Craig understood that—in fact he admired the woman's wisdom and courage and ferocity. But the boy: He was like a son.

Didn't she know who Craig was? Didn't she know he was family? He'd been there when the child was born. Present at every holiday and special occasion, once a week for Bible study, and he had held the child while his parents attended to church business or to their other little ones once they arrived. He had lived in their guest room.

Of course, she had no way of knowing these things: Keisha kept her mother at arm's length, and it had been Craig's impression that Janet Williams preferred it that way as well. As far as she knew, Craig Mitchell was just another concerned and certainly nosy stranger, asking after the boy's well being.

He'd followed them when she'd walked the boy away from the funeral, watched her walk him into the prayer garden, then later down the block to the fried chicken stand, and he remembers that what he wanted more than anything was to join their quiet circle and to embrace them both and tell them that he, too, had been repelled by all the pious grief. But it had been as if the grandmother emitted a force field that repelled his approach. She hadn't even seemed aware of his presence.

Please, he'd wanted to call after them. He's all I have. I'll not survive without him, and Craig had gone home that evening and made the boy's favorite supper—baked mostaccioli with loads of provel cheese and with the burger-sausage mix fried and crumbled finely into the marinara.

"Don't come here anymore," Janet Williams had warned when he dropped off the casserole. She pressed the door closed firmly in his face, and that had been what had broken him.

Donette's gentle hands on his shoulders simultaneously delight and annoy him. It's disturbingly familiar—his father's humble affection—the feather-light caress of the muscle. Simple and reassuring.

"Be encouraged," she says. "Today at the House of Hope is a good day."

He nods. As often, he has no idea what to say to her. Mute as he'd been when he somehow found the courage to return to that house in University City, and he'd made it almost to the door when he realized he didn't know what to say to Janet Williams.

Tell her what exactly? What would she even care to hear from him—about Danny, Keisha, any of it?

That he had been part of their lives. That in almost every way being part of them had been the best time of his life. That he had been there at the birth her grandchildren, each of them, and that he had held them when they were sick—especially Danny—and that they were good and lovely children and that he missed them every day.

That he saw it coming—or believed that he had—and that he had tried to stop it but could not stop it. That he lived every day with that shame.

That her grandson had been a wonderful little boy. (She knew that.) That Danny loved puppies and miniature race cars and was so proud of his brother and of those sisters of his that he never took his eyes off them and he would always make sure their plates and bottles were full before he ate from his own.

That fate is real, that accidents happen. That in an alternative universe—in some luckier and gentler and less capricious one—he might have been the boy's father. How much he wishes that were so.

Chapter **Twelve**

D^{ear}

That was as far as he'd gotten on the letter, because he had no idea how to finish the greeting. Dear Mother? Dear Ms. Davis? Dear Prisoner #01121563. And as far as that went, he isn't even sure about the "Dear" part. He's not locating much endearment in himself, but the best he can figure at this point is to write the woman a letter and find out what the hell she wants.

G is no help. When he mentions his mother to Janet she puts her hands by her ears as if he's swearing at her—a technique only rarely (only once) part of his repertoire. Until recently—until today, in fact—she's gone out of her way to avoid running into him at all. He walks into the kitchen and suddenly something needed doing in the dining room. He'd swear this house had grown secret passageways—bookcases that swung open and magically delivered her from her study to her bedroom—do not pass Go, do not collect two hundred dollars, and whatever you do, do not talk to your grandson.

As of this morning, however, she's hovering. Tapping on the door and calling up the stair with trivial questions, generally making her presence known.

Tap, tap, tap: Snack, sweetie?

Tap, tap, tap: I'm doing a load of whites.

Tap, tap, tap: Severe thunderstorm warning for Washington County. You know what that means.

Actually, he had no idea what that meant. It's St. Louis. It's July. Severe thunderstorm warnings are as common as crabgrass.

As for Ari, he'd gone all moony-eyed and sentimental—no help at all these days. Rather like having a big cow around. He'd taken to bringing over gifts—awful, mushy music downloads, pop songs from way before they were both born that had been a bad idea even at the time they were recorded. We've only just begun, my ass. And he left little reminders of himself around the room, and not even the gross funny kinds like he used to do. In the old days, Daniel might find a Post-it tucked into his underwear drawer with a crude drawing on it. Now it was beanbag animals with actual red hearts sewn to their chests. Gross and disgusting, although not in the good way. Weird, really. Both of them. Just weird.

He's got to get this letter done before Ari arrives for the movies. Settling this once and for all may be the only thing that will return things around here to the normally and pleasantly bizarre status quo.

Hello!

That seemed neutral enough, if perhaps a little on chummy side—like the kind of e-mail you might send to a chat buddy in Portugal. The last thing he needs or wants is a pen pal. (And definitely *no* to the exclamation point.)

There had been five letters to him in the box that G had left on his bed, and it's hard to know what to make of the woman based on their contents. One letter for each of the last five years. None had been addressed to him.

The first she had sent in 2002, and she is no correspondent. The letters are cool and even vague—they sound like something someone might have written as an assignment for class, the teacher ordering everyone to hunker down or else. "And make sure you cover at least three points of interest"—the possibilities for such written on the board in a flourish of cursive letters. Her missives include rudimentary reports on her prison jobs and on the food and on how she's feeling at the time they are written. Nothing that inspires response—and as far as that goes none has been requested. The last letter, dated March 13, 2006, seems to Daniel slightly more engaged than some of the others. While still by no means personal, it at least read as if a real person had written it—as opposed to some letter-writing machine. A line from the letter stuck with him: "Time makes you crazy like a motherfucker." Vulgar and marginally literate to be sure, and because the line had no context, he had no idea what she was talking about. But it at least felt real in some way.

Tap, tap, tap. "It's me. Coming in."

Thanks for knocking. One, of course, never said such things out loud to Janet Williams. Things such as: Thanks for knocking. Or: As if I could stop you, or It's your house.

"What are we doing today?" she asks. She's unusually chirpy—is not even put off, it seems, by the disarray that he sees her making her usual inventory of (and, for the record, it would hardly merit her commentary anyway).

He tells her that Ari is coming over and they're going to "do stuff." She says, "Oh," and her chipper poker face dissolves, if only for a second. He gently—subtly, he hopes—closes the case on the laptop, but she still give it the evil eye, gives him the look that says she knows he's up to something and he's going to be mighty unhappy when she finds out what it is—and he best believe she will.

"I've made . . . plans," she announces. "You're going to like my plans." She strolls to the desk and runs one of her manicured nails around the computer case—the Janet Williams' version of elegant nonchalance.

"Plans?" Daniel inquires. He's lived with this woman long enough to know to be cautious about her "plans." He'd spent a month on stepladders when she'd "planned" to "brighten up that kitchen a bit"; had endured several unpleasant weekends in backyards of obnoxious West County snobs when she'd conceived a "plan" to widen his social horizons by hooking up with some outfit called Jack and Jill.

She's being uncharacteristically cagey about whatever these new plans are; keeps asking when Ari's going home—Ari, who hasn't even shown up yet.

"We're going to the movies or something," he tells her.

"Humph." Like a jealous girlfriend, that sound. She perches on his bed and eyes him up and down. Then, as if summoned, she walks from the room, a woman on a mission.

"Whatever," he says to himself. The others, huddled together on the bed, shake their heads and wag their fingers. He tells them to buzz off. He once again pops open the laptop. Where were we? Oh, yes: the damn letter.

He hits the backspace button, deciding to skip the greeting entirely. Which solves absolutely nothing. *How are you?* he types, and then deletes that as well. He's fairly sure he can guess the answer to that question—something along the lines of "as well as can be expected for someone spending the rest of her life in prison"—also fairly sure that he isn't all that interested.

Fairly sure. Keisha Williams Davis has always been more of a concept to him than an actual flesh-and-blood human being. Like the idea of Antarctica or of the surface of Mars, a person understood that such places existed out there, but they remained abstract and you expected them to stay that way—because who expected to find himself standing on the Ross Ice Shelf or up to your knees in the red dust of a faraway canal? Sometimes she would show up with the others, but the woman who came with them is nothing like the woman in the photos in the box. The one who comes with the others is stylish, sprightly, would smile at the others with her mouth wide open and her teeth parted, as if there were something she was about to announce to everyone but was too charmed by her brood to get the words out. Sometimes the twins needed their hair braided just the way that only she could do, and Say loved her grilled cheese sandwiches more than anything in the world, and she would stand by the stove and grill them up while his brother salivated at the dining room table.

She never seems to know that Daniel is there.

In the picture, in these letters: He doesn't know who this woman is. His lack of memory surprises him. On occasion Janet would joke about something that had fallen through the holes in her ancient brain—the name of a favorite song from back in the day, the location of a recipe—and he wonders if this is what has happened to his memory of his mother. The photos he has been given show a woman with a tight-lipped smile—as if what she'd rather have been doing in that moment was cussing the photographer out. There's a framed photo that must be her senior yearbook picture. Eschewing the coquettishness and glamour of the students in his own high school yearbooks, his mother seems melancholy. She also looks like the sort of person you wouldn't want to mess with.

As for what happened, other than the basic facts he knows very little about it. There's the one-sentence summary he keeps in his head, should he be required ever to tell the story in public: While he was here, she killed the rest of them and now she is in jail. It had taken work, but mostly he'd avoided having to use that line. Other than that it is assorted memories.

He remembers, for example, sitting in his grandmother's bedroom. When the men had come to the door his grandmother had sent him away from the room, but he cannot remember for what reason—is only sure she'd concocted a worthless errand of some kind and that whatever it was he had not bothered doing it. He remembers that he waited there for a long time and that he understood for whatever reason that his patience was important.

He remembers that when G finally came for him, her face had seemed different than before. It seemed looser—as if someone had opened a valve and released some of her air and there was no longer enough pressure to smooth out her features.

"Something has happened," she'd said. She was standing, he remembers, in the doorway, her hands clasped behind her back. He'd been sitting on the edge of her bed. "There's been an . . ." and then she had paused, searching for the word that would do the trick. She had settled at first on the word "accident," and then perhaps not liking the way it had sounded out there in the air, had searched for some different words, almost immediately arriving at the phrase ". . . a . . . mistake . . . certainly."

She told him that the others were gone and that so was his father. *Gone*: She'd had to search for that word as well. He cannot remember any time on that day or on any other day since when she has used the word "dead."

He does not remember what he had done just then, nor, for that matter, much at all about the next few weeks. Bits and pieces, he remembers, snapshot images almost: shopping for a new suit; the big church and the people with cameras; the coffins.

And he remembers, he believes, that after she had told him the news G came to sit by him on the bed and that she had almost certainly pulled him close to her.

"Isn't this something?" she'd said. She'd gotten up after a few minutes, announcing that there were calls to be made. She turned back around and said, "You can stay here," and he remembers not being sure if she meant right now, for the time being, or for always.

She never said a word about his mother.

Over the years, he has acquired and then filed away a few more details of what Keisha Williams Davis did. He's confident that what he knows is the thinnest skeleton of the full story—which is more than enough from his perspective. He knows that Americans—maybe people everywhere—were obsessed with grizzly murders, and he finds this fixation both ghoulish and in some way uncivilized. He'd just started middle school when the towers fell in New York, and that awful Mr. Simmons came into Social Studies class every day that fall with a new, horrifying detail about the way people died, the sort of things a person wished he didn't know. Others in the class seemed to revel in the ugliness—seemed almost turned-on by Simmons' lurid specificity about trapped civilians and the places where rescuers found pieces of dismembered bodies—all the while the same stories repelled him, as did the people who enjoyed hearing them. Maybe you had to have been fodder for sensationalism yourself to understand there was nothing entertaining about tragedy.

He knows that there are books about his mother. He saw one once in Left Bank Books. He'd been in the store, looking for a novel for a world literature class—one of those "student choice" deals (except they give you the list to "choose" from). He'd spotted one of the books on a sale table and had recoiled from it, the way he sometimes did from pictures of snakes in the encyclopedia. And rather than being curious about what was inside, he stood there trying to imagine who would want to read such a thing. When the coast was clear, he'd taken the book and hidden it on a low shelf in a dark corner of the store.

This is your son, Daniel Davis. I am seventeen. I turn eighteen on the 25th of September, in case you forgot. I am a rising senior at

He holds down the delete button all the way back to the first T. As if she cared—that's his first thought. And then he curses at himself for being too smart for such cynicism. Of course, she cares. Maybe it's he who doesn't.

Fucking Ari Birnbaum. Just when you need someone to step up, the boy's a lost cause. Down at the settlement house he'd become positively taciturn—owled around the dump with a big chip on his shoulder, dropping the veneer only for games with the little ones. Here at home he's a big old teddy bear. Vulgar e-mailed photos had given way to dreamy-looking avatars and snippets of poetry from some anthology in Estelle's library.

And how would Ari help anyway? What did he know about dealing with selectively silent grandmothers, or, for that matter, corresponding with their crazy daughters? As if his relations with his own people were so great: His own parents by all evidence could barely stand to have him around, and while Estelle, to her credit, kept him well under hand (and it shames Daniel slightly to realize how much he enjoys this show), having Ari around the house must be like living in a circus cage with a lion. It certainly must exhaust the poor woman—the constant wielding of the chair and the whip. And it's ironic to Daniel that the same things that drive others crazy about the boy—his imperiousness, his bullheadedness, his fundamental misanthropy—Daniel found charming (if charming were an appropriate word for a person who found humor in making fun of the homeless men outside the shelter). Sometimes a good model for unpleasantness came in handy.

You fucking crazy bitch. Who the hell do you think you are, sending these letters to me after what you did? Rot in jail before you rot in hell, and in the meantime leave me and your mother the hell alone.

This one does not get immediately deleted. He kind of wishes he could send it, but knows that G wouldn't approve—even if she probably did concur with the sentiment—a sentiment that he himself only partially owns. Keisha Williams Davis was (is?) crazy: You didn't need a psychiatrist to confirm that. At the settlement house, he had been learning how many fragile people there are in the world—how many are just that close to the edge. Twice in the month he has worked there, he and Ari have had to scramble the kids away from someone who just went off, for no apparent reason. Not that the kids actually needed help: Live like they live and you developed, by all evidence, a sixth sense for spotting deranged trouble makers. The little monsters hit the decks like marines in a combat zone. (His favorite, that little Malik, had pulled Daniel to the floor just yesterday at the sound of a car backfiring.) What you didn't do, he was learning, was blame these poor people for their problems. Just last week, he'd been working the lunch line when he found himself face to face with one of the crazies who the day before had menaced the place with a folding chair, swinging it around and threatening to "kill all you bitches." He'd looked to Craig, who had nodded slightly, and the message had been clear: She's hungry and it's a new day. Craig: There was someone who would understand this problem, but man, he was a busy brother. And he was always shy around Daniel. But Daniel would work on him. He'd warm him up, maybe snatch a few minutes of his time between all the other chaos at the center.

The doorbell rings. Then rings some more. Then rings some more. He knows she's down there. Damnit!

"G! Do you want me to get that? G!" What the hell!

He bounds down the steps and sees G standing in the picture window with her arms crossed.

"What are you looking at?"

"I'm sure I mentioned to a certain person that I had plans today."

And I'm sure I mentioned I had plans of my own. (Not, of course, said out loud.)

"It's Dufus. See?" Ari ambles in looking, in fact, particularly doofy.

"Hey, Mrs. Williams." Lately he'd taken to greeting everyone with "Hey," because he'd seen some sitcom rerun on Nickelodeon where that's what they did. (Mr. Cynicism had decided that it was cool for smart people to embrace retro sitcoms. The less hip the better as far as he was concerned.)

"Ariel," G responds. Janet looks at Ari the way that she always looks at Ari—with her usual varying mixture of amusement and distrust, today slightly more on the distrust side. It's the sort of look teachers reserve for the kinds of student who even though you know they'd steal you blind, you just can't help but love them because they're so damn cute.

"Nice weather, huh?"

Small talk: Daniel wants to kick Ari in the shins.

"It is a lovely day!" G enthuses. Her face lights up—the way it did when she has a brainstorm. She sidles up to Ari and pulls him into a sideways hug, which he receives with his big doofy smile. Damn, Daniel thinks: This is like one of those moments when the battling candidates reconcile on camera "for the good of the party." Weird.

"Let me see what's in the kitchen for my hungry men," she cheers, gathering up her chamois and her can of spray wax. (And while we're on the subject, doesn't she pay someone to dust? Daniel wants to call behind her, but Janet Williams did not entertain rhetorical questions.)

Ari, he can see, has found a way to be both grungy and clean at the same time. Faded T-shirts that fit him tight and seem to go with any of his new jeans. On the way up the steps, Daniel taps him on the ass, hoping to revive the nasty old Ari, but rather than being thrown on the bed and crushed, he's given one of the new intense soul kisses that Ari seems to prefer these days.

"Hey," Ari sighs, in his big-goober country accent. "I've been waiting for that all day."

Romantic, sweet Ari: It took some getting used to. These days he's like one of those dogs—like a boxer or a bulldog—that looked like he might be tough but was really just a big slobbery puppy.

He asks if those are the movie listings on the laptop, makes a grab for it.

"Leave it," Daniel orders. He snatches the laptop from reach and slams it closed.

"Keeping secrets, are we? We both know what happens to boys with secrets." Then he laughs one of his marginally nasty laughs, and Daniel thinks, *OK here comes the old Ari*, and Daniel can feel his shorts filling up.

"Guess what? I got you something." Ari fishes in his pocket and Daniel thinks, *What the hell?*

Ari extends his balled up hand, slowly opens his fingers.

It's a rock.

"Is that a rock?"

"It's not just any rock. It's my favorite rock. From the time we went to the Ozarks when I was a kid. I found it on the shore, polished just like this."

"Let's see!" the others demand, gathering around.

The rock is almost a purple color, flecked with dark bits and shiny bits.

"It's granite, I'm pretty sure. Mostly what you find down there is sandstone." He goes on to point out the creamy streaks that run through the rock, identifying them—he may even have given the chemical makeup, but Daniel isn't listening, really. It's just too weird.

"Thanks," he finally says. He hopes that didn't sound like a question. He adds, "You know, you don't have to give me presents all the time."

Ari grabs him and pulls him down on the bed in the way a parent might do a child to give them a hug. Nothing sexy about it at all, damnit.

"I'm always going to take care of you," Ari says. He kisses him on the head—again, the way a parent might do—and then makes one of those throaty parental grunts of satisfaction, the kind that the mothers down at the settlement house did when they were pleased with the little ones. And Daniel thinks: *What happened to the bet and to the raunchy nasty talk and to practicing for having sex and to all the other fun stuff?* Rather than a boyfriend, Ari is now more like a gigantic plush toy. And, OK, the teddy bear hugs felt good in their own way, but couldn't they be grinding against each other at least a little bit and driving each other to the edge and sweating a lot? And then he thinks, *Fuck this*, and gives Ari a half-tender, half-tough titty twister. It seems to work—judging by that moan, and then Ari squeezes him tighter, like he'd done in the good old days. And then . . .

And then he said:

He said . . .

"I love you," he said.

Which causes Daniel to untangle himself and stand up with the laptop and say:

"Maybe we should check out that Will Smith flick."

"Cool," Ari responds. He's all moony and cow-like again. Daniel's heart beats hard—he isn't sure if it's fear or something else.

"You got the times?" Ari asks.

Daniel reminds him that movies like that one start every hour on the hour as long as they are raking in the cash, and again Ari says, Cool.

"I need a Coke. You want a Coke?"

Daniel shakes his head, which Ari rubs and then kisses before heading down to the refrigerator, and Daniel thinks, *Damn, I probably blew that big time.* Because when the person you love tells you that he loves you, you were probably supposed to say something like "Me too." Which he had not. And now what does Ari think? He's probably down there thinking about how to dump me because I'm such a loser and so pathetic.

Ari ambles back in with a tall glass of soda over ice. From behind his back, he pulls another smaller glass and says, "Ta Da!" He'd gotten really corny, too.

"I figured when you saw how good mine was you'd want one of your own, huh?" Ari pours about half the Coke down his throat, appears not even to swallow. He belches.

"Oh, and . . . Dude . . . check this out: Look what G gave me."

Dude?

Ari unfurls a twenty-dollar bill from his jeans.

"Janet Williams did not just give you twenty dollars." Janet Williams might *loan* Ari twenty dollars, and she *might* give Daniel twenty. Might. If he'd maybe run out of allowance and maybe he'd run out of lunch money and maybe if he'd somehow from some place mustered up the courage to ask. Might. This is a woman who almost certainly had a few pennies of the first dollar she'd ever earned, a woman even panhandlers could tell was a long-shot and rarely bothered asking.

Ari dances the bill in the air like a spokesmodel for the U.S. Treasury.

"G says you and me are to get the hell out of this house and to go out there and have a wonderful day."

OK: weird.

"You know what else G said? She says she's got plans. *Plans*." He says that as if he's announcing the advent of a major secret. "Exciting, huh?"

"I guess," Daniel responds. As it often seemed to do, it just got weirder by the moment around here. He tells Ari that he has to print something up and it will be just a few minutes before they can go.

"You take all the time you need," Ari enthuses, and wraps Daniel in a big hug. In the old days, Daniel would have dumped the Coke over his corny curly head, but the old days are apparently over. Daniel pets him the way that he might stroke a cat.

It is so weird.

He once again untangles himself and maneuvers the laptop from Ari's view.

To Keisha Davis

From Daniel Davis

I received your request for a visit, and I was wondering if you could explain why you are interested in seeing me at this time.

He slides up the cursor to the print icon, then decides on one more line:

I am fine and doing well at your mother's home, where I await your response.

Then he hits "print."

"Hope that's for me," Ari says, all dreamy. If he says one more thing like that Daniel *will* throw a soda on him. He's back there on the bed, snuggling with Daniel's pillow like it's a stuffed animal, sniffing it and cuddling it. The others snuggle around him. That might be a bulge in Ari's jeans, but with Ari it was hard to tell. There was plenty in there under the best of circumstances.

Daniel folds the note and places it in an envelope. It's only fair that Janet see it first.

"Ready?" he asks.

"As a matter of fact, I am. I give up. You win."

"Huh?" Alas, Daniel knows what he means, but it seems like a good idea to buy time.

Ari peels the T-shirt over his head. The soft curly hair that Daniel's hands have spent so much time exploring seems even darker against the paler olive skin on his chest. He's missed sitting by his family's pool this summer—too busy at the settlement house—and Ari had a vague farmer's tan as proof of their indoor lives. Ari pats the bed beside him, and Daniel sits.

"Well?" Ari asks. He seems to be trembling. His eyes are watery and round.

"G's down there." Daniel is trembling too. "She says we should go." He reaches to that chest and runs his hand down its length. "She gave us twenty dollars."

Ari captures the hand and actually brings it to his mouth and kisses it. (Corny!) "We'll wait, then, OK? 'Til you're ready. But, no more bets. I declare you to be the winner."

Daniel kisses him on the cheek, lets himself be held against the boy. He wants so bad to . . . well, to do a lot of things. He places his hand on Ari's crotch and caresses it, but Ari lifts the hand away.

"When you're ready," he says, and Daniel nods.

I love you, too, he thinks, and he wonders if it wouldn't be easier to say the words out loud if today weren't the first time in his life anyone had ever said them to him.

Chapter Thirteen

Estelle lugs that Whole Foods tote for the sole purpose of smuggling in treats for the pastor. She fishes into it and retrieves a thermos of Starbucks and a large hunk of gooey butter cake—one that she had purchased for Janet, but since Janet has here lately been "busy" with some new scheme—and what, pray tell, was that all about?—Estelle hadn't been able to share, so why let a perfectly good snack go to waste?

"We've discussed that guilty look, young man. I'll not have it." The sadly deluded soul seemed to believe it was sinful of him to take a quiet moment to himself, to enjoy a simple treat on occasion. Carpe diem, she'd insisted the first time she'd pulled him out of the main room and into his alcove for a morning snack, and it had been clear to her that this was the first time he'd heard the Latin phrase. They need me out there, he had insisted, despite her own insistence that the world would not end if he took the time for a nibble and a chat. And then he had started in on how it just didn't seem right for him to be eating this sort of thing when all that those poor folks out front got was a cup of soup and maybe—maybe—some fruit cocktail, if a can or two were in the donation bin—which happened almost never, according to him.

"Nonsense," she had chided. "Your own Jesus, he got that foot massage and still had time for a fish fry. Eat."

She had since colluded with the women in the shelter—in particular that Donette, a natural leader if Estelle's ever seen one, as well as the old man who was always around—to help her to help this man to take a moment for himself. So now when she walks in the door Schmidtty winks at her, indicating he'll take over and to get the dear man off of his feet, if only for a few minutes.

Dear. He seemed dear to her.

As she pours the coffee, she sees beneath the guilt a glimmer of pleasure, subdued but there all the same, similar to the bliss that would blossom sometimes beneath Poppa's face. Poppa: a man who savored every bite and who would sometimes allow tears to leak from his eyes at Powell Symphony Hall—but heaven forbid anyone should know that side of him. "It's OK," she would encourage her father, but he'd always shake his head, denying the soft heart that always beat inside him, despite it all.

She cuts the cake into one small square and three larger ones, placing the smaller on her napkin before sliding the foil in his direction. He eyes the door before lifting one to his own napkin. No one is coming, she knows. The boys had cleared part of the abandoned play yard next door and have taken the children outside for a game of circle dodge. The women sit quietly, talking in small groups, flipping through the magazines she has just dropped off, or just sit with their heads lowered, planning the day, perhaps, or just taking a breather from . . . life.

"You're too good to me, Mrs. Birnbaum," the pastor says, shaking his head and brushing a crumb from his goatee. He is serious, she knows, and she also knows he is courting her—or courting Poppa's money, to be honest—but neither of them are innocents as far as these matters are concerned. They both understand the game and its rules.

And while it didn't surprise her that she liked this person—she'd not have come here had she not anticipated as much—it does surprise her how much she enjoys speaking with him, sharing what little time he is able to offer her.

"The gooey butter cake: It's a St. Louis delicacy, wouldn't you agree?"

"Yes, ma'am," he says, and she sweeps her fingers like a broom, encouraging him to take a second of the larger hunks. She finds his reticence charming—remembers spoiling Ari this way. (Ari: She remembers the first time she'd offered him a ten at the movie theater to run up and get himself some popcorn. He'd been thirteen and had startled at the bill, as if there were fire in her hands. What had those people done to the boy? Another one coming unglued, her grandson. Another puzzle to solve.)

"It was an accident, you know. The gooey butter cake. The story goes something like this." And she told him one of the six versions she'd heard—specifically the one about the sleepy baker who'd incorrectly mixed the ingredients for a garden-variety coffee cake. "And so we are blessed," she concludes, indicating again the treat before him and the fact that he should eat up.

"Blessed indeed," he agrees.

She almost gets a smile that time. He is as stingy with the smiles as her grandson, this one. Men who apparently felt like the world might end if they offered up a little sunshine.

"So I've been thinking, Pastor Mitchell, about what you said last time about the women. Why you chose them for your work."

He nods, but rather reluctantly she can tell. She has to admit that the fact that it is difficult for him to discuss his mission charms her, even as he knows that doing so is critical to his goal of securing more funding for it.

"Maybe they chose me," he says.

Estelle chuckles. "That's surprisingly New-Agey for a Christian man."

"There's a lot of overlap between how we spiritual types understand the world," he tells her, and she can see the invisible quotes around *spiritual*. He goes on to talk about the whole idea of being "called," and how there was, in fact, something mystical about that.

"You were called, then?" she asks, and before he responds she watches a cloud darken his features.

"I don't always know how to answer that," he says.

She can tell that this discussion pains the man—this inquiry into the clearly less-than-examined path that has lead him here.

"To be honest it often seems incredibly random to me. If you know what I mean."

She nods once, not so much because she has parsed his meaning, more to keep the man talking. She has learned that, as were most men, he is like a pump: You primed them to get the words flowing, worked them until one or the other of you runs out of energy or interest.

Estelle herself had never worried much about paths. For the most part, hers had been chosen for her. She'd marry, produce children, be happy. She could work if she wanted, move ahead in the world—Poppa believed in the advancement of women, even as much as he claimed to hate feminists. (Goddamn bra burners: What's the world coming to!) But the children, the next generation: that had been the main goal. Fruitful multiplication and all that. And to be happy. When it had been only Aaron to come along, she'd seen the disappointment in Poppa's eyes, but what could be done? So she worked on the work part and on the happy part, and has done well in both, even if she says so herself.

"I heard a voice," the pastor says, and she isn't entirely sure if this speech is being directed at her. "It said to do something. Do *something*. Emphasis on the *something*. So here I am. Doing something."

"Voices, too. Next thing we'll be burning sage and howling at the moon."

Not even a smile: Apparently the subject is beyond humor. He sips at the coffee, savoring the richness of it. One morning dropping the boys off she had accepted what passed for a cup of joe around this joint: Thin as tea, the women conserved the precious generic grind the same way they hoarded pennies, sometimes, she was sure, running the water through twice. Estelle had taken to delivering a couple of five-pound cans with the boys on Monday morning, although she'd still bet they used barely enough coffee to cover the bottom of the filter.

"I would never joke about a person's calling," she says, deciding that she had offended him.

"Don't know that I believe in them myself."

She scoffed at his scorn. "History is full of visionaries. Or at least it's full of people who have heard the voice of God."

"Or it's full of people who are insane."

This time she waves her hand at him, rolls her eyes. In fact, she actually agreed with his cynicism, but it also troubled her, this uncertainty. Didn't we all prefer a healthy amount of self-assuredness in the religious among us? Their confidence—however ill-founded—made it easier for the rest of us skeptics, stimulating our wry amusement at their certainty, all the while facilitating our comfort in the fact that someone, at least, attended the switch as far as spiritual matters were concerned.

"Surely, Pastor Mitchell, you believe that God speaks to us, that he guides our hands."

He shrugs. "Frankly, Mrs. Birnbaum, I don't think it matters whether he speaks to us or not."

Estelle smiles, sits back in the chair, sliding her purse further into her so it won't fall off her lap. "It may be that I prefer my holy men to be a little bit holier."

This time it is his turn to scoff, and she believes that she even saw contempt in his eyes.

"I tease, of course. Forgive the familiarity: It's a family trait, I'm afraid."

Her grandson comes in, panting, sweating, being dragged by one of the pre-schoolers, who was also sweaty and out of breath.

"He says he left something . . ." Ari starts, and then seeing her there, says, "Oh. Hey, Estelle." Ari shoots glances between her and the pastor—the same suspicious glance her father would use when he walked in on her and Bernie having a perfectly chaste glass of lemonade in the kitchen of the house in University Heights.

"What's going on here?" Ari asks her—same accusatory baritone his great grandfather would use.

"Son, that's not a tone we take with any of the women at the House of Hope. Certainly not with your grandmother."

It always scared her, that anger that flashed across her grandson's eyes. Positively murderous, that look. Just as quickly, he sets his face back in the benignly pleasant mode he'd employed before he noticed her there.

"Estelle doesn't mind. Do you Estelle?"

She knows she ought to nip his insolence in the bud, but with Ari you had to play it so carefully, especially here lately. One minute, distraction; the next, a mountain of anger. Last week after she'd gotten him home, he'd gone off—she can't even remember what set him off—and he'd stalked around the house slamming doors and spouting obscenities, and he had even picked up a paperweight, hefted it, tossed it from hand-to-hand.

She'd gotten right in his face; he was quavering with rage. With one hand, she'd peeled the paperweight free, put the finger from the other in his face. "Ariel Birnbaum, so help me God, if you ever . . ."

That's all it took to diffuse him. He'd melted like butter in a hot pan, dropped his head in shame, mumbled over and over again how sorry he was.

"What's the matter, sweetheart?" she had asked him. "Talk to Bubbe, please." You wouldn't understand, she deciphered from the mumbles, and he'd kept repeating it. For a week he'd been volatile in a way she'd never seen—alternating moods with every breath it seemed. He'd backed away from her that day—the day of the paperweight—and when she'd called him down for supper he'd been as pleasant as a spring morning. "Evening, Stell," he'd said, the same way her father always would. Pleasant enough to make her forget (—well, almost—) the quivering mass of muscled anger she'd fronted off earlier in the day.

And what if he hadn't calmed? What then? How far might he go, that Ariel Birnbaum?

The child retrieves his buried treasure—a small green ball—and that saves her from an immediate response to her grandson's impertinence.

"Looks like our friend struck pay dirt," she says—instead of whatever else needed saying. Often enough with the boy it worked best to just change the subject.

"I was wondering where that got to," Ari says, and his sweetness toward the child both touched as well as surprised her—and she commented on it as they charged back out to whatever they were up to out there.

"He's good with them, isn't he?"

The pastor nods in agreement, noted that it was true about both the boys. And then he asks her to tell him about the other boy. "What's the story there?"

"Daniel? What about Daniel?"

Another shrug. "I don't know. Seems like a good kid, doesn't he?"

He is being disingenuous, she knows, but decides to not engage. "They're both good boys, "she tells him. "We are blessed."

"Daniel hangs back. Lets Ari take the lead. Probably hasn't said two words to me this entire summer."

She can certainly believe that about Daniel. He is slow to warm to people—a trait that might be read by some as arrogance, but which Estelle understands to be a kind of intellectual deliberation. He's a young man who takes his time to read people and only after he decides what and who you might be and whether you are worthy would he deign to engage you person-to-person. Only here lately has he even offered a glimmer of himself to Estelle.

"Ari: He's the man with the plan. You drop them off, and Ari's in here asking what needs doing, and if I don't have a list, he finds something anyway. The other one follows the lead."

Which doesn't sound much like Ari either, but who knows anymore with those two?

"Daniel's a fine young man, Pastor Mitchell. It's a . . . touchy time, let us say."

"With his family?" he asks, and Estelle again marvels at how bad he is at being coy. She sips her own coffee rather than respond.

"He lives with his grandmother, right?"

"My best friend Janet. That's correct." It will do none of them any good taking this bait.

"What's your dream for this place?" she asks, and he deflates a bit with the subject change—not easily defeated, this one—and then starts in on his simple-man/simple-dreams spiel about keeping the soup kettle full and blah, blah, blah. She waves that away.

"It's time to get down to business, Craig. May I call you Craig? Good. Then you must call me Estelle. Craig, we both know I'm not here for the comfortable furniture, nor, despite your being a handsome—if inscrutable—man, for the pleasure of your company."

"I'd guessed as much," he agrees.

"Call me a limousine liberal if you want, and I certainly could have dropped you a check and headed on my merry way. And yet, here, instead, I sit."

He squirms with discomfort. Clearly the man needs training in the fundraising department. Down the line she'd get that Shapiro girl from the temple to teach him the art of the "ask," but for now, it is him and her, and she'll have to make the best of it.

"Poppa left me money and instructions. He had a vision, and I've made it no secret that I believe you to have one too. So I'm asking: What's your vision, Craig?"

He raises his eyebrows and twists his mouth wryly. She finds this performance slightly dishonest—cannot entirely believe that his head doesn't explode with dreams for this place—for the whole world for that matter.

"Come on," she chides. "You've got a wish list as long as your arm."

His snigger sounds sad. "Really, Estelle," he says. "Most days it isn't much more than another carrot for the pot." Sincerely, he says that, and she believes it, too. She also picks up on the equivocation.

"Most days," she prompts. "And the others?"

And she actually gets a smile, albeit a cautious one. He presses his eyes tight and sucks on his bottom lip.

"Our friendship is young, Craig Mitchell, so it's probably too soon for you to trust me just yet. Believe me when I tell you that now is the time to dare to dream. Your head won't explode."

He laughs. "Well, you never can tell about that."

She gathers the now empty foil and the thermos into the tote, pulls out another foil packet. "For later," she says. "A little nosh," but he protests that he cannot possibly.

"Then give it to someone who needs a little day brightener. The old man, eh?"

Mitchell nods. He'll want it himself, she bets, but he'll pass along the good fortune. That is his way.

"I'm taking the boys early today, if it's OK with you."

"You're the boss," he replies, which causes Estelle to think he doesn't know much about teenagers. As part of her plan to burn through her unseveranced leave before the big move to Florida, she's taken off part of the afternoon to drop in on Janet. It was a great man who said, Busy is as busy does, but friends are forever. Or something like that, he said.

"I'm cutting you some slack today, Craig, but on our next visit I'll need an answer, yes?"

He nods his consent to the arrangement.

She doesn't know why she feels comfortable doing so, but she places a hand on his cheek and he allows it to linger there in a way that Ari often would not. The brown skin feels smooth where he had shaved, warm to the touch. He is dear; she is sure.

"Dream big, Craig Mitchell. Poppa would want us to."

On the playground, the boys have painted a circle, which the children sit around, Daniel and Ari anchoring the noon and three-o-clock positions. They have organized one of those games that require one of the youngsters to walk the circle tapping the others on the head, calling out silly words, one of which triggers the seated child to jump up and chase him back to the open space. A girl, tapping away, says the secret word to her grandson, who makes a big clumsy show out of rising to chase her. He stumbles and spins—would put Emmet Kelly to shame, that boy—and of course she beats him, just as he intends her to. And it's Ari's turn to say the silly words and tap heads. Impossibly, the children both duck from the tap at the same time as they rise to meet it. Everyone wants his hand on the head.

Oh, how it does her good, watching them play. They have never had this chance, either of these boys, her boys. Couldn't get in, or wouldn't get in, or didn't know how to get in the game. One with a father who seemed incapable of getting down on the floor with the boy ("Play with your son, Aaron! What's the matter with you?"), the other raised by a woman who at his arrival in her life had believed herself to be finished with childrearing—a woman burned down to cinders by a tragedy that defied measurement. (Janet: What to do?) Their faces—Daniel and Ari's—opened wide this way: It is as if she's never seen them before.

Ari taps the other girl—there are only two—and the boys groan in disappointment, but they also know that whoever she is, she will next tap Daniel, which she does, and he clowns as badly as Ari had.

Where are all the girls, she wonders? It is as if the mothers have stored them away somewhere—away from these unmoored and chaotic lives. And all these fatherless boys. All of them. Her heart ached.

Damn you, Aaron, she thinks—her own clueless son, in his own way as bad as the worthless lot who fathered the rest of this tribe— The Tribe of Lost Boys. And she wonders how many types of abandonment are represented in that circle. Men who left. Men who had never been around in the first place. Men, such as Aaron, who had the bad luck of fathering sons who weren't exactly what they had in mind.

"It would be enough, you know," the pastor says, coming up behind her.

"What would be?"

"That. The children there, those smiles. If that's all you do for us, that would be enough."

She reminds him to dream big and signals the time to her boys.

Until this summer, she'd forgotten the smell of boy—the gym locker, sour sock, wet horse thickness of it—and she wishes she'd thrown a tarp over her cloth seats. Ari is soaked as if he'd been standing in the rain, and Daniel's not much better. But that's what auto detailing was for, after all, and she'd have the service stop by on Friday and blow the weekly must from the sedan.

"You boys had fun today," she says—a statement and not a question.

"Hey, Daniel, did you ever play that red-light, blue-light game? We should so play that tomorrow."

As was often the case on these summer afternoons, she might as well not be in the car with these two.

"It's the one that's sort of like freeze tag except you're *it* and you control everything. We're playing that tomorrow. You know what else we should do? We should do some art projects. I'll get a book or something from the library. We'll do some art projects."

Daniel says almost nothing, but how could he have? Formerly mute Ariel—king of the sullen—hardly stops talking on these trips from the settlement house.

"You know, when you pay us, Estelle, we should go to that game store over on Brentwood, and trade in some stuff, huh Daniel? I've got so many I'm sick of. Man."

In her rearview mirror, Daniel sits upright, a little stiff looking. Where Ari has opened up lately, he's been closing in, she has noticed—would stay off in some other place. It's the face of a man working through a puzzle. Sometimes Ari would have to call Daniel's name twice before he responded.

"I can think of three games of yours that should go. Yeah, three."

The big oaf didn't seem to mind the one-sided conversation. What's going on in the back seat isn't indifference, she knows. The child is in trouble, just like Janet is in trouble. As is Ari, for that matter.

Think, Estelle. The boat's sinking and you've got three people drowning on you, however slowly.

"And you know what else I was thinking?"

Still the damn kid goes on babbling, and she wants to tell him, "You are crowding this person. Back off, would you?" The saying of which might cause Ariel to do almost anything, she knows.

A flush of fear washes through her. She's losing her people—the ones who keep her own ship on course.

"What we all could use about now is an afternoon snack," she says, and she pulls into the Steak-N-Shake near the airport—where she finds the drive in backed-up with other late afternoon snackers.

"Ariel, be a love and get us some of those big fries and whatever kind of shakes you kids drink. Bring me a big Coke. Diet. Daniel and I will stay here in the car where it's cool."

Ari is eager as a retriever. "Chocolate, right?" he asks Daniel—although why he bothers she isn't sure, since he doesn't wait for an answer.

The engine lugs from the air conditioning. She turns to the boy in the backseat.

"What are you thinking? Talk to Estelle."

He turns to the window; she can't remember seeing anyone try so hard not to cry. He fails, wipes away what few tears he lets leak. Damn men and their macho silliness. Let it out, for goodness sakes: You've got a right.

It's like this when it fails, that poker face he has inherited from Janet Williams. World-class stoics, these people, and she wonders if this trait is also shared by the boy's mother. Janet's illusory and disarming smile, Daniel's cool, sideways smile that is more like a sneer: two sides of the same coin. But here, today, it's just not doing the job. More tears leak. She would see this look only once more time in her life—this . . . frustrated, helpless rage, this look of abject defeat and helplessness. Not too terribly many years later, he would accompany Ari to her bedside in the assisted living that she would move to when her health began to fail. The look would be for Ari, not for her: He would be too pained to even glance her way.

She reaches back and strokes the arm that she can reach and he lets her.

She pops the clasp on her purse and fishes out the loose end—the other letter from his mother.

"Here," she says, and in answer to the question on his face she says, "That one's addressed to you. From her. It's the last. Of everything."

"It just arrived?"

She shakes her head. "Earlier this year. I held it. Until now. I had my reasons."

His glare of indignation is undercut by a flickering of curiosity. He eyes the envelope.

"Look: Sue me later for the invasion. Grandmother's prerogative. I know you're trying to figure it out. This whole awful mess. That's just another piece of the puzzle."

It contains no answers, she's sure, other than that this mysterious person who was his mother is still quite disturbed, perhaps even more so than she'd been before. It's a jumble of ravings, that letter. She didn't think it would help the boy, but who knew?

"I don't know what's wrong with her," he says, and it's a minute before Estelle understands that he's not talking about his own mother.

"Maybe she's a little scared, yes? Be patient with her."

"I'm trying." The boy sniffs back his pride.

"Listen, my love. We'll get through this. All of it. I promise you."

Which triggers a sob.

"Oh, honey." She strokes his arm some more. "It'll be fine. We've got some rough road ahead, but we'll come through. Tell Estelle that you believe her, what do you say? Huh?"

The best she can get is a nod.

As the big goofy one approaches the car with the drinks, she signals zipped lips to Daniel and then pops the locks to let Ari in.

"Man you wouldn't believe the stupid skank working at the carry-out counter. She's this girl from North, I think, who . . ."

Estelle catches his eye when he hands her the drink. She shakes her head slightly, signaling him to put a cork in it, indicating with her eyes that there were "issues" in the backseat. Ari can be obtuse but he isn't stupid, thank goodness. And now he is alarmed, as perhaps he ought to be. Daniel, bless his heart, is too far off in his own pain to notice that the yammering has stopped.

As she drives down Hanley, the looks that Ari give her are filled with anger and fear. Help me, Estelle: That's what they say. For a moment—just for a moment—she blames the credenza and that daughter of Janet's and the whole out-of-control universe.

But Estelle Hillyer Birnbaum isn't a blamer, really. That hadn't been Poppa's way. Stell, he'd tell her: Stell, you can't fix the past, you can only change the future.

She pulls up in front of Janet's house and although she doesn't have a plan, she believes that she can figure something out. These are all good people. Common sense. A lot of love. A good stern talking to and, when that didn't work, a kick in the pants should do the trick. She pulls in behind Janet's BMW, which has its trunk popped.

"Bring the trash, boys. Ariel, we'll just stay a minute, yes."

Both boys mope up to the door—it would be a rough night at home later on with the big one.

Janet swings open the door. "Hey, everybody!"

Estelle has never seen her this full of good cheer. Stacked next to the door is a set of matching packed bags. "You boys are just in time to help us load."

"Load?" Estelle can't quite disguise the hurt in her voice. "You're . . . going somewhere?"

"I mentioned that, didn't I? I didn't? Well, I know I told someone. Ariel Birnbaum, didn't I tell you I had plans?"

Ariel is furious, can hardly look at the woman.

"Plans! Get a move on, son. Daylight's burning."

"So . . ." Estelle begins, but where to even begin?

"Back tomorrow night. Maybe Friday. We're wild and crazy travelers now, D and I. Aren't we, D?"

As for D (and where on earth had that name come from), the boy looks stunned—as if someone has . . . well, in fact, someone has sprung a surprise trip on him.

"Chicago or bust!" Janet shouts, and hefts one suitcase in each boy's direction. "We'll see you good people . . . well, we'll see you when we see you!"

Estelle watches her friend stride off to her car, the boys in her wake; watches Janet park herself in the passenger seat and wish Ari a good evening—which her grandson is too furious to respond to.

OK, so maybe there's a little more than talking in order here.

Chapter **Fourteen**

Janet pops open an e-mail from Estelle. <Sun-washed cottage in Seaside: Foreclosure! A steal, but we hate the Panhandle, right? Miss you much—miss my noshing buddy. See you soon, yes?>

Well, bless her heart, the Mongols might be at the gates, but Estelle would have her mid-morning nosh. Tell those hordes out there to wait, she'd order Ari, until we ladies finish our blintzes.

<Don't know the Panhandle> she writes in the return e-mail buffer, and shivers at the flicker of light she feels thinking about their plan to quit this place. She wishes, as she would on childhood trips with her family, that she could blink her eyes and wake up in that other place. There *is* an other side to all this mess, she keeps telling herself. There always is. That the other side was better than this one, was as always, a gamble, but what were the chances it could be worse? Whatever: She's got to be done with this, somehow, someday, once and for all. She's ready to push past it once and for all, that's for sure. Unsure as she's ever been, of course, that she's strong enough to do so.

<Redneck Riviera> comes Estelle's response, and it is almost enough to incite a chuckle from Janet. Janet signs off—hardly in the mood these days for lighthearted banter. Even so, she does miss her friend—terribly so. While she might—and maybe even should—clue Estelle into her plans to move Daniel through this mess, she's already burdened her dear friend enough, she believes. This is her mess, after all. Hers and that awful daughter of hers. The fewer people contaminated by this ugliness the better.

She works from home these days—or as often as she can she does. She's chagrined to discover how much of her job can be done from here—chagrined, in that she has been the chief roadblock to telecommuting for the past decade. She's completely rethinking her five-year plan for HR: Instead of new office space, everybody just stays home. They'd rent a room at the Adams Mark for monthly meetings.

And then there's the part of her these days that recognizes five-year plans for the lies that they are—because at any moment you buy someone or someone else buys you and all of your plans go in the trash along with last year's modular furniture. Fuck the phone company anyway.

In the kitchen, Daniel bustles in the cupboards and drawers, pulling out tape and scissors and ancient markers, which he tests on the paper bag that he loads the art supplies into. Every other marker works, and he wisely dumps the dead ones right in the garbage—something she herself has never been able to do. Most of them are older than he is by half, from a short-lived pep squad phase that his mother had immersed herself in, one of so many whims that Janet cannot even remember them all.

"Morning," she says. It's so good to see him. He nods his return greeting, gives her a cautious smile. Then he comes over and wraps his arms around her. How fast the child has grown up on her, and she's oddly conscious of her appearance—this despite her knowledge that many women would kill to look this good at her age and at this time of the day. It's her own benign vanity, this; a little something she's passed on to the boy with pride—even as she knows he is often too obsessed by such things; thus, perhaps, her self-consciousness. It mattered to her that he see her just so; strong, confident, put together.

"Doing a little housework are we?" she asks, untangling herself from the hug.

"Something like that," he mumbles, taking another sip of the coffee he's brewed. Good for him: She herself could use a cup or three, and the boy makes it strong. She knows how soundly he sleeps and the pick-me-up will do him good.

He pulls out a pack of glitter markers with see-through tubes that Keisha used to love to shake in order to watch the silver and gold flecks dance. (Simple pleasures for a simple mind.) He dips the ends into a cup of water to see if they can be revived. So damn messy: the markers and Keisha both. She and that friend of hers would sit here and color in posters encouraging the Lions to GO! and for days after Janet would find the dried confetti remains of those markers stuck to the tines of her dinner forks.

The coffee hits her already sour stomach and she thinks it's probably a good idea to get some food inside her.

"Breakfast?" she offers.

He makes the mumbling sound that means he will eat as long

as someone else is cooking it. At least this one won't care what she serves him. Keisha would have been shouting out her order like this was some damn truck stop.

Miraculously Daniel revives the glitter markers, which Janet can hardly believe. Who said things weren't made to last? She must have spent fifty dollars in the craft store on supplies just for the pep squad—say nothing of the "young inventors" phase, or the punk rock phase, or any of the other ephemeral stages that her daughter passed through (thank God the Bible thumper period had mostly come after she left home); and Janet had to admit that for those few months when for whatever reason the boy's mother had immersed herself in the mechanics of school spirit, she had allowed herself to entertain just a glimmer of optimism that just maybe something would finally take root with Keisha and that her daughter might stay happy for a while. But that didn't happen. The world wouldn't allow it and neither would Keisha.

"You don't mind if I take this stuff, do you?" the boy asks, and she starts to ask him where to, but remembers Estelle's project—the one she went on about endlessly, the way she did with all her "good works" research.

"For the job, right?" she says, hoping it will prompt him for the details. She's been disinclined to visit the House of Hope—who after all, needed a reminder of all that suffering? She'd have to rely on the boy to tell her about the place, but one had to be careful about such things. With these boys, it seemed a bad idea to give them the slightest idea you weren't absolutely on top of everything. Also, given an opening these days, he's liable to start hectoring again about that awful mother of his. He's still sulking, she knows, over their blowout over the letter he insisted sending to Keisha. Although she ought to have anticipated it, she'd been surprised all the same to see it. Elegant and simple and scrupulous in its appropriateness—and she'd of course expect no less from Daniel. Lacking all other standing in the matter, what choice did she have but to go after the prose?

A nod is as good as a wink, she'd mumbled, thrusting the note back in her grandson's face. She knew she'd taken the wrong tack when he'd curled his lip up at her in that way that he did when he knew he had the upper hand. But what could possibly be the right tack here? Stamp her feet? Scream herself hoarse, warning the fool to burn his damn letter and run as far and as fast as he could in any direction where there wasn't a Keisha?

Needless to say, the boy hadn't offered her the satisfaction of a reply—which pissed her off even more—and rather than leave well enough alone, she'd threatened, "You'll be sorry."

The curled lip morphed into a full-fledged sneer. "We'll see." He'd said it with a smile, and ever since he's been, for the most part, cordially mute, even if affectionate in his own odd way.

So, no, Daniel doesn't respond to her queries about the shelter, and she finds herself torn between the part of her who would like to tell him to take his sulkiness elsewhere and the part who would like to—who intends to—engage every waking moment of this boy's life, to keep him too damn busy to bother with any of that . . . foolishness.

The thing with the boy's mother: She never engaged. With anything. Even during the school spirit phase, Janet would see her there at the table, blocking out letters or pasting down cutouts of Lions and it would seem to her that the girl was only halfway present.

She'd connected with some girl, another in a series of temporary friendships (Marcy or Marsha or Martie: Who could keep track?), and Janet remembers thinking that the two of them were the sorts of girls found in pep clubs in schools across America: Mousy or chunky or plain, nowhere near perfect enough to stand in front of the crowd with the pompoms and lead a cheer, Keisha and Marcy—she had been a Marcy—were the kind of girls that the successful girls taught to scream along with them so that there would at least be a critical mass of voices encouraging the team. Pathetic shills: That's all they'd been.

This had been back in the days when Janet believed that if Keisha could just lose that extra ten pounds she would be the one out there in front, assigning girls such as Marcy to have a half dozen posters ready to hang in the halls on the Wednesday before the big game. She'd come in from work and find the two of them at the kitchen table, vulgarly sincere boy-band music blaring from some music countdown show on the television, the two girls industriously coloring away on those posters like the fate of civilization depended on it. She'd be relieved, of course, Janet would, to find

Keisha at home. She daily prayed the prayer that all latchkey parents prayed—that she'd open that door and that her child would be inside, that the rules had been followed, that the child would not blame you for leaving her alone—a class of prayers that it seemed to please God to rebuff, frequently.

She places the bacon between towels in the microwave and breaks eggs into a bowl, a half dozen. No need to ask how many he wants: She's thinking a little more than four for a growing boy. She'll scramble them so it won't look like so much, and then scrape off a small portion for herself. Daniel drops the last of the markers into the bag, then drops two slices of bread into the toaster. He retrieves the butter dish and the orange marmalade he prefers.

"The grape also," she orders. He's wearing, she sees, an older pair of jeans and a white T with some cryptic message on it that she doesn't quite get—the name of some musical group, she presumes. Could be worse, she's sure, and for what it's worth the logo is actually well-designed—and she's a woman who's supervised the design of more than a few corporate logos in her day. It pleases her that both boys took more care in their appearance these days. This one's mother bounced through fashion periods the way she bounced through all of her fads, sometimes a victim of the latest trends (and God have mercy on anyone suggesting girls her size avoid exposing their belly buttons), sometimes not seeming to care at all about her appearance.

Marcy's father taught physics or some other humorless subject at Washington University, and the family lived in the part of U City where Estelle's Poppa had raised her, in the hilly area west of the campus, full of elegant brick homes and ancient trees. Janet had delivered her home one evening after a poster party, and—responsible parent that she was—had seen the girl to the door.

"It's OK," Marcy had tried to discourage her. "It's not like there's anyone in there."

Janet assumed Marcy meant the monsters under the bed had been subdued, the closets checked for serial killers; but when the door opened and the house was absolutely still, she realized the girl's confidence was actually in the fact that there'd be no one home to receive her.

"They're never here," Marcy had said. And the place was a pigsty—like what you'd expect drunken college students to live in: makeshift bookcases, apparently not for the books which had been strewn everywhere, stacked haphazardly and interleaved with sections of the *New York Times*. Augmenting the décor a wide range of overflowing ashtrays and half-dead houseplants—leggy ones, layered with dust and gasping for life in the sorts of slapped together containers that amateur potters sold at the Clayton Art Fair.

She knows now that for Marcy those afternoons in the Williams' kitchen had been something of a respite from her dreary existence in University Heights—that coming home to this empty house with a friend had been so much better than coming home alone to that wallow of filth that her parents inhabited. And it explained why she would light up when Janet came in the door, bearing treats from the bakery and silly stories about life in American telecom. (She particularly appreciated Janet's theory that the entire wired grid had been held together by chewing gum and duct tape and two guys who Janet knew to be beyond retirement age.) Marcy reminded Janet of nursing home residents, the kind who snagged perfect strangers in the hall, chatted them up and seemed so grateful for the moment of grace that the anonymous conversation would be.

Keisha couldn't have been more evil about Janet's attention to the poor creature, would steam with rage whenever Janet talked to anyone she brought around—a rare occasion anyway, her having a friend.

"Come on," she'd say, whenever Janet came into the room, dragging whomever it was upstairs to her bedroom or out of the house entirely, and she'd give Janet one of her trademark scowls, her face screwed up in disgust the same way she did if her eggs were too runny.

Her son preferred them tight as well, and so she'd come to tolerate the rubbery texture herself, had a special nonstick pan she'd purchased at Famous for just this purpose, just because she was sick of ruining her good cookware over a couple of morning eggs. She gives the eggs a final stir: When they're as solid as gum erasers, that's when he'd eat them without fussing.

The toast pops up and Daniel does his usual trick of snatching it hot and flipping it across the room to their plates before his fingers burn—and she wants to say, "I've asked you not to do that," but can't bring herself to do so. Frankly he could plop himself down in that chair and light up a cigarette—even a funny one—and she doubts she'd say anything. As long as he's right here and she knows what the deal is. (She's chagrined not to own the high ground. If it killed her, she'd set this world right again.)

At least the pep squad phase had been a wholesome one for the boy's mother. And while all but the most naïve knew that the wholesomeness of the school-spirit brokers was largely a façade—knew what whores certain cheerleaders were, knew the drunken debauches that made up their weekends as well as the rest of their lives—for the Marcies and Keishas of the world, the reality was that they were dismissed before the parties began—time served—sent home to watch HBO in their pajamas, maybe order in a pizza, before getting to work on next week's campaign while the popular girls conducted their popular lives. Even despite the deep-seated ambivalence that any parent would feel knowing that her child was a server instead of one of those served, Janet had savored the period of calm that arrived with the advent of Keisha's pep squad responsibilities. She knows more than she needs to know of some of the other less wholesome stations on her daughter's teenage travails.

Daniel, her sweet Daniel: He'd never even gotten into the game. Neither server nor served, he was the sort who moved seemingly clueless through the high school fray. He didn't join things—sometimes didn't seem to know there were things to be joined. That Ari was the same. "They're two sides of the same coin," Estelle had told her when she came up with the idea of introducing them, although Janet suspects it ate at the other boy more than it did at Daniel, his social ineptness—if that's what it was. She has no idea really how Daniel feels—knows only that his intellectual competitiveness trumped any interest he might have in the rest of what went on. Perhaps it killed him a little every day—the way it would Janet; the way, she believes, that it had his mother.

Across the table, he curls over the eggs as if guarding them. His expression today reminds her of his mother—a closed-in, wary paranoia; broken here and there with the kind of fake obligatory smile one got at the ticket counter at Lambert Airport. The resemblance troubles her because that expression had always meant trouble, at least whenever it appeared on his mother's face.

"Feeling OK, sweetie?" she asks. She knows he disdained being mothered this way. He shrugs—as if, she thinks, someone else might know better than he does how he's feeling right now. He'd been self-reliant from the start. He never let her dress him or even pick out his clothes, as far as that went. Early on it was as if he had catalogued the tasks that parents do for children and set about learning to do them for himself. When the spirit struck, he made whole meals from scratch—had done so since before junior high. Not just bacon and eggs, but elaborate casseroles, roasted meats with sauces, desserts. He ironed, would mend his own clothes—or she assumed he did. At least he never asked her to repair them. Or maybe he just wore them more carefully than most boys. He'd always had that meticulousness about him.

Keisha: She'd pop a seam daily, and then she'd be in your face, waving it at you and demanding it be fixed immediately. Self-reliance had been as alien to that child as whatever language they speak on Mars.

Marcy, by contrast, was competent the same way Daniel is—(perhaps for the same reasons?) It was she, Janet recalls, who would lay out the task and make a plan for how to execute it. Keisha, a girl who if she had any known leadership skills they had escaped Janet's notice, also happened to be bad in the follower-ship department. God, the girl hated to take orders from anyone—would kick and scream and tantrum over simple requests to pick up after herself or to help clear the dinner plates.

Keisha had been only eight when Wallace had died—suddenly and without warning, of a stroke, and only forty-five years old, the dear man—and Janet sometimes wondered if Keisha didn't secretly blame Janet for his loss, because her willful insubordination always had about it this sense of resentment, as if she were saying "You're the reason *my* Daddy's gone, so clean up your own damn dishes." (But, no, really: Hadn't she always been that way, even when her father was alive?)

Marcy seemed immune to Keisha's high-handedness—to the point that sometimes Janet wondered if the girl had been in some way rather thick.

"Since the background will be dark," Marcy would say, "we

should cut out letters instead of drawing them in." And immediately Keisha would say, "OK, here's what we'll do," and then repeat pretty much word for word Marcy's original plan.

The phone company—most businesses—were full of men and women of the sort Keisha had been, and they were the least favorite people Janet dealt with in life—they made her nuts. She derived no greater pleasure than setting those fools up and driving them into the ground—designing high profile but benign schemes that she was confident they would ruin and for which she would allow them to take unconditional credit, after which, after they crashed and burned, with no evidence of her fingerprints remaining, she'd thrill at their demise.

Keisha's officiousness bothered Marcy not one iota, by all evidence, and for the most part they spent companionable afternoons those happy few months, coloring and cutting and gossiping, no doubt, about the girls who had ordered their industry. Janet's comment on that gossip had probably been the undoing of this transitory and blessed respite, but while it lasted she remembers feeling the way she does about her grandson and Ari. Relieved that someone had busted into the cocoon and found someone inside worth relating to in whatever way. While she has her problems with Ariel—the arrogant smugness, the neurotic vanity, qualities the two boys, in fact, shared—she was coming to love him as much as Estelle always had. He'd made this boy's life better.

"If you're feeling a bit under today, there's no need to go in." Janet Williams, Queen of the Attendance Monitors: She's mortified these words have passed from her lips.

He's rinsing their plates and loading the dishwasher. "Who says I'm not feeling well?" he responds, and she's unsure by his tone how to read this. Occasionally—rarely—he would turn churlish with her and his voice would take on the derisive quality she'd hear other teenagers assume with their parents out in public. If he were mine I'd slap the shit out of him, she always wants to say to those mothers (always with the mothers, that tone; NEVER with the dads). And her instinct in the moment is to jump up and spin him around and say, Who do you think you're speaking to, young man? A scene she had played with his mother weekly if not every day. But she hears something else in his voice as well—Resolve?

Independence? She isn't sure—and it's been so rare that they've gone round with each other. This seems a bad time to change that.

"I'm always happy when you're here," she tells him, and he says "OK."

Ironically, her biggest fight with Daniel had been the mirror opposite of many of her fights with Keisha. It would break her heart, the poor boy up in that room all alone, so with all good intentions she made her suggestion.

"Why don't you get out of here for the evening? Go meet some friends or something. Go to the movies." This had been in the pre-Ari days, before he had any social life whatsoever.

He'd shoved back from the dinner table and seethed for a minute before speaking.

"Don't you ever fucking tell me what to do." That's what he had said to her. The words had sliced through her, with all that they implied about their tentative ownership of each other. He went and slammed himself into his room. Didn't come out for two days. And she remembers thinking, *So OK, there she is: There's that mother of his.* What she'd been waiting for and fearing for almost a decade had finally arrived in all its hate-filled glory.

Over the years, she had rehearsed a number of possible scenarios for what she would do when the inevitable happened—and she had never doubted the inevitability of that day. Apples didn't fall too far from trees, after all, and a tree that rotten was bound to produce poison fruit. In her desk at work was a file packed tight with brochures from the kinds of schools that advertised in the back pages of Sunday magazines, schools promising success for "demanding" learners, and more than one of Janet's scenarios included a trip to the bus depot and a one way ticket to Indiana (where for some inexplicable reason many such schools are based.) She would not—could not—survive another Keisha, and so good riddance it would be for the boy.

She'd heard that same tone in his mother's voice so many times, and Keisha had even said the exact same ugly words to her once. And, oh, how it would enrage Janet when her daughter spoke to her this way. She'd want nothing more than to close her fingers around the wench's neck and squeeze tight and then slap her senseless. It shames her sometimes to remember how often she'd gone there—reared back with her open hand and let the girl have it. And it always seemed to her that doing so was exactly what her daughter had wanted her to do.

She comes up behind Daniel, handing him the juice glasses to rinse. She puts a soft hand on his back. He had a low tolerance for touching, this one. He smiles at her shyly, so she knows he isn't surly. He has never been, really. That one ugly moment with him: She understands now that she had instigated it, reminding him—cruelly if unintentionally—that at that particular moment in his life there were no friends to call—rubbing his face in it, she bet he thought. When after sulking he had emerged from his bedroom, he came down and sat next to her on the sofa in front of the TV neither of them said a thing. She knows that each of them was afraid that the other might completely come apart if either of them spoke. So they sat, as they often would do, silently watching the television world pass by in its merry and disordered way.

He's as sensitive as a bruise, this one, and so is Ari. It scares her. Their saving grace is their goodness. And their fear. As tough as they played it—especially the big one—each, she knows, is in his own way something of a coward. While each would take a bullet for the other, both were easily cowed—the sorts she had no trouble getting an honest time sheet from down at the company.

Keisha, on the other hand, feared nothing. Certainly not her mother's rebuke. Could there ever have lived anyone who took more calculated pleasure at breaking the rules? For a while, post pep squad, she'd briefly taken up smoking, and reformed smoker herself, Janet could tell that her daughter derived no pleasure from the drug, that instead the satisfaction came entirely from the frustration it caused the adults around her—the vice principals who patrolled the girls' lavatories and, in particular, her mother.

But the pep squad days had in fact been a genuine break in the routine, and Janet can even recall a pleasant "Good morning!" or two over breakfast during that time as well as the unbidden offer to help out around the house.

The day it all went wrong, she remembers that at the phone company she had been moving the St. Louis offices through the apex of yet another reorganization—a necessity any time the senior management shuffled, which was frequently. She'd become expert over the years at redesigning charts and jumbling the office manuals in a way that suggested "organizational transformation," all the while allowing people such herself and Estelle the latitude to keep the real work moving forward.

"Afternoon girls," she had said, breezing in the door. Earlier in the day, she'd been promoted into the position that would allow her to eventually become queen of human resources, so she had been feeling particularly pleased with herself—had stopped in at the bakery that used to be on Delmar, near North and South, for some éclairs for herself and for her little spirit-pumpers. Typically, Keisha had loaded one onto a plate for herself, leaving Marcy to fend for herself, but this was a fight conceded by Janet years earlier. The child was just rude, plain and simple.

It had been hoops season—toward the end of it—and cleverly, Marcy had crumpled rounds of orange tissue paper in order to resemble the mottled surface of the balls. Keisha's job was to black magic marker semi-circles on the basketballs in order to complete the effect. Marcy, bless her heart, would discreetly discard the ones that Keisha could not manage to do properly—most of them, if truth be known—and she'd wryly roll her eyes at Janet as she did so, as if to say "What are you gonna do with this kid of yours?"

"How are your parents, Marcy? Busy at the university, no doubt." Marcy's mother ran some sort of ad hoc women's study center that Marcy seemed to know little of and care even less about.

"Same old, same old," Marcy chirped. Girls like Marcy, in Janet's experience came in two varieties. Bitterly standoffish—which would be your garden variety. You saw them everywhere—in libraries and bookstores, at the solo counter at Starbucks—sucking up their disappointment and staring with disdainful pity at people just like them. Rarer were the Marcy types: deviously and deliciously satirical; insiders, somehow, to the larger, cosmic joke their oppressors would take lifetimes to appreciate.

Keisha had mislettered "Friday" (of all things!) and in her good-natured way, Marcy laughed it off.

"It's not like anyone on that team knows the days of the week." She and Janet had laughed, although the joke had passed Keisha by—as did most jokes, for that matter.

"I'm serious, Mrs. Williams. We cheer 'two bits, four bits, six bits,' and I swear half of them count on their fingers."

"Oh, you hush, Marcy. That's too funny." It had been a joy to come home and find Marcy there. A funny-looking little thing, she'd made the most of her pale-skinned and freckled homeliness, dressing herself in ironically childish sweaters and mismatched socks. She had lovely green eyes, Janet recalled—wise and full of sass.

Keisha, of course, had not been charmed and was quickly losing patience with both of them. Had Marcy been sitting there scowling and mocking Janet, Keisha would have been fine, but the harmony between Janet and Marcy had been beyond the evil girl's tolerance.

"You know what else," Keisha interjected. "DJ Simpson's mama is a whore and two other boys on the team gave her fifty dollars and fucked her all night."

Both Janet and Marcy had stayed quiet for a moment—both shocked, Janet knew, at how wrong the girl could be. So typical, though. Not just wrong, but colossally, abysmally, totally inappropriately wrong. And, of course, willfully so.

"Wow," Marcy said, at last breaking the silence.

"Well," Keisha challenged. "It's true. It is."

"Baby, that's not really the point."

"The point is, his mama's a ho, and those boys fucked her for a fifty."

Marcy had hunkered down over her poster the way one does in witness of another family's domestic strife. Some might excuse themselves and quit the premises, but Marcy hadn't owned that brand of spunk. (Janet also suspected she feared becoming victim of some worse behavior should her head be raised.)

For her part Keisha had pushed her markers aside—never, in fact, to return to them.

"This is unbecoming, young lady," Janet had said.

"What, so it's OK for the two of you to make fun of how dumb they are—which some of them aren't, if you want to know something—but it's not OK to say something that I know for a fact because one of them told me."

"Some things are better kept to yourself."

Keisha scoffed. She sat back in the chair and crossed her arms in contempt.

"I guess it just isn't nice," Janet had added, and even at the time, she knew she'd gone a bridge too far. Keisha had mocked her, and Janet remembered how hard it had been to not strike her. And though she knew she should leave it alone, there had always been something about her daughter where her need to have the last word trumped her best judgment otherwise. She said, "Marcy, I apologize for my daughter's discourtesy. I'll leave you girls to your work."

Heading toward the stairs, she heard Keisha's voice—its ugliest, most disdainful tone:

There.

You see what I mean.

See how she is.

I hate that bitch.

Damn, I hate her.

It would be many long years before she saw Marcy again. A year or so back, shopping in the Dierberg's at Brentwood Crossing.

"Mrs. Williams?"

She couldn't recognize the girl that she'd known inside the woman who approached her in the produce aisle. Still not quite pretty, she'd learned the tricks that all smart girls do to work with what God had given her, had styled the mousy brown mess on her head in a way that sent the focus to her best feature—those sparkling green eyes.

And she'd given Janet a hug—which surprised Janet, even as much as it felt wonderful—and told her how good it was to see her and how often she'd thought of her and how much fun those times had been around the table with the bad posters and the sweet treats.

They had not, of course, talked about Keisha. People rarely brought her up. It was better that way.

She was married, Marcy was, living in Ithaca with her math professor husband, and they had two kids and dogs and cats and fish—the whole crazy package, as she'd called it in her classic ironic way. She'd been in town visiting her mother—the father had died—and, guess what? She was taking up tai chi, she and her sons.

Well, good for you, Janet had told her. Good for you, indeed. Here's one who made it through, who proved it was even possible to do so. There might be hope for this boy, who had been at her side on the day she ran into Marcy, to whom she had been unable to explain the rationale for the exuberant bubbly woman in the supermarket. Just someone from the office, she'd lied.

"They'll be here soon," she tells him this morning. Estelle: never sick, never late. He's sitting there with his bag of leftover art supplies, positively bereft he seems to her. "Are you sure you have everything?"

He shrugs, and she doesn't know if he's sure or if he doesn't care.

She'd gotten a card from Marcy, a while after the tragedy. Most, she tucked away immediately, in the credenza, but she'd noted the street address—Midvale—and couldn't resist looking inside.

"Thinking of you, as I often do."

That's what she had written, and Janet had been completely undone by it.

"Are you sure you're feeling all right?" she asks the boy.

He raises his eyes to her slowly, takes his time to read her mood.

"I'm fine," he says, not quite flat, not quite defiant.

"Of course," she responds. "I'm sure you are." She rubs a hand around the small of his back. There's power coursing through this body. She feels it and it electrifies her.

"Do you need something?" he asks—his way of telling her she's in his space.

"Who me?" she teases, and rubs his head—another annoyance, she knows.

Hell if she's going to let another teenager get the better of her.

"Actually, I may need some things. We'll talk when you get home."

She practically shoves him out the door before he can respond, not wanting or needing to deal with the Birnbaum clan on top of everything else on her plate.

More the fool you, young man, if you think I'll let that bitch anywhere near you—Keisha or anyone remotely like Keisha. The answer had been right in front of her all along. Daniel is her best ally in this plan—and he'd thank her in the end. She knew that he would.

And call me manipulative: Tough times call for tough measures. You couldn't be too careful.

She blows a kiss from the window and waves goodbye—waving away also Estelle's beckon.

Oh, hell, yes: They're on Janet time now—all of them. As for Daniel, he'd never know what hit him.

Chapter **Fifteen**

That Ari Birnbaum: It's hard work being him. So many people to keep in check. Just for example, this morning: on the way to work, more or less having to restrain Estelle to keep her from barging in that house to "nosh" with Daniel's grandmother. Practically strangling Daniel to get a civil good morning out of the boy—say nothing of the plan for the day.

"What's up with the markers?" he'd asked. This after having had to look in the bag himself when no explanation of its meaning had been forthcoming. "So don't tell me," he'd had to resort to—and the bitch rolled his eyes. What the hell.

Look at him now, there with those kids. Different story now, and Ari supposes he should be happy about this, but something is off, he knows; you best believe he'd be getting to the bottom of it.

Ari is mopping, but he's not really mopping. The old dude who usually mops is sick or something—wrapped up in a blanket over there in the corner—so the Mitchell prick asked him if he wouldn't please help out with the floor, wipe up the breakfast mess. Sure, why the hell not? Ari agreed. Daniel holds the fort with the little ones while he slops an old rag mop around. Mostly he leans on the handle and watches his boy, but when Mitchell walks by he salutes and smiles and makes a big show out of dancing with the mop. Fuck this mop and fuck that bitch too, but you had to play nice until you found the right time to crush the asshole.

He's closing in on a plan.

He runs the mop through the wringer and decides to take one more decent pass: Do it for the kids, he reminds himself. They're not the problem here. They're good little guys; they deserved a clean floor.

It's hard to keep the accounts on all this—just like Poppa Hillyer warned it would be. Some were innocent, he said. Some were good, some on our side. A person had to be careful. But don't lose sight of the goal.

He rinses off the front sidewalk with the mop water, the same way the old man does. At night asshole drunks puked and pissed out here and all kinds of shit. A couple of the mothers try to catch the anemic shade beneath the smelly old trees that grow out front, having their morning smokes. Ailanthus, that's those trees. In a few minutes, the late van from the job center will pick them up and take them away for the day. They nod and he nods back to them. Minimal appropriate respect—and he can live with that. He knows that some of them hate him because he doesn't have to live the way that their sons do. Some of them are wary of him because they are wary of all men because all the men they know treat them like shit. Men such as the men who are already gathering on the lot for the noon feeding, even though it's hardly nine and they've just washed the last of the cereal bowls. If there's extra after the women and the kids eat, preacher boy offers it to the losers on the lot.

Ari sets the mop upright right next to the front door to dry in the morning sun, rolls the pail back to the storage room.

Daniel has unrolled a piece of butcher paper along the length of one of the dining tables and has the kids busy on the mural. Everyone has a crayon or a marker and a task. It'd be fun to color like that, Ari thinks, but decides he'd only get in the way by getting the kids all stirred up the way he always did, which would make Daniel furious. Daniel's favorite, that little Malik, sits just to his right. Daniel is showing him how to draw what looks like it's going to be dog or something. That kid, he'd stick to Daniel all day like that. Didn't say much usually, just stared up at him with his big dark eyes. Daniel whispers drawing instructions and looks something like an angel himself. Nope, they didn't need him over there.

So he looks for Mitchell to see what's next on the list.

Mitchell sits on the floor next to the old man.

"Let me get a doctor," Mitchell says all quiet-like, but the old man just coughs and shakes his head.

"I'm fine. Let me rest," he says, but even Ari can see that he is not fine. Wrapped in a blanket and shivering, even as stifling as it is in this dump: That can't be a good sign. Mitchell looks up at him; dude looks like he might cry.

"What's wrong with him?" Ari asks as they walk back to the office-thingy, but Mitchell just shrugs.

"So call an ambulance or something."

"It's not so simple."

God, what an asshole this asshole is.

"What's not simple? You pick up the phone and dial 911 and they send an ambulance."

Estelle would pay. Estelle liked the old man.

Asshole Mitchell looks him up and down, like he's checking him out or something. He did that a lot.

"A lot of our people, they have . . . issues. With the system, that is." And then he's talking about how a lot of them trail behind them reams of warrants, bad debts, enemies, just plain chaos. "They're . . . reluctant to check in with 'the man.'"

The man, huh? He's patronizing me, Ari thinks, with his flying quotation marks—and why be surprised, since most guys his age think all teenagers are retards and need the Sesame Street version of the story. Came with the territory. Or, he could be sincere, but it's hard to say with these Bible thumper types. One of the things they taught them at Bible Thumper University was how to put on a convincing performance for the rubes.

"Who knows if Schmidtty is even his real name," Mitchell added, and Ari wants to say, Whatever his name is, he's one sick mother-fucker. Call the goddamn ambulance. But he doesn't say that. Asshole here has all the answers, of course, and isn't about to take advice from the likes of Ari Birnbaum.

"What do you want me to do?" Ari asks, and he realizes that for a minute Mitchell thinks that he means about the old man—he even looks sort of hopeful about the possible answer. Then he says "Oh," and gives Ari the once over again—the old double O (and Ari is positive that he likes what he sees. He's heard all about these fake preacher types and the kinds of things that they really liked).

"It's inventory day. We need to see what's in those cupboards." A job that Schmidtty usually did. He checked in with the food banks to see what might be out there to stock the always-low pantries. Mitchell keeps looking over at the cot while he says this, and if nothing else Ari knows an opportunity when he sees one.

So he turns it on—the old Birnbaum charm. "Say, man, anything to help: You can count on me, right? I'm here for you." He gives the bitch his knowing smile. He'll have him eating out of his hands in no time flat.

Of course the asshole has to give him the whole do-you-think-you-can-handle-counting cans of pork-'n-beans routine—honest to God, how retarded did he think he was?

"Don't count what's on the table. That's for today. This is our look-ahead count, see how we are."

"Sure thing," Ari nods, and then he even repeats the steps of the simple-minded task back to the asshole. Like all preachers, this one loved to hear his own shit repeated back to him.

From what Ari could tell, he'd been in his early twenties when the shit went down with Daniel's family. He's cute in the photos—in a boy-politician kind of way, clean cut and polished—although to Ari it's the look of children playing dress up, trying on the parents' clothes to see how they fit. He must have been a smooth talker back in the day. He is glib on the videotapes, as if every answer has been rehearsed—and Ari has no doubt that they had been. His type never left anything to chance.

For some reason, Deacon Craig Mitchell was the one doing all the talking—at least as far as the New Purpose Temple of Faith was concerned. There he is on the Channel Five Eyewitness News, eyes not too moist, only appropriately so, making the kinds of meaningless everyone-here-is-deeply-saddened-by-this-loss statements that the airlines did when a plane crashed.

You could hardly recognize that Craig Mitchell in the one out there crouched by the old man's bed. He had no facial hair back then, neither had the rest been peppered with gray. The one back then Ari would have punched out by now—the arrogant little prick. This one had learned some humility at least, which Ari imagines a person would do if he fell from some prominent ministry to a shit hole like this one.

Ari cannot believe the crap in these cupboards. Apparently, it made folks feel good to unload on the poor the garbage that they themselves wouldn't eat. Who the fuck eats pickled apples? Certainly not him, and certainly not any of the folks around here—although he imagines that when the pickin's gets slim, it'll be pickled apples and generic peanut butter for the whole crew, although there are only two jars of apples, so he'll be slicing them thin for the little buggers.

Out at the table Daniel shifts the group to the left once again. The project seems to involve moving the kids around in a way to keep any one person from getting too attached to any part of the poster. Daniel and Malik are now working on one of the far ends of the paper. They're calm and quiet out there—the whole crew had been at each other's throats yesterday without Daniel here. (And what's up with that Janet Williams—hauling him away like that?) It's a mutual gift—Daniel calmed them and they calmed Daniel. Only one of many good reasons to nip Janet Williams' "plans" in the bud: Ari can't imagine what that broad's problem is here lately. She's keeping the boy on a short leash and making it shorter every day. First she cut down on the mall trips, then there are no trips at all and you boys just play here at home, and then Estelle says the Williams/Davis family isn't having guests this weekend. And then he's taking a day off from work—which is, for Ari at least, the last straw. Because as much as he's looking to settle up with asshole here, he's sure as hell not spending his summer in this dump without his partner here.

"Well, sometimes a lady just likes to spend a little time with her grandson." That's Estelle's obnoxious explanation—accompanied as it had been by a pinch on the cheek—and he's warned her, "hands off the merchandise."

"And some people are just slackers." And he'd also told her this morning, look, here's the choices: You either drive this fucker over there or I'll drive it over there myself—what's it gonna be, Old Lady? (Of course, he hadn't said those exact words to her, but she sure as hell got the message.)

So they pull in the driveway and she's all of a sudden fishing coffee cake and shit out of that bag she carries.

"What the hell's that?" he asked.

"I'm losing patience, Ariel."

They're saved from an hour and a half noshfest when Janet pretty much shoves Daniel out the door.

The Mitchell asshole comes in to check on the numbers.

"See. I did it just like you said I should. Soups. Vegetable. Canned fish. Staples." Ari points to the stupid tallies on the stupid tally sheet. A chimpanzee could do this job. "You're running way low on jelly, by the way, and not too much better on peanut butter."

Asshole nods and sighs. Ari leans up into him—lets him get a good whiff of the body spray he'd spritzed on this morning—some shit that Hannah had given him, a typically malicious gift from the little bitch. (What had she said? Something like, "Do us all a favor." Gracious as a wild dog with fresh meat. In the car this morning, Estelle: *Someone's smelling fancy, I should say.* She batted her eyes and pursed her lips—an old gal showing she still had game.)

"You know what would be so easy," Ari tells the asshole, "is to put this whole inventory in a database."

It's like Mitchell is deaf or something—that's his response to Ari's brilliance. *What the fuck,* Ari thinks. *I'm gonna work this shit.*

"So what you'd do is, rather than count what's here every time, instead you record it once, and from that point forward add in the new stuff and then delete what you use. You have an accurate count, right at your fingertips."

"I'm familiar with how databases work," Mitchell responded.

You miserable motherfucker, Ari thinks.

"Well, why don't I set one up for you then. I could do it like this." Ari snaps his fingers. "I bet you'd like that, huh?"

Ari bets he'd like a lot of things—hopes his voice implied as much.

When Mitchell rolls his eyes, it's all Ari can do to keep from popping him in the mouth. (Ari actually has never popped anyone in the mouth, but he's been thinking with increasing frequency about doing just that. Here in front of him is his first deserving candidate.)

"Don't databases require computers?" Mitchell asks. The asshole says this like he's talking to one of his moron drunk clients as opposed to the future valedictorian of South High. *A really good way,* Ari thinks, *to lose a few teeth.*

"Why don't you let me and my grandmother worry about a computer? Or two." And then he pets the asshole on his arm. He's been waiting for a few days for the right opportunity to do just that.

Asshole moves himself and his arm out of reach. "I'm thinking that Estelle already does plenty for these folks."

And Ari thinks, *It's Estelle, then, is it? You call her Mrs. Birnbaum, you stupid motherfucker. Better yet, you don't call her at all.*

"Don't worry," he winks. "We'll hook you up." Heading out to round up the crew for the morning games, he gives preacher man one of the special walks he's been practicing.

Preacher man's face these days is harder than the ones in the books and in the news coverage from back then. He's a lot sadder—as well he should be—and not quite as dumb-looking as he'd been when he'd wreaked all that havoc. Back then his face was like all the jerks at South whom Ari hated—that smug, know-it-all smirk—and everything that came out of their mouths they said as if they actually know what they're talking about and as if it's the most important thing that's ever been said by anyone and only a fool wouldn't listen and take notes.

"Deacon Craig Mitchell, pictured here, the close friend and spiritual advisor to the Davis family": All the photos had shit like that written underneath them, and in all those pictures he looked so damn clueless.

Clueless—as if he didn't know that instead of the cyanide, it had been the poison that he'd helped pump into the mind of that crazy Keisha Davis that had ruined so many lives.

But remember, Poppa Hillyer had said: They only pretend innocence, these people. They stand in their pulpits and they preach their Jesus's love. And who is it then telling the Gestapo where to find the Jews? Who sees nothing as the boxcars pass? Don't be fooled, Ariel.

It's hot on the playground, and Ari brings out the big jugs of water for the games. He sees the bums over there eyeing the water and he gives them the evil eye: It's for the little ones, scum.

The games are his specialty. Daniel is the man for the art and the story time and the naps. They're a good team. In so many ways.

They start with a game of In-and-Out. Daniel likes the games with no losers, which this one is, because either you're on the inside team or on the outside team, and loyalties switch back and forth, so the teams stay mixed up pretty good. He starts out, and Daniel starts in—with his little Malik.

The little guys, they like to protect Ari—or like to think that they do.

"Stand in the middle, Awi." (For some reason almost none of them can say the R in his name.) So he stands in the middle while the "out" team aims at him and the little guys jump up and block the balls or catch them. Ari grabs a high one himself, and that Derrick who threw the ball joins the "in" team. Everyone on both teams jumps in excitement because they want him to throw at Daniel. Out there, that Malik cowers behind his boy.

Ari cannot slam him with the ball today. He's just in some way so subdued. He's trying—for the kids, Ari knows—to be cheerful, but Ari knows him and what Ari sees is like the faces you saw in *Newsweek* of people coming and going from courtrooms in those high-profile trials: so distracted that they don't even appear to be in the same space as the mob around them. So he aims at Shantal— she's the biggest—and she catches it like a pro. He high-fives her, and she takes aim at the toughest on the inside.

Ari briefly wonders if it might have been a mistake, Daniel coming here today. But then distracted was a lot better than mute— which he'd been a lot here lately.

It's odd to Ari Birnbaum, the way people won't or can't talk about stuff. How, for example, Estelle cannot or will not talk about what happened to her friend's daughter and her children. It makes more sense, he figures, Daniel's and Janet's silence, but it had not happened to Estelle. All the same, she squelches any and all effort he made to draw her out on the matter. "Not our business, Ariel, to dwell on other people's sadness," she'd say—the use of his whole name as always her indication that the subject was closed and she'd entertain no further inquiries.

Really, all he'd wanted was for her to help him help. And he'd pressed her—yesterday in the car when Daniel skipped work.

"Look, I think Daniel is struggling, and . . ." but she put her hand up.

"Enough. He'll be fine. Trust Grandmother on this one. Give it time. He'll figure it out on his own."

Ari isn't so sure. With the arrival of that box and that hideous request from that Keisha Williams Davis, something had closed in on his boy—it was like those rich people's houses when they pressed the panic button and they retreated into some safe room as the metal barricades locked down around them. Ari is on the outside now and he neither understands nor likes being shut out in this way.

Perhaps some grief is too private to share. Maybe it's like people fear that if they open those dark places to others they'll find themselves trapped more profoundly than before.

Perhaps Poppa Hillyer had been even more courageous than Ari knew: telling his tales, allowing Ari to enter all that evil—and he wonders what Poppa would have him do about all this mess.

Daniel and Malik play along dutifully during duck/duck/goose, the little boy looking to Daniel for guidance on whom to pick when it's his turn. Outside the circle, the bums have gathered around—at first like vultures, Ari thinks—but then he sees that they enjoy watching the little ones be happy. And then Ari feels bad because he'd thought stingily about the water. He excuses himself and goes inside for a stack of paper cups and another big container of water.

During lunch prep, while Ari helps deal out the bologna and cheese, the older ladies are all abuzz about something. From what he gathers something about one of the kids (but those ladies are sure not going to let him in on it). Lunch always sucks here, and there is never enough for him—or Daniel either, he imagines, although Daniel has never complained. One thin sandwich—and you felt guilty taking that. But Estelle made sure they had a big breakfast and fed them again as soon as they left.

The old man is still wrapped up on the cot and Mitchell is still there at his side. Ari approaches and offers them some food.

"I doubt he could get it down," Mitchell says.

"For you, then," Ari offers—they liked it when you gave them food—but Mitchell just shakes his head. He's one of those hard cases who hardly ever seemed to eat anything. Ari can see that the old man has taken a turn for the worse, but he asks anyway: "How is he?"

"He's stopped responding to me."

The old man's color—an unhealthy looking yellow on his best day—is now the color of ash. He's paper dry, still shivering.

"I'm calling my grandmother," Ari says. Fucking ridiculous, this old man here suffering and this asshole not doing anything.

Mitchell says "no" and closes his hand around Ari's phone.

Good, Ari thinks. I got him to touch me. He struggles, but lightly, only to keep the contact going. Let him think he's got me.

"He said no doctors. We should respect that."

Un-fucking-believable. "Well, like your friend 'Estelle' says, sometimes people have to do things they don't like to do." He pulls again, and this time the preacher lets go.

"If you don't mind, I'll respect my brother's wishes."

Oh, so now he gets sanctimonious. Back in the day, by all evidence, he was full of this kind of shit. Ari's been waiting for it.

Ari points at the old man. "He doesn't know what he wants. Look at him." The wheeze Ari heard earlier in the day has subsided to the thinnest of whistles, barely audible. The old man's chest moves but imperceptibly so. "This is criminal."

If he weren't such a good actor, that might be hurt in the preacher's eyes.

"I've known him a long time," he says.

"But a doctor . . ."

". . . probably won't make a difference, young man."

"So you get to play God." As per usual.

"There's a lot you need to learn about the way the world works." Preacher man hardly seems to speaking to Ari when he says this. Then he says, "If you're interested in being useful, you can get me some more cold water so I can wipe his brow."

Anything for you, doll.

Ari knows he's got to be careful. Too much petulance and the plan goes off the rail. So he nods, obsequiously, and takes the bowl to the kitchen.

"Close friend and spiritual advisor": which Ari feels must be a euphemism meaning "the asshole who convinced the crazy bitch that the devil was about to steal her children's souls."

"I visited with the Davis family daily," he'd said. He'd said that on tape and to the newspapers and to the authors of those books. Had my meals with them, he said. Regularly. Said they studied scripture and prayed constantly for the Lord's guidance. Said whatever had happened had been God's will.

It's their delusion, Poppa Hillyer said, that their Lord is behind their madness, when it's their own evil at work, nothing more.

Mitchell's fingerprints were everywhere, though none of the papers dared say so. Only that book—the one called *How Could She?*—had the guts to lay it out straight: That there was something suspicious about Craig Mitchell. Such as: How had he just happened to be the first one there after the murders? And how there had been for years in the New Purpose community whispers about Mitchell and Keisha Davis and how maybe they had been perhaps just "a little too chummy" to quote "more than one source who wishes to remain off-the-record." How at first he played all innocent and did his "God's will" routine ("How could I imagine it would come to something like this?") but had suddenly become taciturn and ultimately "unreachable for comment."

And, well, why the hell not? Who wouldn't hide from a story like this one? You fill some crazy woman's head with visions of demons roasting her babies over a hot fire, and then you're shocked—shocked!—when she takes preventative action.

Ari fills the bowl with water and ice and then rinses out the washcloth for the old man's head.

And then, of course, you get to go on with your life. Move to the city and do "good works" and feel all redeemed and shit.

Fuck no.

"Here," he says, handing the bastard the bowl. "What about them?" Ari asks. The kids back there. He supposes watching the old man suffer was part of their spiritual development.

Mitchell looks like a wrung-out cloth himself. "Get them fed and get them the hell out of here."

"It's story time after lunch."

"Then read them the fucking story under a tree, will you? Please. Just go!"

So a little colorful language from the holy man. Just a preview to a full array of useful peccadilloes, Ari is sure—all of which he intends to uncover and exploit.

Outside they share the shade with the drunks—the ones Ari can't glower away—and Daniel reads a story, that Malik sitting at his feet, staring up in awe and with love. Everyone is listless in the heat, and Daniel's quiet baritone lulls quite a few, including the bums, to sleep.

"How you doing?" he asks his boy when the rest are resting.

"I'm OK," Daniel shrugs.

"I miss hanging around."

Daniel nods. He means "me too," Ari knows, but will still not open those locked gates to anything much beyond benign platitudes. It isn't the time or place to reach over, pull him close and hug him and let him know he'll make it all OK. Instead, he pats him on the shoulder and then goes around to see if it's safe to return to the center.

The ambulance hadn't needed its sirens by all evidence. They load the old man in the back on a gurney. The paramedics hang back the way they did when there wasn't much to be done here.

"You were right about the kids," preacher man says.

"What about him?" Ari asks as the ambulance pulls away, and Mitchell says that he's pretty much gone. "Sorry, man," Ari says, and puts a comforting hand on the pastor's back and holds it there.

"Bring them in out of the heat now," he is ordered, and Ari complies.

Inside, a couple of the older women who serve the lunch every day sit on one of the tables and dab at their eyes. Ari brings out Kool-Aid for the kids. (Every weekend he throws a week's worth of it into the cart when Estelle buys coffee for the place, along with a couple of five-pound bags of sugar. Otherwise, it's tepid tap water around here.)

Things slow down as always for the boys when the mothers roll in from the job centers. Each is eager to spend some time with her own. They are all looking at Daniel, Ari notices. Then he sees it is not Daniel they are eyeing but the boy attached to him, that Malik. Daniel and Ari keep him and themselves occupied with a silly card game. The women keep watch.

Just before Estelle rolls in, so does the last van. Everyone eyes the door. There's everyone who is coming back tonight, and the little boy begins to cry.

"What's wrong?" Daniel asks. "You can tell me. Come on. Don't cry."

Donette, the senior mother here, signals Ari to step over to her.

"The boy's mama," she says. "She ran."

Ari asks her what she means, and she looks at him like he's simple.

"She's been talking about it for weeks now. Girl just broke, I guess."

By now, the place hums like a hive. It's one of those days—too much, too much. Too much for one day. Who could stand it?

Estelle bustles over. "What's going on here?"

Ari tells her about the old man first. She clutches her heart, goes to the pastor, whose ear is already being bent by Donette.

Ari tries to get Daniel's eye, which is filled with panic and pain and fear over his inconsolable young friend.

"You can talk to me," Daniel encourages, but Malik just hangs his head with the tears rolling.

"Daniel." Ari calls his name. "Danny. Dan."

"What is it? What's the matter?" To the child he's saying this: Ari might as well be on another planet.

In the car on the way back to the suburbs, Daniel rides balled up across the back seat. What was that back there? Ari asks himself. What the hell have we done?

Estelle had come out with Donette, the preacher (with his useless, incompetent self) lagging behind them. She had pulled Daniel to standing then bent his ear to her mouth.

"Oh," had been the sound he'd made. As if someone had punched him in the gut, and he'd sat and pulled the little boy up next to him.

"Let's let Pastor Mitchell take over now, son," Estelle told him, but he protested, insisting that someone had to be with this child tonight.

"We'll all watch him," Donette had encouraged. She'd placed herself on the other side of the boy on the bench, but Malik pulled into Daniel harder, away from her and from his fate.

"I'm staying here," Daniel announced.

"Sweetheart, you'll only be in the way here. Let's be on our way, OK?"

"No." He rebuffed her hand as if it were contaminated. She'd then nodded to Ari. Step up! the nod insisted.

"We'll be back tomorrow," was the best Ari could muster for his friend.

Daniel stood with the boy attached to him. "Then we'll take him with us."

"His mother will look for him here," Estelle said, and Ari could sense everyone in the room wincing at the lie, the same way he had done.

"Go now," Pastor Craig said softly. "Come on." Then he too signaled with his eyes that it was time for Ari to step up.

So he did. And he hates himself for that.

When he'd grabbed Daniel around his waist and Donette had done the same to the child, the two of them had howled like animals in a trap.

Come on oh please come on oh come on honey oh please just

come on.

Oh I'm so sorry. I'm so sorry.

At his house, Ari hops out to help him from the car, but he rises, resolved.

"Stay the fuck away from me," he says.

At the front door, he also rebuffs his grandmother's comfort.

"Janet . . ." Estelle calls, but she puts up a hand and shuts the door in their faces.

Fuck, Ari says, and kicks at the wrought iron. Fucking hell. Fuck.

Estelle doesn't reprimand. She wraps her arms around him, which he doesn't notice any more than he notices his grandmother's tears or his own.

Chapter **Sixteen**

Sometimes Poppa placed his fingers to his forehead and said *'Vos ken men ton!* People and their spilt milk." Less about his own fatalism, Estelle believed, than his own personal cry of helplessness. This she understands.

"All we can do are the things that we do," she tried to tell her grandson, there in the passenger seat, filling the car with his own trademarked brand of musky, bitter gloom. And hope that we make good choices. But who could be sure? Hadn't she believed that excavating the past would help her friend? And as far as that went, hadn't Janet believed the same thing—hadn't she asked to be helped to put the past behind her? Perhaps Poppa had been right: *Fartik!* Leave the wounds alone, let them scab over natural. Because see what picking at the old ones has wrought: Janet, a more than ordinarily petulant mass of misdirected energy, sequestered at home, dodging Estelle's calls, on "emergency leave" from the company (a status, Estelle is positive, that has been invented by the woman just for this occasion—Janet: long time believer that liberal leave policies bred slackers); plans for Florida on hold at best (and at a time not only when a lovely and coveted building on Longboat announced a rare opening, but just after a minor dustup of a hurricane washed through the central Keys. But, then, the Keys: not a hotspot for dining and not so much for the shops. Perhaps a bullet dodged, there?).

And these boys! Two teenage boys, raging and raving and out of their minds with . . . whatever! God help us all!

Honestly, this Ariel: She'd send him back to those parents of his—if only for the satisfaction of knowing they'd be the ones enduring his sulks and his outbursts of invective. Just this morning she'd had to say to him, "If Ariel Birnbaum believes for one second that Estelle Birnbaum is a woman who is going to be spoken to in her own home with that kind of language and in that particular tone, then Ariel Birnbaum is a young man who is extraordinarily stupid and is this close to finding out what exactly what Estelle Birnbaum is capable of." She'd left millimeters between her fingers to demonstrate just how close she was to her breaking point. To which the bastard had had the nerve to say "What?" As in, What are you capable of? As in, Do your darnedest, old woman. To which she could only say, "Try me." She'd stepped toward him and he'd had the good sense (Thank God!) to step back. Score one for Estelle. That's the problem with the boy: No one called his bluff. Which is why she's not sending him home to those people. Not only did not even they deserve such barbarism—no one did—but Ari would have both of them bested and beaten by week's end—and that evil sister of his, too. Who but her could handle the boy? (But that face on him: Good Lord.)

"Ariel Birnbaum, what did I say to you about those people at the center not needing along with everything else to deal with your scowling mug."

Unpitying, hard. Sitting here in traffic and you'd think it was round three on one of those boxing matches that Poppa liked to watch, and that Ari had been the one took the last punch in the previous round.

"Would it kill you to smile," she chides, to which he responds with a snort—and one of these days (but not this one) she would tell the child that every face that shows teeth did not qualify as a pleasant one.

"Satisfied?" he asks her—the punishing *satisfied* employed by the male species when whatever civilizing amenity you've shamed them into attending to has finally and reluctantly been attended to.

Which, she knows, is better anyway than some of the other things he'd said to her lately:

Whatever.

Back the hell off.

You want to start something, Estelle?

And then: "Bite me." The child had the nerve to say, "Bite me." To a woman of her age. To his dear grandmother, no less. The world has come to this. (Well, he'd sort of mumbled "Bite me," really, but she was pretty sure that's what she had heard.) All she'd done was to ask the child to please not parade around her house in his underwear only and that she wasn't running the St. Louis County branch of Chippendales—as if a person ever even wanted a free show with breakfast, which she most certainly did not, and had she, she'd have ordered a mimosa instead of this stale orange juice and this isn't Las Vegas, anyway. Bite me, he'd said. If Aaron Birnbaum, that father of his, had ever said "Bite me" to her, there never would have been an Ariel to say it now, because her Bernie would have killed Aaron Birnbaum, and then she would have brought him back from the dead and re-killed him herself.

But as it happens she has declared crisis mode: All the old rules are off. This child is one temper tantrum from ruining his and any number of other people's lives, and she knows that if she pushed back too hard, she'd break him. She considers it a victory that he's still in this car, still headed down to be however marginally useful to the pastor and the women. Because it would not surprise her to wake up on any given morning to find the boy just gone, swallowed up into the world, off to where all the disappeared have gone. At best, he'd survive a week out there, and he wouldn't be one of those lucky enough to come out unscathed, almost certainly not even alive. It's a blessing, then, that every morning this cranky almost-man drags himself to the kitchen and drinks directly from the juice carton and belches and glowers and scratches at himself; a blessing, even, the nasty bulging briefs, stains and all.

The current sulk resulted from her refusal to allow him to "break down the [*f*-word she won't say] door" at the Williams' residence. (Aside from doubting his ability to break anything down, however large he seemed) she had explained to him—rationally and patiently, she believes—that civilized people used doorbells and entered other people's homes when admission was offered, and that no one here needed the Stanley Kowalski routine, and that if he just trusted her things would be back to normal soon and therefore let's just leave these people the lovely surprise basket of treats and continue with our day, and could we do that now, please?

He had seethed at her for a good minute or two. Then he picked up a stone and bounced it off the boy's bedroom window, and then another and another, and Estelle had thought *Good God*, next she'll have to be pricing glazers—and didn't you just know it was a fortune to replace those four-over-four panes. (And mightn't it occur to Mr. Future Valedictorian here that the reason that no one answers the door is that there isn't anyone home?)

<Daniel and I have plans today, OK?>

<Plans?> Every day for a week, this woman with plans, her and

the boy.

<Plans. Love ya. See you soon!>

Estelle had typed back her intention to leave a basket of treats again today, but figured Janet had logged out before that message cleared. In any case, Janet did take the baskets in and seemed to enjoy them—as evidenced by the fact that they came back bare of all but crumbs. She'd replaced yesterday's dregs with the day's offerings: muffins, cocktail peanuts, some of that delicious pomegranate juice from the Whole Foods, a brick of eating cheese, and a nice pâté with the Carr's Biscuits that Janet preferred, some sliced sandwich cheese and deli meats, no biggie. (She'd had Ari stow the perishables in a small cooler she's bought just for this purpose.) On the backseat is a similar basket, albeit somewhat more practical, for the settlement house.

"I hope the service went well," she says to Ari. He has turned into the world's worst conversationalist (conviviality: never his strong suit). But the point, everyone agrees, is to keep these boys talking.

"A service for an old bum," he scoffs.

Estelle suppresses a sigh and a lecture about respect for the dead. Ariel these days never missed an opportunity to pounce on what he felt was a critical response to his nonsense, however much he deserved one. The service had in fact been private and simple. A few words said over the ashes, which were then taken away and stored—where?—until and if a family showed up looking for him. She had paid for the cremation, the city preferring donations to the local med schools and/or a pasteboard box in a common grave at some location they'd prefer not to disclose.

"For what it's worth," she says, "he made a difference with his life here at the end."

Another scoff from Ari and Estelle gives up. She'll not be baited today. She would like to believe that his cynicism is a put-on. She hopes for the boy's sake that it is. Because God help Ariel Birnbaum if it isn't. Poppa told her, "Stell," he said, "it's no way to live. You must believe in your fellow man. Otherwise we're as bad as they are—those animals!"

She pulls in front of the center and watches her grandson deflate the way children did when they discovered today's destination was the dentist office—and the settlement house is far from a surprise to him, coming here these past six weeks. He makes no effort to open his own door, and it has been weeks since he'd opened a door for her.

"Your petulance is tiresome, young man. Bring the basket, please. At your leisure."

Craig Mitchell she finds in the food pantry, organizing the children's cereal for breakfast. It is then for Estelle an immediate and double surprise to—first—discover Ariel right on her heels, placing the basket on the counter, and then—the lollapalooza—to hear a hearty, "Good morning, sir" from Mr. Sunshine.

"Good morning to you too, Ari. What have we here?"

"Just a little something from Estelle and me. No biggie."

Good God, she thinks: *What's he playing at now?*

"For your loss," she adds. "And, again, my condolences. We figured we could all use some cheer today."

She helps Craig slice up the coffee cake and break up the sweet rolls onto serving plates.

"Make sure the coffee is strong," she orders Ari.

"Sure thing, Estelle." He loads up filters for the two large urns she'd purchased at the restaurant supply last week and then heads out to help the women finish storing away the beds and pulling down tables for the meal.

"He's a good kid," the pastor praises.

"Sometimes."

Estelle isn't sure she says that aloud until it garners a response.

"It's a tough age," Craig Mitchell consoles her.

"You sound like you've had experience with teenage boys."

"I used to be one."

She searches for that boy in the weary face in front of her; has a hard time finding him there. He has the dark patches under his eyes of the sleep-deprived or the allergy impaired, the creased brow of the worrywart.

"You'll promise to let me know, Craig, if he's any trouble. What else you don't need on your hands is my big family problem."

He assures her that he could handle Ariel Birnbaum. Estelle is unsure how to hear that remark. There's confidence, yes, but also a macho tone to it—similar to the boy's father—and she wants to warn the man, don't make the mistake my son made. This is not a boy who responds to bullying, however innocuous you think it might be.

"How about the other one?" he asks. "When will I be seeing him again?"

Estelle says that she doesn't know, but doesn't tell him that she doubts he will. Sure, she'll try, but somehow she's feeling Daniel's a lost cause this summer. Janet, by all evidence, plans to keep that young man all to herself. Who's to say which of them, she or her dear friend, has the biggest load: Hers, Ari, is all bundled rage; the other one seemed fragile as a newborn.

"It's a shame. Daniel was great with the kids. He's a natural."

"And look what it got him," she says—another statement she doesn't think she'd said aloud.

"It happens to the best of us. Stick around." A touch of the Ariel Birnbaum cynicism in this man, too. Just as unbecoming.

She hands off a tray of pastries to Donette, who grins and takes a swipe at a dangle of icing.

"Love it!" she coos, and Estelle tells her to knock herself out and that there's plenty and that they'll all be just fine. Donette agrees and dances off with the tray of treats.

"I'm a tough old bird," Estelle tells Craig. "With a grizzled old heart. A little sorrow won't scare Estelle Birnbaum. Believe me."

"I guess that I am always surprised at what gets to a person," he mumbles.

She comes up beside him and gives him a companionable hug. "I am so genuinely sorry for your loss." She holds her arm there until he acknowledges her statement.

"That old buzzard has almost always been a part of this place. I still expect to see him out there, sliding over cots for your grandson to stack. You know the funny thing is: He was a lot of times more trouble than he was worth. He didn't have much strength these last few months. Weak, forgetful. He misplaced things—I'm still looking for my clipboard. It's terrible to say that, right?"

"I always quote the bard: You take the good, you take the bad."

What a pain even a saint like Poppa could be sometimes—a lot of the time—the way he would only eat dark meat even in the chicken salad and complain when your shadow crossed the television set, and God should strike you dead if you touch that remote. When they sat shivah, they had laughed at how ornery and curmudgeonly he could be.

And as for her Bernie: a walking tank of flatulence—just like his son. She'd spend a year in jail to smell one more of his nasty old farts.

"Mr. Schmidt was wonderfully human," she adds, but she doesn't add, And so are you. Mitchell clearly is a man who didn't care to be reminded of that truth, doesn't need to know what she knows of his own hard past.

Ari carries out the milk and juice for the little ones while their mothers queue up for coffee. They nod their stoic good mornings to Estelle, and she tells them it's a beautiful morning and how nice to see everyone and how pretty that color looks on you. It consistently astonishes Estelle the ordinary congeniality among these people living under duress. Yes, sometimes a new woman would come in surly, but eventually most of them mellowed and became a community. It is *this* man's doing, she knows. He set the tone here.

She holds her arms out for the infant of a mother whose turn it is to work the spigot on the urn.

"Aren't we precious," Estelle coos. She walks back with the mother to a place at the end of a table where another toddler waits. She'll look in the basement tonight and see what baby things might still be there from when Ariel had been small. (How fast they grew! It had been way back in the twentieth century that Ari was this size.)

"Enjoy your breakfast, dear. I'll hold him for a while if you don't mind, and it's no trouble at all." Further back still, a third yet if you believed it, her Aaron had been an infant. And now that baby is that man's father. Amazing! She should tell this mother about the magic time machine in her arms.

She observes her grandson wrangling the ones who prefer to have breakfast with him rather than with their mothers. He's learned a lot this past week, she can tell, about how to water the troops and keep them relatively calm. It seems to calm him, as well. A little girl drops her milk, and while the Ari back in the car would have called her an unpleasant name and scolded her, by contrast this Ari tells her that it's OK and wipes up the liquid with a dishtowel he carries in a belt loop just for this purpose. He pours her another cup and teases her until he gets a smile. Confirmation, she assures herself, that this job was a good thing and a right thing. With that boy, you grabbed hold of anything positive and tried to imagine it was a trend.

"And so it continues," Craig says, coming up behind her.

"Somehow I never took you for the philosophical type."

"I am a minister, you know."

Actually, she doesn't know. Those older articles called him "deacon"; the recent ones said "pastor," as had the old man. So did some of the women, although others called him *brother*, but she'd never been sure if that was *brother* as in *brothers-in-Christ* or brother as in *soul brother*. And what did it take anyway to be called reverend or minister or pastor these days? From what she can tell, Christians opened diploma mills for their holy men at about the same rate that her people opened fly-by-night delis. In any case, she's set aside her original plan to dig deeper into his background. It no longer matters to her.

"Any minute now you'll be spouting scripture at me," she says. "Let me get my earplugs." She rattles her giant purse, and she even gets a chuckle from him, albeit a minor one.

"But it surprises you, doesn't it, Estelle: the daily-ness of life. An old man dies. A child disappears into foster care. The sun comes 'round, and we start it all again."

My, he *is* philosophical today. She asks him what he knows about the fate of the child, but the question only seems to trouble him. He tells her that he used to worry over every soul who left that door.

"And then, after you don't sleep for a good long while, you learn that you just . . . can't. You become rather heartless, I'm afraid."

"That's nonsense, my friend. And it's also, if you'll forgive my familiarity, bull."

He asks her how so and she tells him she doesn't believe for a second that he can simply forget any one of these people.

"Each one is here," she says, tapping at his chest through one of the white button-down shirts that he always wears. She points around to the women and their children, now finishing up their meals. "Every one of them." The baby in her arms burbles and examines Estelle's face. She pops her eyes open wide and encourages him.

It's how we are not animals, Poppa used to say. Animals had no hearts. The suffering of others meant nothing to them. They'd kill ten, a thousand, a million: It meant nothing. Animals!

"That child—Malik was it? He tears at your heart just as he tears at mine. As he tears at Daniel's and at everyone's in this room. We must never think it bad that we bleed a little."

"You say that, and yet you saw what it did to them. To Daniel. To the child."

"That sad little boy. We have to believe he's landed someplace where they'll take good care."

The pastor nods.

"As for my Daniel, he will live, the hurt will pass. I guess I think it's the ones who don't hurt we should worry about more."

Poppa said.

"And in any case, we get up each day and make the best of it," Craig tells her.

"And for the sake of this angel and all of those angels over there and all of their mothers, too, that would be a good thing."

"Indeed."

Estelle returns the child to the girl's arms and then helps with the cleanup. The phone company would wait. She anticipates and therefore girds herself to be barked at by Ari when she asks him to please move the horseplay with one of the larger kids to the side so she can clear some bowls, but he only says, "Yes, ma'am." (Ma'am: When had been the last time she'd gotten a *ma'am*? Maybe never.) They fold up all the tables except for the one Ari will use for some project with the kids. Estelle helps wipe it down with the bleach solution. (Her hands! She'll have to use the good lotion tonight, and remember to throw her "living" gloves into the tote.) The women head off to their various vans: school, treatment, job counseling, etc. Estelle cues the pastor that it is time to sit for his meal and a little chat. By now he knows the drill.

"A special treat for you today," she announces. She fishes from the bag an extra hearty cutting off the raspberry coffee cake he'd taken a particular liking to the week before. Happily for Estelle they are way beyond the protest-too-much phase. He digs right in, and the pleasure that the cake and the good coffee give him flashes through his eyes. Estelle finds it moving every time, that naked pleasure. She would never make sense of it—in this man just as she hadn't in Poppa—how the denial of the simple joy of a well made pastry or a perfectly prepared roast became some kind of virtue; equally paradoxical how the inevitable surrender to the pleasure that such things always provided them—when they finally did surrender to it—seemed to resonate to their cores. Her Bernie, by contrast, reveled in pleasure, chased it the way a dog would chase a squirrel—with delight and a tenaciousness that knew no bounds. Never enough with that man—of anything: food or sex or wine or even fresh air. *More!* he would cry: the word she should have had carved on his tombstone.

"There's plenty as always," she encourages the pastor, and once again he assures her that she treats him too, too well.

"You're a constant surprise, Estelle. I would never have expected you to find anything positive about what happened with Daniel and the child."

She tells him he is putting words in her mouth, scolds him for assuming that she is an advocate for stomping on the hearts of random youth.

"You'll see what I mean after you've been around six decades or so. You survive a lot of loss. And every time you lose someone you die a little yourself."

When Bernie had passed, and then when so soon after her Poppa had died too, it had really almost killed her. She had closed herself in—in much the same way she sees Daniel doing now. Slowly, somehow—with a lot of help and a lot of love—she has moved on with her life, but even still, on some days, for no reason that she can predict, a hollow pain cuts through her the way a cold, sharp razor might, and that pain could often bring her to tears. More than once, she'd taken to her bed because of it.

"Do I wish my children's lives be painless? Of course I wish it. But they are alive, and pain is a part of that. I hope for them that they will always be men who experience all of life, which would include the pain, I guess. That is all that I meant."

Craig nods, seeming to understand her point. He sips the special coffee she's sequestered for him and he can barely suppress a grin at its deliciousness.

"For a long time," he says, "I hid from the painful things in my life. The mistakes. The losses."

"You are hiding here, perhaps?"

"At one time, perhaps. At one time, yes."

"But no more, yes. There's no more hiding."

"Sometimes, Estelle, even with the right things in our hearts and with the very best of intentions, we cause great harm in the world."

There are deep secrets inside this man. A part of her wants to excavate, but she's surprised that another part of her is incurious. What can he tell her that she hadn't already discovered?

"I'm aware of the harm that mistakes can cause," she tells him. "Believe me, I am. But tell me: Is this sin we're discussing?"

He shrugs.

"How disappointing. It's a question I've often pondered, and here I am with my spiritual advisor, and the best I can get is an 'I don't know.'"

He scolds her gently about the spiritual advisor joke.

"You tell me, Mrs. Birnbaum: Which does God judge? Our intentions? Our actions? Or the consequences of those actions, intended or otherwise? Let's say I should feed the multitudes, but the fish is tainted and the wine laced with strychnine. Do the points for the luncheon offset demerits for the dead souls?"

"As long as he lived, from the moment I became aware, I would ask my father about the camps. He never would talk to me, Craig, but a detail slipped here and there. A horror beyond horrors: Imagine! But he had a strict code, Poppa did. The good people helped them. The bad ones participated or—worse in Poppa's book—did nothing. Overly simplistic, perhaps, but maybe that's the only way to understand such things."

"So a good Christian man in Poland gathers his neighbors for the purpose of hiding them . . ."

"And people did that, Craig. We know that they did."

". . . but the Nazis discover his cache. So rather than save people, he made it that much easier for them to be rounded up. God judges him how, Estelle?"

"Poppa would bless him, Craig."

"And God?"

"None of us knows about God."

"When I was a young man I used to think that I did. I believed that He spoke to me directly and that His hand guided everything I did."

The boy's mother believed this also, Estelle imagines. Craig's face: much more careworn than the baby-faced man of the news coverage. The handsomeness has survived. What to make of the ironic coincidence of his being here and of her finding him at this time, she has no idea. Once, walking with Poppa on a sidewalk—in Des Moines, Iowa, of all places—they'd run into a man who had been a boy with him in the village back in Poland. They'd hugged and laughed. Could the world be so small? The two of them had cried to each other. And then they had walked away from each other as if their passing on the sidewalk were a regular occurrence, as if no time at all had passed at all and they would see each other again, tomorrow or the next day. They did not even exchange contact information.

"Let me tell you something, Estelle. If someone tells you that God's been talking to him: Run, don't walk, in the other direction as fast as you can."

She assures him that she will do exactly that. What a gummed up mess they've made of this world, all of them and all of their various gods, but she chooses not to repeat those thoughts to Craig.

Instead, she says: "Here's what I think we know. We have in this place of yours dozens of women and half again as many children who had a quiet and safe place to sleep last night and some nourishment."

". . . and then the gas pipes explode or the roof collapses."

Estelle laughs at the man, but she isn't sure he's joking.

"So morbid," she scolds. "I think we can just look at it this way: our hearts, this heart:" She puts her finger in his chest again. "We follow this. We trust this."

"But it's wrong sometime, you'll agree."

Estelle bites her lip in exasperation, even as she maintains her willingness to push on and to puzzle it out with him.

"Maybe sometimes we don't have enough information, yes? Our hearts are good and right, but there are things we don't know. How does that sound?"

"So we're paralyzed, then. Or we stay in the libraries and keep on reading until we know what to do."

"And we die first," they say together, and laugh.

"I think that's immoral," she tells him. "It's the worst kind of intellectual cowardice."

"I think we agree on that."

"More than anything, Poppa hated the cowards. In a perverse way, he had more respect for the Nazis and their collaborators than he did for all the so-called 'Good Germans.' The ones who sat back and watched."

"Because at least they stood for something, even if it was the wrong thing."

"To his death it never made sense to my father that a so-called decent man could stand back and pretend neither to see nor to understand what was going on right in his face. 'Stell,' he'd say, 'it would only take one of them to say *no*. No more. Where was the man to say *no*?'"

"But don't you see, Estelle: That's my point. What if they honestly believed in here [he touched his chest in the same place where she had touched it earlier] that looking the other way was the right thing to do? What if they believed that it was God who told them to look the other way?"

"Maybe it had been. Who knows, maybe it was one of those tests from the Torah—God says to Abraham prove your love by taking the boy up to the summer house and carving him up like a roast."

"And doesn't it surprise you—and frighten you!—that he did what he was told?"

"People do what they're told, Pastor Mitchell. I think that's the point of the story."

"No, ma'am. The story is about faith. And what I'm asking is: What if your faith tells you to do great evil, or to turn your back to it?"

Estelle throws her hands up in surrender. Enough!

"We feed people, Craig. We offer them love and warmth and hope. Like your Jesus did."

"And they killed him for it."

"No one's standing by with any crosses for you. My father's horror was unspeakable to him. Somehow it taught him compassion. Like you, it often makes no sense to me."

He reaches for a legal pad on his desk. "Here are my big dreams," he says, handing it in her direction.

Keep on doing what I'm doing. That was all that he had written.

"Because," he says, "it's like Pandora's Box out there, Estelle. You open the door wider, and there's no end to it. It drowns you. So I feed a few women and give them a place to sleep and I do what I can to help them get back on their feet."

His humility touches her and enrages her and frustrates her and amuses her—all at the same time. A part of her doesn't even believe it. She turns the pad back in his direction.

"This is unacceptable to me," she says, flatly.

He shrugs. "It's all I got."

"Nonsense. And I've had about enough of your silliness," she said, which made him wince. "I scold you with Mr. Mandela's words: 'Who gave you the right to be small?' How dare you?"

"Wasn't Mandela. And maybe all I have is what you see."

Not Mandela? Really? Well it might as well have been—and whoever it was, it applied, and look at this man changing the subject. She scoffed. "That's your vanity speaking. You believe that if you walk away from here that these women won't survive. You're afraid to sleep too soundly because, God forbid, something should happen in the night, and you, Clark Kent, are the only one who can save them. It's vain and it's nonsense. I come to you and tell you I've got a truckload of someone else's money and all that he asked is that the world be better because of it. This is the best you can give me. I say 'No!' to this."

"Perhaps you picked the wrong dump for your truckload of money."

"I chose you, Craig. You. Don't you dare insult me. I know what kind of man you are. Don't you dare."

She fishes in her purse for the tissue he would be needing.

"What if you're wrong?"

"I'm not wrong. I'm not."

He nods in the half-hearted way her grandson did when she tried to reassure him that he was far from the hideous creature he often believed himself to be.

"Now, time's a-wasting, Sir, and mine is as valuable as yours. There's a beach-side condo with my name on it [*and I'd better get*

Janet's name on that mortgage, and maybe also mention the pur-chase] and the sooner we get Poppa's work started the sooner I'm marinating by the pool."

That had to be the answer. Get this done, get Janet moving, set-tle those boys. All of them get on with the lives they deserved.

She orders him again to dream, but he hems and haws and it becomes clear to her she'll have to lead him out of his box.

"Let's forget about global peace and economic justice for a min-ute. What needs to happen tomorrow? Yesterday? Right here?"

He makes the incredulous face that men make when they believe women are being dense. "Well, a building for starters. Someplace that was actually built for what we do here."

She points her chin toward the pad and orders him to write.

"Lord knows this city could use three good-sized family shelters. Ten."

"So you start with two. Or three. Write that down."

"I can't run three shelters."

Estelle laughs at him. She shoves aside the curtain and looks around the building for Donette, whom she spies across the way helping a crew unload a supply of canned vegetables. She beckons her over.

"Step in a minute, sweetheart. Tell this man: Can you run this place, do you think?"

"Well, yes, ma'am, I do a lot here."

"Good for you. You're hired. Give your notice at the store, would you? Good girl."

The girl's knowing smile lets Estelle know that she has both done the right thing and that she has plenty of ideas of how to make the shelter work even better for her fellow residents.

"You're too much, Estelle," Craig sighs. He pulls his hands through his close-cropped salt-n-pepper afro.

"Poppa called me bullheaded. So sue me. But you see my point."

"Absolutely," he tells her. "Estelle Birnbaum is tired of her life in the suburbs, and now she's going to come down here and run my life. Not that anyone asked her to do that."

"Don't flatter yourself. Honestly, you're as bad as that boy out there. A person can't help him either."

"Maybe *he* doesn't need your help either."

She waves her finger in his face. "Oh, no, no, no, no, no, Craig Mitchell. No you don't. Estelle Birnbaum doesn't fold that easy." She gathers together the dregs of their repast and tucks them back into the Whole Foods satchel.

He tells her that she clearly has misapprehended his "whole deal." He isn't about raising money and serving on boards and going to meetings and writing five-year plans.

"What I want to do is just what your grandson is doing over there: reading the children a story. I want to offer comfort to the blond over there because she's just found out that her abusive ex-husband got released from the penitentiary."

"And so you will."

"Not if I'm trying to keep two of these monstrosities afloat. Or even one bigger monstrosity. Nope. I can't do it. End of discussion."

"Vanity. Vanity." She waves her hands in front of him as if waving away smoke. "And I love our discussions. I hope they will always be a part of my life.

"All I'm asking from you is two things. Dream this right. This place. Not cobbled together from spare parts and old cardboard, but dream it *right*. Those babies over there: They deserve your dream. Dream it for them."

"Oh, man, Estelle: How about a cool quiet room just for them, with lots of soft surfaces and soft music and a nurse on call?" He shakes his head as if to shake away the image.

"Write it down," she encourages. "And for the older children, too. And what if the job center were on-site? Or what if you had a whole wing of family-sized bedrooms? Write it down."

"That must be a big truck of money you've got."

It amazes Estelle how little the pastor understands about how such things work. She'll endow a foundation with Poppa's money. The current interest will more than seed a capital campaign for the first building, as well as pay for the staff required to keep the wheels of the operation moving forward while Craig Mitchell continues to do the things that Craig Mitchell likes to do.

"Part of the charm of Estelle Birnbaum is that she knows how to get things done. You already know that, don't you?" The shy half nod and half shrug would be endearing had it not been used on her so often by the boy out there.

"I would never ask you to change your life, Craig. I appreciate you just the way you are."

"But . . . ?" he prompts.

"There are no buts. Please. Trust me."

"But . . . you said there were two things."

"OK then. I do want something else from you. I want you to be contagious."

"Like the plague, huh?"

"Oh absolutely. Allow what Craig Mitchell has to spread—as it did to Mr. Schmidt, like it has to Donette. Let her take what you do here and let her do it for others. And then someone else will do it for someone else."

When he starts to protest, she raises a finger to his lips.

"Dare to be big, why don't you? Do you think you could do that?"

He drops into a distant and sad gaze, out across the room in the direction of the children's area. Ari, they can see, is attempting his own version of art today—much less delicate than Daniel, there's a lot of paint being splattered. But the children are ecstatic.

"You think that God keeps an accounting Estelle?"

"I'll tell you this, Craig Mitchell. Even though I'm a CPA—and very much unlike my Poppa—I don't believe in the big ledger book in the sky. I don't think it works that way."

"How does it work then?"

She reaches onto his desk, for the legal pad and pulls free a virgin sheet.

"Here. This is today. This is what counts."

A blank sheet of paper.

"So the bastards who load the trains and load the gas chambers. The people in Africa with the machetes. They get one of these every day, too."

"We're not Nazis, Craig. And *you* are a *good* man."

She indicates that he should help her rise. (To her own list she adds a decent chair for his office—one that did not lower her to the floor and swallow her up in its must.) She has him escort her over to the children's area so she can wish her grandson a good day.

"With your blessings, Pastor Mitchell, we'll need to have a small ceremony—announcing the Hillyer Family Foundation's major contribution to the House of Hope Capital Campaign. I know it sounds horrifying, but I assure you that it's a necessary evil."

She thinks she hears him mumble something to the effect of "hating that [s-word]." She'll have to do something about these boys and the idea they have that she is the sort of woman around whom they can mumble such things.

"I do it, first, for Poppa. To honor his legacy. Then also to go on notice to a few key people in the philanthropic community that attention must be paid. I've already promised you your work and your vision will be unscathed. I am a woman of my word."

"So a ceremony, huh?"

"Think of it as a celebration for the women and the children. A special day for everyone here who works so hard to make this a community. What do you say?"

Another shrug and nod job.

"Ariel, you'll help won't you? We're planning a Simcha to celebrate House of Hope. We'll take some pictures. Document where we are and where we intend to be."

The boy's face had a diagonal smear of blue. A corresponding pink one ran the length of his beefy arm.

"Sure thing, Estelle. Anything I can do, I'll do it, you know."

She hopes that it has been the kids who opened up that cheer in him. Otherwise . . . well she wouldn't think about otherwise. There is a party to plan, a family to liberate from the demons of the past, bargain condos to bargain even lower, the little matter of a job (oh, well, forget about that stupid job, already!). Oh, and then there's an angry teenager to tame.

She watches him encourage and teach and smile the effortless smile that she has always known is in there. He catches her staring, and his eyes flash momentarily dark in a way that sends a chill through her. He recovers himself—for the children's sake, she imagines. The darkness: That is real, too, she knows.

"Have fun at work, Estelle," he offers.

The coldness she hears beneath those good wishes incites a shudder that she tries to quell and she can't even respond to the boy. She walks away toward her car as fast as she can. Craig offers his own farewell, but she doesn't acknowledge it either. She doesn't look back. She doesn't want to know.

Chapter **Seventeen**

After Pep Club, things went downhill for her daughter. And although it was true that life with Keisha had never been easy, the last year or so of high school proved to be particularly awful. Relatively, in the horror show that is adolescence for so many American families, most would consider Keisha a mild case. Janet had not become a regular in either juvenile court or in the emergency room, although time served on the bench outside the principal's office at University City High School more than made up for being spared the other two. In the place of mayhem, Keisha offered a regularly rotating menu of contrariness and melancholy. It had been awful to be around her, and it was just that simple.

Janet wondered if perhaps there might be a chemical emitted by troubled youth—a similar mechanism to the pheromones that animals use to attract mates and repel predators—because such youngsters everywhere seemed to find each other with little forethought or effort. In the summer between her junior and senior years, Keisha—never a social girl—had suddenly acquired a circle of friends, equally unpleasant and clearly difficult girls, with a few strange boys thrown in for good measure. At least that would describe the few of them Janet had opportunity to meet. Keisha had become more furtive, of course, and in keeping with her mother's worst fear would seldom be home when Janet opened the door to her home after a long day down at the office. She never, therefore, met the friends on her home turf. Instead, St. Louis being in many ways just a big small town, she would come across her daughter out in public somewhere, surrounded by the pack of her scruffy new circle. The girls that she ran with tended to favor sliced-up black clothing and not very well executed asymmetrical hairdos, and the boys dressed similarly, both sexes often enough augmenting their hideous wardrobes with pounds of chains, hanging and clanking from belt loops or strung around their necks—for no purpose that Janet could possibly imagine, all that metal. In this group, cosmetics knew no gender bounds—and as far as that went there was something distinctively feminine emanating from the boys she'd see around her daughter during this phase.

The first time she'd come across Keisha with her "friends" had been a hot June afternoon in the summer of '87. After work, she had been driving up Delmar on the way to her favorite bakery, when she spotted a familiar shape in front of Streetside Records. How odd, she has always thought, that what she had first recognized was a shape; it had taken her a minute before she realized that the reason for its familiarity was because the shape belonged to her daughter. Her husband's people had been haunchy. As did Wallace, they carried all of their weight in their noticeably bulky thighs, and what Janet had seen had been a large, square person standing as if she'd just dismounted a horse. *Oh. That's Keisha,* she'd thought to herself, and even then it hadn't immediately occurred to her to be upset by the sight of her there—a place she had no permission to be, even if it had been the middle of the day.

Still early in the summer and Keisha had already worn her out—the daily battles over where she belonged (in the house) and doing what (helping maintain the place—at the very least picking up after herself). Even as she had pulled the car to the curb, Janet realized she'd be wasting her time; all the same she was not a woman used to ignoring facts, and the fact in this case was right in front of her: her daughter milling about aimlessly on the sidewalk with the sorts of people who would surely turn even the most permissive of parents into nervous wrecks.

"Keisha," she'd said. She had not raised her voice or been accusatory or scolding in her tone. "Keisha. May I speak to you for a minute, please."

Even despite Janet's restraint, the look her daughter offered her had positively dripped with venom.

"Lady. Lady. Lady. Lady." A boy tugged on her jacket—silk for summer, and he wasn't the sort of person you wanted touching your clothing, regardless of fabric. "Lady. Lady. Lady."

"Keisha. I'm speaking to you."

"Lady. Lady. Lady." She looked at the boy—a mistake—which provided him the excuse to ask her for a dollar. This apparently had been the funniest thing that happened to this crowd in months, because suddenly she'd been surrounded by laughter, the bullying, derisive kind.

The girls were all hard looking, in a way that Keisha mostly had not been—or at least was not unless she decided to look hard, which with this crowd she did. One or two of them might be pretty if they put some effort into it, as was true for her daughter, but they seemed to have intentionally chosen styles that highlighted their worst features—unflattering haircuts; ill-fitting, filthy clothes; too much of the wrong colors of makeup for their skin tones. They shared with Keisha a predilection for fixing on their faces cynical sneers, one lip curled up until it more or less forced an eye closed. Everyone looked like she smelled something.

"Who's this bitch?" asked one of these charmers.

In both her personal as well as her professional life, few things brought Janet more pleasure than reducing such people to size. Yet somehow, on that day, she had been rendered defenseless. She could only think to call on her daughter for support.

"Keisha," she said again, and she had hoped (and even then she had known that doing so had been futile) that her daughter would rise to the occasion. "Chill, ya'll, it's just my mom," or more fiercely perhaps, "Check how you speak to my family."

Instead, Keisha stood there, impassively, her face set with the same hate-filled detachment as the others.

"That's your mom?" one of the girls asked Keisha, emphasizing the *that* and the *mom* part, as if the fact of Janet being mother to her friend were the most ridiculous thing in the world.

A few years earlier, before Keisha grew to be her equal in size—to outweigh her, in fact—Janet would have thought nothing of walking up to her daughter and dragging her out of there, by the hair if necessary, or by the ear. She had momentarily calculated the odds that she'd prevail in the battle on this particular day, but quickly disabused herself of the scheme. She'd seen other parents fight with their children in public and had always been repelled by such behavior, had zero desire to be seen as the sort of person who aired her dirty laundry on a busy sidewalk in the Loop. And while she knew that taking the little wench down a few notches would offer great satisfaction, more likely it also stood the chance to further impair whatever remained of the already faltering connection between them.

On her healthiest day, when she cuts herself slack, Janet takes quiet pride at her moments of magnanimity, times when she'd taken the high road with Keisha, when the low road would have offered so much more pleasure. Steering Daniel away from a positively hideous impressionist mess, she directs him to a cubist sculpture that has always pleased her, even despite its somewhat vulgar subject matter. She can almost muster a smile at the memory of the younger Janet crossing her arms benignly and offering her daughter a ride.

"It's such a hot one this afternoon," she had said. "I thought I'd carry you up to the house if you wanted."

What virtue! The inane pride of the "good sports" on the losing team: stand up guys who despite their shame sucked it up and walked across the field to shake their opponents' hands. And while they might not have that World Series ring, they would always know they'd played well and had been men about it. The Greatest American Heroes meet the greatest American chumps, and once again Janet found herself on the side of the mortified.

As for her offer, well you'd have thought that she suggested taking the whole sorry lot of them around the corner to the toddler park and pushing them on the baby swings, so derisive had been the laughter at her proposition.

"She's high," one of them had scoffed, and she had wondered how many of them actually had taken something that day. She'd never known the degree of Keisha's use or experimentation, or even if that had been part of the pathology. She had always doubted that her daughter had even dabbled in drugs—Keisha enjoyed being in control too much to allow the lowering of her guard. She'd hate to miss the opportunity to take advantage of someone else. But Janet had no idea, really. Whether chemically induced or otherwise, her daughter was often someone she couldn't recognize.

"I'll see you at home then," she had said to her, and she'd headed back to her car.

"Hey!" Keisha had called, running up behind her. "Hey!"

It had been the *Hey* Janet had heard street toughs use after taking offense when you rebuffed their nasty advances or refused to fund their drinking habits. The *Hey* of pool-cue-wielding belligerents outside the sorts of bars that women like Janet did not frequent. She turned to face the girl, who scolded her, saying:

"I don't need you coming down here embarrassing me in front of my friends."

In hindsight, an almost reasonable and certainly typical complaint for a young adult—and she'd even used a reasonable voice level and tone with her mother. But she had also supplemented her grievance with a whole array of overblown physical gestures—goose-necking and fingers-in-the-face and hands in the air—designed clearly to communicate to the rabble what a tough little bitch she was to stand up to the old cow.

Janet remembers being completely undone by this performance. It was absurd and embarrassing—like finding oneself in a bad movie or on one of those hidden camera shows—and she had even looked around the same way people did on those shows when the naked shill walks up to you asking for directions to the mayor's office, scanning around to see if anyone else saw the ridiculous situation you found yourself in, to confirm you weren't hallucinating.

She'd raised her arms in surrender and had even chuckled a bit.

"You know my rules," she'd said and continued on to the car.

To everyone's surprise, Keisha followed her and had gone to the passenger door and waited to be let in. Of course, she'd made a big display out of slamming the door, once again supplemented with some exquisitely overblown body language.

And thus they had gone Petrofsky's—and it had been much as if the whole scene back there in the street had never gone down. Neither of them said a word about it. They selected their treats—Keisha asking almost demurely for a crème puff and, ridiculously enough, for an iced cookie in the shape of Big Bird. Janet paid the bill and the two of them retreated from the heat to the cool comforts of their house on Teasdale Avenue, settling into their evening routines—Janet upstairs; Keisha down; the kitchen, a neutral zone, which for some reason had become the only acceptable place to exchange a civil word.

This was in the days before Estelle came on the scene, and as part of the routine lunchroom "family" banter Janet would seek advice from her co-workers in the Human Resources department. She had been canny enough at least to couch her dilemma in the that-darn-gal, good-humored way in which her colleagues discussed their own children's antics, although major curfew violations and unspeakable rudeness didn't as easily lend themselves to the spirit of fun. She'd say, for example, "Girl, let me tell you what Miss Keisha did: helped herself to fifty dollars from my purse. Can you believe that?" She'd sit back and wait for the commiseration—which never came—hoping that perhaps one of her co-workers had a similar hard case on her hands, and had also come across the secret cure to adolescence. It quickly became clear to her that as far as her co-workers were concerned, Janet had the hardest row to hoe. While the wrecked cars and ruptured appendices of other people's offspring brought challenges, Keisha Williams must be the devil incarnate, and if Janet Williams knew what was good for her, she would cut her losses and get the poor girl professional help.

"Oh, Janet, I can't believe she said something like that to you. How awful for you. How genuinely awful."

After a while, she just stopped talking about Keisha at all. People didn't get it. They believed that children were blank slates, emerged from the womb ripe for the molding, and if you just did the right things for them, they'd grow up happy and healthy and sane. If things got rough, you relied on prayer and all other manner of magical thinking, waving your wands and chanting the magic words until little Junior or Sal saw the light and set to the golden path.

They didn't understand. Some people—people such as Keisha—were just the way that they were: ornery, difficult—evil even. Her colleagues would look at Janet as if somehow something she had done along the way had poisoned this child and made her the seething bundle of spite that she was. No, Janet wanted to say. I did not. She came out this way.

Had they been in the nursery? Had they heard the child fuss and holler? Two hours old and already bitterly angry at the world, when all that had been done to her was soothing massages and the offer of a breast to suckle. They didn't understand.

Daniel's sneer at a second-rate Picasso pleases her to no end—my how he was coming along on these little tutorials.

"Sign that man's name on a couple of stray pencil marks and sell it for a million bucks."

"Looks that way," he concurs.

She nods toward the mid-century and they amble on their way.

In that hot summer of '87, Janet became obsessed with following her daughter. She had convinced herself—her early rationale—that on the road just ahead of the girl trouble lurked in the bushes ready to waylay her and to ruin whatever future she might salvage, and didn't one read regularly in the *Post* of young people just like those in front of the record store meeting some bad end, either something done to them or some unspeakable plot cooked up by their ringleader and executed by the rank-and-file, something grizzly involving vivisection, candles, and sodomy?

Whatever mystery might have existed concerning the behavior of Keisha and her crew had quickly been laid bare. Their antics consisted primarily of clustering together and being unpleasant—preferably in some public place where people wished you wouldn't and weren't.

It surprised Janet how easy it had been to keep tabs on her daughter. As it happened they limited the businesses they chose to torment to a favored few: record stores, vintage clothing vendors, "smoking paraphernalia" shops, and rather soon it became clear to Janet that however unsightly these young people were, their behavior was relatively innocent—in fact, the best she could tell they offered a certain cachet to some of their chosen locations, places wishing to suggest that their ordinary wares had the same edge to them as emanated from the riffraff out front.

And yet, even despite feeling relatively content that her daughter had not been out looting and pillaging, she could not stop following her. As fall approached and Keisha's senior year began, a Saturday morning in September or October would find Janet parked down the block on Delmar or South Grand, just out of sight of her daughter and her friends, just watching.

Observing the oversized, awkward girl, down in front of those shops, posing and pacing and stomping from foot to foot as the weather turned cold, Janet could never have guessed that in less than two years she would be a married woman, a holier-than-thou-art church goer, dressed in the sorts of cheap and dowdy suits that the office temps down at the company wore, the mother of an adorable son.

The group of friends down the block, she came to understand, had no consistent membership. Children came and went for no apparent reason. At the center of the group, a core that seemed to include Keisha remained consistent. Other than panhandling, their primary occupation seemed to be smoking cigarettes and blocking the sidewalk. Keisha, she could tell, didn't really smoke—the puffed out cheeks the telltale sign of a non-inhaler—and she supposed that should offer some comfort. In those days, you took it where you could find it.

Clearly, there was little conversation among them, or if they did talk, their affect was flat and unanimated. Mostly they were listless. Keisha, ironically enough to Janet, seemed the liveliest of the bunch, albeit her bursts of animation she limited to strings of invective hurled at passing cars—for no reason that Janet could ever decipher. Cars with young drivers, cars with old drivers, foreign-looking people, cops: There was no discernible pattern. Now and again the spirit would strike and Keisha stepped to the curb and let fly the abuse. And, Good Lord, Janet had thought, what if someone took offense? What if some nut job stopped the car and jumped out and went after the girl? She realized then that this was exactly what they wanted, those kids, Keisha in particular. She'd love to front off some loser who dared take umbrage at being called a sack of one thing or another. (Keisha had a fondness for calling people sacks of things.)

And with the mildest of shame, Janet remembers entertaining sometimes the wish that one of those drivers would take care of business—stop the car, that is, and put that child in her place. Standing in front of those insufferable Pollack drip jobs (that for a reason she cannot possibly fathom seem to have entranced her grandson), it saddens her to realize how unlikable her daughter had been. How little she had liked her herself.

So, no, over the course of the winter, the behavior had not escalated, even though had it done so no one would have been surprised in the least, certainly not Janet. Instead, just day after day of the general obnoxiousness that was Keisha.

It had been Janet's inclination to skip teachers' conferences altogether that fall, but the company had been in one of its occasional "good corporate citizen" modes, and had been encouraging the employees to "take time for the children." (Looked good on paper, but in fact it had been part of a larger scheme designed by a team led by Janet to counter that pesky "family leave" business, which at the time kept rearing its ugly head in various legislatures.) As a senior member of the human resources team, it behooved her to set an example.

Thus, she'd endured in early November a particularly humiliating evening of educational professionals shaking their heads and clicking their tongues at her daughter's squandered "potential." *Sullen* and *inattentive* had been the popular epithets that year, and she'd heard them from every teacher as a description of Keisha's delightful presence in their classes.

"And your daughter is honestly capable of doing so much better than this."

What she remembered most about the evening was how hard it had been to know how to respond to those people—what her demeanor should be, whether or not to defend her daughter, and if so to what degree. She remembered being on the one hand keenly aware of her parental instincts kicking in—the desire to hold up the stop sign and say "Just one damn minute here: That's my baby you're talking about. Surely there must be some kind of mistake." Because it was common knowledge that these people had problems with fairness—and how dare they pile on her child in this way and with such vigor.

An even more compelling instinct, however, had been what she had known even then to be an extraordinarily selfish one: to defend herself against the attack. She'd wanted to ask those people, Why the hell are you blaming me for this? You think it's my fault the girl is the way that she is?

Of course, that's what they thought. Always, every time, still. And as they browse the museum's rather paltry collection of contemporary art, she finds herself filling with resentment and rage. It wasn't fair. She had honestly done the best that she could, every step along the way. She knows that she did. And what did all that hard work get you?

She suggests to Daniel that they try the new Wolfgang Puck place for lunch. It's down in the new addition behind the museum.

She had settled on powerlessness that night; had decided that she had no choice except to play the role of the helpless adult, just like the loser parents who had always disgusted her, the sorts of people who, as she had done that night, sat there at the teachers' desks and whined, "I just don't know what to do with the girl." Because they didn't, and neither did she.

She'd felt a resounding sense of déjà vu that night. Thirteen years of sitting across from these people. The chairs had gotten bigger, but the litany remained consistent. Younger more vigorous versions of Janet would revel in the irony: You, whose job it is to deal with this child, have the nerve to ask me, who pays your salary, what to do about her. But by November of '87 she was way beyond that. She'd defaulted to the helpless mother routine because at the time it felt better to be thought incompetent rather than complicit. And yes, of course, incompetence equaled complicity, but she understood that the limited imagination of most public school teachers allowed for a narrow range of explanations, and over the years she'd learned to find at least a token of comfort in their second-rate pity.

Which is what it had always been: horribly pitiful and sad.

"This joint's not so bad." Daniel's pronouncement that today's outing has met his high standards.

"You'll like the Met a lot better," she says, and then suppresses cringes at her mistake: She hasn't yet told him about next week's tickets to New York. It's to be another surprise!

Spring with Keisha had been anti-climactic. Janet hadn't known of course that her daughter would save the genuinely awful stuff for down the road a piece. Even so, she remembered this as the most stressful time of all—not because of what actually happened but because of the constant potential that it might.

Living with Keisha was like living with an erratic alarm clock: You knew the damn thing would go off eventually, you just couldn't predict when it would. So Janet spent the spring of her daughter's senior year on tenterhooks, expecting any minute that the phone would ring and that the voice on the other end would speak some horrifying truth.

Eight years later when the bad news finally came—to her front door, as it happened, rather than across her company's wires—she had put the boy to bed and undressed herself and had allowed herself to savor a moment of trashy relief: So there it is, she thought. It's happened and it's over. The feeling had been like that moment after the nurse finally pierces your skin with the needle—the anticipation always worse than the fact of it.

But that awful spring there had only been the waiting for the needle, and so every time the phone rang at work or a siren screamed down Hanley Road, she would gird herself for the impending assault.

That spring's only disaster had, in retrospect, been a minor one. Janet opened the door one day in April to find an array of garbage strewn at the bottom of the stairs and up their length. Pets—viciously unruly dogs, perhaps—might explain the nature of the mess. Clothes, posters, bedding: everything shredded, and she followed the trail up to her daughter's bedroom.

She found Keisha sitting in the middle of a pile of the remainder of her clothes and bedding, snipping at them with the scissors. She was crying, but in a detached and cool sort of way.

"What on earth?" Janet asked her. "What is it, sweetheart?"

"They all hate me, Mama. Why?"

Janet had lowered herself into the mess and gathered the child into her arms to comfort her. She couldn't remember the last time Keisha had let herself be held in that way.

She'd said all the things one would expect: that mother was there for her and how everything would be OK. She's sure that for at least a few moments they had both believed her.

"The young people you'll be in school with will also have spent time in such places," she tells her grandson. He nods—ironically, she thinks.

"But not in such good company."

She's not sure if that's sarcasm or if he's buttering her up for something.

"I promised you every advantage."

Again, the ambiguous nod. "So much culture, so little time."

There's a weariness in his tone: So, yes, he is growing tired of her relentless schedule. But so be it.

In the middle of the summer after graduation, she'd answered the door, Keisha had, and there had been two young evangelists on the other side, one of them the man who would become this boy's father. Within six weeks, she had become an enthusiastic recruit to the New Purpose Temple of Faith and acolyte to the charismatic young deacon who had charmed her with his fancy talk. She had been an easy mark, Janet knew—a lonely unpleasant girl getting attention from a good-looking young man. Up until then, boys such as Jerrold Davis had surely never given her the time of day.

Contrary had yielded to self-righteous.

"When I pray tonight, Mother, I'll ask Jesus for help with your drinking problem."

While at the time being lectured for her heathendom had seemed a vast improvement over verbal abuse and indifference, Janet eventually came to understand that they were two sides of the same coin.

Janet would sip her occasional glass of wine and say simply, "You do that, Baby."

The following June Keisha married Jerrold Davis in a wedding that even now it chagrins Janet to have funded, tradition or no. Three hours of whooping and hollering in the corrugated barn that those people called a church, followed by a dry reception in the "fellowship" hall next door to it. Janet would have sprung for the Coronado Ballroom—your child only married once—but no, they had to be in that stifling hangar, which smelled of chalk and sweat socks. And apparently their particular Jesus had issues with filet—which she would have also have happily paid for. She'd choked down an austere meal of dried, unseasoned chicken breast, plain broccoli, and plain white rice. (And paid pretty much the same as the filet would have cost her in the first place.)

She believes that the relief that she felt to see the taillights of the car hauling away her daughter's few possessions is common to all parents. Goodbye and good luck: That had been her wish. She converted Keisha's room to a guest suite.

In a little over five years, she converted it again for the boy.

Janet jangles her keys—her signal that it's time for him to hustle it up and finish that Kobe beef burger. She thinks she's just heard "hold your horses"—unsure, since it's both arcane and uncharacteristic.

"Oh, humor an old lady, would you? This is my last full summer with you."

Is that a sigh or a scoff?

He says: "I'm thinking that I might do another shift at House of

Hope. Like maybe tomorrow."

And thus it is her turn to scoff.

"Tomorrow? Really? I've got passes to the Gates of Heaven show up at the Art Institute and tickets on the morning train. They'll only be in the country for a while, so it's a golden opportunity. We've got to be at the station at dawn, so it's an early night for us.

He looks at her like she's lost her mind—and certainly she has, if only a little. Tough times make even tough old birds like her a little crazy sometimes.

"Janet Williams isn't about to send her grandson off to the Ivy League lest he's been exposed to every cultural advantage." She caresses his back just before she pops the locks on the BMW. They're late for a lecture at the History Center. "You'll thank me one day."

Neither will he ever set foot again in any center run by that Craig Mitchell.

They'll never get their hands on this boy. Never: not the preachers or the bashers or the bullies or any of them. Never. And particularly not that mother of his. She'd sooner kill him herself than let that witch sink her claws into him.

Chapter **Eighteen**

M ove it, Buster.
We haven't got all night.
Don't you people ever sleep? What's so funny?
You.
Seriously, people. I need my rest. The woman is running me ragged.
So rest already.
Don't let us stop you.
A question or two first, if you don't mind.
It'll only take a minute.
We wouldn't want to disrupt your precious beauty sleep.
OK, but just for the record, you are disrupting me. We can agree on that, right?
Petulance doesn't become you, big brother.
Whatever.
And speaking of "whatever," first question: What's your dang problem, anyway?
Yeah.
Yeah.
Right now my problem is that the three of you . . .
Objection!
Sustained. The witness will answer the questions and refrain from personal attacks.
Whose idea was it to give the baby the gavel?
Objection! Your honor!
Young man, don't think I won't charge you with contempt.
What I wouldn't give for a normal family. Honestly, I have no idea what you people are talking about.
Would the clerk please read from the transcript? Page 12,874, please.
It says right here: "I love you."
The prosecution rests, Your Honor.
The defendant is found guilty and sentenced to . . . What should we fix his sentence at? I'm only eight months. And I was a preemie.
Wait! You didn't give me a chance to defend myself.

What's the defense for stupidity?
The boy told you he loved you. And you said? What?
Not so chatty any more, are you?
Please note for the record, Your Honor, that Mr. Davis refused to answer the question.
So noted. Miriam Davis, please call your next witness.
Wait a minute. Wasn't I just already convicted? What about my witnesses?
You don't need any witnesses. Everybody saw you.
He said: Oh, Danny, I love you. Kiss, kiss, kiss, kiss, kiss.
That's not how it happened.
Such a dreamboat, that Ari.
And then this one said:
Nothing.
Where did you get a word like dreamboat?
You prefer Studmuffin.
Bonedaddy.
Mr. Bulgypants.
We don't know what any of these words mean.
Honestly.
I can't even talk yet, remember?
OK, now I am officially vexed.
If I were you, I'd order us to leave.
It's not like you listen to anything *I* say.
Well, that is true. You've got to give him that much.
So we're done here, then?
Oh, hardly.
You're a mess, Brother.
We may have to convene a grand jury.
This isn't helping. I've got a long day ahead of me.
Speaking of which . . .
You and her: If there ever were two people with issues.
What does this picture remind you of?
What picture? Where?
Over here.
The boy is always looking in the wrong places.
When I say a word, you say the first thing that comes into your mind.

So we're playing doctor?
Open your mouth and say "Ah!"
Show us yours and we'll show you ours.
This is gross.
So I'm to understand that you think this is gross.
I think we're frustrating the poor boy.
He frustrates himself.
You know what? You're right about that.
No, she isn't. And there's no call for eye rolling.
Whatever, Mr. Whatever.
As if a bunch of children . . .
Your Honor: I'd like to add age discrimination to the bill.
So charged. Has anyone seen my pacifier?
Life: It's a lot more complicated than any of you would know. Sorry.
Didn't it used to be hanging around my neck on a string?
Is he talking down to us because he's our older brother or is he talking down to us because we're not really here?
He's talking down to us because he talks to everybody that way.
I do not.
Found it! Was a snake it woulda bit me.
You certainly talk to her that way.
I don't want to go to some dumb museum. I just want to go with Ari. Kiss, kiss, kiss, kiss, kiss.
I never said that to her.
But you thought that. In her direction.
That Ari is kind of cute though.
He's a dreamboat.
It's complicated.
Being a dreamboat is complicated?
It's all complicated, if you must know.
Or. Or, maybe it's simple and you make it complicated.
Say for instance there are things that she and me need to discuss and she's not willing to discuss them.
Danny, Danny, Danny. Why is everything always about Danny?
If you'll be seated, I'm ready with a verdict.
We already did this part.

In the matter of Daniel Davis versus the world, what say you?

Your Honor, we the people say: Beware of him who thinks too much.

I thought he was Your Honor. And that's not a verdict.

Is so.

Is not.

Is so.

No, it's not. It's a fortune. I saw you break it out of that cookie. And what's the baby doing with a fortune cookie anyway? Would someone keep an eye on this baby, for God's sake.

They're good for teething.

I don't have any teeth. See.

And so you put little pieces of cookies on the gums and you chew. Like this.

See.

It's simple.

A lot of things are a lot more simple than you think.

And that's the verdict. It's simple.

That wasn't what he said.

He's a baby.

Yes it is. Hosea, tell her what you said.

Ga, ga, goo, goo.

Whatever.

Whatever, whatever.

Look, I'm going to sleep now.

Don't let us stop you.

Don't think about pink elephants.

Where's my pink elephant?

Check the string around your neck.

Thanks, bro.

Now will you leave. Please.

OK, we'll leave. But before we go, I have just one more question.

One more. That's it. Promise.

Promise.

One more. OK then.

Daniel Davis: Who's Your Daddy?

Oh! Oh! I know! I know!

Yes, Hosea Davis. Who's his Daddy?

Ari Birnbaum.

That's right! And aren't you a big old precious thing. Yes, you are. Yes, you are. Tell your big brother "goodnight."

Big Brother Goodnight.

Tell him we'll see him tomorrow.

Ga, ga, goo, goo.

"Rise and shine, sweetheart. Tour bus leaves in forty-five minutes."

You've got to be kidding me.

No rest for the wicked, huh bro?

Get your shower. We'll see you on the bus.

Chapter **Nineteen**

For maybe only the second time in his life Craig Mitchell wakes to find other folks at the controls of the wild ride that is his life, he a mere passenger on that ride, clutching tightly and not particularly looking forward to the whole series of dips and turns he knows wait up and over the horizon. Just hang on and trust me, Estelle says, and she hands him another list of things to be done before the gala announcing the Hillyer Family Foundation's Women-and-Children-First Initiative. ("Too much to do, too little time! Ten days and counting.")

(*Maybe* because maybe the dark years don't count. A wild ride to be sure, those years on the street, but maybe it didn't count if you were too disconnected from reality to understand how genuinely crazy it was.)

This time as well as the first he'd been wide-awake and even punched the ticket himself, all the while knowing that anything might happen—and him not ever having been the sort of person who reveled in uncertainty. This time and the first his gut had told him it just might go badly for him. But the thing about these rides: Once they lower the bar, there's no backing out. The metal rod locked down tight when he'd signed onto Estelle Birnbaum's plans for her father's legacy. He couldn't stop now even if he wanted to; almost certainly wouldn't if he could. When it gets crazy—as it has gotten crazy today—in his mind he casts ahead nine months, two years, five, and he imagines all the sheltered mothers and their little ones. If Craig Mitchell is found crushed and broken track-side, well, quoting Estelle, it's the cost of doing business. But don't you worry: I've got this covered, my friend, she says, begging his trust—and she is the sort of woman who tends to inspire confidence. He's belted in tight, figures the best-case scenario is a mild case of whiplash. He will survive.

Over at "her" counter—a space in the pantry she's cleared for a gala "office"—Estelle tantrums over the latest fiasco.

"Tell me there are more photos," she says. An order as well as a lament. She waves a folder he'd handed her containing the few images taken over the years, waves it as if it were on fire, as if doing so might dislodge a Polaroid or two. He's not been running pony rides these past five years, but those aren't the exact words he chooses to remind her of why he's not documented more of the work.

"Here's a nice one," he offers, handing her a framed snapshot, which he kept on his desk, a group photo from about two years back that one of the women had taken. She'd been one of those large-spirited people that passed through now and again. Down on my luck, dammit, but that don't stop me from saying good morning to you. Her life she hauled around in a ratty old silver backpack, the shoulder holsters of which had blackened with grime, and before she moved on to the next temporary cot she'd fished from her gear an ancient camera and gathered the residents for a photo, promising copies to one and all. Damn if she hadn't sent them, in an envelope from some no-name motel in Memphis, and she scrawled on the note her love for all of God's creations.

"We'll make this our opening. Or closing. Or . . . what do you think, Ariel?"

The grandson, who she has assigned to build some sort of audio/visual extravaganza—to impress the rubes with the checkbooks as to the worthy cause their monies will join her father's money to support—can barely manage an audible response. He looks like shit—like he's slept in the gutter or been holed up in some roadhouse drinking and smoking everything in sight. Clearly, he has zero interest in Estelle's project.

The boy's degeneracy surprises Craig not one bit. The suburbs of America are chock full of privileged burnouts like Ariel Birnbaum. If the boy's lucky, Estelle will buy him a month in one of those treatment resorts before his liver gives out or he wraps himself and his Porsche around an oak tree that happens into his path.

"What's that, young man?" Estelle asks. The boy has mumbled something under his breath, as per usual.

Craig can't resist: He turns from his own work in hopes of seeing Estelle backhand the bastard but good for once.

"Nothing," Ari responds.

"You said 'it sucks.' Grandma's not deaf. Let me tell you something, Mr. . . . Mr. . . . Mr. . . . " and the normally quick tongued Estelle is so anxious and so geared up about this gala—and so not going to waste her time on the fool—that she can't even fish up an appropriate sobriquet for the boy.

(How about Mr. Teenage Skid Row 2007, Craig doesn't suggest: It's not his place, neither can he be bothered.)

Donette sidles up to the boy and coos, "Give a working man a break, Mrs. B." She fingers his curls with her nails. Surprisingly enough to Craig the boy seems to enjoy her teasing and flirting. He blushes and smiles and his mood seems to improve—even if he does still look like hell.

"Can I borrow him?" Donette asks.

"Be my guest," Estelle encourages—as if someone has offered to extract a diseased tooth.

"Follow me, Hot Stuff."

The cloud of gloom moves off with Donette, who delivers him to a table full of mothers and kids making posters for the event.

"Do yourself a favor, Craig: Get your tubes tied."

"I'll do that," he tells Estelle, who's exploiting this respite from her grandson as an opportunity for their coffee break. She unrolls the lushest caramel rolls he has ever seen—dripping with pecans and glossy with goo they are. He retrieves their mugs and pours the coffee and cannot wait to dig in.

"Enough! A real break today. No Simchas. No teenagers. Let's talk about something else. How's your love life?"

"Same as yours, I imagine."

"I don't know what you've heard, Mr. Mitchell."

"Rumor has it."

"And every word is true, I promise you. I get you set up here, get these boys of ours packed off to school; then me and Janet are off to Florida, and I'll tell you this: there's no looking back and things in Sunshine State will never be the same again."

Craig has no doubt. No doubt there is a whole lot of life left in this broad, and from everything he knows about Janet Williams, she's still a live wire, too. Estelle looks at him as if he were being a bad boy.

"Not answering personal questions, I take it."

His mouth is strings of caramel so he is saved from answering.

"A nice-looking young man like you."

He smiles his thanks at that. Would it surprise this woman to know that Keisha Williams Davis had been the last woman he'd loved? The only one; his other wild ride, the one that almost killed him.

"A person stays busy," he tells Estelle after a swallow of coffee.

She was pretty, but she didn't know it, Keisha was. Uncomfortable in her own skin, as if she were an alien who'd been dropped into her body by mistake, constantly smoothing her skirt or tugging at the hem of a jacket or a blouse. She'd squirm and adjust her hips trying for a better purchase. Like Ariel Birnbaum, joy did not come easy to her, but when she did smile, which she would do sometimes—rarely—when her guard was down, she would dazzle you.

Back on that other roller coaster, early on during their time in the church they had been referred to as the Three Musketeers. Inseparable. None of them had been popular in high school. He gathered from the few times she would open up about her past that, like him, Keisha had been a loner; and as for Jerrold, his parents didn't approve of friends outside New Purpose, and during its early years, children had been rare—either not in his age group or, worse, more shut down than he had been in terms of the boundaries. The sorts of kids who thought comic books tempted scandal and who suspected any conversation that wasn't about Jesus.

The days had been full of evangelism, the three of them dropped off in some subdivision with briefcases full of crudely produced tracts announcing the New Purpose Temple of Faith's particular take on the Good News. At the time their ministry had seemed powerfully exciting to Craig, but now he is aware that it had merely been another version of the same-old-same-old: Jesus will love you more at our church than at the one down the road. He can still remember the feel of those flyers, printed so cheaply that the moisture from your fingers dissolved the ink and blurred the obnoxiously sentimental artwork. Enough lambs on those circulars you'd think they'd been selling discount mattresses rather than salvation, or at least the promise of it.

He'd done most of the preaching back then, Craig had. Poor Jerrold proved incapable of memorizing the canned presentations, and too frequently his fumblings with note cards produced the wrong effect: derisive laughter where one had hoped for humility and the relief one finds at being delivered from eternal damnation.

As for Keisha, while the promises flowed from Craig like bacon grease from a hot skillet, in her mouth the words sounded stilted and unconvincing. It had been clear her heart wasn't in it—not in those early days, at least—and that she'd as soon be hawking two-buck chocolate bars or raffles for a new Honda. But she'd be there every morning, dressed and on the curb in front of her mother's house, ready for another day of work.

"Hey, girl," they'd both call, as Craig relinquished shotgun and Keisha climbed in front next to Jerrold.

"Hey yourselves," would always be her response. Sometimes she would bounce in her seat like a small child on her way to a big surprise, begging to know where they were headed. (As if one worn out working class suburb were somehow more stimulating than the one down the highway.) Even when mellow her pleasure at being out with the two young men had been palpable and he imagines that she would have come with them regardless of their mission.

And despite the shortcomings of two-thirds of the team, they'd found success harrowing the rocky soil of suburban St. Louis. By the time the new sanctuary had been consecrated that fall (Jerrold's father and several other long-time members pompously carrying banners that the youth group had constructed on an ancient sewing machine) the pews had been full. Reverend Brickell had smartly targeted neighborhoods full of strivers—black folks whose desire to have the best of everything extended to being part of the hottest new church in town. Who better to shill that dream than the three of them—young folks whose radiated wholesomeness had been exceeded only by their actual innocence and naiveté.

Craig's belief in the basic decency and nobility of their work kept him motivated through the late summer and into the fall. He knew that Jerrold also believed, and Craig imagined that on her best days Keisha believed also. She'd never said as much, but she would, when they found willing converts, smile at them warmly and in a way that said she couldn't be happier they had agreed to step forward for salvation.

Because none of them had been extroverts, they relied on each other for the courage to knock on those doors and to deal with the not infrequent rudeness and sometimes outright hostility. Jerrold would knock and he and Keisha would offer a hearty greeting, which cued Craig to begin the standard spiel:

"Good morning (sir or ma'am)! We just wanted to know if you knew how much Jesus loves you?" The three teenagers' breath would be held in anticipation of the response. On a good day most of the doors went unanswered, or if they had been answered their presentation received a quiet "No, thank you," and they would—after the standard consolation prize of a condescending "God bless you anyway"—move on down the block.

They had many bad days.

Meanness hurt: the slammed doors, the cursing, the people who relished this convenient opportunity to unload their hostility toward any and all churches on a clutch of hapless teenagers.

"I ought to go up there and knock him upside his head," Keisha threatened, as they walked away from a particularly nasty piece of work, a man who had lectured them both thoroughly and harshly about the foolishness of signing onto 'the white man's religion.'

"A dirty old sack of shit," she continued.

This had been early in October, and neither he nor Jerrold had seen this side of the girl, and they both fell over laughing, mostly to have the tension relieved. For weeks they'd simply taken what had been dished out to them.

They'd been working in Spanish Lake, in a part of the county recently colonized by families fleeing the death throes of the city. Houses sat well back from the sidewalk-free streets in this subdivision, and it had been unusually hot for October. Craig remembered being exhausted that day, and as for Keisha, she'd walked pointedly in the opposite direction of the next bungalow and in the direction of Jerrold's car.

"Where you going?" Jerrold called after her. His tone had been bemused, if a little irritated.

"To take these shoes off my feet and make myself a little more comfortable. For a minute. Because I want to. Because I can. If you don't got a problem with that." She popped the chunky short heels from her feet and attempted to continue on—alas, the sun-warmed asphalt proved instantly too much for her stocking feet, and she hobbled back into her footwear.

"I thought we'd finish this block," Jerrold suggested.

"And I thought I'd sit my ass in the car for a minute.'

Jerrold raised his eyebrows in Craig's direction and then curled his lips to the side. Craig had been unsure how to read this expression, which was unusual because Jerrold was nothing if not transparent. The eyebrows and curled lips had been muted additions to the boy's always-placid exterior. He limited his range of expressions to variants on a vacant yet wide-eyed simper, either goofy-looking or alluring depending on a person's mood when he read it. Craig had noticed this flat bliss on the faces of many religious types over the years. People like Jerrold (and Keisha, toward the end) who might smile at you, but it would be the sort of smile you saw molded onto the faces of plastic dolls in the discount store. Not quite believable and perhaps even a little bit scary. Emotions were dangerous things, after all, and joy at the wrong moment or misplaced anger might instantly render one's keys to the kingdom revoked. Therefore, the only place that feelings would flow with impunity would be in the sanctuary, where it would not be uncommon to see grown men cry and see women swooning with ecstasy. But run into a New Purpose member on the street and they were like people on too much medication: It was as if their full range of emotions had been locked away alongside their disappointments at not living in fancy mansions or driving the newest SUV. God would provide in his long-promised kingdom (and apparently he would also tell you how to emote and for what reason).

Certainly Craig had been as taken aback by Keisha's sudden spunk as Jerrold had been. Until that moment she'd had been an easygoing and even pleasant young lady—had never talked much at all, frankly, before that afternoon—save some almost comically childish outbursts proclaiming her adoration for one of the songs on the gospel disc or her "are we there yet" excitement over impending lunch breaks or the ride to each day's territory. Oh, and of course to deliver the prepared text when it would be her turn to do so—which she'd always recited from memory in a refined monotone that had put Craig in mind of the voice of directory assistance. The sudden appearance of ghetto girl had been a surprise indeed.

Jerrold had shrugged and indicated they should follow her. Which they did.

At the car, Keisha leaned against the fender and fished a stick of spearmint from her purse and proceeded to chew with enthusiasm.

(She had not offered any to the boys.)

Keisha knew just as Craig knew the telltale signs that Jerrold was getting himself up for one of his impromptu lectures—the deep inhalation, the rearing back of the head—so she cut him off at the pass:

"Why don't we go do something or something? Huh?"

"We are doing something. We're spreading the Good News."

Keisha rolled her eyes. Some people.

"Do something," she said. "Like go to the movies, do something; or go to the mall do something; or go . . . I don't know. Bowling. Something."

For just a moment, the vacant façade cracked, and a little of the hidden Jerrold leaked through to the light. Let's humor the bitch, his smirk announced—and, yes, Craig had been pretty sure *bitch* would have been the word behind that expression. He'd been intrigued by the girl, Jerrold had, and certainly game for her little plan. But he had also been genuinely pissed off. That much was clear. Here was a young man under his father's orders to do everything he could to become the leader of the thriving new congregation, and, raised with a heavy hand, he'd not been one to defy that father. This *bitch* might be more trouble than she was worth, but Jerrold had also been nineteen and headstrong and open to what he imagined was a momentary diversion from his path.

"All right, then," he had said, and he'd removed his suit coat and actually rolled up his sleeves.

Keisha, clearly anticipating a different response to her rebellion, at first did a double take, and then grabbed hold of her victory, saying, "Let's go then," directing them toward their fate.

Since bowling was cheap, relatively, bowling it was, and as it happened, one of their brethren worked the shoe counter at a place off 270 in North County. So in they went for their free footwear, watery Cokes and as much mayhem as three good kids could muster.

It had been awkward at first. Until that afternoon, every bit of their time together had been spent in the church or doing the church's business or coming and going from church. For the first few frames they'd sat together as stiff as spinsters on a blind date. But on Keisha's fourth turn, she'd run up to the line and—because she had insisted on selecting the ball she found pretty rather than the ball that actually fit—her fingers became stuck and she'd fallen face-first onto the lane.

"Fuck," she'd screamed.

As un-Christian-like as it had been, the boys had dissolved in laughter and Keisha had broken up as well. She laid there on the alley, vibrating with laughter—a sight, then, that became funnier than the fall itself. As they both would come to discover, physical comedy was her thing. She mocked walks, did pratfalls and—when not frozen up with icy disdain—had an elastic face which one minute she'd stretch into open-mouth incredulity only to follow it moments later with crossed-eyed goofiness.

"Help me up!" she bellowed. "Help me up, godammit." She flailed and waved and thrashed like a kite trying to catch a draft. Both boys grabbed her arms and pulled, and the three of them collapsed together into the booths.

"I get a do-over," she announced, and that time she'd not even bothered with the finger holes. She sashayed up to the line and shoved the ball forward with both hands. It was a strike.

"Psyche!" she shouted. "In your face, sucker."

"All right then," Jerrold said—never a man to walk away from a challenge. Such a vain young man: He'd posed surely the way he'd seen the pros do it on ESPN on Saturday afternoons. "Let me show you how the big boys play." He rolled the ball right down the gutter; with the second ball, he'd clipped two pins on the corner.

"Uh, huh. That's what I figured. How 'bout you, Scarecrow? What you got for Keisha?"

Less an athlete even than the others had been, Craig figured being an intentional fool was his best bet, so he'd sauntered to the line and, as did bowling hams everywhere, spun around at the last minute and fired the ball between his legs. And he'd knocked down about half the pins—to his own surprise and to Jerrold's clear disgust.

"It's on now!" Keisha pronounced, and she'd offered Craig a high five.

"But don't even get cocky," she'd warned him.

"Loser takes the first door in the morning," said Jerrold, announcing the stake.

"Then it'll be an easy day for me," she said, and proceeded to best them both on the next three frames.

Her face had been wide-open for most of that long afternoon and her genuine beauty had shown through. She'd flashed her teeth as she'd teased and flirted with the boys. Despite his limited experience with such matters, Craig had picked up enough (from television mostly) to know that she'd never win awards as a coquette. What might impress as alluring on a more delicate girl came across as wooden and vulgar when Keisha attempted it. And as they came to learn that afternoon, that foul mouth also supported a viciously sharp tongue, one that wouldn't think twice about asking you to direct your beady eyes elsewhere or to get the fuck out of her face. As things went, her nasty comment about Craig's skinniness had been relatively mild, and despite his deep sensitivity about his body, he'd forgiven her. She was a street brawler, Keisha was, and she employed her best weapon—her mouth—to swing wildly at whatever happened to be in her path. She meant the things she said only to the extent that they served their purpose, which was to mark her turf and to let everyone know who they were messing with.

Even despite the rude outbursts, she'd been a pleasure to be with that afternoon. Like a plant starved for sunlight, she billowed in the light of the attention of the two young men—who teased her by calling her "Mama" and "Baby Girl" and "Miss Keisha" and "Sugar."

"Sugar: You're damn right I'm sweet, and everybody here knows it."

"I bet she was special, whoever she was," Estelle says to him.

Craig nods, fairly sure he's not been speaking aloud about the girl. He doesn't actually know what the woman knows about her friend's daughter or about his connection to her.

"As for love, here's where I stand," Estelle says, packing her things and readying to head down to her "real" office. "I'm thinking life is short and we should grab it by the bucketsful. As much as we can hold. Our lives should be absolutely full."

Craig had never felt more full of love than in that afternoon at the bowling alley. As if it were this morning he can remember sitting in the booth with his friends and the way that he had had to sit on his hands to still their vibration, so ecstatic he had been about having these people in his life.

"Ariel, darling, come here for a minute, please."

The boy looks up from where he is regaling the kids with some hilarious story that they can't get enough of. He signals his imminent arrival to his grandmother, and again it strikes Craig the way an open face can transform a person. You'd not know it was the same boy who glowered around here sometimes. But then, who knew what was real in anyone; whether it was the face shown in public, the face from the unguarded moment, or some hidden face—an almost certainly darker one—that would reveal itself without warning and at the most inopportune time? He'd thought he'd known Keisha and Jerrold, but he couldn't have been more wrong.

Toward the end of the game, the dynamic had shifted.

"Let me show you how to do that right, Sweetness," Jerrold had offered, believing despite all evidence to the contrary that he had something to offer as a bowling instructor.

"I'm all yours," she responded. She gave a little shimmy and opened her arms in welcome—a performance earning all its erotic charge from its brazen unsuitableness to this body and this girl and this audience.

After he'd wrapped his arms around her—ostensibly to "correct her stance"—he'd caught Craig's eye, that ain't-I-nasty-and-clever look boys direct to their buddies in moments such as this one.

"Like this?" Keisha asked, adjusting in one direction, "or this?" adjusting in the next.

Being naïve, it had taken Craig a moment to understand what had happened and the way their worlds had just altered course, and before he could summon a rebuttal—some smooth way of his own to let it be known that he, too, was in the game—his friends had settled together on the banquette, this time with Jerrold's arm thrown over Keisha's shoulder with clear proprietary intent, the gleam of victory in his eyes.

"No hard feelings?" Jerrold had asked, later that evening in the car. They'd dropped Keisha off first—which would be the last time that would happen. Jerrold had the hulking physicality of the sort of men who filled whatever space they occupied—by the volume of air they consumed and the way they seemed barely contained by their clothes or by the rules and strictures that governed the civil among us.

"What?" Estelle's grandson: his response to her summons, another hulk, this one. He towers over the woman—six-foot-something over her diminutive not-quite five—and his voice drips with uncalled for impatience and scorn.

Estelle doesn't bat an eye. Tough as cheap steak—else the best poker face he's seen.

"Listen, you. I need to see some progress on that presentation today. And behave. Do you hear me? Be-have."

"Whatever," the boy responds, and it's all Craig can do to not deck him. All the same, Estelle pulls him down for a goodbye kiss, and he uncharacteristically allows it. Ten minutes later, he's snoring on Craig's cot. Not my problem, thinks Craig, and he cannot even imagine how one might get a boy like this in hand.

Jerrold's exact words that night for what he'd sworn he'd do with Keisha.

"I'm going to get that young lady in hand," he'd told Craig. "You mark my words."

Craig didn't remember responding to this pronouncement. The entire day had stunned him and left him awash in a range of feelings he'd been ill equipped to deal with by his doting yet uncomplicated parents. So much pleasure and love and disappointment and envy: What on earth did people do or say in such moments? Jerrold, in any case, had not required a response and had continued on in full sermon mode.

"There's a fine Christian woman inside that girl. She'll make a fine Christian wife. She just needs some guidance, you know. The way all women do. You know what I'm saying."

A statement not a question, that was—although Craig hadn't at the time a clue what Jerrold meant. He's often chagrined these days to remember how ignorant he'd been about religion and how little he understood the principles of his chosen faith community. Comforted by fellowship, soothed by platitude, he'd signed right on—no questions asked— and disappeared into the flock.

"'A woman should learn in quietness and full submission. I do not permit a woman to teach or to have authority over a man; she must be silent.' It's in there, son. First Timothy. The problem with a lot of women is that no one ever took them in hand. I'm gonna shape her up. You mark my words." He'd reached over and patted Craig's shoulder. He'd left his hand to linger there, had rubbed it around a bit.

"Of course, we've got plans for you, too," Jerrold added.

And whatever circumspection he ought to have felt at such news had been overwhelmed by the happiness he felt at knowing he'd continue in some way to be part of the day's earlier joys.

"People *like* you, Craig Mitchell. Me: They appreciate. Or they tolerate or they give me my due, but people *like* you. They listen to you and respect you."

Another thing Craig hadn't known how to respond to. He'd been susceptible—hadn't they all been then?—to the slightest flattery, to the most meager attention and affection. He imagines he had mumbled some kind of thanks to this nonsense.

"We need you," Jerrold continued, fingers still massaging Craig's shoulder. "The church needs you. I need you. I don't think I can do this alone."

Had that been Jerrold's ambition speaking or his father's ambition speaking for him? Craig had never been privileged to the master plan, had only known that an empire had been dreamed for his friend and a plan had been in place to achieve that empire. He'd just been excited to be along for the ride. Hindsight tells him that, just like every other hormone-crazed adolescent, he'd been drunk with the excitement of his first female friendship. His first real friends of any kind, really.

But if not for Keisha, he now understands, he would have been long gone from New Purpose—would have long since lost interest in the new church and the oddly stuffy people who gathered around it. If not for her, he'd perhaps have gone ahead and enrolled at Florissant Valley, as he'd thought he might do back in high school. Kill a few years in the community college until another plan revealed itself to him. Or, who knows, maybe he'd simply have moved away from here—gone to California or New York, to those places of dreams—if not, that is, for the advent of these people and the power they'd had in his life.

If not for Jerrold, too, he had to admit. Craig might be anywhere and doing anything.

But speculation about alternatives came up short as they always did with black boys who were for whatever reason unable to imagine alternative lives. They had held out their hands, Jerrold and Keisha had, and beckoned him to come their way, so he followed them. He might have taken any hand offered, but no others had been, so he followed Keisha and Jerrold.

A brashly spirited girl, whom he'd suspected all along had not been the innocent she portrayed. A handsome and placidly ineffectual young man—one who possessed a self-confidence that Craig himself could never muster.

Diffident and skinny and nervous and geeky Craig Mitchell.

Come with us, they'd offered. They'd opened their arms and he walked into them.

Craig remembers not being able to sleep that night. Because he had never loved anyone the way he loved Keisha Williams, he didn't know if the sickness he felt was part of it or not. But he remembers not minding the ache, not nearly as much as he'd minded being unable to finish the stories about their lives together. He'd never been able to imagine much beyond the time they'd spent knocking on doors or hanging out in bowling alleys. Twenty years later and his prescience still astounds him: How, after all, could anyone imagine such an ending as Keisha had created for them all, imagine Jerrold being gone, imagine himself as an all but forgotten footnote to such a horrific tale.

He had, in fact, sometimes imagined an alternative version: he and Jerrold off running some opulent and reverent church. But then, the reality that had been Jerrold always short-circuited such fantasies. What an ignorant man he had been. Not that it had mattered much to Craig back then. All he knew was that he had two wonderful friends. He loved them both. He'd gotten on the ride willingly and believes that even knowing what he knows now he would do so again.

Except next time he'd stop the crazy bitch.

Chapter **Twenty**

Yes, Grandmother. No, Grandmother. Good night, Grandmother Birnbaum, and God bless you, too, Estelle.

The woman's really getting under his skin. He figures if this is what it's going to be like from now on, he might as well move back to Twin Oaks.

The young man will have the broccoli with that, please.

No, the young man won't.

Close that refrigerator door.

It makes an old lady sick, the way certain people chew—I didn't invest in that plush robe in order to see your giblets hanging out—and you'll drive when I'm good and ready for you to drive, and for the record, your father's the one with the insurance."

"I don't want any skulking around in there, Ariel Birnbaum. Turn off that computer, close the lights, and get a decent night's sleep. Bubbe loves you, always."

Love you too, Estelle. He won't give her the satisfaction of the spoken version of that. Maybe tomorrow. Maybe if she's not riding his ass like an infected wood tick.

What luck: nasty photos, and the color matches perfectly. He pastes Craig's head onto one with the guy sprawled on the bed with his dick in his hand. Too bad this guy is buff: Mitchell's all skin and bones. But hard to find naked brown guys. (Maybe if they saw Daniel Davis, huh?) It's the thought that counts anyway.

About midnight he cat-foots it to Estelle's door to check for her telltale snore. Estelle does a quiet rasping, the sound of someone clearing a popcorn hull from the back of her tongue, only incessant.

"Later, doll," he whispers, saluting her in the dark, and he picks his way down the stairs, avoiding with care the tread that squeaks.

He incapacitates the alarm and then wheels the ancient Schwinn through the side door of the garage, tossing the tarp he's been hiding it under onto the hood of the Lexus.

The path he's planned takes him out the cul-de-sac and up Spoede toward Olive. He again debates between the shortcut through Monsanto versus the open assault on a main thoroughfare; decides the private cops on campus just might be more vigi-

lant than the county cops. So it's Olive across Lindbergh, Old Bon-
homme to Price, Ladue until the turn off to Daniel's place. He'll
not be caught. He can't be caught. But every time a car approaches
he feels himself cowering over the bike (as if that would make him
less visible—Duh!). Good thing the sidewalks roll up around 9:00,
and the only other fools out are closing-time drunks and the night-
owl types who just have to have a Slurpee during the rerun of Leno.

The bike must have been his father's, he figures, but he can't
imagine how it survived all those years in Estelle's garage. As far
as that goes, he can't imagine his father being on a bike. And why
hadn't Estelle sold the damn thing or had it hauled away by one
of her charities? You couldn't figure with Estelle. The house is
like a magazine ad for luxury goods. If you're going to sit there
in those undies, let Grandmother open you up a garbage bag. It's
no bother—unlike re-upholstering. Of course, she did change the
upholstery every year anyway, and tucked in closets Ari'd found
remnants of various other phases of her lives. Beanie babies, a
diet book by a woman named Power, a CB radio of all things! And
maybe Estelle had had a fitness phase, or perhaps his father had
delivered the paper up and down these same rolling hills. Or had
the man even lived in this particular house? You think your only
son would know which house you'd grown up in.

It had taken a couple of days to get the bicycle back in shape.
He'd done what he could with it, but Ari's a lost cause as far as old-
school mechanics are concerned, so he'd wheeled it to the shop in
Creve Couer and told them to give it the once over. ("Damn, a vintage Schwinn! You want us to put some streamers in the handle-
bars for you?" Assholes.) But they'd gotten it together; it's ugly but
functional. He'd make better time, he imagined, if the thing didn't
weigh a ton, but it's the getting there that mattered. How long
since he'd ridden one of these? He hasn't a clue. Pushing through
pitch-black suburbs, he knows he'll be sore in the morning—can
already feel the chafing on his thighs—but that's the cost of doing
business, as Estelle herself would say.

Up ahead a county cruiser flashes through the intersection at
Dielman, and his first instinct is to run the bike up into a hedgerow,
but it's clear they're not after him. He wonders what his dad would
say if he did get hauled in on curfew. Bastard might not even show

up. He ought have made a deal with Estelle: I get busted—for anything—don't even call him. He kicks himself for not doing so.

He honestly can't recall seeing the alarm code box in Janet's house, but takes no chances: Janet Williams impressed you as the sort of woman who would blow you away with her magnum first and then call the U-City police—all the while looking for a coaster to rest the warm gun upon. Around the side he sees Danny's window cracked open, and he hunts down a stone to rouse him and get him to come open the damn door. No answer—as usual here lately.

An articulated ladder rusts against the alley garage, hidden from view by the fountaining hostas and tiger lilies. As quietly as he can he pulls it free and then dances it over to the side of the house. How did it even work? His dad, Estelle, probably every Jew in America hired shit done. But the mechanism was simple enough, so he opens the ladder full and aims the hooked end at the ledge outside Danny's window.

Or seemed simple anyway, as halfway up the bitch slides closed on him. He's on the ground, and the clatter of metal will surely send someone running his way. But no one comes, and he figures the loudest thing anyway is the stream of filth he directs at the ladder and at every other damn thing wrong with the world.

OK, then: So feet are hooks and hooks are feet and the latches with the mouse ears swing around and lock the two halves together. Two minutes later, he's up again, in the window—a regular second story man.

Except, he'd not accounted for the other side of the window, and it's dark in there and he's groping around—feeling nothing—hanging into the room with his upper torso and hanging out of it with his legs.

"What the hell," he says, and he propels himself into the bedroom like a swimmer would—feet kicking behind him for power. Which dislodges the ladder, of course, which clatters against a fence, which leaves him stranded, none of which he worries about just then because he's misjudged the distance down—it's closer than he thought—and the revolution-and-a-half tumble he's done is as humiliating as is the shoe or book or whatever it is lodged painfully against his ass.

"Son of a bitch."

And surely by now the alarms clang and the neighbors load their pistols. Estelle will pull up in the Lexus and he'll be exiled to Twin Oaks for the rest of his life. Son of a bitch, indeed.

But none of that happens.

Up on the bed, Daniel rustles quietly, turning in his sleep. Ari stays still, a moment longer, just in case, just listens to his boy. And when there are no sirens and when Janet isn't at the door, he slithers over to the bed and pulls himself onto it.

"Hey buddy," he says. "Hey." He tousles Daniel lightly, and then slightly more vigorously. Daniel moans, peels open an eye.

"Hey," Ari says again, and he starts to tell tonight's adventures, but Daniel interrupts.

"Hurry," Daniel whispers—or Ari thinks he hears hurry. He's hardly awake, Daniel is. Voice thin as tissue, nor air to ripple one.

"Come on," Daniel orders. "They're waiting. The others."

Ari doesn't know any others, but a surprisingly strong hand pulls him closer and he relaxes against his friend.

"Beautiful, aren't they?" Danny whispers.

"Sure," Ari agrees. The boy's sigh of pleasure and contentment as he relaxes against him has made this night worth it—all the chafing and scrapes and tumbles and risk. He holds him for a very long time.

Everything's in place, he tells his boy. He's all set up for the big take down.

You could tell with guys. Some guys. The way they looked at you. Sideways, kinda. Half smirky, a flash of something in their eyes. (At least he thinks that's what it means.)

You know the guys: Scout leaders. Priests. Soccer coaches.

The Craig Mitchells of the world.

Like bank robbers, they are—they go where the money is. A day, a couple more days at most, and he's all mine. I'll time it so Estelle catches him rubbing on me. Watch that money dry up like Estelle's baked chicken.

And, if that doesn't work, there'll be a nice surprise waiting for him during Estelle's slide show. That'll bring in the donations.

Daniel's way off in his own world—doesn't seem much interested in Ari's brilliant plans—but Ari is restless and excited with a prospect of revenge. So off he goes: some exploratory fun. Might as well.

"Back soon," he says, tucking Daniel away in the top sheet.

Janet Williams sleeps bolt upright in her bed, a book (it appears she's made zero progress in) dangling precariously from her hips. She stirs and Ari ducks from the doorframe and the book tumbles to the floor. As it happens, a minor adjustment only for Janet, and when Ari's brave enough to look again he sees she's moved just the slightest bit, has lolled her head to the opposite side, so that the stream of drool runs west now instead of east. The lamp there on the nightstand must be blocked from the outside by blackout curtains, the same ones Estelle has on her windows. (He'd bet they bought them at the same time: "Two for one: They'll deal!") He'd noted no light from here when he'd cased the joint—and he kind of liked that phrase, with all its connotations of Ari, the professional badass, and for a moment—just a moment—he entertains the idea of sidling over to that chest-of-drawers and of rummaging around in it for . . . What? Diamonds, maybe? A couple of hundred in loose bills?

Instead, boldly, he approaches Janet and retrieves the book to a more stable place on the bed—a trashy bestseller it is. Not much of a reader, according to her grandson: the sort of person who bought the books that she heard she was supposed to be reading and then threw them out if they didn't match the wallpaper. Janet Williams would die, he knew, him seeing her like this: makeup free, wrapped in terry cloth, rolled and trussed in every kid of curler. It's where Daniel got his vanity, right here in this bed—Daniel, his Danny. A boy who fussed over invisible scuffs on the heels of his shoes and would stay in the house rather than be seen in an imperceptibly wrinkled shirt.

How pretty she must have been—another gift to her grandson: the flawless skin and the wide, flat nose with its delicately hooped nostrils. How pretty she is—curlers and drool be damned.

And she looks so uncomfortable, slumped like that. Poppa Hillyer would be found this way, more often than not: sound asleep in one of the chairs in his grandmother's living room. Why don't you lie down, Poppa? he'd ask, and Poppa would say he was just being vigilant. You had to keep an eye out—and don't you forget it, sonny boy.

More than anything what Ari wants to do right now is to rear-range the pillows and lay her back on her bed, gather her bedding, make sure she's cozy. It's not his place, however: What is she to him, after all? The mother of the mother of the person that he loves. He's not sure that gives you rights.

What he can do is take care of that empty coffee cup. Make sure that everything's in good shape for their morning. He knows they'll be busy.

He gathers the cup and an empty water glass and then collects enough tableware from Daniel's room to dress the windows at the Pottery Barn. He wipes a ring from beneath a carafe of wa-ter, oblivious that this action would be the unconscious trigger for what would be the most powerful moment of déjà vu he would experience in his life. Many years later, in a hotel at a Mexican resort where he and Daniel had gathered for a summer vacation with their grown children, picking up a sweating carafe of water and wiping away the ring with his hand he'd be gobsmacked by the feeling he'd lived the moment before.

Downstairs he feels his way forward like the stereotypical zom-bie, remembering with feet and extended fingers the way this world has been arranged. Appointed like a palace and camera-ready at all times: A showplace! exclaims Estelle. Here is the leather wingback and just in front of it the hassock that allows Janet to lounge com-fortably. Here is the candlestick lamp—which boldly he switches on. Tuesday's stack of mail nests on the arm of the sofa—so busy they have been these two they have not even taken time to sort through. Ari feels not one tinge of guilt over fingering through the circulars and catalogs and credit card solicitations. By force of habit he crumples the "have you seen me?" flyer and takes it to the kitchen to be tossed.

Time for a snack. In the refrigerator he finds the remnants of a salami that Estelle had thrown in the morning basket a week or so back. And there's some of that smoked Gouda. He does a rudimen-tary search for crackers, but finding none he decides to dig right in. He gnaws a chunk of salami—fuck a knife. And he knows where those crackers are, too—and he wonders if he's up for a life with a person who leaves crumbs in the bed.

The salami is good plain—Estelle and her dang basket. You had to love her.

"I think these people are perfectly capable of going to the grocery store," he'd grumbled to her the last time she'd dropped one by. She looked at him as if he were crazy and ordered him to ring the bell.

It's a crapshoot: Some mornings they're here, some mornings they're gone. Even if they catch them, they're always on the go.

"Gotta run," Janet will cheer, listing the day's destination: this museum or that history center or some other science museum. Daniel always shrugs and loads his and Janet's supplies for the day—says to humor the old girl—she's just feeling bad about her crazy ass daughter. The two of them disappear once again. Who knew there was so much to see in the Midwest?

"What about me?" he'd asked Estelle last week after yet another futile drive-by. She'd again looked at him as if he were an idiot.

"Patience," she'd encouraged.

Patience my ass. If he cannot spend the day with Danny, he can spend the night.

He empties his snack dregs into the garbage—which is full, of course. So he runs it out to the big bin, just outside the mudroom, where it's ready to be rolled to the curb. He folds his grandmother's festive red plaid dishtowels and then places the basket by the front door to be exchanged for the next one (which he, ironically enough to him, will switch on an upcoming drive-by sometime later this week).

It's coming on 4:30 and Estelle will be up in time for *Morning Edition*. His time is running short, he knows. He pages through a fashion magazine on the counter. A seedy perfume ad gives him a great idea for a photo of a slide show—so it's off to the S & M sites for just the right body to crib. He rifles through a stack of catalogs.

You're snooping, Ariel: That's what Estelle would say.

So sue me already.

Janet Williams by all evidence is one of those ladies who liked to shop the catalogs. Just like his mother—a woman who, being queen of all things medical in the Western Hemisphere, did not have time to spend in an actual store with actual other humans.

In the center of the kitchen island he spies a letter for Daniel—from the College Board—and for Ari finding it feels like some sort of punishment from God, and he can't even imagine what he's done to deserve this temptation. It's all he can do to not stick his finger under this flap and check out those preliminary scores, and it *is* sort of his right, really, isn't it? OK, so he already knows the answer—and if they aren't perfect, then poor Janet Williams is in for more than a bit of unpleasantness. Logic, which is derailed by the memory of his father's non-response to his own perfect scores earlier this week.

("No surprise there, I guess.")

The angel bests the devil this time, and Ari takes the letter upstairs to deliver personally.

"Hey. Hey, buddy."

A sigh-ish moan or a moan-ish sigh from Daniel.

"But we could stay here," he mumbles.

"I bet this says you'll be going anywhere you want." He places the letter inside the laptop on Daniel's desk. He so wants to wake this boy, but he seems to be relishing this sleep.

Ari drops down next to his friend, reaches down and holds his hand, kissing it, then massaging it.

It's perverse to Ari that love should hurt this way. His heart feels wrenched like a sodden towel—twisted and drained of every ounce of life. If he stays here another minute he will never leave this place.

"I've got to go," he tells Daniel, "but I'm coming every day, OK? I promise. Every night, I'll always be here for you."

"Come every day. Don't forget."

"I won't. We'll figure it out. I promise"

"We already had mostaccioli."

"Looks like you guys had lots of good food. But I'll get Estelle to bring us some."

"She doesn't like it when we play in here. Let's go out, OK?"

"We'll go out. I promise."

Ari kisses his forehead, says "Later," which agitates Daniel's sleep somehow.

"Don't," Daniel begs. "Come back."

Outside, the first blush of dawn backlights the trees. It will take a bunch of luck of a kind he's never possessed to climb those stairs before Estelle climbs down for her morning coffee.

He soothes the boy's brow, and when Daniel finally stills a bit,

Ari slides away.

Backtracking, the hills feel like mountains, and had he not known Estelle would send him packing he'd have called her himself and demanded a ride. Has he ever been this tired?

Just then he is crushed with the weight of all that sadness in the Williams house.

Bloody fucking hell. And goddamn you Craig Mitchell. Dead babies, a whole bunch of other lives ruined, and somehow you get to skate.

You'll know when it's time, Poppa Hillyer said. And when it's time, take your stand. Be ready.

But, so many of them, Poppa. How do we fight?

One at a time, sonny boy. We fight them one at a time. We start with the ones who hurt our family.

But how will we know when they come?

Sonny boy, you'll know them when you see them. As common as crows and just as obvious and vulgar. You'll know when it hurts your heart.

It hurts. My heart.

Then you know. No turned cheeks next time.

No turned cheeks, I promise.

He covers the bike and the lawnmower and lets himself back into the laundry room. Upstairs, floorboards creak and the muted sound of public radio news filters down the steps. The automatic coffee maker drips its last few ounces, and he is ten minutes too late to pretend to have been asleep, neither does he care. Let her do her worst.

And just when he's set to surrender he hears her voice—the morning call to his father, of course—a saving grace, and who'd have thunk it.

You've not forgotten your vitamins, Aaron, darling. They work you so hard at that hospital, you poor thing.

A little indigestion is all—the usual, no biggie. We ate Mexican last night—the boy insisted, so there you go.

Yes. Yes. A lovely place. On Olive. Authentic—real Spanish people in there and everything.

What did I say?

What did I say?

So. So it's Mexican. So report me to the Post Dispatch. *How's my granddaughter?*

Mother doesn't like the sound of that.

She's a tough customer, that one. Don't let her fool you.

He's fine.

Yes, I said he's fine. He's a good boy, Aaron.

Yes, I'd tell you. And you took your supplements. Just a second: Ariel Birnbaum, the shower should be running now. Don't make me come in there.

"Yeah. Whatever." He fills his voice with phlegm to sound groggy.

I swear he's just like you, Aaron: Mr. Sleepyhead, that one. You took the zinc, sweetheart, you're sure? And the fish oil. You can't be too careful. Am I right?

Am I right?

Tell Mother she's right.

Well, of course I am.

Have the tuna today at the hospital. No deli meats. Promise Mother.

OK, Love.

OK, sweetheart.

Mother loves you, too. Talk to you in the morning.

Love you.

"Love you too, Estelle."

Chapter **Twenty-One**

It chagrined Craig, the rush of thrill he felt when Ari opened the door for his grandmother. Alas, it isn't the lovely company of his friend Estelle that catches him up each morning; rather it is the possibility that the other boy will arrive again with these friends. It's the thrill of anticipation he imagines the gambler must feel waiting for that final card to turn.

Today, as is so often the case at the blackjack table, anticipation gives way to disappointment. It's Ari and Estelle only—as it has been for the past month or so. Neither does Estelle have time today to share a visit over coffee.

"Rushed off my feet, my darlings," she announces. She thrusts a tote bag in Craig's direction and yanks her grandson's head down in order to smack her lips against his cheek. "Be good," she orders. Ari Birnbaum grumbles and rolls his eyes and drags himself over to where the women are setting up breakfast. He grabs an armload of cereal boxes and takes them to the table where the little ones await his service. He knows the routines as well as any of them.

Craig hauls the tote bag and his disappointment back to the alcove; feels like a fool for feeling this disappointed—disappointment about something he neither controls nor has any reason to expect will happen. Those few weeks earlier this summer with Daniel Davis had been merely an unexpected boon, a windfall. That the boy might ever be a part of his life again . . . well, only a fool would imagine such a thing.

Donette has arranged an outing for the families—to the children's garden and to a picnic in the park. Estelle had been begged (or more likely had volunteered) to spring for a bus and admission fees. Ariel Birnbaum lugs boxes of sandwiches and jugs of lemonade out to the sidewalk and passes them up to Donette, who is arranging food and people into seats. When everyone and everything is loaded, Craig watches Donette flirt with Ari, cajoling him to climb the steps to the bus.

"I'll see you when I see you, Baby," Ari shouts, just before the doors flap shut. He waves the group on their way and turns back toward the door of the center. Craig watches what looks like genuine delight dissolve into something more sinister.

Great: Look what I get to spend the day with.

"Thought you'd go with the kids," he prompts.

"Thought I'd stay here with you," Ari responds.

Discomfited by Ari's sneer, Craig turns on his heel and heads to the office. Quiet days such as these are rare to nonexistent, and he relishes the opportunity to focus down and move some of the unrelenting paper off his desk. He hears Ari clomping along behind him, figures maybe if he ignores him he'll go find some way to amuse himself. No such luck. As Craig sorts through the various piles of paper on his desk, he can feel Ari's eyes on his back, hear him back there, breathing thickly.

"Where is your friend these days?" Craig asks.

"I'm his keeper, huh?"

This is what passes for a response. He was in some sort of a mood today, Ari, but wasn't he always? The lug had no more sense of civil discourse than a child raised by wolves. How many times already this summer had Craig had to rebuke the boy for the way he'd spoken to his grandmother?

"He's well, I hope?" Craig prompts. Perhaps a bit of persistence . . . They've played this scene about once a week since the other boy stopped coming to work. Craig figures one of these days he'll catch Ari in a charitable mood, but today is not to be that day.

"If you're so interested . . ." is his standard response, and Craig is fairly positive Ari knows that, no, *he* cannot call; is also sure that Ari knows the reasons why that is true. Nothing that Ari or his grandmother have said this summer would confirm this belief that they know his connection to Danny's mother, but he feels in his gut that it is true. One mention of Craig's name to Danny's grandmother and that would have been that. Janet Williams's hatred for everything even remotely affiliated with the New Purpose Temple of Faith would never cool. Clearly Estelle had told her who her grandson's boss was, and while he didn't know much about the Williams woman, he was pretty sure she'd sooner the boy do almost anything else rather than spend time with the likes of him.

"So," Ari says, lingering in the door. He's one of those people who talked in shorthand. One-word phrases, grunts, head nods. The arrogant assumption: that the rest of us owned the same codebook.

'Sup.

Hey.

Humph.

So.

In this case "so" means: "So what do you want done, Dude?" and to Craig's chagrin he has spent enough time with this horrible person to have mastered his private language.

"That floor out there . . ." Craig shakes his head and blows an exaggerated whistle through his teeth. "If you don't mind." A person practically had to peel his shoe up after every step. Things got away from them around here, often enough routine maintenance. "Full time custodian," he sketched onto Estelle's list, forty some items and growing by the hour.

"Sure thing," the boy chirps. A bad actor this one: cannot quite muster the fake delight at having just been ordered to swab a filthy all-purpose room. Ari was one of those young men who despite his best efforts wore his true feelings the same way a clown wore whiteface. Large and expressive brown eyes he had—eyes that tended to flash with anger or water over easily whenever his emotions would be stoked, which seemed to happen with some frequency. Joy, pleasure, happiness: These by all evidence were hard to find in his life, and the fake-ass warm smiles here recently had been readily betrayed by the cold contempt in his eyes.

All things considered, Craig imagines he prefers this young man's naked resentment to Jerrold Davis's inexpressive cool. Danny's father's face most often betrayed absolutely nothing, neither pleasure nor anger nor confusion. And yet, it proved to be a mistake to confuse that equanimity with lack of interest. He could hug and he could lash out, too; both would come quick and neither could be predicted. The troubled and dark side of his friend as it emerged had surprised Craig; he'd not anticipated Jerrold's violent rages.

He had blackened Keisha's eye only the one time of which Craig had been aware. That there might have been others seemed likely, but Craig had no evidence to support that belief. He noticed the bruise at a New Year's Eve party at Jerrold's parents' house in St. Charles. Keisha had made a valiant attempt with her makeup, but she'd been new to the cosmetic arts, and because New Purpose held vanity (at least in women) in the same esteem they did Hollywood films, there'd been no one around to demonstrate the technique for concealing unsightly discolorations. (Where had Janet Williams been, he has often wondered. Had she not known? Or perhaps she simply hadn't cared.) Keisha did the best she could, however, and those who didn't know her might assume she had slept badly or, ironically enough, misapplied her mascara. Maybe Craig had been the only one present that night who had recognized the dark shadow for what it was. He'd approached her to ask her if everything was all right.

"Fine," she'd responded, in that tight-lipped way she had of dismissing people she'd rather not be bothered with. Her eyes had communicated the opposite of fine, but pressing the girl seemed ill advised. Jerrold had hovered all night, leaving little opportunity for private conversation. Now and again he'd catch Craig's eye and an I-told-you-so sparkle would be flashed in Craig's direction, leaving him to feel both guilt as well as complicity in the girl's suffering.

At midnight they'd gathered with their glasses of sparkling cider and welcomed 1988. Jerrold's father had an announcement to make.

"In appreciation of all his hard work, as of this new year Reverend Brickell has promoted our Jerrold to the position of Assistant Pastor." A round of "Hallelujahs" and a few Praise Jesus-es. Jerrold stood at the center of the circle, Keisha's hand folded into his; him, bathed in love and admiration; she looking sheepish and uncomfortable, the expression of someone discovered browsing the wrong books in the wrong kind of bookstore.

"He's pretty much our minister-in-waiting, is what he is," the father bragged, and the man had oozed the arrogant pride of any father whose long-standing dream had finally come true. "Not that we wish our dear reverend ill, but . . ." and a hearty chuckle passed through the room—an appropriately subdued one, as none gathered wanted to seem overly eager for Jerrold's inevitable rise to the throne.

Even at the time, it had occurred to Craig to want to ask about the formal training that even he knew many ministers received. What about seminary or divinity school or . . . hell, even some kind of correspondence course? But it had been the wrong time and these the wrong people for such questions. As was often the case back then, at any social gathering, everyone with the exception of Craig and Keisha would be part of the extended Davis clan—people who also formed the core of the early New Purpose community, people for whom this announcement had been extra sweet. They clapped and cheered and hugged their boy, who reveled in being admired as well as adored. Theirs had been the unconditional joy of the triumphant; the not quite secret vanity of the blue-ribbon winner who in the photo of herself and her banana cream pie is unable to conceal her belief in the supremacy of her wares. And despite knowing the emperor had no clothes, Craig had shaken his friend's hand and congratulated him on his success.

"You deserve it," he lied. Each outing with Jerrold revealed the young man as more the empty suit than the one preceding it. What Craig had believed six months earlier to be a discourse limited by faith had in fact been closed in by Jerrold's very real limitations. He'd talked about nothing but Jesus because there had been nothing else in his head. He was simple—in surprising ways, he was. He didn't know, for example, the most rudimentary things about food—that ice cream was made from cow's milk or whether chicken was meat or dairy. ("It's a different color. Than hamburger, I mean. So I wasn't sure.") What he did know was how to wear a nice suit and to look good in it while he said all the right things to his elders and betters. He could stand in that pulpit and call out to his personal savior in his uplifting tenor, that unexpectedly musical voice of his that might even have softened those structural steel beams that arced above the new sanctuary. And he knew who to have next to him to complete the illusion. He knew when to step aside and allow Craig to deliver the substance of the sermon or to bear the heart of the witness.

"It's you and me all the way, brother," he'd said in response to Craig's congratulations—which, for what it's worth, had been genuine. Disillusionment came later; cynicism later still. As for love: It wasn't the blindness that got you, it was the stupidity, and he'd managed to persuade himself that night—even as Jerrold winked at him and even as Keisha stiffened her shoulders to suppress a cringe—that surely she must have bumped into the bedpost or walked into an open cabinet. The alternative had been unthinkable, so he embraced the version that offered the greatest comfort.

He saw it all the time here at the shelter.

"It's Not What It Looks Like": The abused woman's theme song.

And of course it almost always was and is; and had he been a man and stepped up . . .

But he had not been, and now he has a large and obnoxious teenager leering at him from the doorway

"Mind if I get comfortable?" Ari asks. A few minutes with the mop and he's already dripping with sweat, and before waiting for Craig's answer and with all the finesse of a seasoned porn star, he strips down to his wife beater (unfortunate name in this place), tossing his denim shirt on Craig's bed.

"You know where I am," he said, strutting off with the mop.

Unbidden, the word "sleazy" wanders through Craig's brain. He realizes that should Jerrold Davis walk in this room right this minute, that same word would no doubt cross his mind. That he hadn't thought so back in the day was symptomatic of the entire mess. Everything at New Purpose had been upside-down, although at the time he'd had only the vaguest notion. Community meant shunning the outside world. Fellowship meant abandoning your family. Family meant using your fist. And no, he hadn't been blind to those distortions: It was the language that got in the way.

"It's right here in the Book," they'd hector, and while not the brightest bulb in the store, Jerrold had possessed an uncanny ability to dredge up the exact chapter and verse to justify his every mood.

"'And the woman shall be the helpmate of the man.' It says right here": the quote he'd thrown in Craig's face the one time he'd dared approach him about his treatment of the girl.

Possibly he'd have been more diligent in protecting Keisha had his own circumstances not turned. In the fall of '88, early in November, Shirley Mitchell succumbed to her pulmonary disorder, his father following in quick succession. It was his heart, the doctor had told Craig, who had already known that. Of course it had been broken, losing the love of his life, a woman he'd shared a bed with for more than four decades. They'd lost hope of having a child, and then Craig had come along, a mid-life baby, the great miracle of their lives. They'd been bonded, the three of them, in that way unique to older parents and their late arrivals. It was love, but it was a lonely love—like being on a lifeboat in the middle of the sea. The sea too big, the boat too small; the fear of being left behind, the fear of being found—because God knew what else might be out there in the world and isn't it so much better right here with just us? To Craig's great shame, he had abandoned them first—sulking away into the world of the New Purpose Temple of Faith. Perhaps they had merely reciprocated.

"We're your family now," Jerrold said, less an offer than a direction. Benumbed with grief, he'd allowed the young minister to wrest the services from his parents' beloved Shiloh Temple. New Purpose filled one evening with the celebration of the life of a man that almost none of them had known while he was alive.

Later, after the burial and the wake, after he'd wrapped the last pans of food and stowed them away in the refrigerator of his parents' home, the bell rang and he opened the door to Keisha. There was no sign of Jerrold (and he had never learned how she had gotten herself to his house).

She threw her arms around him and began sobbing—something she'd not done at either of his parents' services.

"I'm so sorry," she wailed. "So very sorry."

He held her and thanked her and told her it was OK. "They're in a better place now," he assured her, repeating the obnoxious platitude that had been offered him repeatedly over the past month. It hadn't seemed to help her any more than it helped him: On she sobbed. "I don't know what I would do if she left me," she whimpered, and Craig assured her that would never happen.

"She'll always be there. Don't you worry about that."

They sat on the broken-down sofa in the living room and she allowed him to keep an arm around her even after she had relaxed into his side. Life with Keisha meant allowing certain ironies to slide by uncommented upon—such as that of him comforting her on the day his own father had been put into the ground. He hadn't read it as selfishness on her part; her grief had been genuine, he could tell. The very idea of being forsaken seemed intolerable to the girl—a truth that made her future actions only that much more inexplicable.

"You'll need help sorting their things," she offered, and stood to lead the way into his parents' bedroom.

He remembers how taken aback he'd been by this. He'd been a dry-eyed stoic during the ordeal—the trial of both funerals, actually, very much his father's son in that respect—but her uncharacteristic initiative and generosity had done him in.

"I . . . can't . . ." he'd stammered, unable to even tell her how heartbreakingly impossible he found the idea of settling the humble affairs of the people he loved, and he had broken down for the first time. His was a choking, violent cry, one he has surrendered to few times in his life: on that night and then again on that other night six short years later.

(Those tiny, tiny coffins: God in heaven!)

"Let me look," Keisha had offered, caressing his shoulder. He sat alone in the quiet house and listened to her open and close closets and drawers; him hurt and ashamed, remembering all the times over the past few months when he'd come in, giddily high from the enjoyment of his friends. Here they'd be, Eugene and Shirley Mitchell. Sitting. Just sitting. Him on this couch, her in that chair. Companionable. Silent.

Hey there, son.

Did you have a good day?

A love that crushed and smothered him so that he often could not breathe in that house. One day you came in and it was gone. How could that be? How did it just evaporate like that? Where did it go and how would you ever find it again?

Keisha remained in his parents' bedroom for a long time, and when he went to see why, he found her in the bed, her dress arrayed carefully over the back of a chair, her other garments on the seat.

"Come on," she said, patting the sheet beside her. Neither a command, nor had there been anything alluring or seductive about her directive.

His memory of that evening has nothing to do with sexual pleasure nor even of the sensation of skin on skin or the co-mingling of their scents, their mutual breath. In place of the long-anticipated thrill of discovery came a dislocation in time and place. For a moment he'd not known who he was or who this woman above him on the bed could be, and when he did know them he imagined their fully-grown, perhaps middle-aged selves. Keisha would grow into one of the formidably solid women one often encountered in the teller's cage at the bank or running the office at the local elementary school. He'd remain lean and lanky his entire life, and they'd enjoy taking cruises together or driving off in the car to the kind of low-key resorts where every restaurant is an all-you-can-eat buffet.

She hadn't rushed away that night; even so, her departure had an abrupt and premature feeling about it. She had shaken her way into her clothes, and when it became clear that she had nothing to say, he'd asked, "What now?"

"What now what?" had been her response, offered with all the standard Keisha cold-eyed contempt. He'd said nothing else to her. He heard her pull the front door closed behind her and he rolled over and fell asleep.

Weeks later, the holiday season: customary time for Davis family announcements. They'd been gathered again in the large basement room that Mrs. Davis with no sense of irony insisted be called "the rathskeller."

"I've asked this very special young lady to marry me, and she's agreed to make me the happiest man in the world."

Keisha had allowed herself to be drawn into Jerrold for one of those sideways hugs—a rather risqué display among members of a church who disdained public displays of affection. A kiss would have been out of the question. From somewhere she'd mustered up the semblance of a smile.

"You'll be best man, of course," Jerrold proclaimed, drawing Craig into the trio. Flashbulbs popped and once again praise had been offered for the provident gift of the impending union.

Later, while Jerrold entertained his aunts with a hearty round of carols, Craig managed a minute alone with her. She'd avoided him entirely since their night together, off always with one or another of the women who had moments earlier become her future in-laws (or at least according to Jerrold she had been).

She'd stationed herself behind a punch bowl, docilely ladling out paper cups full of the insipid fruit punch served at all Davis/New Purpose occasions. She'd been surrounded by a herd of the littlest members of the clan, all of whom had been pleased to have someone attend to their thirst. It had been a warm December evening and the little ones had been in and out of the patio doors, chasing each other around the spacious backyard.

"So cute," she'd simpered, smiling at one of the nieces, and he remembers being unsure of her sincerity. Her face had seemed earnest, but as a response to the quotidian, "cute" hadn't ever been part of her repertoire.

"What the hell, Keisha?"

She'd scanned him up and down with her eyes, coolly, as if he were some stranger walked up to her in a bar: disdainful and dismissive. Across the wood-paneled basement, over beyond the pool table and the sitting area where Mrs. Davis sometimes held her women's Bible reading group, Keisha's fiancé belted out an overwrought version of "O Holy Night." The blond-wood upright piano had been ever so slightly out of tune but could barely be heard anyway over the resounding vocals of the groom-to-be.

"You can't marry him."

"What are you, my mama now?"

He didn't know what he was to her. What rights did that give you, putting your penis in a person? Who was to say that he owed this woman anything?

But they were connected. The great curse of his life, that would be.

He opened his mouth to speak again, but she anticipated the words just as he found them.

"This isn't about you," she scolded, but mildly, barely disturbing her simper. He sometimes wonders if what he'd sensed at the time to be compassion in that scold had been something closer to triumph.

"But I would take care of you," he remembers mumbling, and to her credit she hadn't scoffed at the feebleness of his plea. What she had done was to pull her lips into a tight, false smile—the way people did when humoring small children.

"It needs to be someone stronger than me." She poured two glasses of punch for one of the aunts come over from the piano.

"Bless you, child," the older woman had said. It had always been clear to Craig that they had never quite approved of the girl. None of the Davises had. She'd come to them coarse, was too large, and not nearly pretty enough. Nothing like the fair-skinned, long-tressed goddess they'd always imagined would someday wed their golden child and become First Lady of the New Purpose Temple of Faith.

"They don't even like you," he'd grumbled in a way that even he knew sounded petulant.

"They never do," had been her reply. The determined resolve in her voice masked the bitterness he knew must also be there.

"Oh night divine!" Jerrold bellowed, and after not-too-humbly accepting his applause, he began staggering in their direction, drunk, clearly, on something other than the punch. He had that way about him: So overcome by happiness or by the delight of simply being Jerrold he would lurch about and glad-hand everyone within his reach.

Sensing it might be his last chance, Craig had turned to Keisha, but again his thoughts had been intercepted.

"I know you will," she said.

He wondered if she'd known how hard he'd tried to keep that promise.

"My two favorite people," Jerrold enthused. He grabbed them both and kissed them both on the lips. "The Three Musketeers, forever!"

Well, hardly.

Sometimes he cannot recall Jerrold's face—only the bear-like physicality of him. Frequently his parents fade, too—which makes him sad—but when he prays, it's them he sees, prayer as much an exercise in memory as anything else.

Keisha, well he'd mostly like to forget that face, but she is imprinted on him like a fresh tattoo. She's always there, often enough with the expression she'd offered him when he'd promised he "had her back": simultaneously defiant and vulnerable it had been.

Ari Birnbaum comes shlumping into his office. "Bet you can smell me, huh?"

Craig looks up from the computer into which he is entering Estelle's list. The boy, glossy as a seal, drains ribbons of sweat onto the floor. As a matter of fact, Craig can smell him—although he's unsure what kind of question that is. The boy raises his arm and tucks his own head into his pit and audibly sniffs. He wrinkles his nose the way wine snobs do when they're trying to pin down the peculiar bouquet of a discount chardonnay.

"Ripe," Ari pronounces, and the look on his face Craig sees is the same look he sees boys this age give their girlfriends after they flick a booger in her direction.

"You finished out there?" he asks, not willing to pursue whatever the hell Ari's line of conversation portends, but Ari is undaunted.

"Summer funk and body spray: nectar of the gods."

What is that, Craig wonders: a sneer or a grimace or is he constipated or what? Time to divert:

"You never mentioned when your friend might be coming back."

"Didn't I?" Ari responds. He glares at Craig and before strutting off to the pantry runs his hands up and down his sodden body as if checking for lumps. Whatever its intended effect, it causes in Craig a wave of nausea.

Craig had cradled this boy's friend on the night he'd been born, Jerrold handing him the newborn the minute the nurses wrapped him and pronounced him a bundle of health. He'd never held a baby before and at first he'd been intimidated, but he found himself quickly relaxing and settling into what would be his role for the next five years.

"Hey, little buddy."

"His name is Daniel," Keisha snapped. By all evidence delivery had left her in a foul mood, albeit a benign one as far as Keisha's bad moods were concerned.

"Hello, Daniel." So tiny, he had been. So calm.

One of the aunts stuck her head in the door.

"The last thing I need," Keisha grumbled. "Them bitches snooping around here and I've just had my insides ripped out."

"You better check yourself," Jerrold grumbled back at her. All the same, he worked his magic to hustle the gathering throng from the door. Craig heard him in the hall, charming them with his tale of the rush to the hospital and tantalizing them with the promise of the baby, who would be visiting them any minute now, just give us a minute to get things cleaned up in there.

All the cleaning and such had been done before Craig had been admitted to the room. He sat in the chair by the bed and offered Daniel to Keisha. She scoffed but then smiled weakly and pulled the baby to her, her face full of fascination and fear.

"I can't believe he's finally here," Craig said, unable to stop staring at those sleepy brown eyes and at those tiny, tiny fingers.

"Why? It's not like he's yours."

Typical Keisha graciousness. She'd gotten consistently less charming since the engagement party. More accurately, she ricocheted between flat-eyed blankness and a harder-edged rendering of her usual sharp-tongued, sullen self. Unpleasantness aside, he preferred the feisty girl in the bed to the zombie version of her.

"Are you happy?" he asked her.

"Another motherfucker wants to tell me how I should feel. Don't I look happy?"

"You know, the Lord says . . ."

"Don't. Don't even." That hatred in her eyes she usually reserved for her husband, so he raised his hands in surrender and rose to wish her well and to take his leave. She'd worn him out again, as she often had over the past year. Often enough he would decide to walk away forever. It just wasn't worth it: the hateful faces, the verbal abuse, the mean-spirited snarkiness about everything and everyone, dealt out only because she felt like it and because she could. But as she often did she somehow sensed his leaving and she stopped him.

"Don't go," she said—an order really. "Don't leave me here with them."

So he stayed and watched—as he had often done over the previous year—as she played the role of dutiful wife, daughter-in-law, good churchwoman, and, now, mother. She offered the baby up to the Davises, gently admonishing each when it was time to share the wealth.

"Give Grandpa a turn," she'd purr, and around the circle Daniel went. That they noticed the cynical gleam in her eyes, he doubted. It was for him, he knew. See what a bad girl I am. See how I've got them fooled.

Fooled? Well, maybe. To be honest, Craig didn't believe they saw her at all. For the Davis family, she was a cipher. An inconvenience at best—just a questionable choice on their Jerrold's part, one that with any luck would disappear the way summer colds did: quietly, often in the night, and with little evidence of ever having been present. All the same, throughout the betrothal and well into Danny's first year, as far as Keisha was concerned it was her game and she had the home field advantage.

Shortly after Danny'd been born, Craig happened upon Keisha in the garden outside the church, casually puffing away on her cigarette and even more casually gliding the stroller back and forth, with her foot.

"I don't think your husband would approve," he'd told her, for which he got the finger as a reply. He reached into the carriage and lifted Danny into his arms.

"Am I missing anything?" she asked, nodding back at the church. Tuesday nights were organizational, and the various New Purpose committees met to plan fellowship or organize the ushers or select music for the choir. As future First Lady, she'd be expected, of course, to play an active role in the running of the place; alas, she'd already demonstrated her lack of leadership potential. She'd be one of those women forever placed behind the steam table, a dollop of green beans on every tray—and heaven forbid someone else not be standing by with the refill. She'd not know what to do should she run out.

So, no, she hadn't missed a thing, neither was she missed—and he told her so, despite being pretty sure she already knew it. She'd pretend not to care, but she was hardly stupid. She knew well the importance of appearances at New Purpose, and had there been even the remotest chance someone might come looking for her, she'd not have parked herself in that shoddy little garden, brazenly indulging in the forbidden weed. Even so, he pushed her on it.

"I'm not sure what you think you're playing at," he said.

Her habit since the engagement party had been to cut him dead with her eyes and then pretend he'd said nothing to her at all, but for some reason on this particular night she took him on.

"I'm not going to tell you again. I know what I'm doing."

He nodded at her—not to agree, but to acknowledge the ever-present Keisha self-confidence. Frustrating as hell and misdirected at almost every turn, but certainly not to be denied. He rocked the baby in his arms and made goo-goo noises at it. What a sweet baby he had been.

"You think you know me and my husband, but you don't know anything."

"I know that you're unhappy a lot of the time."

She crushed the cigarette with the same foot that had rocked the carriage, a foot shod in the inelegant, clunky-heeled shoes the New Purpose sisters preferred. Around them the dispiriting garden struggled into spring life. "The Contemplative Grotto" they called it, but all the garden put him in mind of was the problem black folks had maintaining their lawns.

"Jerrold says I need to pray more, is all. Says it's the demons in me. He says if I pray more and I come proper when I talk to him, I'll be released and everything will change. You believe that, don't you?"

For a moment he'd been unsure which "him" had been the referent of her sentence. Most days back then he did believe something of the kind. But hadn't it been just like Keisha to leverage her predicament on someone else's faith?

The baby blew spit bubbles and burbled. Craig smiled at it. "I think you are who you are," he told both of them.

"Just fine the way I am, huh?"

"If you're fine with you. That's all that matters."

She waved her hand at him and pinched her brow, something she'd never done in the past, and he'd wondered if that was something her mother did when she was upset—gather the skin above the bridge of her nose and pinch.

"You know what? Fuck you, Craig Mitchell. And that's the demons talking, in case you're interested."

For some reason at that moment he lifted the baby to his face and kissed it in the same place its mother had been pinching herself. With the clunky shoe, she shoved the stroller in his direction.

"Do us a favor and take this whole mess inside. Mama's got some praying to do." She fished the cigarettes from the diaper bag and tossed that his way as well.

In his pious moments, he believes that it had been a battle with the demons he'd watched those next five years. On the dark days there'd be the Keisha of the garden—in your face and obnoxiously so. When the angels won, the Keisha who emerged sat obediently on the front pew, a placid but vacant smile on her face. Toward the end it had been angels all the way, or so it had seemed. But it was an illusion.

Anymore he didn't have many pious days; hadn't had them in a long time. That kind of piety was for children, and surely part of growing up had been learning to appreciate the gray in what he'd been taught was a black and white world.

He couldn't exactly say how it was that Jerrold had broken the girl—this despite having watched it happen. Yes, he'd known of the heavy hand, of course, but there'd been something more to it. Something deep, something more treacherous.

Perhaps it had been sexual. When the spirit struck him (as it too often did), Jerrold offered sophomoric reports on his masculine prowess and his wife's insatiability.

"She's all over that shit, my man. Yowls like a cat and keeps me working *all* night."

The babies, a testament to that industry, arrived like clockwork. (Birth control: another New Purpose no-no.)

Sometimes he believed it had been the children who'd undone her. They overwhelmed her, constantly. So many hands and mouths and dirty bottoms and people who just needed to be held for a minute or two.

"Please, God!" she'd beg, and pinch her brow. She'd squeeze her eyes closed like a child making a wish at a birthday party.

One horribly hectic afternoon, one of the girls—that Miriam or that Sarah (those poor, poor girls)—had sprayed a mouth of carrots on her mother, squealing in delight at some antic her big brother had performed.

"Dammit! Dammit!" her mother had screamed, and Craig, there as he often would be to assist her husband with church business, had been sure she'd been going to strike the girl, and he'd stepped toward them to intervene. But the angels had won. Keisha dropped her head into her hands.

"I just can't," she cried.

"Let me," he offered.

He'd taken the spoon and finished the feeding. When Miriam spit—or it had been Sarah?—he burbled back at her—and he'd looked up to see if Keisha enjoyed the show. But she was gone, nowhere in sight.

So they became Craig's job, then: Danny, the two girls and the one still inside of her. No formal agreement this, just the way

things played out over time. Like the elderly neighbor's grass needed mowing: You didn't ask, you just did. He practically lived there
anyway.

Ari Birnbaum, whose boundaries seem to have shrunk by half
here lately, sidles up and leans down, exhaling his hot boy-breath
on Craig.

"IM-ing?' he asks.

Not your goddamn business, Craig thinks, but sets his face to
neutral. There's no percentage in pissing off Estelle by pissing off
her grandson—and anyway: It could be that the boy knows how
to make this damn computer work. Craig has promised Estelle
to hand her a printout of his "wish list" when she returns to pick
up her grandson. "Not that it's final," she assured him, "we'll be
adding to it forever, of course." Surely the boy knows a thing or
two about computers, but Craig can't quite bring himself to ask.
There's beholden and then there's beholden.

"Stuck?" the boy queries.

Craig's been pressing the *print* icon but to no effect. He's of the
generation of folks who passed through school moments before
devices such as this computer dropped like acorns on classrooms
and bedrooms around the world. Reluctantly he acknowledges
that he does need help. The boy wraps around him like a golf pro
coaching backswings.

"Do this. This. This, this, and this. Then this. You're good to go."

His scent overwhelms Craig so much that one "this" is the same
as the next one. The boy lingers there as if there are more commands to execute, but the printed list is all Craig needs.

"You tense?" the boy asks.

"Not particularly."

"I'm feeling tension," he announces, and proceeds to dig his fingers into Craig's shoulders.

He's clumsy, this boy, and certainly indelicate, but the massage
does feels good. The thick fingers press into points that haven't
been touched forever.

And the boy says, "You like that, huh?" And there's a nasty edge
to it. And his fingers reach around, and the last person who touched
him there was her.

"What the hell," he says, shoving back his chair.

"Come on," the boy entices: The embattled face betrays the lascivious voice. "You know you want to," he growls.

Craig shoves him. "Get the hell away from me."

And Estelle has returned. "What's the meaning of this?"

"What the hell's the matter with you?"

"You saw what he did," the boy cries. A real cry.

"I saw nothing, sweetheart. You calm yourself." She reaches out to comfort the boy and he swats at her.

"If you ever touch this woman . . ."

This time he'd not walk away. Never again.

"Let me," she says, and she turns and waves a silent finger in the boy's face, ordering him on his way, waving to Craig her goodbyes and see-you-tomorrows.

She herds the brute off with her big purse, assuring Craig she'd handle it.

"It's fine, Craig. It's fine," she says. "I've got him in hand."

Good luck with that, he thinks, hoping her words are truer than the last time he'd heard them.

Chapter **Twenty-Two**

C rack of dawn.
   Maybe if I ignore this woman she will go away. He, of course, knows better. Tenacious like a bulldog, this woman.

"Up and at 'em!" She tosses something or the other on the bed, and whatever it is winds itself into the sheet even as he unwinds himself from it.

More so each day she channels those chipper matrons from black-and-white sitcoms: Aunt Bea with a better personal shopper. Her speech she peppers with phrases such as "Top of the Morning!" and words such as "piffle" and "land-a-Goshen"—words and phrases that would have generated in the old Janet Williams a fit of bone shattering cringes.

He mumbles, "How 'bout today if we just . . ."

"Stuff and nonsense!" she cheers, cutting him off. The well-honed authoritarian directness of her tone as always casts a layer of frost over her newly-minted cheery locutions, and he has showered and is drying himself before he is once again vexed at how easily he yields to her velvet intimidation.

Behind him in the mirror, his brother (the girls allow him privacy when he's dressing) cocks his head to the side and grins with wry disappointment. Hosea trills his fingers with a shooing motion, encouraging Daniel to go ahead and get on with it, to set about the business of humoring the old girl.

Easy for you to say.

But he *will* wear his jeans today. Two hours on the plane, he's wearing his jeans—damn what she says about the way "decent ladies and gentlemen dress for travel." He folds the letter into his back pocket. Perhaps today will be the day.

As she opens her mouth to demand them—because heaven forbid an idiot like him could carry two slips of paper—he hands her the passes he's printed that will allow them to board in group A.

"Ah, for the days of first class." She plucks the papers from his fingers and charges out the door in front him, shouting in her wake reminders of light switches and deadbolts. Go! Go! his sisters encourage—same trilling fingers as their brother.

Onboard Janet Williams commands a businessman to relinquish his seat—"so she can keep an eye on her grandson." The man finds this as funny as his sisters do. Daniel keeps his face neutral: Alienating this woman will not get him anywhere that he needs to be.

"Many, many years ago," she says, "long before you were born, your grandfather and I would travel all the time. I'm sure I've already told you all this."

She has told him nothing. She folds his hand in hers as if he were still five years old. Hers are lotion-soft as he always remembers them to be, and he knows that when he lifts his fingers to his face that the fragrance will have lingered. She reclines her seat and her nostalgia seems to subdue what has been for his entire life a busily troubled expression. She melts as she relaxes.

"We went to Paris, you know, my Wallace and I did. Oh, Daniel: It is glorious. Everything you've heard is true. A city just made for people like you and me." She inhales deeply and rests her head against the window. "We'll go one of these days, we will. Soon, yes?" Her breathing evens.

She would want me, he knows, to stir her—ladies did not sleep and drool on a public conveyance. Instead, Mimi is on hand with a pillow (—but Mimi is a flight attendant now). She places the pillow so gently that G does not object; G mumbles a quiet Thank You.

He only knows who Wallace is because he had once pointed at the photograph on her dresser and asked about the man pictured there. "Oh, that's my husband Wallace," she'd responded—quite matter-of-factly as he recalls it, the same way she might identify the engraving on a coin or the celebrity cover of *Essence*. He's of mixed minds as to her orientation to the past. Even as much as she is stymied by the enormous and ugly muddle that is everything about his mother, Daniel imagines that if there had never been a Keisha his grandmother is the sort who would be disinclined to make a fetish out of her history. She owned no photo albums he had ever been able to locate, few pictures other than the wedding photo. Anniversaries and birthdays seemed to hold no value whatsoever in her universe; she mustered only minimal enthusiasm for Daniel's, zero for her own.

(Ari Birnbaum, on the other hand: Every birthday was a jubilee.

Most especially his own, of course. He'd jump up and down and clap his hands and enthuse over even the lamest of gifts: socks, stationery, educational software.)

Daniel declines soft drinks for himself and his grandmother, and he fights the sleep that threatens to consume him as readily as it has done her.

Poor deluded thing. Could she honestly have believed that all this constant motion would keep the past at bay? As it is, this summer's manic tourism has been nothing more really than a sometimes-diverting variation on a theme—cultural attractions substituted for human resources and power shopping. What has been accomplished other than wearing them down to flinders? He knows no more about anything now than he ever has—certainly no more about this woman asleep beside him on the plane. He knows:

She is an only child (although he believes there might have been siblings who died at birth or in infancy. He has no idea why he believes that.) She was not born in St. Louis, but he doesn't know if she lived here as a child.

She is a graduate of the University of Missouri and she also spent time at Washington University—although he doesn't know exactly when she was at Wash U. or for what purpose she might have attended there.

Her own parents were "literate if not extremely well educated." This distinction—hers—is not one that he completely understands, but this information has been emphasized regularly during the tour. "The opportunities you'll have: Unimaginable to them—and yet I know they dreamed them for you. Do you understand?" (Actually, he did rather.)

She was a hottie; he's seen the wedding photo. They'd have been all over her back in the day.

She's lived in her house since at least when his mother was a baby. She'd once referred to an upstairs room as "the nursery."

She has always and only worked for the phone company. This is not, he knows, complacency. This is instead forbearance and determination. She made a plan and she stuck it out. She would not have it otherwise.

She hates liver; will only drink whole milk.

She doesn't suffer fools.

She adored a well-made silk suit (witness today's lovely summer white!).

This is about as much as he can say. She would have him say less—would certainly allow no mention of her love of trashy novels, of her (inexplicable to him) worship of the actor Robert Mitchum—to say nothing of an almost murderous antipathy toward things religious.

"You let me sit up here asleep," she says, swatting at him. An accusation, a damnation: For just a moment the summer's labored and synthetic sweetness is nowhere to be found. In the aisle the others tease him by wagging their fingers at him. Naughty, naughty Danny.

He offers a futile "sorry." She fumbles for her compact and repairs what she can in the tight confines of the plane, dusting and swiping, all the while mumbling her complaints about "some people" who "didn't have the sense God gave lint."

"Tell him, Grandma!"

What use, then, the rebuke of ghosts.

They are the day's first visitors to the galleries, and they arrive with Daniel not so much forgiven as back on duty. Culture insists—the slacking of incompetents be damned. Shaking free the arm she's decreed be presented to him for her (patently unneeded) assistance whenever they walk in public, she advances on the front desk of the museum.

"Mrs. Janet Williams. I spoke with your supervisor."

She does not, of course, extend her hand when presenting herself, and Daniel tries to imagine how this young man understands what he's been confronted with. Pierced-eared and fashionably coiffed with highlights—almost certainly an "art student"—were there reference points in his world for a woman such as this one? Did the tucked away offices of the Nelson-Atkins swarm with similarly elegant creatures—middle-aged empresses, straight-backed, impeccably turned out in the best Country Club Plaza had to offer, the merest hint of Chanel wafting from their wrists? At the very least he's been trained well, this clerk: The very model of obsequious attention, he assures Mrs. Janet Williams that she has been expected, is heartily welcomed, and he makes a big deal of offering her the "highly exclusive" VIP tour, should that be to her liking.

"My grandson and I will make our own way, thank you very much." She accepts from him her pre-paid credentials and museum guides. She passes Daniel his share along with a wink advising he note the way she handles these people. He's observed such performances all summer and, in fact, for as long as he can remember—her ability to cow the most supercilious maître d' or to shame the full can of soda from the stingiest flight attendant. Only Estelle Birnbaum seemed her match, frankly. Two old ladies who scared the shit out of almost anyone they chose to.

"European first?" she asks, and since it is not really a question she leads the way in the direction they've been pointed. Her heels snap like dice against the terrazzo; You'd think she owned the joint.

"Humph!" Her dismissal of a depiction of the martyring of St. Sebastian. Daniel figures they won't be buying.

"I guess it's just that I find these old masters—all this iconography and heraldry and all these muddy brown landscapes—I find them all so . . . turgid. I'm right about that, am I not?"

And before Daniel can muster a tactful way to undercut her dismissal of centuries of western art, she says:

"The thing about being cultured gentlemen is not so much that you young men embrace everything you see but that you, first, have, in fact, seen it, and that you are therefore able to offer an informed opinion as to why you find it distasteful, repugnant, or, even possibly, enchanting. I'm sure you agree."

She snaps away towards impressionism.

Daniel massages his temples in front of a Gauguin. Across the room there is clearing of the throat.

Yes, I guess I will stand here and look at this painting all day if I feel like it. He doesn't say this to the woman—instead gives her his most placating simper. She should patent these: these Janet Williams Thirty-Minute Tours of the Great Cultural Institutions of the Midwest.

"Well," she prompts. Practically bouncing on her heels so eager she is to get on to the next artist, the next century, the next museum.

"I *am* looking at this," he tells her.

He is *not* looking at this, but she would have no way of knowing that. He simpers at her again. She sighs. The veneer on her pleasant demeanor is wearing thin. She's just this side of having a fit on him, he knows—and so be it. The storm is long overdue.

He rests his eyes on the stunningly lurid raspberry color on the dress of the woman in the painting, stills his entire body, offering it momentary respite from the constant motion of this other woman. Nonstop for weeks this has been. Memphis, Des Moines, Chicago, with a bonus side trip to New York thrown in for good measure. Botanical gardens; planetaria; small town historical societies; the site of Winston Churchill's "Iron Curtain" speech; the Mormon settlement at Nauvoo; Abraham Lincoln's boyhood home, ditto Harry Truman's, ditto Bill Clinton's. He's seen fences supposedly painted by fictional characters being painted by children dressed up as those fictional characters—has, as one would expect, been offered his own turn at the brush: "It's fun!" Dinosaur bones preceding lunch at the Palmer House preceding *Sunday on the Island of the Grand Jete* preceding more fish than should fit into an aquarium that size. Five state capitol buildings. The plinth in the center of the center of downtown Indianapolis. Even fucking Graceland, for God's sake.

(OK, so Graceland was his idea. Only another of many failed attempts to poke a hole in this summer's unrelenting . . . enthusiasm. She loved it, of course ["You had to admit there was something about the boy."], and Graceland had been *great*! He can't wait to show that Ari Birnbaum.)

Today it's Kansas City. Again. They soldier on.

"Oh, look!" she chirps. He angles his head in the direction she's pointing but does not look.

She asks, "Doesn't it remind you of the Manet we saw at the Met?"

He allows a noncommittal noise to leak from the back of his throat. Across the gallery one of his sisters issues a disappointed sigh. It's Sarah, and she squinches her face up in a way that means he'd best behave himself. He ignores her: Even that bunch is on his nerves any more.

What could Sarah or any of them know about Janet Williams and her full-court press? Day after merciless day of the woman's insistent optimism, of her energy without bounds.

His grandmother sidles up and embraces him from the side.

"We're so lucky, you and me. *I'm* so lucky."

She steers him through the rest of the exhibits, loosely clutching his arm. Noticeably spent of chatter, there is only the occasional "Good Day," directed with vigor to fellow patrons whose eye she manages to catch.

She's showing me off, Daniel suspects, and then immediately admonishes himself for having that thought. This is who she is, he understands, and this is how she has always seen herself: elegantly strolling in a quiet place with a man on her arm. At home in a place like this, just as if that were her name over the door.

Lunch, she announces, they will be having here in the museum—a sign she's wearing down that she feels no need to have him drive her to a certainly tonier establishment she's selected and already printed out maps for. None of her selections ever serves what he wants and needs, really; sick to death of various terrines and all manner of precious sauce, he craves something rough-edged and rustic: burgers, ribs, buffalo wings, steak. The closest on this menu is a not too gussied up club sandwich, so he orders that and listens to his grandmother interrogate the server about the exact preparation of today's fish special. Coffee is poured and she commands the server to leave the carafe. Her radiance barely masks her exhaustion.

The letter burns a hole in his pocket. He sits forward to retrieve it from his jeans and there behind his grandmother's chair his siblings shake their head in warning. They point at her firmly—you'd think she was on fire or something—but he cannot understand what they are getting at.

"What?" his grandmother asks. "Is there something on me?" She brushes at nonexistent crumbs.

Damn kids—but they've no interest in his reproach: They are apoplectic about the letter—which he quietly places on the table, angles it so G can see the letterhead.

How is it possible she sits up straighter? She looks at him like he's called her a vulgar name.

"I wanted to ask you . . ."

"No." She feigns a nonchalant sip from her coffee cup, offers a pleasant smile to another passing diner.

Returning the cup to its saucer, she offers her lips an unnecessary dabbing before sliding her chair back from the table.

"Let me tell you one thing. You do not do this. Not me, you don't. Hell, no."

"I . . . I . . ." he stammers. He's unsure what he is saying, but no matter. She's up, reaching across the table and clamping a hand over his mouth. A French tip snags his chin and he feels sliced open, but later there is no blood, only a royal red gouge. She's hot with fury—like standing by a wood burning stove—and she couldn't give a fuck about the scene she's making. Let 'em look, goddamnit.

She stays in his face, relenting only after he folds the letter away. Then she deflates into her chair, but only back to her standard regal nonchalance. The picture of equanimity: Just that fast it is like it has never happened.

The clearly alarmed server is beckoned and ordered to bring some more rolls. "For the boy."

More than gouged he feels slapped. Humiliated. And that is exactly her intention, he knows. Aggression met with force; she'd sooner snuff him than alter her course—or his, as far as that goes.

Behind her the others are all we-told-you-so, with their shrugs and their sardonically curled lips. Eat! they mime. Buck up! Keep this train moving forward!

He stuffs wedges of the quartered sandwich into his mouth and his grandmother keeps the bites of trout moving from plate to fork to face. Mouthfuls of food preclude conversation, and Daniel can't imagine what else there is to be said. Janet Williams makes all the noises she makes when she savors her food. She sparkles and flashes her eyes in his direction.

What about my chin, bitch?

A change of venue helps, and strolling the American Jazz Museum she clutches his elbow and draws him even closer. They read about Bird and listen to his music, and she says in an almost conspiratorial whisper, "Don't ever forget that you need to know this, *too*."

He knows that she is not talking about these recordings. She's never been one to play music in the house.

Talk to her, Mimi mimes. The others nod with enthusiasm

About what, exactly?

Let's see: There's my weird-ass boyfriend who keeps breaking into our house at night. There's our crazy-ass mother—and we already know that's a non-starter.

"Do you think it was different to be around back then?" They are in front of a display of photos of this neighborhood back when it was alive and kicking. Kansas City's seen better days, from what he can tell. Where did all these people go?

"She," his grandmother says, directing one of her razor nails to a woman posed in front of a jazz club, "looks just a bit like my mother." She gives him her isn't-that-interesting smile, and that's about all she has to say about the matter.

Again she falls asleep on the plane and—he cannot help it—he does as well. The others allow him his rest for once: They nap in the aisle and in the overhead bins.

Jostled awake for landing he finds himself tucked into her side.

"You let me sleep again. I don't know what I'm going to do with you."

These may have been the first words she ever said to him. Her customary tease.

For the most part he cannot remember not being with this woman. A few memories he has, however, of when she'd bring him to her house—him alone and never any of the others. He'd ask for more milk and she'd pinch his cheek and rub his head and say, I don't know what I'm going to do with you.

What she did with him a lot of the times was often not much of anything. Or perhaps it depends on how you look at it. She liked to sit on the couch with him and turn the pages of a magazine. Sometimes they would just sit. How much she seemed to relish the quiet. As far as that went, he'd never minded it much himself.

Barbecue, he insists when she asks his request for dinner.

"Too rich," she warns. "Too messy."

"Shouldn't have asked then," he mumbles.

Sarah kicks the back of his seat.

"I swear, certain people get cranky when they're tired. All right, then, Mr. Big Stuff. Skip our exit and take the next. I'll show you some barbecue."

They head north from UMSL and off into some neighborhoods he had no idea existed.

"Ah, yes, Red *is* cooking today," she says, and she orders him to get them a picnic table. What looks to have been a converted gas station swarms with people, hours past the normal dinner hour. Lurid signage announces the offerings and irregular hours, and behind the booth two giant pits are being worked hard by men who are sweaty and grease-spattered with the effort.

"Rib tips, pork steaks, potato salad, beans." She presents her selections as if they were Tiffany jewels. She welcomes him to knock himself out.

It's out of this world; He can't get enough. Janet Williams concurs. She forks free dainty bites from the meat taking extra care to drip free the sauce before bringing them to her lips. Even so, she is mummified in layers of paper towels. ("I'm not messing with my silk.") She smacks her lips. "Sometimes you've just got to smack your lips," she says.

Returning to the table with another order of the rib tips her eyes are aglow. She waves her finger at him.

"Shame on you, bringing me up here with all this good food."

Shame on you, the others agree. They are teasing, too.

Janet Williams is luminous. Even in the late summer twilight—even there amidst all the wood smoke, there in the vinegar/pepper air, even as the others stand in attendance behind their grandmother in the same way that the angels do behind Mary in the paintings back there in the Nelson—what he ought to have known all along suddenly couldn't be any clearer.

For so many years, this has been all she's ever wanted or needed. Him.

Here, or any place like here.

This: the quiet companionship. This . . . simplicity.

Hallelujah, the others mime—finally the boy gets it. They disappear into the parking lot.

This: Not that or then. None of that other. Never again.

But as for that . . .

"G," he says. "I just wanted to . . ."

But she has dipped a finger into the sauce and she touches it to his lips. Blink and you'd miss the shake of her head, the wink. She trills her fingers: Eat! Eat!

So he eats.

"Next summer this time we'll be packing you boys off to school."

She fans her eyes as if the tears will start, but he's never seen tears from this woman. "Time!" she exclaims—the same way Estelle exclaims "Oy!" She shakes her head and proffers a not-particularly-convincing shudder. Even the best actress has her off nights.

"Time!" she exclaims again.

Time, indeed, he agrees. He raises a bone to his lips; savors the smoke, savors the lavender.

Chapter **Twenty-Three**

That Ari Birnbaum flies his bike down one steep hill on Price
Road and then coasts up the next one. Midnight and he has the
streets to himself, so he rides the midline, owns the damn street.
The finally cooled night air keeps him dry and the residual heat
in the asphalt bubbles up to keep him from freezing. Twice county cops have eyeballed him, but neither squad bothered stopping.
Only marginally swarthy, the Birnbaum boy; not traveling with a
pack. He figures they note one lone male and will only circle back
and shoot him if the night goes dull on them. He's a regular anyway: this, his nightly path, the shortest from Estelle's to Janet's.
Twenty minutes if he pumps hard on the long hills instead of walking the bike. And he's not really alone; he's become part of the
secret fraternity of night riders—the swing-shift Mexican busboys
who sometimes ride in tandem from the swanky Frontenac restaurants to their homes in Overland and to other places north and
more modest; anorexic cross-country racers whose skeletal faces
flash past in the amber streetlights of Olivette, grim determination
set in their laser-focused eyes.

Once, just after he'd begun his nightly excursions, cruising up
and out of one of the valleys, he'd found himself on the same tra-
jectory as one of those speed-racer types. Ari, hypnotized by the
rush of the wind and the rhythm of the wheels; the racer, high on
adrenaline and pain; and neither had spotted the other in time.
They'd just missed crashing and only Ari had fallen, and the other
rider had circled back to him, initially Ari believed, to give him a
hand up, but that hadn't been the case. Rather than helping him,
he had shoved Ari back to the pavement and called him an asshole.
So he lay there, Ari had done, unsure of whether to scramble away
or to rise and to punch it out, but he'd been buff and tattooed and
pierced, the other rider, so Ari averted his eyes from the hate-filled
glare and awaited his fate. The man radiated heat and Ari heard
him take a long drink of water, heard splashing against the asphalt
but had been unsure if it had been the water or if the guy had been
peeing. And then the energy shifted.

"What's your name?" the rider asked.

Ari looked up from where he sat Indian-style in the middle of the street and what he saw in the hollow-socketed eyes gave him more than a bit of a charge. As of yet he remained unsure of how such things worked, but he'd been confident enough he could win this round if he wanted to that he rose and faced the man off.

"Ari," he said. Nothing more. Let him ask, the asshole. He took the water bottle right out of the rider's hand and shot a stream of the cool liquid down his throat. In exchange and under the guise of "making sure you're all right, OK?" biker-boy caressed the beefy muscles on Ari's upper arm.

"Get yourself some reflectors, OK, Ari?"

"I'll look into that."

That it went no further Ari chalked up to them both having other agendas that night—the rider to grind away at his already wasted frame until there was nothing left but air; Ari to get to Daniel.

He bought no reflectors, but every night, including this one, he eyed the fleeting figures rocketing his way. On this night, two or three glide past him. They are familiar only in the way that they all looked alike, with their shaved heads and knotted calves. He does have his own water bottle now, and without stopping he takes a long swallow, the same way the hardcore riders do. Another one will notice him one day, and he has the power, he knows to do whatever needs doing (Craig Mitchell be damned). They'll notice him and he'll not be pushed away. Never again will he be pushed away.

As he's done every night he entertains a moment's worry as to whether Janet might have in some way absconded with the ladder, but Janet, he knows, is another one with her own agenda—as unconcerned about ladders as she is unaware of his late night presence in her house. Sunup—and often enough earlier—she's got herself and Daniel packed off on another "cultural expedition" from which they return long after suppertime. The two of them she runs like marathoners, stopping, by all evidence, only for meals at the best restaurant closest to wherever their little jaunts have taken them. Foil swans materialize every evening in the fridge—twisted inside of them morsels of lobster and scallops and the tenderest nuggets of filet imaginable. Ari anticipates scavenging the leftovers again tonight; figures it will be a long time before Estelle springs for such a meal for him—not after the business with her beloved Craig Mitchell.

"How's my presentation going?" she had asked him, pointedly ignoring, he'd noted, his oh-so-carefully planned dust up with the Mitchell bastard—which he knows she'd witnessed, since he'd timed it that way.

Ignore me, Ari had thought, and I'll ignore you as well. It's a two-way street. He stared from the car window and willed the ride home to be over.

"Your slides will be at the heart of Poppa's celebration. I want socks knocked off, nothing less."

It would knock something off, that's for sure. He didn't say that, of course, just grunted at her. There were more ways than one to fix Craig Mitchell. Thank God for Photoshop.

"Honestly, Ariel. I don't know what's the matter with you sometimes."

"I'm not the one with the problem." Let her take that any way she wanted to hear it.

"I'm hearing a tone in this car." Her universal conversation stopper, employed most frequently on Ari's mother who dared rebut the woman's advice on childrearing.

Despite (or maybe even because of) knowing how much it got under her skin, he'd mumbled the word *whatever*, and added something to the effect of, "It's not like you listen to me anyway."

She'd taken a deep breath—inhale, exhale—and then pumped the volume to loud on her NPR show. She danced her nails on the steering wheel to the not-so-musical intonations of talking heads on the subject of oil prices.

He'd tried to burn a hole in her head with his glare, but she'd have none of it. Stalemate.

As he'd learned to do in order to avoid the more aggressive Clayton police, as soon as he crossed under 170, he cut up across the parking lot by the Kinkos and back into the neighborhood abutting U-City.

He climbs the ladder with confidence these days and easily slides the window open, rolling himself onto the chair he has left by the window just for this purpose.

"Hey, buddy," he says, wrapping himself around the boy on the bed. He's warm, Daniel is. He sleeps so soundly these days that Ari cannot wake him, and he has tried—oh, how he has tried. Daniel's breath is hardly there, but, as he does almost every night, he reaches without waking and pulls Ari's arms around him.

I almost had him today, Ari whispers. Almost, but, well . . . there was a little timing issue. But don't you worry. I'll get the bastard.

When I'm done with him, he won't know what hit him.

"You don't even know," he'd whispered at his grandmother. Sometimes he hated the woman.

Her turn to ignore him, by all evidence. She'd barely stifled a smirk.

"You don't know anything about Craig Mitchell."

She had reached over and petted his arm as if he were some stupid kid. She'd shaken her head, sighed, seemed to fish for the right words.

"Sweetheart," she tried.

"Precious," she tried.

She settled on *darling*.

"My darling, on some days—many days—I think you are the most intelligent man I have ever known. Other days: not so much." She continued her petting.

"I am not wrong, Grandmother. I am not wrong. I read it. I read that box. You know I read it. And you know I'm not wrong."

"Ariel, you saw what you wanted to see. It happens all the time— even to smart boys like you."

"He was there. She listened to him. Keisha Williams Davis. He could have saved those babies. He could have saved all of them. And now all he wants is your money."

Out of the hand she petted him with she made a stop sign. "Even so, Ariel. God doesn't need your help. Even if it's true, you'll not be judge and jury of this man. And while we're on the subject, if I want to stop my car right here in the middle of Highway 70 and burn Poppa's money on a bonfire, that's of no concern to you either."

"You'll see," he mumbled. Whether or not she heard him she pinched him on his arm anyway—the tender spot inside the elbow. She'd turned up the radio again and drove them home. Fuck whatever Ari has to say—and so what would be new about that?

In bed, in his arms, Daniel sighs and moans. He's so still that he hardly seems to be there at all. Ari himself fights sleep, but he mustn't fall. There's so much to tell this boy. Sure, he'd be disappointed about Plan A, but the Photoshop scheme is well underway and foolproof—and won't Estelle just adore those charming photos of her supplicant.

The boy next to him sighs and beckons hard: Come join the dream, so he does fall, and he lands hard in a world both familiar and strange.

Daniel and . . . oh, so *they* are the others . . . wait on a busy street corner—an oddly resonant corner that Ari cannot place. He's been here before, he thinks, but he cannot remember when or why. It's a place that is all red brick and ivy; funky storefronts and tattooed people like the night boys with their bikes. Like the biker boys, everyone here is happy to see him.

Daniel and the others beckon the new boy to come.

We're off to the garden, the girl cheers, one of the twins. She's Daniel's favorite for now: Sarah.

She's pretty, Ari tells Daniel. Daniel is proud. Sometimes they look alike—exactly alike—Daniel and Sarah. Or, rather, sometimes they all look alike, all four children, even those who are not twinned. Other times they are vague—all but Daniel—and don't have faces at all. Sarah waves her long arms like a traffic cop.

Move it, Hoss, she orders their brother. Some days sullen, some days bright, that boy, Hosea. Typical five-year-old (or ten-year-old, or then he is an infant in the stroller). Today is a sullen day.

What's the garden, Ari asks? Which garden?

Who is this other person? Who is this man?

This way. The one with the Climatron. They follow the other girl, Miriam, the loud one who seems to know where she's going.

This is our friend, she says. He helps us. She says it in a sassy way.

Just like her mother, they say. The people on the street say this, and they all shake their heads, but in a friendly way. That darn Mimi.

How could that be true? Ari wonders. That's not what people said at all.

We all live under glass, Mimi says.

The man sees them all across the busy street. His arms he circles around them all.

See, the children tell Ari. It's OK, see?

See, Daniel says. He couldn't be prouder. He says to Ari, Didn't I tell you they were great? All of them.

You did? Ari wonders.

But you were children. They were babies. The littlest one, had he even been walking?

It frustrates Daniel, Ari's forgetfulness, but he wraps an arm around his friend's shoulder and they hustle down the oak-lined street after the others.

Miriam and Hosea bicker. You'd think they were married. Something or someone sucks, according to his brother, but his sister assures us they are the bomb.

That's not how we say it now, thinks Ari, a thought that disappoints Daniel. As for the man, he surrounds them. Ari knows who he is.

The children's faces blur in and out of focus. Mostly they are flat and halftones, like the photos in the books. They run ahead on legs that are sometimes short and sometimes long. Off into the fog they run. The man shoos them ahead and signals Ari and Daniel to stop: He'll take it from here.

Ari protests: Why is he here? They do not belong to you.

Daniel only smiles. Maybe it's time.

Run, Daniel encourages. The young ones get farther ahead. They're mostly small now, only every third step do they spring up to teenage-size. (Once, they are adults.) They lope ahead and the brownstones fade to gray. Daniel is weak now and hardly able to stand. The man fades, too, waving everyone where they belong. "Go!" his mouth seems to order them.

No, Wait! Daniel pleads. Hang on, he calls after the others. Now they are the others of the photo album. Frozen, on their parents' laps. Sometimes Daniel is in the picture and sometimes he's been cut away.

They need us. We belong with them.

No, Ari knows. We do not.

Help me, Daniel begs. His legs mire in the molasses.

You're fine, the man says. He helps Ari hold onto the boy.

In Ari's arms Daniel convulses and struggles, but Ari is paralyzed.

Wide-awake—all but his body, which is trapped in the dream with his boy and with those others. He fights his helplessness, willing his arms to release or his legs to kick or his lungs to take in air. They will not.

So it's like this, he understands, and relaxes, resolved to his fate—which is to wake, covered in sweat and gasping.

Daniel has sprayed vomit onto his pillow. He sputters, coughs.

"Fuck," barks Ari. He runs first to find a washcloth. Then he runs back and pushes at the boy's shoulder.

"Wake up," he orders. "Daniel."

He runs back for the washcloth, but then he runs to Janet's room.

"Help. Please, help me."

She remembers him and then she stumbles after him.

"Oh, dear," she says. "Well, so much for those late night stops at the barbecue stand." She looks at Ari and shrugs sheepishly and coquettishly, the way his sister did when her father busts her on her usual foolishness.

Ari hands her the washcloth. She rubs it around the boy's face. He fights it the same way a toddler would, as if it were made of sandpaper and the mess were a mark of pride.

"Get over here," Ari orders Estelle, who has answered on the first ring.

"In the name of God," she implores, outrage melded with resolve he hears in her voice. She knows where he is, of course.

"And I just don't know what all this fuss is about," Janet protests, mildly. "Honestly, you boys."

Daniel blinks himself awake, by all evidence unsure of which world he's woken into. His grandmother strips the pillowcase and swabs away at the sheet.

"I told the fool to order the mild sauce," she says. "Does he listen?" She says this with a wry grin on her face, touches Ari on the arm as if he's her co-conspirator in this mess. "You know how he is."

Ari does—even at the same time he doesn't understand one single thing about this family and whatever their whole deal is.

"You OK in there?" he asks his friend.

"I think they left," Daniel mumbles, still in that other place.

"I know."

"I wonder where the hell they got off to this time?"

"They're gone, buddy. Let them go."

Daniel sighs and rests his head on Ari's chest.

"Why don't you get some ginger ale into him," Janet orders. She hustles them all in the direction of the kitchen.

While the washer rumbles away, Janet Williams sermonizes as to how a person just can't trust these hole-in-the-wall barbecue joints—although the potato salad was out of this world! They make it with just the right mix of salad dressing and mustard. But the baked beans: too runny. She prefers hers tight, a little crust on them even.

"Oh, hey, girl!" she says to Estelle, who has let herself in through the front door.

Ari can practically see the wheels spinning in his grandmother's head; it takes her only a minute to tally this all up, note her miscalculation, and to set in place the reconfiguration of all their lives.

"You," she says to Ari. "Get the rest of that soda into the boy and then get him dressed, will you? I'll be right up. We'll deal with your other problem later, but if I have to have the Creve Couer police lock us in from the outside every night, don't think I won't do it."

"You," she ordered Janet. "Let's break in that new Samsonite—and remember, boys, to stick with your name brands. The Birnbaums don't buy cheap suitcases."

Many years later, running between the A and D concourses in the Atlanta airport, the wheel had broken off the rolling overnight bag Ari had purchased at some discount store just off the turnpike in Jersey. He'd been in one of his (frequent) frugal phases and figured with the beating these things took with all his traveling, why invest in something fancy, and he'd only brought it along on this trip in order carry back gifts from Florida for the kids.

So there he was, dragging the bag along the people mover—sparks shooting behind, probably—who had time to look?—cursing the goddamn thing and cursing himself for buying it in the first place and then further cursing himself because he could already hear Danny when he arrived home that night: laughing at him and once again reminding him that he was the tightest Jew on the planet—more or less a regular refrain in their ongoing comic duet of mildly offensive racial and religious humor. And in that moment this entire night had come back to him—or, rather, two specific things had come back. Estelle's advice about luggage, of course: Damn, she had always been right, and may God offer her rest.

The other thing: He'd never understood Janet's easy acquiescence to his grandmother's orders. From all he knew of her from all these years as part of her family, it had never made sense to him, but that's what had happened. (Even now, even just this morning, there in assisted living, the damn woman would not be coerced to breakfast. "Nobody tells Janet Williams when to eat!") Yet, when ordered to do so she had pulled down those suitcases and loaded up the things that she and Daniel needed for their first few days in Creve Couer. Ari hadn't known that night that the Williams family would never return to that house in University City, and he doubted that Daniel had known it either. He'd helped the ladies load the bags into the car and then had parked himself next to the by-then cranky Daniel in the backseat. (He would always be someone resentful of having his sleep interrupted—for any reason.)

(Oh, another thing he remembered: In his peculiarly overprotective zeal, he'd done the reach-around on Daniel, but only with the intention of grabbing the belt and buckling the boy in. "Back off, perv," Daniel grumbled, pushing him to his side of the car, and then he'd made this sound with his lips. It was that sound—that expulsion of air, somewhere between a raspberry and a scoff, classic Danny, it was—that had been his first indication that everything would be all right. No, they'd not been out of the woods yet, but they would be fine.)

But all the while that they'd packed and all the way back to his grandmother's place, he'd not heard Janet one time put up a fuss or otherwise mount an argument about Estelle Birnbaum's spontaneous and outrageous plan to combine the two households on the spot.

He'd mulled this over frequently in those many years since, and he'd always concluded the same thing: Sometimes we mortgaged our own free will.

For spite. For laziness. Because we're dim-witted or because there is some other reason that we cannot be trusted to do the right thing—or wouldn't know the right thing if it smacked us in the eye. For rage. And sometimes for love.

He would often remember how before he'd run off to Daniel's on that peculiar late night, Estelle had knocked on his bedroom door and she had perched herself at the edge of his bed. He'd been chilly to her, of course, seething as he had done over her lack of insight into the human condition—which nevertheless the damn woman insisted on lording over him despite the superiority of his ever-infinite wisdom. All the same, she'd lovingly run a manicured fingernail around his brow and across his stubbly chin—half temptress and half saint she was. The other great love of his life.

"You're a good man, too," she said. "I'm counting on you."

How hard he had fought to hold his face tough.

An idiot, he'd been: a fucking fool.

But, he didn't know about mortgages back then, nor had he learned about forgiveness. So when he did disappoint her—quite soon thereafter, as it happened, on the dear woman's biggest day, no less—he had not understood that she would be able to love him again, and the prospect of her permanent disdain had nearly killed him. But she did love him, of course, as she always had, and she told him she would not tolerate his insistence that he did not deserve that love.

"You listen up, mister: I give it and you take it. Unconditional. That's the way it works."

"But . . ." he'd protest. But as she always would do until the end of her life she put that manicured finger to his lips. There in that same room in that same assisted living she'd done it.

"Shhhhh! Not necessary."

She read everyone's mind, all the time, the damn woman, and damn if she wasn't right. Or 99.5 percent of the time she'd be right.

But even the best sometimes fail to see the truth, and, alas, this one part she had never gotten quite right: All those years she had always assumed that what he'd wanted was her forgiveness. Silly old woman. It had never occurred to her that he might want her to tell him how to forgive himself.

Chapter **Twenty-Four**

So, all right then, she says to herself. We're back on track, moving right along—and in the right direction, too. At least she thinks they are. Or hopes they are. Or . . . or what you better do is not get too far ahead of yourself, Estelle Birnbaum. The Human Bulldozer, Poppa had called her—and if the first rule is *no doubts*, the second rule is the one about not counting chickens. In any case it felt like the right track to her.

Sometimes you had to be the person who said, "Enough already." Let's get this thing set right, else a couple of us will be on the locked ward at Malcolm Bliss, the rest sharing cells with that deranged woman.

Her mistake, she understands now, was assuming that intelligent people, left to their own devices, would manage just fine— something, for the record, she had never assumed to be true of the generally idiotic riffraff down at the phone company. But *these* people are not idiots. Which goes to show a person, did it not? And so, all right, then: lesson learned. Estelle Birnbaum, back at the helm—and there'll be plenty changes in this operation, believe you me. This morning she gives each one—Janet, Daniel, and that darn slippery Ariel Birnbaum (and let him scowl at me one more time: a certain little pisher will wish he'd worn a cup)—his or her own revised marching orders. She'd drag them—all of them—up and over this hurdle, as Moses' wife said, "As God is my witness!" (Or perhaps that had been Abraham's wife said that or maybe one of the girlfriends. They all had both in that story. It was Sodom *and* Gomorrah both back then, 24/7. Worse than daytime television.)

Should there be doubts—and not that she was looking for doubts and not that she'd tolerate any that happened along on their own— but on the off chance there might be doubts, these would only concern the fact that she's not entirely sure what the hell's wrong with all these people in the first place, or with that Craig Mitchell either, as far as that goes—and while we're on the subject let me slice off his chunk of this coffee cake and tuck it in next to the thermos. But what did it matter? They're in trouble: and what's Estelle Birnbaum's specialty if not helping those in need? (I give and I give!)

She'd clear this little rough patch the way her gardener had cleared that tired patch of daylilies last week, and it's no bother at all. Really. She's here to serve.

And, so, OK, yes, she's fairly sure . . . no, positive . . . that all this chaos had been spawned by that awful Keisha Davis Williams. And who would imagine a person could leave so many . . . residuals, yes, that was the word . . . in her wake? And, God in heaven: such residue. Like a store-brand fabric softener, that girl.

Janet had been half right, at least; she'd had half of Poppa's formula correct. You put it away and you moved on with your life. Except the dear woman hadn't put it away, not really: The books were still open on this particular account.

Well, cookie, let me tell you one thing, and for your own good I suggest you listen up: Estelle Birnbaum's a gal who knows a thing or two about closing a set of books. And she kicks herself, because she has been running ledgers since Methuselah was Pope, and she can't believe she's forgotten rule number one.

"Stell," Poppa would say: none of this crap like accidentally this receipt you should somehow forget because it accidentally on purpose slides beneath the bench. None of this.

The boy has always been the key. Her boy. Her other boy. Her Daniel.

She folds the map she's printed and sets out the coffee service—and, because life is short and because, as the president says, "A spoon full of sugar . . ."—the loveliest—the loveliest—Caramel Honeybee stolen she has seen on display at Schnucks IN HER LIFE, and if that icing were any thicker, they'd all end up in Barnes/Jewish on the diabetes ward—wired up, but in bliss. It's that good. They might as well enjoy a slice or three while talking about the hard parts. Who's to know?

And, there she is anyway, Mistress of Good Timing, arriving just as the first slice tumbles onto the dessert plate. (Such icing!) How lovely Janet looks.

"Is that new?" Could this be the perfect summer dress—all flouncy and flowery and comfortable-looking?

"This old thing," Janet teases—a good sign that is. "Actually I got it in New York. My grandson helped me pick it out. You like?"

"Saks? Bloomies? The boy has an eye, yes?"

"He's coming along nicely, I think."

Estelle extends the plate with her—yes, trademarked—make-yourself-at home sweep. As always Janet accepts the treat as if it's Estelle's fault she's about to swoon with delight—it is that good. So far so good—and perhaps there's not much to be said or done here at all.

"And, of course, no worries, right, darling," she tells her friend. "You and me. Nosh a little, talk a little. Like always."

"Absolutely," Janet says, waving her hand in dismissal of whatever protest she'll not be making this morning—which relieves Estelle to no end, since, in fact, perhaps she has at least some cause to fuss a bit.

Because—and in the interest of a thorough and accurate closing of these particular books—it must be noted that she, Estelle Birnbaum, is not entirely beyond blame in these matters. Estelle Birnbaum: Queen of the Laissez Faire. Live and let live. When had that ever been a good idea? And may God have mercy on her as well. Judge Judy: Feel free to throw the book at me. Kiss today goodbye, and yes, Your Honor, it *is* what I did for love. Up the river with this sorry old woman. (And when you do send me up, one request, please: a suite—with a view if it's no bother—and, also, if you wouldn't mind, one next to that lovely Keisha Williams Davis—and a few minutes alone with the young lady, as long as I'm asking. There's some matters I'd like to discuss with the girl. I'll page you when we're through.)

She slid one of the lists she's sketched out this morning to her friend. (Another specialty: the list! Poppa'd been right, the girl's talents—had there been no end to them!)

"Realtors," she tells Janet. "And I had your girl fax me your relo specialists. The last four there. U-City/Clayton border: It's a hot market—you'll be flush. Enough for the wet mule and the matches to burn it with. Poppa used to say that, you know."

Poppa, who also might say, Whoa! Estelle: Gear down. Pay it out in small parcels (Poppa's rule). But, hey, desperate times . . . And a punch to the gut is a punch to the gut, whether you throw it now or ten minutes from now. And you don't see Janet Williams putting up a fight. She might be taking on water, our Janet, but this is a practical gal, my friend is. She knows better than to swim away from a perfectly good life preserver when it's tossed her way.

And, should any further evidence be required, Janet takes a pen and marks through one of the realtor's names. "I don't like her attitude," she snipes, and she dabs at a place where her concealer has clumped.

My dear, sweet, and lovely, lovely friend. Just look at the state of you. Exhausted from running from it all—for all these years. Enough. You know, don't you, they're as much for me as they are for you, all these changes. I've grown accustomed to your face—and I can't even remember who said that one.

She hadn't expected this friend. At this point in her life. Who would? You travel your road, you have a good life with a good dear man and you raise your child and you make your way in the world. By a certain age, it's you and the hot water bottle and the same old faces from the synagogue. And then this . . . person . . . comes along, and what do you know? It's the long lost sister you never had. Who knew?

Poppa might say, Face it, Stell: The woman's as big a witch as you are, although I'm not sure how that's possible. You're stuck with her.

Poppa: such a kidder!

And—come on—it's not like it's all been sunshine and lollipops—take a look: The woman has baggage. Good God, did the woman have baggage! But, hey, which of us didn't?

(Just, as for example—among certain others, mind you—the six-foot-something and who knows how many hundreds of pounds of wander-around-the-city-all-night baggage out there in the other room, and she'd be dealing with Mr. Ariel Birnbaum directly and personally, next, but let him sweat for a minute or twenty. She wasn't in any rush. And you'd better believe *he* wasn't going any-where, soon or perhaps ever, and you could cash a check on that. She'll co-sign.)

And standing in the door, then, is another one about worn out with the whole mess. Their Daniel. Eyeing the coffee cake, of course and why not? But there's no need to offer him any. These boys, they'll vacuum the dregs like yesterday's lint, rip the tray in half and suck the icing until the Styrofoam melts in their mouths. Darling boys. You had to love them.

Be with you in a minute, she signals.

But, first things first, and speaking of you'll owe me:

"I did have one favor to ask. A small one. No bother, I'm sure. If you'd be so kind."

Janet nodded.

"I'm going to need my running buddy. At House of Hope next week . . ."

And would you look at the face on this woman! As if I'd asked her to work my shift on dollar-beer night at Lacy Garters—not that Estelle had been in a "Gentlemen's Club" or to dollar-beer night or even knew what went on in such places. She's only saying.

The boy puts his hand on his grandmother's shoulder. Comforting her? Encouraging her? Holding her back? Who's to say with these crazy people?

"My friend, please. I need you. I wouldn't ask." She angles the coffee cake in their direction, points to another slice. Sometimes it helped to sweeten the pot.

"That man . . ." Janet says, and then she cringes.

"Yes, I know. *That man.*" She raises her hand in surrender. Ari and that man. Janet and that man. Everybody and that man—that poor, poor man. Another person who couldn't close the books.

Look, people: Just take him to the mall and nail him up, would you please. Be done with it.

And there it is: closed. Another unreconcilable in the ledgers. She'd had this feeling that Janet knew that Craig Mitchell ran the House of Hope, although she certainly hadn't learned it from Estelle. As soon as Estelle herself had figured it out she'd also figured it was not a good idea not to upset her dear friend. It's the boy who told her. It had to be.

"This isn't about Craig Mitchell. It's about me. About *me* this time. Next week I honor Poppa's life and I leave my father's mark on this world. The world: You know it wasn't always nice to him. But he overcame. He did. And this is what he wanted. Something good for the people. And I want for Poppa that it be absolutely perfect. *And* I want the people I love around me when I launch his dream. All the people I love. All of you."

Her friend is like she's received the worst news of her life. Crushed over with disappointment or grief or pain. She shakes her head. Not a "No" Estelle knows, but an "As much as I'd like to, maybe I can't do that for you."

"We'll help you, sweetheart. Won't we help her?" she asks. The boy doesn't speak and she doubts his grandmother could have seen his almost imperceptible nod. His hand is pressed into his grandmother's shoulder and he is considering her as if she were a puzzle and if he stared at her long enough he would solve her. It interests him, this puzzle, and his is the face of a young man who is sure that he owns the tools to figure her out. All he needed to do was to think about her.

And, boy, do you, Daniel. You own those tools. You were born with them.

And right here is the last piece of your puzzle. She lifts the road atlas from the table: She'll deal with him next. Now. No time like the present, and tomorrow is another day.

"We'll all think on it, eh?" she tells Janet, and before ordering the boy to follow her she sighs and clears her throat and opens her mouth for a taste of her own medicine.

"As long as we're clearing decks—and wasn't it one of the founding fathers who said 'Let he who is without sin build a glass house'?" I, Estelle Birnbaum—regrettably—have my own confession to make at this time."

As per her father's suggestion, she paused to allow her audience to prepare to receive their blow. (Alas, and as Poppa would also say, a tough room, this: these darn stoics. She might as well be talking to deaf people.)

"Where to even begin. OK, out with it Estelle. There's this little matter of a . . . condo. There: I said it. Gulf-side. On an island. 2/2, en-suite, plush, updated kitchen, pool—heated for the chilly months—plenty of parking, and a Publix just up the block. Also: ours. There I said it. Done. Bought and paid for. You'll owe me. My deepest regrets. Sincerely, Estelle Birnbaum. I await my punishment."

Done, because she's seen this look on Janet's face countless times, and between us this is not a good thing, let me tell you. This is the one with the pursed lips and the arched left brow; the one reserved for those think-they-know-so-much gals down at the phone company; gals who assumed that if they kept those gums flapping and kept on adding words to the explanation as to why they rolled in at 9:17 every morning, Janet might give them a pass. Then her head starts goose-necking, and she forgets who she is and how far she's come in the world, and then everyone knows what comes next: She rolls back in that chair and she pushes up out of it and she leans up over whoever had the bad judgment to be in this predicament in the first place and she says, "[*b*-word that Estelle won't say or think], keep talking that [*s*-word that Estelle won't say or think] in my office, and see if I don't come across this desk and break my foot off in your [*a*-word that Estelle won't say or think].

It isn't pretty.

But it is a good sign. The old Janet's well on her way back.

"The boy and I will give you a moment."

Leave her to marinate a while.

She pulls Daniel by the arm into the dining room and closes the door. Here the accounting had begun, so here let it end. She places the map between them and taps it absentmindedly with her ring finger.

"Rough times, eh? Talk to Estelle, sweetheart. How are you holding up?"

He shrugs.

These big boys and their big shrugs. What she didn't know about men and their shoulder blades. Poppa. Bernie. Aaron. Ari. Now this one. Eternal torment, and why me?

You say to these men, What do you mean "I don't know?" and they say, "I never said 'I don't know,'" and you say "But you shrugged," and then they shrug. What could you do? It's like the boy in the Torah who pushes the big rock up the hill only to have it fall down again—Silas, or what did it matter what they called him. They drove a person crazy. You wring their necks and you end up in the suite next to this one's mother. (And she'll take the shrugs any day, in case you're interested. She's sure the food's better out here, to say nothing of the company.)

"It's only us here, so Estelle's gonna talk to you man-to-man, and I'm sure you won't mind. There's no need for rehash, so bottom line: You got dealt a bad hand. A royal mess, and not a face card in the bunch. And even so, you played that hand like it was aces. Anybody else would have folded. Or broken. But not our Daniel, you know what I'm saying? Tell Estelle she's right."

Only a half shrug this time, and (and it's progress, and you don't spend your life with these men and not savor the small wins) the tiniest sliver of a smile—even if the eyes are misting over (and don't let the tears come, cause these boys, they close up on you like a bankrupt shoe store, and then you're back to square one. Oy! These marshmallow men! Just before he died she had sat with her Poppa and watched a rerun of *West Side Story*—the man loved a musical—sunrise, sunset—so shoot him. So the boy dies and there's A Place For Him and all of that, and she looks over and who should be blubbering like a baby. What in the world? Poppa, please, she tells him: It's just a bunch of Spanish people. Who else wore clothes like that? The Wood girl: She's not even singing!)

("Bernstein, Stell: He gets you every time.")

But the one in front of her will hold it together today. She wills him to.

"So we need to make a deal, you and I. Because you have been so strong, we're able to do that."

He nods. More progress. Keep it coming.

"It's this: I will help you, but I need you to help her. You need to step up now, young man. We both know this is something you can do."

"Help how?"

Words! Miracle of miracles!

"Your grandmother is a tough, smart cookie. Toughest and smartest that I know—and, trust me, precious: Estelle Birnbaum has been around the block once or twice, and I mean that in the polite way only, of course. Our Janet there: She's the best. But the old girl misses the mark now and again, if you get my drift—just like the rest of us do. Like me and you and don't get me started on your friend there in the other room."

Like everyone, the boy's a sucker for a taste of backbiting.

"All she wanted to do was protect you. We both know that."

"G can be fierce. You wouldn't want to cross her."

"From your mouth to God's ear, and has Estelle got stories for you. Find me sometime. We'll dish."

(Like the data-entry clerk and the box of fake letterhead. Or the half-naked office manager, the copy machine, and the hot glue gun.

The boy will positively die.)

Good old, tough and diligent and hard-hitting and fierce Janet Williams. The unspeakable happens (she can't even imagine, Estelle can't, these children being taken: this boy or that other one or even that horrible Hannah) and the woman does what needed doing: She steps up. She takes the one that could not be killed and builds a whole life for him. She pushes forward as if the whole mess had never happened.

There's the one little problem. The one thing she could not fix or erase or in any way make go disappear, whichever of her tricks she employed.

"You remember a lot of things. I know. You were there. Not for the worst part. God is merciful, then. But you were there."

"I remember everything."

"My Poppa, he would never talk about that time. In the camps, you know. 'Stell: I forget all that,' he'd say. But I knew he was lying. People don't forget. So, no, of course you remember."

"It wasn't all bad, not all the time. They were so great. The others. And then there was him. You know what, Estelle? For a long time I thought I made him up. Because he disappeared. I'd thought that I'd imagined that there was this man who used to come and stay with us all the time. Until I saw him—when we went to House of Hope—I had forgotten he was real. He was there all the time. He wasn't so bad."

"He's a good man. You need to tell *her* that—when she's ready, eh? But, not just now. That's not how you help her now."

Later, sometime, they would discuss the fact that his grandmother might never be able to deal with Craig Mitchell, but now is not the time for such talk.

"How do I help her now?"

"One thing is all: Grandmother needs to understand that *you're* OK. That's your job for now."

When he laughs—ironic and sardonic for sure, but a laugh is a laugh, and you take the victories where they come—his teeth show and his eyes light up. And, God in heaven, will you look at this boy. Movie star gorgeous—and a brain on him, too.

"I'm OK?" he asks. Mostly only a joke, thank God.

We should all be so OK. But she says:

"Everyone's got issues. Trust me on this."

He nods. Who better to know about issues, after all.

"Estelle's got to be honest with you, Daniel. It's not going to be easy. She's so afraid."

"Of what?"

She slides the map in his direction.

"It will help us navigate to the prison. You and me, yes? Her, in there, she's come as far as she can with you with this. Time to let her let it go."

He nods again and she understands the he has most certainly already figured some of this out for himself.

"So you think I should go? See her, that is."

"Oh, sweet boy. I don't know. You don't mind if Estelle calls you sweet boy. I honestly don't know if seeing her will help you or hurt you. But old Estelle here, she's a girl who likes to place a wager now and again—and not that I'm encouraging that sort of thing in others. Still: I'm betting it wouldn't hurt. Who knows and we'll see."

"She's crazy, Estelle."

Estelle bites her lips and looks to the stars before these next words. May God forgive me if I'm wrong to say so, but:

"She's also your mother."

The boy leans up and kisses her on the cheek.

"People forget that sometimes," he says.

And, OK, so hold it together, Estelle. There's one more customer in line this morning—and one who didn't particularly respond well to blubbering. She stands and turns her back for a moment, pretends to fish through her giant purse.

Don't let them see you weak, these boys. They'll eat you alive.

"So we go soon, yes? Me and you—and we keep her out of it."

He gives her the "sure" shrug. (Is the repertoire infinite?) And then,"I tried to talk to him, too, you know." He whispers this.

Him? Which him?

Oh, that him.

"Well, him. That's a special case, I'm afraid."

The boy rolls his eyes. He knows about special cases.

Ari may be slightly older, she wants to tell him about his friend, but in so many ways he is so much younger than you. Estelle's men: blustery, transparent, arrogant, sentimental. As easy to operate as a German sedan.

"Be patient, eh? They come around."

She pulls his head close, kisses his scalp and then rubs it in good.

Which he allows! There's just no telling with these boys.

"And while we're on the subject, your friend and I have some unfinished business."

"Estelle?"

"Yes, love of life."

"Ari was trying to do the right thing."

She shushes him. "The road to hell. Grandmother knows he's a good boy, but I'll make you another deal: You don't tell him I said that, and I promise to go easy on him."

"But you do plan to rough him up a little, right. Just to be on the safe side."

"Oh, absolutely. Listen: No one sneaks out on Estelle Birnbaum's watch and gets away with it. And now that you're under this roof, I suggest you remember that." She catches the tip of his earlobe between two nails.

You correct a little, you tease a little.

They both eye the map, still spinning around in his fingers.

"Hide that. Hide it good. And then I've got another suggestion: You go on back there in the kitchen with her and make like you're real busy with some things. Cook us all a meal, why don't you."

(The boy's stroganoff: To die for!)

"Let her think you need her help with it. We both know how she is, yes?"

Ah, that smile! Again! Could a heart stand it?

Alas, there's no rest for the wicked. It's the curse of the competent. On to the young Master Birnbaum.

"You," she barks, and he startles like a jittery con on his first heist. Slams the laptop shut. The face, then, is classic Birnbaum disdain— and if you smell something, buddy, it's your upper lip.

"So Estelle walks in on what this time: Porn? Identity theft? International espionage?"

Not a shrug, not a smirk (God forbid a smile for your only living grandparent—a woman who loves you more than life itself!).

In its place, the frosty, dead-eyed Birnbaum glare.

How to even play this hand?

Strong-arm him and he's out that door in a shot.

Talk it out?

With *this* Philadelphia lawyer? Thanks but no thanks.

She could soft pedal, but for Ariel Birnbaum soft equaled weak—and Ariel had no respect for weakness. And if you lost his respect . . . Well, ask the boy's father about lost respect. Her poor Aaron. Poor, sweet, ineffectual, long-suffering Aaron Joel Birnbaum.

"The boy doesn't listen, Ma."

No, Aaron. He doesn't respect you, is more like it, but how did a mother say something like that to her son? Neither would she stand by and watch the boy's reign of terror. Tantrums like a D-list actress, this one. There'd not be any bullies in this family, emotional or otherwise, not as long as she drew breath. She brought him here, took him in hand. It's not been easy, but it had to be done.

Ari puts his head down on the desk covering the laptop. For today's performance he's selected a particularly unfortunate combination of the Hillyer slump (Poppa collapsed on a desk full of invoices) and the Birnbaum sulk ("Why can't I get a date, Ma?"). He has at least stayed here in the office where she has parked him for the day—and if he knows what's good for him, he'd better have that PowerPoint ready to view.

"Not speaking to Estelle, I gather."

And why would one expect a reply to that? So, all right, she figures, I guess it's time for the big guns. A little shameless flirting, and what could it hurt?

"Say, what do you say just you and me make a run up to the mall and pick you out something nice for the Simcha? Something classy and pricey, too. You should look good while you're running the show."

It's the oldest trick in the book: Soften them up with merchandise and then drop the guilt trip on them over hot fudge sundaes.

She's in touching range now: Like exotic birds, sometimes you had to sneak up on these boys—and she dares tickle her fingernails through those luscious, luscious curls.

"Knock it off."

"Well, all right then: Aren't we Mr. Grumpus, today."

And there it is again: that same dismissive scoff thing. But rudeness is not the matter at hand just now. A boy out in the streets at night is.

She perches herself sidesaddle on the corner of her desk—something he's been warned never to do. We're all rebels here today; that's the message here. Ari faces away from her. She senses what she thinks is a trembling, but he is not trembling. Instead, something—some kind of energy or . . . something—pulses off him like heat. He'll not back down, she knows—not until, at the very least, he gets what he believes to be his due.

Oh, all right, then Estelle. He is due. And it's her own darned pride in the way. But it's a lesson the boy needs to learn.

"I'm sorry, Ariel, that I didn't pay more attention."

He flips his head around. Still reclined, still sulking, of course. But facing, at last, in the right direction, and he mumbles:

"Popsicles in hell tonight, I guess."

"Why don't you not press your luck, how about it?"

And, of course, as expected, he sits up, in full prosecutorial mode—and if he points that finger at her, she'll snap it off like a dried twig.

"You know, if you'd only . . ." but she cut him off.

"How about if we don't do it this way. Maybe this once let's try it different, you and me."

"Sure, Estelle. And how about maybe you listen to me in the first place once in a while."

So this is how it happens. This is how you could kill your children—and she wills her hand not to slice across his face with her nails.

But you are teaching him, Estelle. He doesn't know, the boy. Because you didn't teach the father this.

"Our friends are healing now. Let's all help each other move past. This is me, giving that a try. How about you?"

"But . . ."

"No, Ariel. No *buts*. *I'm sorry* means I'm ready to move on. *But* keeps us both from doing that. I'm sorry."

And the dismissive snort again, but he seems to be letting it go. He slumps back over the computer.

"Anything happens to him and I'm not responsible for my actions. I just want you to know that."

Mercy! The melodrama with this one: You could sell soap during the commercial breaks!

"Duly noted. May we proceed with our next item?"

"You're the one with the agenda."

(And how dare he mumble that? Or anything. Under his breath. To a woman her age. A woman who couldn't love him more if she'd squeezed him from her own womb. To any woman.)

"And today's agenda is all old business, I'm afraid. Hear me when I tell you that I'll not have teenage boys sneaking in and out of this house at all hours of the night. It's not going to happen."

Because what would she do, these precious angels. Dead in some gutter or paralyzed in some hospital or just disappeared from her life. How would she bear it? How had Janet? And she could say that to the boy—but she already knew what he'd say in response. (They're so transparent!) Nothing is going to happen to us. We can take care of ourselves. We're invincible! And denying that to them would be a waste of breath. Instead, you made yourself as myth-ologically big and bad as you were able to—twice the size of this house. And you leaned into these big boys and you put the fear of God in them and hoped for the best. At least she has drawn the line.

And, alas, they *will* step across it these two. One of these days. This line or the one next to it. Because that's what boys do. You move the line and they move their enormous feet. With these boys you call a stalemate a win; and a win, therefore, is when the line isn't at the edge of a cliff and they choose to step over anyway. Just because you said not to.

Luckily the only argument she gets is the eye-rolling scoff. No biggie: He'd responded the same way when she demanded he not scratch himself "down there" in her presence.

Look at this boy: trying so hard to be tough. And so hard to be good. There are bad boys in the world, and as much as it might break his heart to hear it, Ariel Birnbaum is not one of them.

As for the real bad boys and girls, one need only go back in that kitchen and ask a certain mother.

She tickles her fingers into the boy's hair again. "A little condi-tioner wouldn't kill a person, maybe."

He swats her hand away, but he smiles. Smiles from two men in one morning. A certified enchantress, she is.

"Say, you know what else I was thinking: The whole gang of us take a week off and head on down to Florida for little vacation. Break in the new condo. Our first family vacation together, the four of us. What do you say?"

"We can go surfing."

More a question than a comment, and she tells him it's a lovely idea—does not tell him she cannot imagine how a young man uncoordinated to the point of tripping over his own feet thought he'd be riding on top of a wave. But what did she know? Who's to say he wasn't made for the ocean?

That stunning lack of physical grace: another gift from his father. That, and the kind of stubborn self-righteousness most often found on the sort of men who ran passenger liners into icebergs and national economies into the ground. Like two rams in the same pasture, running headlong into each other every chance they got, because . . . well, they forgot why. It's a habit and it feels good. Mirror images, neither noticing anything in the other except the thing that annoyed him most about himself. A son who hates the geeky nebbish who allows himself to be bossed about by his wife (because he loves the woman, stupid). The father exasperated by his clumsy geek of a son (who cannot remember back even twenty years when it had been he with the almost mustache and the inflamed back and the feeling that you were the one person that the entire world was out to get). Ornery. Vindictive. Two men who heard "Pass the peas" as an invitation to debate. Neither of whom for so many years now had shown each other their whipped cream centers, that treacley sweetness with which often Aaron smothered her, his lionhearted love. Rain just a little of it down on the boy, she has wanted to order her son, in order that he should know that allowing those emotions to show will not kill him. Let him win so he will be able to lose to others. Forgive him so that he can forgive himself.

"We could ride the rollercoasters maybe," he says. Just a little boy, he is, who thinks he's too big to say the word *Disney*.

"We'll go to the parks and you boys can ride all day long," she tweaks his cheek—and he lets her! These boys: They're a sucker for a soft-touch grandma.

"Let's just get this Simcha over and behind us, and it's off to the beach we go. Have you added that picture I found of Poppa holding you when you were a baby? I want it in there as we transition into the *Fiddler* medley."

"Figures . . . you still giving that man your money."

And so off we go again with *that man*: Janet can hold the nails while this one pounds them in.

"My *father's* money will assure that some young people much less fortunate than you, along with their families, have a safe and comfortable bed to sleep in, wholesome meals, and maybe the hope of a place of their own someday." Estelle says this to her grandson who has two homes, one with a pool, both with central air, and he's welcome in both as long as he draws breath. Enough with that disgusting noise. "If I needed your approval for this, I'd have sent you a memo, and don't waste your time checking your in-box. And—and here's hoping it's for the last time, and merely for reiteration purposes—if Estelle Birnbaum wants to spend her money on the champagne flight to Uranus, I'd like to see you try and stop me."

Great! A chuckle instead of a scoff. Now you're cooking with gas, Estelle. Your teenagers love the Uranus jokes. Slightly off-color without being blue.

"Well, I can stop it if I wanted to," he mumbles through his giggles.

"It's done, Ariel. Let it go."

"What do you mean it's done?"

"I mean it's done. The foundation's established. The board's slated. You're nominated. You, your father and mother. Hannah. Janet. And Daniel. Craig. And Donette. And about a dozen of the richest folks old Estelle here could charm out of some fast cash. So all of us. We are all now The Hiram Hillyer Family Fund, in support of needy families. We're going to do amazing things, my love."

"So he talked you into it after all." That wry smile, she is choosing to believe, is his placated one and not the cynical one.

"More like the other way around, since you're so nosy. And not that it changes things one way or another. You've finished the PowerPoint, then?"

"Yes, I finished your damn slide show," he sing-songs, so she grabs her second hunk of tender ear-lobe flesh of the day—except this time she puts some English on it.

"You'll make me proud. Yes? Yes, you will. Grandmother knows."

"Wanna see it?" He pops open the laptop and starts it warming up.

"You know what I want? Surprise me. The pictures of my Poppa and the House of Hope and the children and the music and the words—you found the speeches, yes? Dr. King and Mrs. Roosevelt and the reading of Anne Frank?"

"It's all in there. The Barber Adagio, and Poppa's Song of Joy."

"Oh! I cannot wait. Oh, dear one: Almost four years I've worked on Poppa's dream. I searched high and low for the right place and the right people and for the way that all his hard work could touch other people's lives. I've finally done it. All I want is for Poppa to be proud of me."

And, OK, so the boy sees her cry a little. He wraps her into his big and beefy arms. See: not so difficult.

"I'm proud of you, Stell."

Poppa's voice through the darling boy's lips. She's died and in heaven.

The boy melts in her arms, a big sloppy popsicle, not in hell, but here in her arms. He's done with it, then. Released, she can tell— and his whole body relaxes. What a burden when it's your job to right every wrong.

"So we're fine, then?" she asks him. "Everyone is good, yes?"

He nods. He is done.

"Navy slacks I'm thinking for Simcha, what do you say?"

"Poppa liked plaid."

Please: not on your best day, plaid. On these giant legs?

"Off then with you. To the kitchen. Help him with lunch back there. Shopping after work. You boys keep an eye on her while I'm out. No car trips—tell her 'Estelle's orders!'"

As in, "Leave this house, the pair of you, and they'll be two new baritones in the boys' choir in hell."

What a day, what a morning, what a life, what a world!

What a grandmother couldn't accomplish: Give her a brain, a decent manicure, and throw in a dose of intestinal fortitude—which couldn't hurt either.

Just look: all the little ducks in a row.

She is strong. She is invincible. She is—Estelle Birnbaum. She appreciates the accolades but next time bring a cheesecake.

Chapter **Twenty-Five**

It's no surprise that neither boy shows up to work, but it is a surprise when Estelle calls and invites him to a meeting at her house to finalize the gala for the new foundation. She'd seemed genuinely hurt at his (however polite) begging off. At a loss for any rational reason not to go to his benefactor's home he'd concocted a lame excuse about something needed doing around the shelter, an excuse he'd regretted almost immediately, even as he watched Estelle's face crumple with the disappointing transparency of his lie. Who these days knew better than she the routines of this place and how easily they might have done without him for an afternoon?

His lame excuse: Well, it was better anyway, he figured, than the real reason he'd declined. Surely it would have made no sense to this woman that he wasn't sure he remembered how to be in an actual house. He'd spent time in so few in his life; two of them, to be exact—subtracting, as he did, the odd basement cot or attic floor.

Silly, of course. What could possibly happen, after all? Sit in the wrong chair? Speak too admiringly of the décor? But what's a person to do: He owned one of those irrational fears people have. Of using the restroom in public or of distant thunder. He understands this; all the same he cannot accept his friend's gracious offer, so instead he accepted her tight-lipped displeasure.

There had been his parents' home, of course, and then there had been the Davis family house—a gift from the congregation to the newlyweds. At some point it had become less trouble to stash Craig in the guest room after the late nights at the temple than to drive him back to Overland. He'd wake each morning and start breakfast for the entire crew. His hosts, by all evidence, had no knowledge of how a kitchen worked.

The pattern had been that after clearing the dishes he would sit down with Jerrold to plan a sensible day's service to the temple, and then off they'd go to take care of business. Jerrold couldn't get enough of visiting those shut-ins and dropping by hospital rooms to check on the infirmed—had been known often enough to stop by the homes of strangers who had been named by congregants as being in need of ministering. More often than not this left Craig with the more nuanced, more diplomatic work of the temple: negotiating with printers, making sure the usher board had the flowers arranged for the following Sunday, settling disputes over which color choir robes best highlighted a sister's skin.

Things between Keisha and the children continued to deteriorate. Ordinary behavior would send the woman into fits. A spoon dropped from a high chair. A too frequently wet diaper. The garden-variety crankiness of the garden-variety toddler. Craig couldn't imagine what went on while they were at work. He decided he'd damn well better find out.

"I'm gonna work from here today," he announced. This was a morning in the early fall of '94.

Jerrold had no response, as per usual. When he'd first met the man, he'd understood these silences to be a mark of strength, characteristic of the kind of a man who needn't be bothered with idle chitchat. In fact, Jerrold owned no conversation skills. So, as was necessary, Craig had prompted him:

"Did you hear me?"

"Something about here? Working here?"

No listening skills, either.

"Yeah, something like that. You see, Keisha needs a hand. With the little ones."

Which *had* caught Jerrold's ear—or at least his wife's name had.

"Let's just keep praying for her. She's praying hard, too."

"And she can use a hand. And we'll pray."

The left side of Jerrold's face twitched as he thought it over. Or what passed for thinking with him.

"I'm still counting on you, of course."

Of course, Craig assured him. He hadn't in the least been surprised that Jerrold's primary concern had been his ministry and not the health of his wife and children. Nor had Craig disappointed his friend. Each Sunday's remarks had been researched and written, programs designed and printed and at the ready on the pews, the pews themselves gleaming, the list of folks needing a visit and/ or a prayer processed and printed along with maps marking the locations of the various nursing homes and hospitals. He could do all that and keep an eye on Keisha and the kids, no problem. Thank God, they'd all been dutiful nappers—even and especially Keisha.

One-on-one she had been fine with the children, if not entirely enthusiastic. He'd keep the others busy while another one got fed or diapered or bathed or bounced on her mother's lap—which she'd sometimes deign to do.

Sometimes even one was too much, and she'd wander away—for hours sometimes. She'd return, smelling of smoke and her head hung in shame—often enough just in time to head to the temple for the evening.

"Sorry," she'd mumble, and he'd tell her not to be. It was no trouble at all. How he loved those afternoons when she'd disappear: not having to walk on eggshells around her, him just rolling on the floor with the children, singing silly songs to the girls and cuddling them when they got cranky. The diapers and the spilled milk and the sometimes incessant wailing: all of it. He loved all of it.

Big brother Danny made it easy. He watched those girls like a hawk, seemed to know when they were hungry and always knew when to get the clean diapers out.

"Mimi's wet," he'd say—perhaps even his first words to Craig.

When Craig arrived in the morning (when he'd not slept over) Danny would meet him at the door and lead him to what needed doing first for the little ones. The child had been on to his mother—almost from the start, it seemed, he'd been on to her. That much had been clear. Certainly children have a sixth sense about such things. Craig saw it all the time at the shelter: mothers like chickens without the brains to come in out of a hailstorm, guided by their seven-year-olds through the rudiments of the day.

Not quite four, and there he had been, Danny, leading Craig to poor Sarah, stewing in her own juices on the "great room" floor of that ticky-tacky Florissant house, her mother up to her elbows in mashed peas, multi-tasking not her forte, not by a long shot. When he didn't have words—and early on not even that precocious boy had been up to "She forgot to buy Cheerios"—he'd shake the box at Craig, rattling the last few *O*s, before handing it over with a big smile on his face.

If he'd needed any other proof—and he didn't—on the day the last baby had been born, Craig had dressed the others in their Sunday best and delivered them to meet their new brother, Hosea. Boldly, Danny had stridden to his mother's bed and lifted his arms for the baby. That she handed him to the child spoke volumes—and she'd done so without batting an eye. Perhaps she'd anticipated the next move: Danny had immediately placed the baby boy in Craig's arms.

"Here," he said.

Keisha, in angelic mode, stared coolly out the windows toward South St. Louis.

Back to Florissant they all went, and he watched—helpless to the point of oblivion—Keisha Williams Davis's increasingly rapid withdrawal from reality.

Now and again the grandmother would step in—the other grandmother, Janet Williams. The phone would ring and there she'd be, belligerently demanding to speak with her daughter. What bizarre conversations those must have been, or at least the half he'd eavesdropped on would be. She had one of those voices, Janet Williams did, that carried over the phone lines, and from across the room he could hear the amplified rasping of her squawks. And while he couldn't make out exact words, he could tell they'd be coercive—something the daughter had done or hadn't done or needed to do or to stop doing. By this point in her craziness, such words washed over her daughter like a soft spring shower, bliss-eyed Keisha receiving them as if bread from heaven. She'd respond:

"Is hell really in the center of the earth, mother, or do you think it's far away? Like on another planet or something."

Or,

"I need an A-line skirt, below the knee. Get me an A-line skirt, mother. Navy blue."

Disparate statements like these, often enough back-to-back and disjointed in a way that defied normal conversational conventions.

For her own obscure reasons, on those rare occasions her mother would decide she needed to come over there, Keisha would make sure that Craig was somewhere else; she'd invent errands or just order him away for the day, giving him her patented evil eye and telling him to "take his ornery self on somewhere." It couldn't have been more than a half dozen times that happened, and Janet Williams would often take Danny with her when she left. Craig would return to a miserable baby and a pair of out-of control toddlers.

"Where's our Danny boy?" he'd ask, and Keisha would always take a minute to figure out who that might be.

"Oh," she'd say. "*She* took him." And then she'd smirk—as pleased, it seemed, to be rid of her son as she was oblivious to how much she needed him to manage his siblings.

As for the Davis clan, they kept a cool distance from the mess. In addition to biblical counsel about the sacrosanct "man as head of his household," like liberal parents with an unruly teenager, they stood back and watched her toying with the rope they seemed to hope would hang her one day—better she should learn her lesson the hard way. Maybe if they'd known they'd get their wish . . .

Many days, when she wasn't out walking, she'd sit at the dining room table and hum to herself and rock and page through the Bible, flipping the tissue pages with an index finger damped from the moisture on her lower lip.

"Can I get you anything?" he'd ask, and in reply she'd ask for help with her demons.

"What do we do about all the evil in the world?" she would ask. Things such as that, and he'd remind her that we'd all been redeemed and that all we had to do was ask for His love and forgiveness. She'd shake her head and look at him quizzically.

"It adds up. It all adds up. Too much for Him. Too much." More flipping and more pinching at the bridge of her nose.

Still, and despite her, he cherishes those days and remembers them as the happiest of his life. Baby Hosea was a plump bundle of giggles. His sisters smothered him with affection, the way all little girls will with a fat and happy baby to love. Just after noon, on the warmer days they would gather on the porch, the baby in his arms, the little girls at his side, and they'd wait for the bus to drop off their brother from kindergarten.

"Hello! Hello, everyone," he'd cheer, and they'd all be so happy to see him, too.

There's something shameful about loving a child so much. Like a sports car or a dream house: It's a love made of pride—and maybe that was the problem. The object of that love: It's perfect and you can't imagine it could be otherwise (even as all the evidence in the world told you it most certainly could be otherwise). Look what I have, a love like that said. As if your being so blessed in some way depended on the admiration by others of your good fortune.

And Danny was far from perfect, of course. He shared his mother's willfulness, and he sometimes seemed to be obtuse in the same way his father was—although in Danny's case it was just for show—and he thought nothing of exploiting the worst of his inherited traits to achieve his goals. If Danny wanted to finish coloring, Danny simply didn't hear the request to clear the table for supper. "Crayons? I thought these were pencils." Craig would gently close the book and gather the colors. Danny never whined—instead he would flare his nose and purse his lips ever so slightly—just to let you know that he had a list and that your name was on it.

But that was merely the cost of doing business, and a minor cost it was. The cost of having Daniel Davis in your life. And the benefits made every pain worth it. Why, just to listen to him talk! He talked all the time, all afternoon long, spinning out his absurd tales for his sisters and for anyone else who would listen. "Tell us a story," they'd beg, and he would never say no.

Had that been the greatest pleasure of Craig's life, sitting those many afternoons and listening to a child tell rambling and pointless tales?

When Craig had been a child there'd been a song on the radio constantly—a sweetly sentimental thing about a blind boy, also named Daniel. The chorus, the part about stars, had always stuck with him, and he'd sit and watch his boy and he wondered how the songwriter had anticipated this boy's being in the world. A star in the face of the sky. That's what he'd been.

Or is?

Yes, is. What a life they all have these days that he would doubt this for even a second.

On one of those idyllic afternoons the boy's mother had come into that house on Keevan Lane and found then all playing quietly on the floor. She'd stood there trembling, and shaking her head, and then the tears coursed her face.

It told, didn't it, that her children had not been alarmed at their mother's turmoil, but it hadn't been uncommon for her to be in one heightened emotional state or another. They continued to play—all but Danny, who interrupted his drawing to retrieve the box of tissue from the bathroom.

(Had Danny shaken his head after handing them off to her? Could that have actually happened or is it just something Craig wishes had happened?)

"What is it?" Craig asked her. She'd been holding her shoulders back and her hands, palms open, faced front. The position she used when she had something to say.

"Why are they so bad?" she asked. The question hadn't seemed directed to anyone in the room.

"Why is who so bad?" he prompted. The sick feeling began—the one that, in fact has not left his stomach since that afternoon.

"You know who. Them." She pointed at the children, each of them in turn. To Miriam. To Sarah. To the baby. To Daniel. Her breathing became heavy—that angry-Keisha heavy breathing—but her voice remained composed.

"Danny was just telling us a story about Twisty the Squirrel. Why don't you sit and listen."

She pinched her brow and squeezed her brow.

"Satan will pitch them into the fiery furnace. There's so much evil in this world. Everyone is bad." She shook and trembled.

And then her son said, "It's her. She's the bad one." Out of the side of his mouth he'd said it. In Craig's direction. For Craig's ears.

"What did you say to me?" Dark Keisha is back. The Keisha of the garden. "What did you say to me, little boy?"

"You need to calm down, Keisha."

"I want to know what he said to me. Let him say it again." She stepped in the direction of the boy. Shoulders squared and fists clenched. The others were crying by then. Craig pulled up to his knees and pulled the boy behind him.

"You calm down," he ordered.

She reached around him and flailed at the boy, but Craig held her off with his arm—though barely. She'd been strong as an ox back then. And it was then that she popped Craig in the eye.

"Not in my damn house, you won't tell me what to do. Not in my house." She thrashed away at Craig. Danny pushed his sisters to the bedroom and then came back for the baby.

"Where do you think you're going?" she fumed at the boy. By then Craig had pulled himself up and had better leverage on her. He put himself between the woman and her son.

"Get out of my way, Craig. I'll fix your ass but good, little boy. Get out of my damn way." And then she called after her son again.

"Daniel!"

"Leave them be."

"Daniel! You stop when I tell you to stop, you hear me? Craig Mitchell, I swear . . ."

Which is when Jerrold had come in the door, but Keisha hadn't noticed him. She continued yelling after her son.

"You'll be sorry, you little bastard. I'll send you to *her* house and then you'll be sorry. For the rest of your natural life."

"What's going on here?"

"Get *this* nigger out of my house." She shoved Craig. "Now!"

Craig turned to Jerrold and said quietly, "You've got a big problem here. She's lost it. Completely."

"Get him out. Get him out. Get him out."

Jerrold put a hand on Craig's shoulder and guided him to the door. "It's OK," he said, his usual cool tone. "It's OK, brother. I've got this. I've got her in hand. You go, all right? It's OK."

Another face seared in his memory would be Jerrold's at the moment he had closed the door: the I'm-in-charge-here, self-assured pose of the career politician on a bad news day—head tilted slightly to the side and bottom lip bitten in determination.

"I'll call you," he promised Craig, pointing him in the direction of his car.

It was the last time he saw Jerrold alive.

That night, the first of countless sleepless nights—years of them— all night, while he waited for the phone to ring, he replayed the whole thing in his head, from the day Shirley Mitchell had opened one door to the moment Jerrold closed the other, piecing it together and rewriting the parts that just seemed so wrong. But he could not rewrite it, not even the terrible ending that he hadn't yet heard but that he somehow knew was right around the bend. He lay there and waited for it, and when the phone rang and it was Keisha on the line, he knew the worst had happened before she told him to come.

My Danny. Where's my Danny?

Someplace you'll never get him.

He'd only sobbed that one other time. All these other times over the years, as has happened today, the stinging tears would dance around his eyelashes and his sinuses would swell shut. Allergies, he would explain.

He had managed to go many, many years without thinking of them.

Or, rather, he'd gone years without constantly reliving the whole sorry tale. Bits and pieces were always with him: a girl's laugh, a baby's tiny fingers, the inexplicable and uncanny good grace that is visited on certain little boys.

And here they are, all of them, landed on him again. The lot of them—in all of their messy, inscrutable, contrary, tender, obnoxious, horrible, wondrous glory. The joy. The grief. The hate and love.

For twelve years the story has ended in that garden—that awful garden—where he watched the Williams woman walk away with the boy and him unable to follow them. Craig's imagination had frozen them there, and over the years when Danny would visit him, it would always be the Danny in that suit, or a younger one, or a younger one still.

And then he walks in this shelter. Daniel Davis. Lord in Heaven. The story goes on. Jesus! What a life this is!

He dials Estelle's number and then he hangs up just as it rings. He daren't ask his dear friend's help.

And so—and despite how often he'd been rebuffed all these years—he prays once again that God will deliver the boy to him, just one more time—in his dreams or through that door—it doesn't matter. It's a little thing, really, Lord: this reminder that there are silver linings, however tarnished we allow them to become. Just a bite-sized nugget of hope, a morsel of nourishment to a humble servant. That my stomach might at last still itself; that I might finally pass the night in peace.

Chapter **Twenty-Six**

Blame it on the love. On the clumsy slippery delicious kind; or on the soap and the lather and what two boys could do with things like that; on the icy slick tiles against which the big boy collapses in pleasure before pulling the other one down on top of him as they drain each other and all of the hot water from the heater in the basement. The grandmothers will have fits: two such nasty clean boys. Not an ounce left for laundry or dishes. They giggle and squeal like the others, and stuff washcloths in their mouths against their calls of delight. When you couldn't scream it seemed your legs came out from under you. Or maybe that's just the clumsy one. All bets are off, of course. Two have won and two have lost and neither can remember what or why they had bet. (Although, often, but not until they are together for a long, long time, one will remind the other of his unadulterated and bald-faced lust as well as his unseemly lack of self-control—evidenced all those years back in his inability to just say no. They'll laugh and tease about it: the non-contagious and private humor of the long-mated.)

Or a simple lapse of judgment, perhaps: Many years later, Ari would blame the persistent blind spot he'd had since he was a little boy; that tenacious and unflattering character flaw of his that he would never be fully able to best, not even with Daniel's help. For the rest of his life he would find himself at cross purposes with family and neighbors and fellow jurists over what might easily be resolved if only he could be made to understand some fact or reality that would be instantly obvious to ordinary mortals. What was about to happen became part of an inventory of mistakes that he would always trace back to this flaw of his. Oh, how often he would have to be saved from himself by the people who would love him over the years. And oh how blessed he would be by their common sense; at the luck of their timing; at the grace of their forgiveness. This day would offer some of each, if not nearly enough of all.

And it is ironic that as they dried themselves from the shower and helped each other dress that he has finally come to believe what Daniel tells him about Craig Mitchell and the selfless way that he had helped the Davis children all those years ago. But the die had been cast: He'd cast them himself. Which would be his fate also in life: almost always to have known better, to have often enough been his own worst enemy.

It would be their habit in life to dress this way, these men: to tie each other's ties and to straighten seams and attend to stray pieces of lint. As long as there would be curls to arrange on the other man's head, Daniel would do the arranging of them.

It is this specific familiarity that Estelle interrupts to direct the boy to come see to his grandmother—who will not put on the dress Estelle has selected for her to wear today (shopped high and low for it—and just imagine the garbage she had to sort through to find this gem!), will not even open her bedroom door on a morning such as this, and they may be friends but a person could only take so much, you understand, so be a doll and go in there and move things along, would you. Time waits for no one.

The grooming embarrasses her more than finding them in the shower might have done, the naked vanity of their attendance to one another, the peculiarly narcissistic intimacy of such love.

"Bring her when she's ready," she orders one; the other she suggests get a move on, she hasn't got all day, and some people were worse than his father, no names mentioned, who'd be a week and a half getting dressed for a trip to the Dierbergs—not that it made any difference: outfits such as a homeless person might choose, and the man a successful surgeon, but who would even know that? Don't get me started. And don't forget that computer.

Such love: It would never not gall her for the rest of her life the way that when these two were together there wasn't anyone else in the world. As if she hasn't spoken to them at all; she knows they have heard her. An obsessive, selfish love this. Certainly worthy of blame.

"Move it," she orders. "The both of you." She shoos them with her hands and is not above swatting either or both of these young men. How's she the only one who can read a clock around this house?

Blame it on the love or blame it on her haste that he does not erase the other file, did not erase it all the many times he's had a chance to. Maybe, he kids himself, he will show it to Daniel someday; maybe they will all have a good laugh. But, no, never, and he will do that now, but there is a transition in the music to perfect and Estelle needs calming about a caterer and this boy is just so hot and needs attending to and so he will do it now. And he will do it now and now. And she is calling and he mustn't forget a thing and he grabs the cords and cables and there she is waiting.

Must be the love, Estelle figures, and she clutches to her heart a strong hand, because how is it possible that this big beautiful man on the stairs is both her father and her son and also neither of those men, come to escort her on a day such as this, and why not?

"Move it yourself, Toots," he teases, and he pecks her on the cheek, and—miracle of miracles—he's Bernie Birnbaum, too, the last man who called her that name.

"So we go then," she says, but not without his Daniel he insists. Exclusionary, jealous and sophomoric love, and not even their own children would affect that. (But they would wallow in it, all three of those kids—draw strength from it the same way a tree taps water from the ground.)

"He'll bring her later. You come. I need you, and hurry."

The boy gives her a look that, while she really ought to (because what sort of person looks at his beloved grandmother with a face like that) but has no time to address this just now—and if she had a dollar . . . She drags him to the car and speeds away to the city.

Blame it on the way that for the rest of his life Ariel Birnbaum could be fully confident of only one thing: that the other one had his back. Or blame it on the speeding car.

There may be blame, but Daniel has no interest in it. He sits beside her on the bed, the dress Estelle picked for her resting neatly on the duvet. He might ask her what the problem is and she might beg his forgiveness, but that has never been nor ever will be their way with each other. Counseling and confession are not a part of their repertoire.

A unique love, a specific one. Two people who often enough found their greatest comfort in the quiet strength of the other. He liked it when she cooked for him, which she had never been any good at. She liked to take him to restaurants, because who better than she knew her own inadequacies in the kitchen? She liked to watch the boy eat.

She liked him to tell her stories.

You should not blame it on this story:

He was almost always there, you know. It's weird how I'd forgotten that and forgotten him. Until that day at the center, when that other boy's mother left him. The day that I told you who he was. But I think he lived at our house. Do you remember that?

And when she does not answer, he continues:

Every day when I got off the bus from kindergarten, they'd be waiting on the porch. Craig Mitchell and the others. Sometimes the girls would sing a song for me, one that he taught them. The baby would bounce on his lap. I remember that.

And I remember he would roll out long strips of white paper for us to color on sometimes, and he'd make us rotate around that paper so that all of the drawing belonged to everyone. Even Hosea would crawl around with his big fat crayon and leave his mark. But mostly he would just chew on it.

The love: It is the worst story she has heard in her life. An awful thing. Unbearable. Worse even than those men at her door—Craig Mitchell and the other one. How could we live in a world where people knocked on your door with such news or even where such things could happen?

She rocks. She holds a hand against her face on the side where he sits, pressing with that hand.

He cooked dinner. He was a good cook. Macaroni and cheese. Mostaccioli. Sometimes after school he would just make tomato soup and grilled cheese sandwiches. The girls were always fussy about how they wanted those cooked. Not too brown but not too white either.

Enough! He is torturing her. She squeezes his arm, willing him to please stop this savagery.

He squeezes back. Yes, it's enough for now. He stands and gathers the dress from the bed. Structured and simple and elegant: There is no more perfect garment for this woman. A rosy peach to warm her brown skin. There'll be other times for other stories, but for now they have business.

"They're expecting us," he tells her.

Another time for the afternoon at the garden and another time for the birthday party at the zoo and another time for how good it felt to just have someone hug you and let you hold his hand.

She shakes her head. "I don't think I can," she whispers.

How could he know about the kind of love that made you alter the story in ways that made you feel better, however slightly, from an intolerable one to one that at least allowed you to move forward? What did he know about inventing a whole life after erasing another one, and how dare he remind her that she'd done so: It's spiteful, is what it is! And she's someone knows about spite, Janet Williams.

"Put it on," he orders her, and she jumps up. Oh, no; oh hell no!; not this again; not ever; not in her lifetime. No more impertinent teenagers in her world. Never again. She draws back her hand to slap the one who dared speak to her way. But: Look—it is not she. He is not her.

Look: This is no impudent child, this one. This is a man. A man who had not and will not become the person she was always afraid that he might.

"They need us. Come on, then."

And what to blame for how the world shifted? Suddenly, the way it always seemed to do for her. For how one second she's a woman in charge of an abandoned boy and in the immediate next second she is this woman in this house, being lovingly attended to by this man.

She dresses: for love of this man and for the love of her friend.

"Wear these," the man tells her, and he fastens a string of pearls around her neck—the ones Wallace gave her as an anniversary present. He fusses with her sleeve, fusses with her collar.

"We look amazing," he tells her.

They do, and she suppresses a smile at his easy vanity—suppresses pride at raising this prince. She loves how he will never cower. Blame it on their beauty and pride.

Daniel drives her to the Chase Park Plaza, where behind tables full of punch and cookies and finger sandwiches and crudités the most unfortunate women he knows stand, mouths agape, awed by the grandeur of the Khorassan Room and overwhelmed with the love of strangers. It is a fleeting love, they know, and tomorrow these lovers will move on to the symphony ball or to the fundraiser for a candidate governor, but it buoys them, reminding them at least of the possibility of love and goodness—the existence of which has been proved to them daily by *that* man, their brother—

if only by his mere presence. He's not much on the words, Craig Mitchell, but he is there, by God, he is always there.

Look at him, they whisper to each other. Glorious in the charcoal jacket and gray slacks that the Jewish woman bought for him. And who could blame her for her goodness to him, and didn't they fit him well, and wouldn't they all buy for this man had they the means to do so? These skinny men and their hard-to-fit little butts; but just look at their brother! Hell, no, they don't blame the woman and mostly they are blameless themselves today. They greet the money people with warmth, humbled not by circumstance but buoyed in the face of what they know to be God's manifest grace in their lives. Later—soon—after their shock and rage, they will be the first to understand and forgive, will do so almost instantly. People make mistakes, are too quick to blame.

Craig Mitchell has never owned clothes so well tailored as these and he is ashamed to admit how much he loves them; chagrined at his vanity when he admits to himself that he *does* look good in them. The generosity and love in this room overwhelm him, too, even if they do not surprise him. In his darkest moments there has always been love—if only the remembered kind. There will always be love—and this is both a promise as well as prescience on this part. Foreknowledge that is a gift to him, given so that in the dark times that inevitably come he will be able to push through and continue with the work. Blame it on the way he saw some things coming and did not see others.

It's the love that always saves him—or the memory of love—and he watches the door, eager to see if it returns today, with Estelle. He is anxious, and he blames it on this always unrealistic expectation of his that it would return, or that when it did return to him that this time it would stay. How foolish his disappointment, how naïve his hope. It had been, after all, a borrowed love, a temporary one. He had been a stand in. And when Estelle arrives with only her grandson in tow, he blames his unrealistic expectation for crushing his heart a little. He will never blame the love.

"Look at all the love," Estelle Birnbaum announces, as she enters the room, her father dead all these years and so many should come out to honor him.

"They love you, Stell," her Ari tells her, and will you look at the mug on the boy. So proud: and who could blame him?

Later, she would.

But for now there is work.

"The woman in the gray suit is the mayor's liaison," she tells him—because it was never too soon to learn how to work a room, and who better from? "Estelle's on her way to make nice. You: Get the show set up. I want to knock 'em dead."

Be careful what you wish for—and to that extent she blames herself.

From his station in front of the dais, he networks into the hotel's system and projects the photo of Poppa Hillyer onto the screen behind the podium. The photo file is next to the file about Poppa's life, which is next to the *good* House of Hope file, which is next to the bad one. The bad file, the one that shows what a bad boy such as Ariel could do with the help of Photoshop and his favorite porn site. That Ari Birnbaum: It's the kind of organized and mischievous boy he is. There's a shiver of glee runs through him when he thinks about the bad file and he thinks about what it would feel like to do something so bad as to click on that file right this very minute. I could do that, he tells himself. Shock people, crush someone. Blame it on the same hormones that made other boys become paratroopers and other ones drive fast without their headlights on.

Above him Poppa Hillyer is the size of a billboard. It's a photo of the painting from above the fireplace in Estelle's home office, and he's done a good job of reproducing it here—if he doesn't say so himself. He is good that way. He has built these files to his grandmother's specifications, even as he built the naughty one, the one he would *never* use. He is not a bad boy, only likes to think he might be.

His father and sister come up behind and greet him and exclaim over the picture and the ballroom decorated with children's art, their grandmother and mother at the center of it all; Estelle: of the handful of checks and the biggest smile any of them has ever seen.

"Don't touch it," he admonishes the man bent down to examine his rig. Because what would he do if his father saw the bad file and why hadn't it even occurred to him he might? Blame it on loving someone who you always disappointed and on how that made you nervous enough to trip over your own feet for no reason.

"Touchy as always," Hannah says, and his father laughs anemically—because he is afraid of this witch and therefore can muster no other response. Ari turns to the door of the ballroom because inside him there is another Ari, the fat and ugly and clumsy one that no one ever wanted, and if Daniel doesn't come in that door the other Ari will take over again and then anything could happen. Blame that other Ari.

Donette comes by and after pinning them up with boutonnières and corsages leads his people away to seats for the honored guests. He's relieved, if still a bit sweaty, and he watches the door for the person who has already begun to teach him how to be a son and a brother. (A lifetime's work, that.)

Estelle radiates love and everyone here today is a little in love with her. It strikes them all the uncanny resemblance between the face projected behind her and her own face. Daddy's little girl, and the emotion she feels threatens to spill over, and she admonishes herself to hold it together because the head of a serious family foundation did not blubber and kvell and otherwise make herself into a spectacle, even if she did have already in her hand pledges and checks—actual legal tender—somewhere in the half-million dollar neighborhood—a very nice neighborhood, indeed—and evidently all you had to do is mention Hiram Hillyer's name and have the limo standing by for the trip to the bank. She watches the door, too, because your best friend should know whose daughter she shares a home with.

The presentation starts and she does weep—and she blames the boy. She'd given him stacks of photo albums, and, yes, the photos are there, but also from somewhere he has found the movies of her Poppa, and there he is: Look. It's the eighty-fifth birthday party. Look. Poppa blows out the candles. The song "Unforgettable" plays and, well, Nat King Cole: What are you gonna do? And then there is him who made this show, bundled into his great grandfather's arms. The look on Poppa's face that day: proud and humbled and disbelieving—all at the same time. The unbearable beauty of this. She blames the boy.

The clip startles Ari as well—the giant baby up there who is him. And then there is Poppa Hillyer, who . . . and how could this be . . . seems to be looking back and forth between the Ari in his arms to the Ari he is now. Come on, Poppa says to Ari: Use that brain God gave you. Think!

Or sometimes it's a matter of timing—such as the way that at the exact same moment he and Estelle had noticed the startlingly handsome young man in the door with the regal woman on his arm. They had not been aware of each other's faces, of the way that they had simultaneously opened with pure joy; neither had either been aware of the other's laughing with delight.

The man at the podium does notice, and as Craig Mitchell moves the audience to tears with his accounting of his years at the House of Hope, they are unaware that the passion in his voice is as much for these women and children that he loves as it is for that boy in the back of the room. The one he knew would return—because hadn't he always, whether in dreams or in visions or here in the flesh? He laughs—the audience assumes at another of his tired old tales of loaves and fishes, this one concerning a single can of bean soup and a bag of stale Wonder Bread.

"Hey, we've got pictures. Mr. Birnbaum, if you please."

Not the Mr. Birnbaum, whose daughter has never been so embarrassed in her entire life, Daddy, and would you please stop blowing your nose and, no, I don't have any more tissues and why is that even my job and where's Mom anyway when you're all weepy like this, *God!*; but the other Mr. Birnbaum, the one who remembered a particularly dirty joke he'd seen on the Internet and is eager to lean over and whisper it in that boy's ear, his breath hot and moist and soft with nastiness. People would see the two of them in that configuration for many decades to come: standing at the edge of a crowd in some ballroom just like this one, the taller one bent to the other one's ear, intensely and furtively whispering something that it clearly delighted him to share. The more handsome one would tilt his head up, but only slightly, to receive the whisper, eyes sparkling and nose twitching slightly, a face of smug pleasure.

"Go! Go!" Estelle signals him. She's at the door now, welcoming her friend, eager to show Janet the glory that is the House of Hope.

"Chill," he signals back. "We're among friends."

Blame it on being so drunk with love you didn't even know your own name.

So, no, he had not intended to click on that file. That wrong file.

Blame it on having worked the kinks out of the good file and the kinks out of the bad file and on having made most of both identical. Blame it on the way that ambivalence of any kind has a way of punishing us in the end.

Here are the kids and here is the House of Hope. Here are more kids and here are the children's mothers. Here is a child. Here is Craig Mitchell. Here is a mother. Here is Craig Mitchell.

And then here is Craig Mitchell. Or at least here is Craig Mitchell's face.

Ari is turned toward Daniel when the slide covers the screen. He does not hear the gasp: love being both blind and deaf in these boys.

It takes a minute before Janet understands what she sees on the screen—because it is as illogical and out-of-place as it is vulgar and offensive—but her confusion is temporary. She knows exactly what those photos are because she's a woman who knows more than a little something about spite. She hears the noise from Estelle, and she grabs for her friend's arm, because she knows a little something about rage, too, but it's too late. The woman takes off after her grandson.

The look on Danny's face confuses Ari and scares him a little—because he has not yet realized what he's done. Danny's face: Violated. Offended. Fury directed at Ari. It's his father's voice breaks the spell.

"What did you do, Ariel?" Broken and heartbroken.

As he turns to see his handiwork, the first blow from her purse catches him in the neck.

"Animal," she screams, and she swings the purse again. "You animal."

I didn't mean it, he tries to say, but the purse hits his mouth.

"Animal." It's the only language she has anymore. This animal. This goddamn animal.

"God in heaven," says Janet. "Have mercy."

And while He might not be merciful—or maybe not readily so—PowerPoint can be, and the program cycles back to the photo of Poppa Birnbaum, where it parks, as designed by the brilliant young man. But the damage is done.

"Animal."

The boy curls on the floor in a ball, both against the blows and because he is the other Ari now—the sad little fat one.

"Mama, please," his father cries. "He didn't mean it. I know he didn't mean it."

"Animal," she screams. She's too tired to swing the purse.

"That's enough, honey," Janet says, gathering her into her arms. "It's over now. You come on with me."

Janet Williams didn't do spectacle, and she figures the best thing right now is to get this woman across the hall to that little coffee shop and get one of those pastries into her—maybe one of those kiwi tarts. The strawberries looked so fresh. Things here were quickly moving back to control. Some girl has picked up with the entertainment and the other girls are circulating with trays, passing around the hard stuff.

"You come with me, sweetheart."

On the dais, Donette has moved their brother to the side and taken the microphone herself.

"Jesus is my portion," she sings, and she tries not to giggle. Once, before she lost her apartment, she'd stayed up late watching a movie and looking after a sick child. She doesn't remember much about that show, except that one of the women in there—Nell Carter, that's who it was—sang this song and another woman in an adjacent jail cell told her to shut the hell up. It was the jail part made it funny. She'll finish this one and then she'll start "Oh, Happy Day." There's a lot of white folks here today and they like those sing-along kind of songs. The other girls can make a chorus. Then she'd invite everyone to step over and see the architectural model of the Davis Memorial Family Center.

And sing along they did, for the most part forgetting all about the broken boy on the floor, the one being cradled by the man who is his father.

Nor do they notice the other boy, who extends his hand in Craig Mitchell's direction.

"I remember you now," he says. "I thought I'd tell you that."

Craig doesn't understand how it could be possible that this is the same hand and the same suit from the other time the boy had come to him, from the time in the alley. He trembles and he knows people think he's been undone by the filthy display—hideous bodies more hideous than his own with his head pasted on them. Those obscene collages.

But, look: He'd seen so much worse in his life. The obscenity of hungry children and of families with no place to sleep on cold nights. How a government and an entire society could stand by and pretend like they didn't see it and that it didn't matter. The complacent ravings of a political culture that offered comfort to the ignorant masses by explaining how poverty was more than anything else a character flaw and that the Lord helped those who helped themselves.

"You took us to the zoo one time. Remember?"

He nods because he cannot speak. He remembers everything.

The boy sits beside him. They smile at each other. He nods some more. People hand him checks and ask him when they will break ground. What a wonderful world it is. No one is to blame, really. They both know that, and they will never again not be part of one another's lives in some way.

Someone who Daniel recognizes from the grandmothers' work hands Craig a check, but Daniel doesn't know the man's name.

"Is this your son?" the man asks Craig, because who else could be comforting him this way—holding his hand with one hand and rubbing his back with the other.

And it doesn't occur to either of them that the puzzlement over the question that is reflected on both their faces might seem irrational.

But, hey, love—like spite—*is* irrational. They both had known that for almost as long as either could remember, just as they'd also understood how the unconditional embrace of one always triumphed over the unintended consequences of the other.

But this is just some nice man with a check, and what did he care what they knew. For now, Craig points to the beautiful and unlikely man by his side.

"You mean this guy. Well, sure, he might as well be."

Later

Epilogue

Honestly! Such a noise! She closes the door to the mudroom that separated the lock-out from the main part of the condo. They kept that door closed the two times they'd rented the studio, but with family here, who thought to shut it? But she's learned her lesson now—you can be sure of that—and she'd just as soon not be told about whatever in the hell is going on in there. Next time she'd let Estelle inquire for her own damn self if the boys are up and ready for breakfast.

"They're up all right," she tells her friend, who shushes her—the morning calls to St. Louis taking precedence over the smut report.

Listen. Listen to Estelle when she's talking, sweetheart.

No.

We've been through this. No. You'll purchase nothing out of your own pocket, do you hear me. Forbidden.

Why? The man asks me why. For the last time, because you never get the receipts to Donette. That's why. Because I said so.

How do I know? Estelle has her ways.

Listen. Case closed. OK, darling. Next subject. Have you eaten?

Why? Because I know you, that's why. Answer my question, and why not every day?

Why do I even bother? Listen: When I'm done with you, you're to march into that dining hall and eat. Toast and coffee—that's all I ask. And some bacon, while you're in there. An egg maybe, too. OK.

Listen, you tell Donette I'll see her at the board meeting next week, OK?

OK, sweetheart.

OK, sweetheart.

No, Estelle knows. She knows.

I'm sure it will.

OK, sweetheart.

Yes, the boys got in just fine last night. Our two spring breakers. They're doing fine. Just fine.

Uh, huh.

Yes, I let the poor dears sleep, but they'll be up and at it before you know it.

The spring breakers had been up and in fact at it for quite some time by then. In contrast to the tenderness of their languid bedtime sex, morning sex had a rough edge to it. Daniel taunts Ari with a peacock feather from a (they both agree) vulgar arrangement on the chest of drawers. Tickles from the soft end alternate with jabs from the shaft. The vanes of the feather have become glued together with sweat, so it's mostly jabbing at this point. Since the bite on Daniel's chest stands to become infected, he feels no compunction about poking Ari hard and repeatedly. Ari lies prone; his the spent, pissed-off face of a defeated boxer, his lips pouted with rage and disgust.

"You're a sexy motherfucker, aren't you?" Daniel says to him. (Poke. Poke.) "Aren't you?" (Poke. Poke.)

In reply he gets a growl and a grimace.

The peacock feathers compete with hosts of Florida kitsch as objects of their disdain, but for the most part the condo was well decorated—all except for the carpet in the lock-out. The ladies had chosen to cover the floor in an industrial grade Berber—the better to be worn down by what they'd imagine to be regular renters of the studio. Since both grandmothers had decided it was more trouble than it was worth to have strange people sharing their mudroom, their days as landlord have ended.

It's the same, hard-wearing, uninspiring carpet from the visitors' room in the prison, where Danny has visited Keisha perhaps ten times over the last few years. He'd stopped counting and it was hard to keep track. The visits ran into each other—the way days here at the beach sometimes would, with one day the same as the next for the most part (although the ladies seemed to keep plenty busy, what with their charity work and shopping and book clubs and, and, and, and, and). They would bring his mother in, and at first she'd be chained to her chair—about which he'd complained to the guard—who told him it was for his own safety. He'd asked her doctor to intervene, sardonically goading the woman, saying, "She's already had her shot at me. What could she possibly do?" So they agreed to allow her to see him unfettered—but "someone will be watching you at all times. For your protection. You have no idea what your mother's like."

Whatever.

She would saunter in as if on some picnic, tugging at her clothes and simpering and talking trash about people he assumed were her fellow inmates.

"Have you heard of logorrhea?" the doctor asked him. Melanie or Maria or something she said he could call her—and he always had to resist saying to the woman, bitch, I'm headed off to Harvard on a full ride. Don't you fucking dare talk down to me, and why don't you have somebody look at that mole on your neck?

But, yes, apparently his mother did tend to run on at the mouth. She talked for the entire visit, and there was nothing conversational about it—perhaps the primary reason the visits ran together.

Since he'd moved to New England for school, the visits had slowed down some. Not that she'd noticed. The guard walked her into that room with the one-way mirror and she started in as if he'd just stepped out for coffee.

Ari and his grandmother refused to accompany him on these trips, refused to discuss why they wouldn't go, and also refused to hear his reports on the visit, such as they might be. Which had bothered him the first few times, the times he'd been accompanied by Estelle. But after a while he no longer cared. It was just as well the topic was off limits—because were they to ask him why he went to see her, he doubted he could tell them. His original curiosity had given way to an inkling of obligation, which itself had been so slight it had collapsed by the third or fourth visit. What had it become? Habit? Or maybe it's his own peculiar form of charity. Himself, his presence: something he could offer now and again to this wretched abandoned woman who had made herself so alone in the world. He felt nothing for her really, not even pity, but he doubted Ari and Janet would believe that. Doubted they believed that when he was off in Massachusetts he hardly thought about her at all.

When eight years later, he got the call from the prison about her death, he'd still felt nothing.

"She choked," he'd told Ari. "On a piece of chicken."

They were living in DC at the time while Ari clerked for the court and Daniel had an internship at the Folger. Ari had long settled in with law, but Danny would never, in fact, settle. Librarian. Poet. Pianist. Shoemaker. Webmaster. Chef. And all those years raising the kids. Often enough simultaneously, he would do these jobs. (Alas, no one, not even his disciplined grandmother, had mentioned to the boy that you were supposed to pick *one* job and stick with it to the end. Therefore he had never been particularly troubled by his peripatetic career path, only occasionally put off by the puzzled expression on people's faces when he'd tell them he'd moved on from that gig because "I did that already.")

Daniel sat with his arms crossed, not nearly as vexed by the Keisha news as he had been entertained by the way Ari had continued to step around the corner to look at him—to see what? If he was kidding or if the news had broken him or . . . what? It wasn't until the eighth or ninth step around the corner that Ari had managed to ask, "You OK?"

He was fine, he told his partner.

"Except . . ." Ari stammered. "Except . . . what about Janet?" Which led to more pacing which would lead into raging and tears.

"Fuck! Fuck! Fuck!" Ari cried, and he banged himself in the head with his hands. "This will break her heart. We have to go down there." And he'd gone off to call the airlines.

For a man with one of the most coveted clerking jobs in America, damn he was dumb sometimes. The question was not how to tell his grandmother but whether or not to tell her at all.

But he would leave that all to Ari, as he often did. Ari doted on the ladies—more so with every passing year. He lavished them with gifts—fresh flowers for no reason, and regular shipments from any and every decadent bakery with a UPS account. And a daily phone call for no reason whatsoever.

Daniel would slip away that night to St. Louis and arrange to have her interred next to her husband and children. He had not been surprised to find her burial expenses prepaid; the tasteful if bland coffin selected and arrangements made to have her name inscribed on the existing tombstone. Alone at her graveside, he had mourned for a woman that he remembered knowing only occasionally and rarely. On that trip to the zoo, for instance, when he remembers turning around on the train (or was that a tram?) and seeing her holding her baby and smiling the same, innocent smile of his sisters. It was as if she'd never been to the zoo before—any zoo—and the idea that you could ride around on a silly train and look at the antelope was the most wonderful thing imaginable.

The pictures of his sisters hang in the hallway of the condo leading from the mudroom and studio. The one of Hosea sits on his grandmother's nightstand. Daniel winks at the girls as he always does and comes out to find fresh coffee and the usual array of rolls—from a little secret place in Bradenton, tucked away, only a few of us know about: To die for! Ari struts behind him in only a Speedo. He scratches at himself and rearranges the merchandise. Estelle clutches her chest.

"Again with the Chippendales! Some clothes would kill you?"

"We're going right to the beach. And you ladies know you like it."

Which causes Janet to gasp, and she doesn't even know where to look. Here in her own house. This is a good-looking man, no doubt about that. He'd give Wallace a run—and Wallace was no dog.

But this is Ari! A college boy, no less. Oh, it was all so confusing sometimes. She'll just go out on the main balcony. That's what she'll do. Out into that eternal sunshine. It wears you out sometimes, all this brightness, but she's grown to love it these past three years.

It isn't too long before the boys are down there on the beach. The condo is a penthouse ("Prime, corner unit, and a steal!) but the building's only two stories, so there those boys are, right there—you could practically touch them from here.

Is it a trashy daydream or is it suddenly years later and there they are on that beach, still, joined this time by their children—two daughters and a son. Daniel builds sandcastles with the boy while the girls keep the Frisbee comically from their other dad. Some other children join them (but it *is* impossible that those children could be here!).

"Aren't they something?" Estelle asks her. She hands her a fresh cup of tea. "Two big strong handsome college men. We done good, kid.

Janet sniffs and nods.

"You sure you're OK?"

"I'm fine," Janet told her.

"Yes, you are. Just fine." She hugged her from the side and they sipped their tea and watched their boys trying to drown each other in the Gulf of Mexico.

Janet had been fine: as fine as she would ever be right up to the end of her life, and that, frankly, was always a little less than fine. It wasn't that she had never been able to let go of what had sullied her otherwise lovely life; instead it was being unable to understand *why* she couldn't let go. She'd finally figured that out, almost at the very end.

That Ari Birnbaum had come down to see her, alone, as he often did, her own grandson unable to bear her final decline, his lifetime quota for such loss already long spent. As always he'd passed the first hour or so appraising the apartment, Ari had, and fussing at the staff about things that were not to his liking: the supply of cottage cheese run too low or a streaked mirror over the bathroom vanity.

"I'm paying all this money so you can live in a dump, G? Hell no! Listen, day or night, something here's not to your liking, you call me. I'll remind these assholes who owns the joint."

He did own the joint, actually, part of it at least—significant stock, that is, in the corporation who owned the joint—and, for the record, it had been no dump. It shamed her sometimes, such extravagance, when she knew the way that most older people lived. But fighting these boys: What good had it ever done?

Inspection duties complete, it would be her turn to be fussed over.

"It's time for brunch. I'm looking. Do I see brunch? No. Time to eat, G."

"All my life I have eaten when I want to eat, and I'm not changing that for these people in here or for you, Ariel Birnbaum. Bring me that shopping bag so I can tell you what's what."

With this one you always had to go over twice the contents of the bag of presents to be sent back with him to Hartford.

"This one is extra. For my big girl. To start high school with. Don't let the other two see. They'll think I'm playing favorites." Which they both knew she was—and who couldn't love Stella K? All the fire of her great grandmothers and all the heart of her two dads.

It surprises Janet to admit that this dad has turned into the man he has. Unable to be still—as has been true for as long as she has known the boy—he strides around the apartment, popping his gum and entertaining her with his run-on sentences about who'd been in front of him in court and how some people: You just couldn't believe them, G.

They'd be lucky to plea their cause in front of Judge Birnbaum—his family court renowned for its fairness and for its dedication to doing the right thing for everyone concerned. His stubbornness he had channeled into a resolute single-mindedness about children's safety and welfare, and the arrogant selfishness provided the impunity to bully the system into doing its part to look after the vulnerable.

"I barged my way into the bastard's office and I told him to get off his ass and go get those babies like I told him to. Danny and me have this cop neighbor, the one I told you about, and I had him there for backup just in case."

Just look at the boy smirk. As pleased to have done right by those babies as he is disappointed not to have further humiliated some poor social worker. Esteemed universally and respected enough he can close the court and cancel classes at the law school to come see her for a day or two.

"Why don't you sit somewhere or something? You make a person crazy with all that strutting around."

There's a flash of the classic offended face, which dissolves quickly into the solicitous sweet boy—the one for so long seen only by her grandson and her best friend. He has, in fact, surrounded himself with tough-talking women—pugnacious clerks and legal secretaries selected not only for their competence but because they refuse to be intimidated by him. The one exception, the housekeeper and nanny, whose West African sweetness oozed through the phone when she answered it. Chimi, Janet knows, disapproves of their lifestyle, not on moral grounds so much as because it seems such a waste to her—a woman from a country with a dearth of eligible men—that two fully functioning males with all their limbs intact aren't helping out by taking on a wife or three. And who wouldn't want a husband such as this one?

"Am I making you uncomfortable, sweetheart? I'm so sorry. Here," he said, as he made yet another awkward attempt to fluff her pillows and rest her back against them.

"I'm not helpless. I can do that myself," she scolds, not so much to stop his fussing—rather, he's so damn bad at such things and is about to break her back with all his unnecessary arrangements.

357

Her poor child: wasn't a blessed thing you could do about his clumsiness—other than try to stay out of his way. But as Stella K liked to say, "Some people got the dads who coached the team and some got the dads who wrote the check for the uniforms. You don't hear me complaining."

And because he believed, she knew, that his money and power could do just about anything, there came a time in every conversation with him, whether in person or on the phone, when he demanded a report on her health.

"So, tell me how you're doing, G. Really. Give it to me straight. No bullshit. You're talking to a judge here."

Among other things she was damn near ninety years old and sometimes her bones just hurt. For no reason. Old bones just hurt sometimes, and, thankfully, a lot of the time they did not. Yesterday's hour in the outlet mall felt like a month, and she didn't eat much these days because, frankly, she often forgot to, and everything tasted the same anyway. She still liked her ice cream, and she'd have to remember to have him get some of that strawberry he found her with the whole berries in it. She liked to let the fruit melt and then mash them with her spoon—or sometimes she'd melt them in her mouth. And she slept a lot—and she felt a nap coming on just then.

That Ariel Birnbaum: He'd wear you out every time.

"I'm fine," she would tell him, and for the first time in almost a half a century she really meant it. "I figured something out."

"Tell me," he prompted.

Oh, how she cherished the way he would often just perch there on the edge of her bed, holding her hand or gently stroking her arm.

"Well, Mr. Nosy." (Always in someone's business, this one: snooping in your file cabinets and reading other people's mail. Estelle once had to put mousetraps in her dresser drawers!) "If you must know, what I finally figured out is that I'm never going to figure it out."

He sighed and nodded, sadly.

(Look at this! Who is this middle-aged man?)

"She took the secret to her grave, I guess," Ariel guessed.

Janet had not responded to that, nor had his misunderstanding surprised her. He was, after all, a rational and learned man, and his humanist heart had long ago vanquished his cynical mind. Despite what would be paraded before him in court each day, he still believed that people were decent and that if you just asked the right questions you would be able to figure it all out.

It seemed too late somehow—late in the day, late in their relationship, late in life—to explain to him that she had never really been interested in why her daughter had done such a terrible thing. Keisha was . . . Keisha. The Lord made her for a reason, she supposed, but, again, she hadn't held her breath for that answer either.

Well, actually, she did know why there had to be a Keisha. Every one of them did. His name was Daniel, and the thing that she'd really puzzled over all these years: She'd never been able to understand where the damn boy had come from. It had been neither a physiological nor an epistemological question—however related it might have been to his unlikely heritage and parenting. Maybe it had been closer to a spiritual concern: Why is he here? Sure, you could ask that about any and all of us, except in his case it's the *he* that she emphasizes. He has always been marvelous to her, a thing of mysterious wonder. And it's comforting to her as she falls asleep—as comforting as Ari's touch—to be able to finally after all these years stop wondering why and to just be happy that he is.

And, therefore, and most importantly, she had also been able to let go of that other awful question: The "What if" one—and a genuinely trashy question it is.

Even so, people all over the world hugged their loved ones every day and asked the same thing themselves. What if it had been you on that bus that slid off the road? Or: What if you'd been in the towers the day they came down?

Sometimes it isn't a question at all. Sometimes it's being a bothersome old woman who calls around the country every morning reminding those who needed reminding to take their vitamins and eat their toast. Estelle stands by the dearest friend of her life as they watch two beautiful boys play in the surf and she can hardly breathe she is so verklempt—because how could life have given you such gifts as these and are we sure those trunks are the right size for the boy? (They're large down there, the Birnbaum men.) Sometimes it's like that.

Sometimes it's like her friend Janet, who also cannot take her eyes off the children. The little ones run here and there, and the two men seem attentive enough, but still: They're just babies, those little ones out there with all that water and all that shoreline. And they're impulsive, these kids. Everybody knows that. The waves on Coquina Beach are known to be unpredictable and she's heard reports of riptides. But, Danny—her sweet, sweet Danny—stands between the ocean and the little ones, and he catches any and all who try run past him. All the same, she wishes that they would all move up closer to the condo. It never hurt to err on the side of safety and, after all, a person couldn't be too careful.

About the Author

David Haynes earned a B.A. in literature from Macalester College, Minnesota, in 1977 and an M.A. from Hamline University, Minnesota, in 1989. A former fifth and sixth grade teacher, he served as a teacher in residence at the National Board for Professional Teaching Standards. Haynes also served on the leadership team at the experimental Saturn School of Tomorrow. His book *Right by My Side* (New Rivers Press, 1993) was a winner in the 1992 Minnesota Voices Project and was selected by the American Library Association as one of 1994's best books for young adults. Two of Haynes' stories have been recorded for the National Public Radio series "Selected Shorts." In 1996 *Granta* magazine named Haynes as one of the best young American novelists. Haynes is currently an associate professor and the director of creative writing at Southern Methodist University in Dallas, Texas. He also teaches regularly in the Warren Wilson MFA Program for Writers and has taught in the MFA programs at the University of Missouri-St. Louis, Hamline University; the Writer's Center in Bethesda, MD; and the Writers' Garret in Dallas. His teaching interests include gender, class, race, and generational differences—themes that he explores in great depth in his seventh novel, *A Star in the Face of the Sky*.

Acknowledgements

My gratitude to SMU for the Ford Research Fellowship and to Dedman College and the English Department for providing additional valuable support during the completion of this novel. Like most of my work, this book would not exist without the quiet spaces provided by The Virginia Center for the Creative Arts, The Ragdale Foundation, Centrum, and the Writer's Colony at Dairy Hollow. I am deeply in their debt. And to all of the writers in the community of the MFA Program for Writers at Warren Wilson College, thank you for continuing to teach me all the things that I didn't know I needed to know.